faint promise of rain

faint promise of rain

anjali mitter duva

Published 2014
Printed in the United States of America
ISBN: 978-1-938314-97-1
Library of Congress Control Number: 2014936029

For information, address:
She Writes Press
1563 Solano Ave #546
Berkeley, CA 94707

In memory of
my paternal grandmother, Protiva Mitter,
a woman of grace and inner strength,
and of
my maternal grandfather, Maurice Sagoff,
poet and storyteller extraordinaire.

Don't grieve. Anything you lose comes around in another form.

Jalal ad-Din Muhammad Rumi

Jaisalmer in Rajasthan

Barabagh

Thar Desert

Half Day Journey

Gadisar Lake

The Citadel

The Temple

Adhira's Home

Himalayas

One Day Journey

Delhi

Hindustan

Derikot

× Jaisalmer
Mt Abu
Rajasthan

Adhira

1611

In Rajasthan, where I was born, a child of five is likely never to have seen rain. For hundreds of years, the monsoons have been elusive. In the children's rooms in the royal palace, not far from what used to be my family's home, the walls are painted with black and blue cloud designs, so the little ones will not be afraid when the skies finally break open. But for less fortunate children, such as my brothers and sister, the day of their first rain can mean an intensity of both fear and hope. And for adults whose lives are connected to the rhythms and cycles of beliefs they cannot always explain, these storms can signify both portent and promise. So when the skies darkened and the heavy drops fell as I was born, it is no wonder that some considered it a sign that I had been chosen.

Of course, I began—as all children do—accepting my lot in life. It was the only life I knew, ruled by the decisions of my father, dance master at the temple to Lord Krishna just outside the citadel of Jaisalmer. When I was old enough, I began to understand, contrary to what he'd told me, that I could have a hand in creating my own path. And although I struggled greatly along the way, the deities must have approved of my choices, for many, many years later they made me special after all.

I am not sure why they acted as they did, or how they chose what knowledge to grant me and what to keep concealed, but I was given insight into the thoughts and feelings of others. Was it a moment of selfishness on the part of Brahma, Vishnu, and Shiva? Was it for our dance? I cannot presume that it was just for me. Whatever the reason, I came, in hindsight, to know the minds and hearts of some of those closest to me when I was a child, a knowledge that allows me to tell this story.

It is not my story alone, therefore, but it is mine alone to tell.

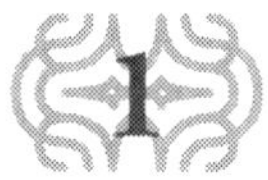

Mahendra

Summer 1554

For five long years, the rains had failed to come. For months, my brother Mahendra had watched the lake's water level drop far below the steps that used to lead into it from the sandy path, leaving ever-smaller brown rings along the shore. The grasses in the temple courtyard crackled in the wind, yellow and brittle. Within two days of being painted, decorative designs on the outer walls of the scattered huts, made with a paste of white lime, flaked off and blew away. And out beyond the city limits, where Mahendra often sought refuge from what he felt were his burdens, even the camels swayed languorously over the hazy dunes, dragging their flat feet across the searing sand as their drivers *ut-ut*ted them in irritation, eager to set up camp in the cold relief of night.

The morning Ma announced that I, her last child, would arrive, our father—Bapu to us—summoned my brother to go to the temple to pray for a safe birth. Mahendra crossed the still-dark room to wake five-year-old Hari Dev, whose crippled legs poked awkwardly out from under his blanket.

Bapu cleared his throat. "Not Hari Dev. He need not come."

"But, Bapu, what if he has one of his fits?"

There was a brief silence, the type in which Bapu weighed the knowledge of his heart against the desire of his mind. "Fine," he said.

Bapu's footsteps retreated into the darkness, followed by the clicking of the bead curtain hanging in the front entrance. Mahendra shook Hari Dev awake and pulled two shawls off his bedding, and together they joined Bapu in the courtyard, where the babul tree and the pots of rice and lentils and the near-empty water jug stood neatly in the gray-blue darkness that precedes dawn.

Bapu nodded. "Good. No disappearing games today."

"Yes, Bapu." Mahendra bit his upper lip, where a few sparse hairs were sprouting. By the end of the summer, he would have a genuine mustache, and then he would advance his plan.

"The temple is what holds us all together, son." Bapu rubbed his hands for warmth. "Today is an auspicious day. You will see. The child on her way will be our salvation. For a long time I have worried about the fate of this temple, but she will save it."

Mahendra glowered behind Bapu's back. He imagined the day Bapu, the temple dance master, would acknowledge to him that his son had chosen the right course, that in fact it was his to choose, and that battle was indeed as glorious as dance. But it was a different glory that each one sought.

Bapu handed Mahendra a clay cup of water, cooled by the desert night. Mahendra drank half, then gave the rest to Hari Dev. The chill in the air smelled metallic. They set out wordlessly for the temple, Bapu walking as always with a distinct sense of purpose, Hari Dev struggling to keep up on his shriveled legs, and Mahendra following close behind.

It was not so much for me that Mahendra had agreed to pray at the temple. Rather, he was worried about Ma. He was right, for her childbearing years were drawing to a close. Our sister, Padmini, had been born twenty years earlier. As for his sister-to-be—for Ma said I would be a girl, and Ma had never been wrong about such things—Mahendra thought perhaps it would be for the best if, like Hari, I was unable to dance. It was a thought Mahendra knew he should not have, but he could not deny his feeling. If the gods decreed that I be unable to dance, then Bapu would finally remove his blinders and accept that none of his children would follow in his footsteps, and life would be easier for everyone.

It was still dark when they reached the temple. Bapu pointed to a corner of the outer courtyard.

"Sit here and wait for us, Hari."

"Can't he come in?" Mahendra asked, although he knew the answer.

Bapu shook his head and gestured upward.

Mahendra spoke before Bapu could say it. "I know. The earth and the sky are his temple."

"Exactly." As Bapu entered the temple, Mahendra turned to Hari Dev.

Hari Dev shrugged. "It's all right. It's my legs. He doesn't like to see them in the temple."

Hearing Hari Dev say this so clearly hurt Mahendra more than the time he had cut his own palm, sealing with blood his promise to himself to become a warrior. Yet Hari Dev was content on the dusty ground. This was one thing everyone in the family knew.

Mahendra scuffed his foot against a loose stone and looked toward the temple. "We'll be back soon," he said, and patted Hari Dev's head. He left him sitting in the red dirt, worrying an ant hole with a twig, his legs tucked under him.

Mahendra entered the temple as Bapu slipped quietly around the carved sandstone pillars of the inner courtyard. In front of him was a lithe and graceful dancer, not the tired, bony old man he saw at home, whose presence lately had suffused the air with tension. The gods had made Bapu a dancer; not even Mahendra could deny that. Bapu knelt in prayer before the main shrine to our Lord Krishna, oblivious to the stone floor's chill. For his chosen ones, the earth melts away in Krishna's presence. Mahendra wrapped his shawl tightly around his narrow shoulders, slender as Bapu's, and shivered.

He kept to the side while Bapu danced. He leaned against a pillar, tracing the contour of a carved elephant, weaving a story. In his mind, the elephant took life, and he rode it across the desert, leading a charge against the Muslims and returning home triumphantly as the Raja's favorite warrior. In the years to come, my fingers would trace the same nooks and ridges of the temple pillars, drawing from them a different inspiration.

The sound of an urn clattering to the ground echoed through the chambers, and peals of laughter followed. The *devadasis*, the girls and women wedded to Lord Krishna who danced for the temple, were readying themselves for the day. The slightest of frowns momentarily marred Bapu's peaceful expression. Mahendra knew what he was thinking, could even hear the words in his mind: *The temple is no place for giddiness and giggles. You are servants of God, after all. You are the embodiment of the divine.*

But the giggles stirred something pleasant in Mahendra as his mind wandered to the *devadasi* quarters, where no men were allowed. The *devadasis* always went to the men's homes or to other meeting places; they never received them at the temple. Mahendra wondered what it was like when they were out of sight of the priest and Bapu, and away from the men who paid the temple for their favors. What did the *devadasis* do? It was a world forbidden to Mahendra, and thus he could only imagine what any young man would imagine. He pictured an unclothed *devadasi*, Chandrabai in particular, with her eyes soft as sand and curves smooth as dunes, pouring a jug of water on her head, the cascade of her hair clinging to her breasts. He imagined the *devadasis* washing together. They appeared to him as a riot of bare arms and legs, inner thighs and slender necks, unraveling lengths of silk and cotton.

Bapu's voice cut through his fantasies. "Mahendra, what are you doing?"

My brother shook himself from his daydream, his face on fire. Hurriedly, he joined Bapu in front of the blue wooden statuette of Lord Krishna nestled in an alcove in the sandstone wall. He breathed deeply to cleanse his mind, ashamed for having those thoughts right there, in the temple. And about the *devadasis*!

"Sing with me," Bapu said. "You will need to know how to do all this when you take my place."

A familiar tightness clamped around Mahendra's chest. He clenched his fist around the scar in his palm. He joined Bapu in singing a prayer, but while his voice fed Bapu's like a stream feeds a river, their hearts were far apart.

They performed a ritual that had long been second nature to Mahendra. Singing a melody in sixteen beats, they brought their palms together in front of the statuette of Lord Krishna and bowed to his all-knowing presence. Mahendra looked up and searched his face for a sign of reassurance. As always, Lord Krishna's expression emanated peace, yet something about the eyes on this day looked different. Mahendra chided himself for thinking that they glowed as though Lord Krishna saw something dazzling, but he could not turn his own eyes away. I have felt Lord Krishna's love from the moment those eyes alighted on me, but that love has come at a price.

"Do you see that, too?" Bapu whispered in Mahendra's ear. "It is a sign of what is about to happen."

Mahendra, never one to believe in signs, stood. "Shall I fetch Hari Dev?" he asked, eager for an excuse to break the chamber's spell. Besides, Hari Dev had been alone long enough.

"Oh, yes. He can join us now. Krishna's will is done. There is no changing it."

Mahendra crossed the chamber and walked through the pillared main hall. He had just stepped into the courtyard when Hari Dev lurched into him, whimpering, and wrapped his arms around Mahendra's legs. Dark clouds rumbled in the distance against the lightening sky. Clouds! The air smelled rich, fertile. Across the courtyard, Sundaran, the temple cook, gesticulated wildly. On Mahendra's arms, the hairs rose like the quills of a crested porcupine.

He pointed. "Look, Hari!"

Hari Dev's face was wet against Mahendra's legs while Krishna's eyes danced in his mind. And for a moment Mahendra almost lent credence to Bapu's belief that one unfortunate child could suppress the rains and another blessed one could bring their return.

Mahendra pushed Hari into the temple. "Come inside."

Bapu was singing. His voice was strong, resonating throughout the chambers. His face was radiant as he thanked Lord Krishna for watching over the *devadasis* and his family. And then he reached for a small bundle tied into the folds of his white *dhoti*. Mahendra watched as Bapu carefully unwrapped the layers of cotton cloth and revealed four dried apricots.

Bapu giggled. Mahendra thought he sounded like a little girl, and was torn between amusement and scorn. I wish he could have felt the same lightness of heart that Bapu's rare laughter gave me. Hari Dev lifted his face from Mahendra's legs and watched our father.

"I found them in the sand," Bapu said, placing two of the shriveled fruits on the brass tray at Lord Krishna's feet. "They must have fallen from a Persian caravan on its way to the market." He grinned. "Do you want one? Look, I have scraped off the sand."

Bapu sat cross-legged on the floor and motioned for my brothers to sit with him. He handed one apricot to Mahendra and kept one for himself. As so often happened, Hari Dev went without. Bapu and Mahendra each bit into theirs and, unknowingly, both felt the same thing: a tingle beneath the tongue, a reawakened sense of hope in life's richness. The rush of saliva, the flood of feelings, moved Mahendra to stand and dance, despite himself, in thanks to Lord Krishna. He chose the story of Krishna and the serpent Kaliya, although the reason escaped him.

With rippling arms and hands, Mahendra created the river Jamuna. His arms encircled the girth of a tree trunk, and his fingertips formed the bright flowers on the branches. Then, with one turn, he became little boy Krishna, the cowherd, playing along the river with his friends, and Mahendra recalled himself as a young, carefree boy before his dance training had begun. Krishna tossed a wooden ball up in the air and caught it, to the beat of an imagined melody. And then, full of mischief, he climbed the tree. But all of a sudden, he lost his balance. As he reached to regain his hold, his ball fell into the water.

Then Mahendra was Krishna's friends on the riverbank. Eyes wide, hands at his cheeks, heels drumming fear on the ground, Mahendra called out to Krishna not to fetch the ball, for surely the water serpent Kaliya had it now. His hands fanned over his head, he showed Kaliya's hundred and ten hoods, and for my brother the serpent's threat became that of Muslim armies invading our land.

Once again Mahendra became Krishna, now a savior, his expression serene. He jumped into the water, pushing aside the water grasses to search for the ball. Then Mahendra was the serpent Kaliya, rising in anger, his body undulating. Mahendra's arms showed the serpent coiling around Krishna, the foreign army encircling our citadel. But Krishna assumed his divine powers and grew to such a size that Kaliya had to release him.

Mahendra was the furious serpent, vomiting poison. Mahendra was his furious self, letting loose his rage in the pounding of his feet. Then he was Krishna, jumping onto the serpent's heads. Krishna assumed the weight of the universe, and Kaliya slowly began to die. At this, Kaliya recognized the greatness of Krishna and lowered his body to the ground. In my brother's eyes, Kaliya melted into an image of my father, then that of a foreign soldier with red eyes. In the end, Mahendra was Krishna again, placing his hand on Kaliya's heads to pardon him but banishing him forever from the river Jamuna. It would not be as easy, however, for him to forgive Bapu or the Muslims.

Mahendra kept his eyes closed, his body at ease for the first time in a long while. In the fleeting moment of stillness after a dance, he almost understood how dancing was divine, how one could spend a lifetime searching to hold on to that feeling of lightness. A weight was lifted, the intensity of his anger faded, the burden of Bapu's expectations lessened. He tried not to let himself think, simply to feel, to make the moment last.

But for him, it did not.

Bapu rose. "*Wah*, wonderful, my son. Wonderful. I was beginning to doubt, but now I am sure again. You have the dance within you. Just think! One day you will be your sister's teacher, the teacher of all the *devadasis*. I know there are very few now, but this will change, you will see."

Despite the gray early light that filtered between the pillars through the cutouts in the ceiling, Mahendra felt a lid had been slammed down on a well, with him at the bottom. He wanted to shout to Bapu that no child of Ma, who wasn't a dancer herself, could be a *devadasi*, that if he tried to force the condition upon me, he would only bring more misfortune to the family. Just see what Padmini had done, turning her back on all of them and breaking a piece of Ma's heart. He wanted to shake Bapu by the shoulders and ask him if he ever thought about what the Muslim invaders would do to the *devadasis* when they captured the temple. Did he really want that for his own daughter?

I know now that my life might have taken a different turn had my brother not changed his own path. Our actions are all connected, whether we want them to be or not. But what exactly my life would have become, only Lord Krishna can answer, and I have chosen not to ask that of him. I am thankful not to have been given the knowledge of what would have been—only of what was.

While Hari Dev sat in a corner of the chamber, counting the birds he could find in the pillar carvings, Mahendra began to clear the offerings from the previous evening's prayer. He felt a strong need to move away from Bapu. He picked up the puckered remnants of a fruit, and it fell apart into a sticky mess in his fingers, oozing an amber liquid and giving off a sweet, pungent smell. He had a vision of Chandrabai and a thought that he knew was not appropriate to be having at the temple.

The heat rose once again to his face, but he turned to the other items around the shrine. The copper plates that had held the fruit were dented and tarnished. The urns containing the sacred water were chipped at the mouth and cracking along the base. The temple was a place of glory, but Mahendra did not see this. To him, it simply looked more and more piteous.

"What are you making that long face for, *beta*? This is a time to rejoice."

Mahendra turned to see Bapu approaching. He gestured at the plates and urns, at a loss for words.

"What?" Bapu looked around.

"Everything is falling apart."

"Don't worry, better times are coming. Great things. Here, you missed a piece of fruit."

Mahendra wanted to hurl something to the ground and watch it shatter. He heard Chandrabai calling to another *devadasi* from behind the temple. Exhaling, he sat by Hari Dev at the foot of one of the pillars and took his hand, stroking it. Hari leaned into him.

Bapu lit a stick of sandalwood incense and sat in silence for a while, meditating. Birds twittered and the sun shortened the shadows, its strengthening rays gradually warming Mahendra's back as they slid into the temple through the openings between the pillars. Outside, the clouds approached, and in our home, within the liquid warmth of Ma's body, my arrival drew near as well.

"*Bhai*, is Ma all right?" Hari Dev's voice was quiet.

Mahendra touched his arm lightly. "Yes, don't worry, she will be fine."

"And after the baby comes, will she smile more again?"

"I don't know. I hope so."

"And will Bapu be nicer?"

"Maybe. I hope that, too."

"Will you stay home more?"

Mahendra did not answer.

"Will our new sister become a *devadasi*?" Hari Dev continued.

Mahendra sighed and looked across the chamber. The *devadasis* had been a part of his world his entire life, belonging to the temple like the dunes belong to the desert, but lately he had begun to understand that their existence was not as simple as the shifting of sand under the wind. The response of his body to the sight of Chandrabai had awakened him to the other side of their lives, the side no one spoke of openly at the temple. Mahendra looked over at Bapu, who was still meditating.

"I hope not," he said to Hari Dev in a very quiet whisper.

"Why not?"

Mahendra looked into little Hari's trusting brown eyes and instantly regretted his words. He thought of Padmini, the sister Hari Dev did not even know we had, and found something to say.

"I think *devadasis* have to do a lot of things they don't want to do."

"Oh."

My brothers were sitting there, wrapped in the silence created by Bapu's meditation, when Saiprasad-ji the priest arrived, his feet slap-slapping the smooth floor as he made his way heavily to the shrine. Bapu rose and bowed to Saiprasad-ji, then motioned for his sons to do the same. The priest uttered a prayer and rang the brass bell.

The jangle of bangles, the click of toe rings on the stone floor, and a stream of chatter signaled the arrival of the remaining seven *devadasis*. Ten years earlier, in times of peace and plenty, there had been twenty-four of them. But drought, disease, and diminishing faith had taken their toll. Fewer girls had been born to the existing *devadasis*, and fewer families had given their daughters to the temple. They fell silent as they entered the chamber, bowing solemnly, but their eyes sparkled with excitement. They had seen the clouds as well. Chandrabai was the last to enter, and Mahendra drank in her presence as he would a cup of water.

Dutifully, the youngest *devadasis* swept the floor, arranged flowers, and chased away a family of desert coursers in a flurry of flapping wings, red cotton, and orange wool. Mahendra watched Chandrabai overseeing their work, the way her arms moved as she swept, the curve of her back. In this way, and in his belief that nothing could stand in his way, he was very much like all the other men. Then he noticed that Saiprasad-ji was watching Chandrabai as well. Intently. Too intently, Mahendra thought, although his own expression had been one of similar lust. He glanced at Bapu, who was blissfully putting on his dance bells, and at the other *devadasis*, who were intently avoiding the priest's gaze. Within a few moments, Saiprasad-ji had turned around and left the chamber. Mahendra watched Hari Dev stare at the priest's receding back.

The *devadasis* took turns to bow to our Lord Krishna and touch their teacher's feet.

Bapu beckoned to my brother. "Come, dance next to me."

Mahendra took his position and held himself as tall as possible. Chandrabai stood in the front row, just a few paces away from him, on purpose, he hoped. As he took in the garments she wore, a *ghaghra* and *choli* of peacock blue, the hem grazing her bare feet, he had an unwelcome vision of her elderly and wrinkled patron removing them. Looking through her and through the other *devadasis*, he tried to focus on the rhythm Bapu was tapping out with his feet. But his gaze faltered for a moment, his feet fumbled, and he saw Manavi-ji, the senior *devadasi* and Chandrabai's grandmother, look quickly from him to Chandrabai, frowning.

Afterward, Mahendra sat by Bapu's side, wondering about that look. He did not fully understand the depth of Manavi-ji's wisdom, but he knew enough to take note of her expression. Bapu was speaking to the *devadasis*, reminding them of their importance as vessels for communicating the divine, as bestowers of good fortune at weddings and births, of which there would be many if the rains did arrive. Bapu was reminding them of their oath to Krishna, their lord, their husband, as if any of them could ever forget.

My brother could not concentrate on Bapu's words, nor did he feel the need to. He looked around at the *devadasis*, occasionally daring to steal a look at Chandrabai, who stared consistently away from him. Manavi-ji now paid him no attention. He wondered if he had imagined her frown. But he had not. He pictured Chandrabai escaping with him, the nights they would spend together in the desert, the riches he, as the unequaled hero of Jaisalmer, would bestow upon her. Unexpectedly, his eyes met hers, and she shook her head almost imperceptibly.

And then, as if in answer to the storm within him, a gust of wind blew through the chamber, carrying on it droplets of moisture. At last! Even Bapu could not ignore it. Smiling, he declared the dance lesson over. The calls of Sundaran and the rest of the dwindling temple staff—the gardener, the watchmen, the accountant—echoed from the kitchen.

Mahendra leaped to his feet. He watched the *devadasis* bow hurriedly and leave, returning to their quarters. Chandrabai did not so much as look over at him. Manavi-ji rose gingerly and wrapped the end of her sari over her head, the green cloth framing her light eyes. She smiled at Bapu, and he smiled back, and Mahendra glimpsed for a moment the depth of their feelings and wondered at the way these two people, who had lived so closely for so many years yet, as tradition decreed, had never touched, could speak to each other without words. He felt the nobility of their comportment and the baseness of his lust for Chandrabai. It was one of those moments, so rare for him, in which he sensed the power of the temple, of faith, of dance. If only he had been able to hold on to them, to ground himself in them like a tree with deep roots. But like the spiraling powder designs on the temple floor on holy days, the moment for him was ephemeral, carried away on the breeze.

"Look," Bapu said. Beyond the temple entrance, the sky was darkening. Swirls of red dust danced on the floor and settled briefly on the central shrine, only to be picked up by the next gust of wind. Frightened, Hari Dev reached for our brother's hand. Mahendra lifted him up and carried him to the entrance. There, Bapu and Mahendra paused and gathered the white cloth of their *dhotis* around them as the wind whipped them against their legs. The first rolls of thunder rumbled in the distance, and Hari Dev broke into sobs, his arms tight around Mahendra's neck.

Bapu stroked Hari Dev's back awkwardly. "*Beta*, do not be afraid. Lord Krishna has finally answered our prayers."

"But why is it so loud?" Hari Dev's voice trembled.

Mahendra set him down on the floor and touched his arm. "It's the sound of Lord Indra traveling toward us across the sky in his chariot. It's going to rain soon. Your first rain."

They remained there for a moment, squatting on the sun-warmed floor at the temple entrance, looking out through the gateway, past the scrub bushes and the burial ground, to the desert beyond. Humid, heavy air filled their chests.

Bapu broke the spell. "We must go. The child is coming."

Mahendra did not doubt Bapu now. Hari Dev took Bapu's hand as they rose. As he always did when he was upset, he counted out loud. One step, two steps, three steps, four. Mahendra followed them as they eased their way down, one slowed by the passage of time, one by misshapen legs. It was a rare sight, Bapu comforting Hari Dev like this. But then, it was a rare sight to see the desert so transformed. An orange darkness had descended. The dry leaves of the *khajeri* trees and scrub bushes whipped in the wind. The first, heavy drops of rain splashed to the ground, vanishing into steam on the hot stone of the temple. Hari Dev let out a cry when the first drop fell on him, and Bapu laughed aloud. It was a sound Mahendra had almost forgotten. He wondered which to feel: our brother's fear or our father's joy. The eerie brightness of Lord Krishna's eyes still burned in his mind.

They hurried past the western end of Ghadisar Lake toward

home, on the outskirts of the citadel. A flock of cranes rose from the water and scattered raucously into the wind. Goats ran bleating in circles, uncontrolled, getting underfoot. On an ordinary day, the formidable walls of the citadel would be visible now, orange-brown sandstone fortifications rising up from the ochre sand, cut out against the dazzlingly blue sky. But now, with the rumbling black clouds and pouring rain, everything was dark and gray-brown. The air smelled of mud and ash. Mahendra and Bapu pulled Hari Dev along past a cluster of huts where women scurried, pulling in clothing and setting out pots to catch the rain. They passed the irrigation well, its mouth gaping open like that of a thirsty beast. Hari Dev was slowing them down. Mahendra picked him up and ran. By the time they reached our hut's courtyard, ropes of rain were splashing to the ground, weaving braids of red and brown in the dirt.

"Ma!" Mahendra called out, setting Hari Dev down on a rug as soon as they were under shelter, in the main living room.

"It's time," a voice answered him from Ma and Bapu's sleeping room. "Don't come in."

It was the midwife, about whom Mahendra had forgotten. A single oil lamp burned on the floor, by the prayer space, casting shadows across the rugs and cushions. Hari Dev sniffled and leaned his damp head against Mahendra, sucking his thumb.

Then Bapu came running in, rivulets of water trickling down his nearly bald head, his *dhoti* drenched and clinging to his legs. He rushed into the bedroom. There was a murmur of voices, a brief argument, and then the midwife was in the doorway, holding a lamp, beckoning Mahendra to come in, her eyes dark and wide. He hesitated. He was not supposed to see what was happening. He did not want to see it. But he heard Ma's weak voice calling for him, and so, instructing Hari Dev to stay where he was, Mahendra went into the bedroom.

Immediately, a metallic smell pressed against him in the dimness. Ma lay moaning on a sheet, her eyes shut. Mahendra panicked. He looked to Bapu, whose face betrayed his own feelings about the ways of flesh and blood.

Ma opened her eyes. Mahendra imagined that they met his gaze.

It was so easy to forget that her eyesight was weak. She smiled and held up her hand to hold his.

"I wanted you to be here. Both of you." She paused for a moment, and Mahendra tried to look anywhere but at her face.

The midwife squatted between Ma's legs, her knees jutting out awkwardly from her orange sari like bony twigs. The oil lamp by her side cast her distorted shadow, frog-like, on the packed-mud wall. The rain beat down, drumming an irregular rhythm on the roof.

Ma, still holding Mahendra's hand, took a breath and continued. "It is time for you to know some things."

"Girija?" Bapu uttered just one word, Ma's name, but his voice carried in it both caution and warning.

"It's all right." Ma pulled Mahendra down until he was kneeling on the floor. A fine sheen of perspiration on her face caught the lamplight. Bapu knelt on the other side of her, by her head, their bodies so close to each other, their sixteen-year age difference was striking. Ma's voice was a strained whisper.

"You are each so sure of what you think. That you, my son, can change a life, yours or someone else's. That you, my husband, can tell someone who they are meant or not meant to be." She paused for a moment, breathed in and out. "Either way, this is where it all begins."

Ma's grip on Mahendra's hand tightened even more, and she squeezed her eyes shut. His hand was going numb. With her next words, Ma's voice fell to a whisper.

"This is a new beginning for us all." Ma's eyes were always weak, but her vision was always great. "What shall we make of it?"

Mahendra looked over at Bapu, willing him to do something. Bapu looked paralyzed. Ma was the only person at the time who could have this effect on him.

"Bapu!"

Bapu shook his head, reached across Ma's body to pry her hand loose from Mahendra's, and placed it instead on the coil of cloth the midwife held out. Then he stroked Ma's forehead. Mahendra had never seen Bapu make such a gesture of tenderness. He turned his own head away.

"The rain has come," Bapu continued. "This child shall stay, and this child shall dance."

Mahendra backed away from Ma as her body contorted.

"She's coming now—I can feel her." Ma twisted her face and opened her eyes. Bapu was whispering, his lips moving in prayer, his hands folded together.

"O Lord Krishna . . . " The words floated into the air.

"Gandar!" Ma called out Bapu's name sharply, without the respectful suffix *-ji* that everyone else attached to it, which always caught Mahendra by surprise. But it pleased him, as well, that Ma was one who dared to break the rules. "I think you have prayed enough. If you're going to stay here, be prepared to help. Now."

The midwife was peering down, encouraging Ma to push me out. Mahendra's stomach turned, and he stood, backing away even more. There was a shout, and the midwife received me, small and glistening, in her hands. My cries filled the hut. Mahendra's eyes watered. He blinked and turned toward the doorway. There, several paces inside the room, was Hari Dev, huddled against the wall, wide-eyed and shivering, weak legs tucked under him. Beside him a thin trickle of our mother's blood swirled into a pool of rainwater.

Chandrabai
1555

They named me Adhira, born of lightning and rain. Adhira of the liquid eyes and shimmering hair. Adhira, who came early to end the drought and restore life to the desert, said Bapu. The rains lasted only two weeks, but during that time they were plentiful. Months after my birth, a pair of *chinkara* still lived by the lake, their dark horns glinting in the sunlight. Fox tracks had soon appeared alongside their hoof marks. Families of birds had returned to the temple grounds, pecking at newly green bushes. Lizards, indolent for months, darted in and out of view, chasing succulent beetles and mosquitoes. Water filled the wells around the city, and women gathered at their edges, balancing jugs on their heads.

Now, six months later, on the day before the Janmashtami festival to honor our Lord Krishna, Chandrabai was sitting by me. We were alone in the courtyard of the temple, in the shadow that the back wall threw upon the ground, a merciful respite from the ardor of Surya the Sun. Bapu was resting in the dance chamber and had asked Chandrabai to watch over me. The still air of early afternoon hung quietly over the temple. Even the insects were hiding, in the cracks between stones, in dry dirt holes.

Chandrabai watched me lying on a folded piece of cotton cloth, enjoying the tranquility of the moment. She was fifteen, and it was only a matter of chance that she had not yet had a child of her own, although in the *devadasi* quarters, there were already whispers on the subject.

"Come, Adhi, do you want to play?" She picked me up under my arms and pulled me to a standing position. There she held me for a moment, wondering at the lightness she felt in her own body. She sat me down and let go of me, and the sensation faded. It was the same sensation I have felt within me, as if the droplets of my blood were humming in unison with Lord Krishna's flute.

"Do you want to dance?" she said in a whisper. She held me up again and moved me from side to side, watching my little feet tap the floor. The sensation returned to her. Softly, she hummed a melody that Bapu often sang during dance lessons and sat me in the crook of her crossed legs. She felt my warmth against her stomach and chest, and she gently rested her chin on my head.

"Where is your brother?" She stroked the wispy curls at the base of my neck. "He left so suddenly, a few months back. He wouldn't even tell me where he was going. All he said was that he was fulfilling his real duty."

Chandrabai looked around the courtyard. "But his duty is here, isn't it? To the temple, to dance? To me, and to you?" She clasped her hands tight around me. "He'll be back tomorrow for the festival, at least. He can't possibly miss it. And we'll keep him here, right?" She rubbed her cheek on the top of my head, breathing in my milky smell. "You and I, we'll keep him here."

She stood me up again and turned me toward her. She looked into my face, seeking some validation of her belief in my brother. A hawk flew overhead and cawed loudly. It swooped down, landed briefly on the courtyard wall, cocked its head toward us, then took off again, circling once before disappearing from view.

"Chandrabai!" Sundaran the cook came running into the courtyard. "A messenger is here. Your patron has called for you."

Chandrabai closed her eyes. She nodded to Sundaran, who shrugged apologetically with a half smile. Then she stood, placed me on her hip, and returned me to Bapu, who was waking with a yawn, before heading toward the citadel.

She walked as slowly as she could. Two years earlier, when she had come of age, she had been given no say in her choice of patron, because of the lean times. It had pained Manavi-ji, but she had agreed to the highest bidder for her granddaughter. It had been an unusual moment of weakness, when Manavi-ji had first begun to feel unwell—although she had still told no one—and then it was too late. Now Chandrabai passed the lake and glanced at the women at its edges, envying them their afternoon of washing clothes together as she herself made her way toward the explorations of her patron.

She lingered a moment at the arched entrance to the lake, as a hawk swooped to the mirrored surface. Was it the same one she'd seen at the temple? Continuing on the path toward the citadel, she entertained a frequent daydream of hers. We have all, at times, sought refuge this way in our minds. Had Mahendra been able to do the same when the circumstances of his existence were too difficult for him, it might well have saved him, and our family. In Chandrabai's daydream, she thought of Mahendra, recalling their first, flustered encounter in the unused guard house behind the temple. Since that first time, he'd appeared more and more in her thoughts and dreams. For the six weeks the rains had lasted, she had seen him every day at the temple, had watched the muscles of his shoulders and calves as she danced, then felt them under her fingers during their unions. For her, it had been a glorious summer.

She climbed the long flagstone steps to the entrance of the citadel. Her throat tightened. This was always where it became difficult, when she was only a few moments away from her patron's home. The sun was still high overhead, and there was little shade in the narrow streets. Most people were indoors. She had overheard shards of conversations among some of the temple staff about foreigners and invasions, but she saw no evidence of either one around her—just the usual midday torpor and the smell of dung and spices. By the time she reached the ornate, carved door of her patron's home, drops of perspiration beaded on her temples and trickled between her breasts. She did not wipe them off; her patron enjoyed her that way. Closing her eyes for a moment before knocking on the door, she set her mind loose, willing it not to notice what her body was about to endure, in the way, like so many generations before ours, she had begun practicing soon after her coming-of-age ceremony.

Inside, a female servant, head bowed, led her up the dark, stone stairwell to the patron's chamber. He sat bare-chested, dark and shriveled like a piece of bark, on his wide bed, propped against a multitude of red and saffron cushions, amid an expanse of yellow silk. His legs emerged from his *dhoti* like twigs. The smell of his coconut body oil hung heavily in the air. His lips parted in a grin to reveal his betel nut–stained teeth as he leaned forward.

"Ah, my precious. It has been torture awaiting you since the day before yesterday." He waved the servant away. "Come fast to me, or my poor old body might no longer be able to contain itself."

Chandrabai swallowed hard and stepped forward, propelling herself into the evening and her reunion with Mahendra. For the remainder of the afternoon, she imagined that the bare skin against hers was his, smooth and taut. She imagined that the lips on her breast were Mahendra's, that the scratching she felt on her thigh was from the wiry hairs above Mahendra's upper lip. But in the depths of her need, what sprang to her mind was our Lord Krishna and his lover Radha, playful and happy, and dance, and the strains of a flute. That was her true sanctuary.

When he was finished, the patron reached under his pillows and pulled out a coin purse. He pressed it into Chandrabai's hand, folded her fingers over it, and brought them to his lips.

"For the festival tomorrow. Please give my regards to Saiprasad-ji. And there is a new outfit for you."

"Thank you," Chandrabai murmured, reaching for her own clothing. She dressed hurriedly while his eyes followed her every gesture. On her way home, she stopped at the lake to wash her face, rinsing the taste of her patron off her mouth, and felt the whole afternoon flowing away from her in the drops of water falling back into the lake.

Back at the temple, she found a swarm of activity. The *devadasis* were preparing for the festival. Her mother, Jayarani, and her aunt Devika were readying the inner sanctum, cleaning it and adorning our beloved Krishna with flowers. Chandrabai, her body tainted by her activities with her patron—sanctioned as they were—would not be allowed into the inner sanctum until the next day. Guilt for the times she had entered it after doing the same things with Mahendra washed over her. Her station as a *devadasi* did not allow her to have relations with a man who was not her patron or otherwise a financial supporter of the temple. As if she could make amends for her behavior, she threw herself into helping the youngest four *devadasis* with their preparations, recalling with envy the days when she was as they were, worried only about such little things as hair ribbons and bangles.

Saiprasad-ji bellowed from across the chamber. "Chandrabai!"

"Yes, Swami-ji." She used the term of respect that such men of erudition and religious standing usually deserve and always require. She looked behind her, to ensure that she was not alone, and avoided the priest's eyes.

"I need your grandmother, please. Go fetch her." Saiprasad-ji wiped a trickle of ever-present perspiration off his cheek.

Chandrabai put down her broom and went in search of Manavi-ji. She headed straight to the garden, where Manavi-ji often went to rest for a while on the wooden bench in the shade of the wall. Chandrabai approached the garden from the rear to enter through the little gate by the bench. As she neared it, she heard the voice of my mother, reaching over the high stone wall, and something about its tone made her remain out of sight.

"I can see it coming, Manavi," Ma was saying. "The way he looks at her, the way he sings to her and tells her the stories of the great epics. Even though she is just a few months old."

"It is hard not to. Just look at the girl. And the temple—"

Ma let out a sigh. "Don't tell me these things! I hear them all the time from my husband. I know the temple needs more *devadasis*. But she does not have to be one. And you are the only one who can give her a choice."

Pebbles crunched underfoot as Ma stood. Chandrabai took a few steps back, but when she found she could no longer hear, she approached once more. Ma was speaking again.

"Adhira is a gift. We won't have any more children. I know what you are going to say. If she wants to dance, so be it. I'm not asking anyone to prevent her from dancing. But what will happen when Gandar is gone? When you, Manavi, are gone?"

Chandrabai did not understand what Ma was talking about. Holding her bangles in place, she lowered herself against the wall directly behind the bench and sat down. She wondered if her teacher, my Bapu, was leaving soon, and if that meant Mahendra would return. Or perhaps, she worried, there was something truly wrong with her grandmother.

Ma continued, relentless. "Who will make sure Adhira is taken care of? If you bind her to the temple, what will happen if the temple is destroyed?"

Chandrabai felt a hollowness in her stomach at these words, imagining savage men running amok as the temple's walls and pillars crumbled. The flutter of joyous excitement in the temple chambers just up the path now seemed worlds away.

Manavi-ji spoke softly. Her voice was heavy. "Girija *ben*," she said, using the sisterly term of endearment, "it is too early to know what will happen. To any of us. Maybe . . . " Her last words were lost to Chandrabai as a breeze rustled the dry leaves.

"Please no, Manavi. Stroking my hair won't comfort me. Not now. Gandar will begin to train Adhira as soon as she's ready. I have to think of a way. . . . "

"Girija. Think of your other children. There are times to let go and times to hold on. What's that noise?"

A spider had crawled over Chandrabai's foot, and without thinking she had kicked it away, sending a small rock flying and knocking against another one. She scrambled to her feet, pulled some wisps of hair out of her braid, and started to breathe heavily, hoping the two women would believe that she had just run down the path.

"It's me, Dadima!" she said as she entered the garden. "Saiprasad-ji sent me to find you."

She sat down heavily on the bench next to her grandmother. Ma was carrying me, and I was watching Chandrabai.

Manavi-ji laughed and tucked Chandrabai's hair behind her ears. "What, did you just run all the way from the citadel?"

Ma resettled me on her hip. "I should go. I know you two have a lot to do. Hari, where are you?"

From the far end of the garden, where the gardener had planted some medicinal herbs, Hari Dev's limping form emerged. He liked to play there, to sit among the plants and make his wooden elephants and camels walk through their stalks. Sometimes Chandrabai heard him talking to himself, counting or whispering words she did not understand. Mahendra had told her about our brother's occasional fits, but he had not had a single one since my arrival.

When Hari Dev reached us, he raised his head to brush my leg with his lips. I have felt many lips against me, but those of my little big brother are the only ones that have ever held the essence of devotion.

Ma put her hand on his shoulder so that he could be her guide. She turned back to Manavi-ji. "Please think about it. You are the only person who can allow a change here."

My brother led us out of the garden, our shadows long and narrow behind us. Two other ghostly shadows followed behind us: Mahendra and Padmini. Chandrabai turned to her grandmother.

"What did Girija-ji want you to think about?"

Manavi-ji sighed. "She wants me to think about the future."

"Oh. So what was that about allowing a change?"

Manavi-ji turned and gave Chandrabai a long look, as if deciding whether she was ready to hear what she was about to say. She was thin and frail. Chandrabai straightened her back and tried to look as serious as she could, hoping her grandmother would deem her old enough to confide in. Something rustled behind a bush, and a peacock emerged, its trailing tail feathers raising a cloud of dust.

"The time will come," Manavi-ji said, "when Gandar-ji will have to ask for my blessing to make Adhira a *devadasi*, because she was not born one, unlike you. And I will have to decide what to do."

"And what will that be?"

Manavi-ji shrugged. "It's not all in my hands. There are things happening, out there." She waved in the direction of the desert. Then she turned to Chandrabai and took hold of her hands. The frail appearance of her fingers belied the strength of her grip. Her gray eyes bored into Chandrabai.

"There will be some hard times ahead. And we *devadasis* are very special. Our dance, our bodies, the stories we tell, the music and faith we inspire, they call forth the divine in others. Do you understand that?"

Chandrabai nodded. Yet the intensity of her *dadima*'s gaze frightened her. She did not truly understand.

"We help people see the divine. Never forget this." Manavi-ji let go of Chandrabai's hands. Chandrabai recalled the light sensation she'd felt earlier when she'd held me, and wanted to ask if she herself had been that way as a baby. But her grandmother had retreated into herself, her head turned toward the peacock pecking at the hard ground.

"Then why did Girija-ji speak about making different choices?" Chandrabai blurted out.

"Oh oh! I thought you ran straight down from the temple to fetch me!" Manavi-ji's serious face now broke into a smile. "How did you hear Girija-ji?"

Chandrabai's face reddened, and she looked down at her bare feet.

"Maybe I'd like to make a choice," she whispered.

"Well, you are already a *devadasi*, Chandra. No one can change that."

"No, I know." Chandrabai lifted her head but did not look at her grandmother's face. "I just meant . . . "

"What is it?"

"Well, what if there were someone, you know, someone I wanted to be with?" Chandrabai felt the heat rising to her face.

Manavi-ji's face lost its tenderness. "Mahendra?"

Chandrabai nodded.

Her grandmother let out a breath. "I was afraid of that. Chandra, it's not a good idea."

Chandrabai closed her eyes. To her, it was not an idea at all. It was not something that she had simply decided. It was a necessity.

She opened her eyes. "Why not?"

Manavi-ji shook her head. "Just forget about him."

"I don't think I can. I don't want to." Chandrabai looked down at her hands, which blurred with sudden tears.

Manavi-ji put her hand on her back. "In any case, Gandar-ji would not allow it. If he knew, he would make you choose."

"So I do have a choice?"

"Mahendra or the temple."

Chandrabai wiped her eyes and looked up at Manavi-ji. The temple was her home, the meaning to her life, the place where she knew she belonged. Her grandmother watched her, slowly shaking her head.

Chandrabai stood. "I don't want to talk about this anymore. Let's go. Saiprasad-ji asked to speak with you."

Together they left the garden and walked up the path to the temple. The sun had dropped below the horizon. The day watchmen were ceding their place to the night watchmen at the entrance to the grounds, but here at the side, the guardhouse was empty. There were just two guards left. Not long before, there had been eight, but the temple manager had sent six away. Chandrabai wondered why the *devadasis* were no longer worth protecting.

She and Manavi-ji walked quietly past the outer dance area and into the inner courtyard. Three sticks of incense burned at the entrance to the shrine. Three spirals of blue smoke mingled and melted into the twilight. The air was cooling, but Chandrabai's bare feet felt the day's warmth retained in the stone floor. This was home. She stood for a while in the courtyard, waiting for her *dadima* to catch up to her, enjoying the emptiness. Tomorrow, the temple would teem with devotees, pilgrims, and city residents. The Raja of Jaisalmer himself would be present, accompanied by his royal retinue. For now, however, the evening stillness was all that filled the courtyards and chambers.

From the outer sanctum came the resonant, rhythmic jingle of *ghunghru*, a dancer's ankle bells. Chandrabai knew, from the sound's depth, that it was her guru, my father, the only dancer to wear as many as two hundred little bells on each ankle. The sound made her smile, and she and Manavi-ji moved toward it. The oil lamps cast a warm glow on the cream-colored stone. The air smelled sweetly of incense and cumin. Chandrabai watched the shadows of the carved nymphs, elephants, and monkeys dancing in the breeze and felt lucky to be in this moment.

Bapu stood with his back to them, facing the entrance to Lord Krishna's shrine. His head was bowed, his hands were joined at the palms in front of him, and his eyes were closed in meditation. Manavi-ji held out her hand to Chandrabai, who helped her ease herself down against the pillar. Gathering their skirts and shawls around them against the chill in the air, they sat at the pillar's base. Chandrabai was witnessing the divine about which her grandmother had been speaking. Shame washed over her at the thought of what she had done, and hoped to do again soon, with her guru's son.

Bapu slowly raised his head, and from him came the rich, many-layered sound *aum*. It swelled from deep within him, rose through his chest, was formed by his lips, and emerged to fill the room with its calm intensity. It wrapped itself around each pillar, expanded to the ceiling, found every crevice in the carvings and in Chandrabai's body, hummed through the marble and her bones, until she felt as one with her teacher and the temple. Then Bapu began to sing, paying respect to the trinity of Brahma the Creator, Vishnu the Preserver, and Maheshvara the Destroyer. Next, he invoked the five elements of Sky, Wind, Fire, Water, and Earth.

Moving slowly across the floor, Bapu danced. Chandrabai could not see his face, but she knew, simply from the easy set of his shoulders, the peace he had attained. She watched him dance a poem to our beloved Lord Krishna, his hand gestures indicating the mark of sandalwood paste on Krishna's forehead; the glittering crown that adorns his head; the conch, discus, mace, and lotus he holds in his glorious hands.

Bapu came to a standstill at the center of the room, still facing away. Chandrabai glanced at her grandmother to see if they should say something, but Manavi-ji bore a look of faraway longing that robbed Chandrabai of any words. A murmur to the left broke the spell. Turning toward it, she saw Hari Dev sitting with his legs folded under him, and me nestled in his lap under a wool blanket. My head against my brother's chest, I watched my father. It was a perfect place to be. And as always in my presence, Hari Dev was tranquil.

"Help me up," Manavi-ji said, and Chandrabai held her arm as she rose.

"Manavi! I did not know you were there," Bapu said, turning toward them.

They sat with him when he joined us. My father slowly uncoiled the rows of bells from his ankles, and my brother stroked my hair. Then a familiar slapping sound and the tinkle of the prayer bell sounded. Saiprasad-ji.

Chandrabai jumped up.

"What is this? Were you bitten by a snake?" Bapu was laughing, but my brother began to suck his thumb. Chandrabai noticed that my lip curled down.

Saiprasad-ji entered the chamber. "Good evening. What luck to find you all here. Look at this baby, your precious gift to the temple. We are all blessed." He beamed at us, then turned to Chandrabai. "Just the girl I was looking for. It's time to put Lord Krishna to sleep and close the temple for the night. Come snuff out the lamps."

Chandrabai knew what this meant. All the *devadasis* did. A lump formed in her throat.

"I thought . . . " She glanced at her grandmother. "I thought you needed to speak with Dadima."

"What is this?" Bapu said once again, this time the laughter draining from his voice. "You must go with the priest."

Manavi-ji stepped forward. "Well, why don't I do it? I haven't closed the temple for quite a while. Swami-ji, come with me, and we can speak about the festival preparations."

"No! We cannot have this kind of disrespect from a *devadasi.* Chandrabai must do it if Swami-ji asked her. Go!"

Manavi-ji gave Chandrabai an apologetic look but urged her forward with a nod.

"Yes, Gandar-ji," Chandrabai said.

"Good girl." Saiprasad-ji fell in step behind her. "All this fuss for nothing. What are you making that sad camel face for? Come, let's start at the back of the temple. We'll be done in no time."

They crossed the outer chamber, passed the smaller shrines, and walked toward the dance chamber at the back of the temple, away from the kitchen and the guard house, where the watchmen and Sundaran the cook would be. Away from Manavi-ji, her teacher, Hari Dev, and me. She heard our voices fading.

She turned to face the priest. "I can do it alone, Swami-ji."

His small eyes, nestled deep in his face, narrowed slightly at her. "Oh no, I'll come with you and do some as well. Faster that way, right?"

"Which ones will you be doing?" She hoped that he would step in front of her and that she could then follow. He did not.

He held his ground. "Oh, you get started with the lamps in the dance chamber."

Chandrabai's pulse quickened as she walked forward. She kept him in her peripheral sight as she fetched a pile of covers for the oil lamps, but when she reached up to a high ledge upon which one of the lamps sat, she felt him approaching. His wheezing breath sounded close to her ear, followed by another sound.

A small voice. "Chandra *didi*?"

Saiprasad-ji turned around and stumbled a few steps away. Chandrabai turned as well. Hari Dev was standing in the entrance, apology and alarm blending on his pointed little face. Darling Hari Dev.

"Hari?" Saiprasad-ji wiped his forehead with his arm. "What are you doing here? Why are you not with your Bapu?"

Hari Dev shrugged and looked down.

"It's all right." Chandrabai handed him the lamp covers. "Here, do you want to hold these for me?"

Saiprasad-ji frowned. Hari Dev nodded and limped forward, cradling the stack of lamp covers against his chest. Together, they extinguished all but three lamps, and by the time they headed out of the dance chamber, the priest was gone.

A sickening sensation of unease still lingered with Chandrabai when, early the next morning, she made her way to the temple kitchen. She could still hear, even feel, the priest's moist breath near her ear. She remembered the look on Hari Dev's face. Years later, as she watched me dance, these memories would surface, fitting together like fragments of a puzzle.

In the kitchen, Sundaran the cook was sifting through a large pot of uncooked rice, inspecting it for insects. Beside him was a mound of freshly made coconut sweets.

"Chandra, there you are!" Manavi-ji appeared from the back of the kitchen. Chandrabai stood in the doorway, rubbing sleep from her eyes and looking warily around for the priest, even though it was too early for him to be about.

"Come, this is the best place to be on festival mornings." Manavi-ji beckoned her granddaughter in. "Better than with the girls and their squabbles."

The voices of the girls drifted into the kitchen from the courtyard in the *devadasi* quarters. On occasion, that of Jayarani, Chandrabai's mother, rose above the chatter. Chandrabai, now a woman, was no longer part of their world. She lingered in the doorway.

"Come, Chandra." Her *dadima* pulled her gently in.

Sundaran grinned as he looked up from the rice. "Here, Chandra baby, I'll give you some nice sweet. Special-special one." He pointed to the pile of coconut balls.

Chandra had to smile. Sundaran always put aside something sweet and tasty especially for her on festival days. Next to the growing mound of sweets, rice and vegetables were piled on mats, ready to be prepared for the pilgrims, some of whom would have walked several days from distant villages in the desert. Chandrabai's mouth watered as she squatted to help chop some okra. The food was still plentiful, thanks to the previous summer's rains. No one knew how short-lived that bounty would be.

"Dadima?"

"Yes? Is something bothering you?"

Chandrabai looked over at Sundaran.

He smiled at her, stood slowly, and stretched his arms. "I'll just go and check on the water supplies. Make sure all the jugs are full."

Chandrabai watched him leave, then turned to her grandmother. She dug her fingers into the dry stickiness of the chopped okra.

"Is Adhira special?" she asked quietly.

Manavi-ji, squatting on the floor by her, looked into her face. "Of course. So are you."

"No, no. Not like that. Really special. Like . . . magic." Chandrabai avoided her grandmother's look.

"Why do you ask?"

Chandrabai pulled her hand out of the okra and pressed her

thumb and forefingers together. Gummy strings stretched between them.

"Yesterday, when I went to blow out the lamps . . . "

"Did Saiprasad-ji do something?" Manavi-ji's voice was sharp.

"No, not really. Not more than usual. Has he ever done more to anyone? Would he?"

"No. I don't believe he would. Not after so many years. But what's this to do with Adhira?"

"I think Adhira protected me," Chandrabai whispered.

"How?"

"By sending Hari Dev to find me."

Manavi-ji sat back on her heels and nodded slowly.

"Does Mahendra know?" Chandrabai now looked at her grandmother. "About Adhira being so special?"

"Mahendra?"

Chandrabai shrugged once more. "Maybe he would come back and stay?"

"I thought I told you to forget about him, Chandra."

"I know, Dadima. But it's not that easy."

"I know, *beti*, I know," Manavi-ji said with a sigh.

Chandrabai stood and wiped her hands on her skirt. She looked at the food around her and, believing Mahendra would return to the temple for the festival, decided to prepare a special plate for him.

"Manavi-ji! The court gifts have arrived!" One of the girls came running, her long braid flying behind her, and held on to the side of the doorway to stop herself from skidding into the kitchen. She stood in the entrance, jumping up and down, unable to contain herself. "They've brought all the offerings!"

"Go." Manavi-ji waved toward Chandrabai. "Tell them where to put everything. I'd rather stay sitting here."

Chandrabai looked at Dadima's tired face, but she could not worry, not now, not when there were gifts to receive. She ran out to the temple entrance.

Outside the gates, a small crowd had formed. Against the sky, tinged pink by Surya the Sun, rose the silhouette of an elephant, a slender driver sitting on its neck and cloth-bound bundles tied onto its back. Two court attendants stood by its trunk. Dust still hung in the air behind the elephant, kicked up by its large feet. Children who had followed it down from the citadel stood shyly to the side, some daring to reach out as if to touch the creature, but too far from it to make contact. Chandrabai assumed an air of studied authority and nodded to the elephant driver, who clambered onto the bundles and began to hand items down to the attendants.

Chandrabai told the attendants where to take the offerings. Many of the items were intended for the *devadasis*. But the bundles were even smaller than in recent years. There were copper bowls of deep orange and red saffron threads to flavor rice, and silver ornaments for the younger dancers, but there were no gold platters upon which to rest garlands or the prayer bell. There were fine sticks of sandalwood incense for ritual ceremonies, but there were no bolts of silk for new costumes. A *devadasi* is a *devadasi* without any belongings, but to Chandrabai, the diminished offerings were disconcerting.

Later, after the midday meal and rest time, under the silhouettes of the thorny *babul* trees at the back of the temple, the gardener gathered orange marigolds and yellow *jendu*, gently dropping the flowers onto red cloths, which Chandrabai brought in to the *devadasi* girls by the armful. They were cool and soft, and Chandrabai held them against her skin. Rested, bathed, dressed, and jeweled, the girls sat in a circle in the outer courtyard, their oiled and combed heads bent in concentration over the garlands they strung. As they completed them, Chandrabai placed them in the inner sanctum, around the images of our beloved Lord Krishna, and in the shrines throughout the temple.

By the time the pilgrims began to stream into the outer courtyard, Surya's last rays were slanting into the temple's pillared main chamber. The temple hummed with activity like a beehive at dusk. Lord Krishna was born at midnight; the festivities would take place throughout the night. Chandrabai's heart pounded, her desire to dance and her desire for Mahendra beating a frenzied and confusing rhythm.

She returned to the kitchen to find Manavi-ji but saw only Sundaran.

"Gone to her quarters, she said," Sundaran told Chandrabai. His already lined forehead was creased into additional furrows.

Chandrabai swallowed. "I think she is fine. Don't worry." She hoped to sound convincing.

Sundaran shrugged. "Well, go, then. I don't need any more help. Everything is ready."

Chandrabai hesitated, wanting to ask him what he thought was wrong with her grandmother. But he was just a cook, and it would not have been proper to solicit his opinion. Instead, she found two large clay bowls and filled each one with a plentiful amount of rice, vegetables, lentils, and sweets. One for Manavi-ji, and one for Mahendra. She would bring Mahendra his after the performance, when they might slip away unnoticed for a while. She covered the bowls with a palm leaf and tucked them onto an empty shelf. Sundaran knew not to ask what she was doing.

She left the kitchen to join the other *devadasis*. The courtyard echoed with the sounds of walking sticks tapping against stone, clay cups of water for thirsty travelers shattering dully on the floor and scraping across the stone under the groundskeeper's broom. Occasionally, the voices of the faithful rose up in devotional song. From somewhere near the temple well came the tapping, twanging sounds of the drummers and musicians tuning their instruments. Chandrabai's pulse quickened. She hurried to her place with the *devadasis* in the inner courtyard, where Bapu was reviewing with them the plan for the evening.

"Remember, pour your whole being into the dance." Bapu looked up briefly at Chandrabai, then continued. "Dance in such a way that you become one with everything. Reward these pilgrims for their faith. Some have worn away the very skin on the soles of their feet just to be here tonight."

Bapu paced back and forth, possessed by an untamed energy. Then Chandrabai noticed me, strapped to his lower back like a bundle, held tight with an extra length of *dhoti*. Chandrabai stifled a laugh. How odd it was to see a man, her teacher, carrying a baby like this! She glanced over at her mother as she sat down beside her on the floor. Jayarani shook her head ever so slightly.

"Jayarani! What are you frowning about?"

"Nothing, Guru-ji. I am just reminding myself that while this is a joyous occasion, it is a serious one as well."

"Right!" Bapu waved an arm in the air. "Very serious. Now, Jayarani, you will be dancing tonight."

Chandrabai looked from her mother to her teacher while something plummeted inside her.

"Ma," she blurted out, "I thought I was dancing tonight!"

Jayarani shook her head and held her finger to her lips.

"We must make our celebration of Lord Krishna as pure as possible," Bapu said pointedly.

Tears springing to her eyes, Chandrabai finally understood. She was still too unclean from her time with her patron the day before. She could not take part in any sacred acts for another full day. It was, yet again that day, an instance of her wishes being foiled by the circumstances of her position. A variation on a theme. In dance, such a variation, a *kaida*, is a thing of great beauty. But Chandrabai saw no beauty in the *kaida* of her life.

"It's not fair," she whispered, wiping at her eyes. She imagined Mahendra among the pilgrims, looking desperately for her, giving her one last chance, not finding her, leaving.

Bapu's voice was soft. "I know, Chandra. It is disappointing. But you have Lord Krishna in your heart; you do not need to dance to feel his love." He turned to the other *devadasis* and motioned for them to rise. "Come, the devotees are waiting."

Chandrabai fell in step behind them. Ahead of her, I clung to Bapu's back. *Like a hump on a bull,* Chandrabai thought, scowling. If this was the effect I was having on Bapu, making him even stricter, then maybe, she thought, I was not such a blessing after all. The grasses may have greened and the lake filled, but Mahendra had left and Manavi-ji had tired, all following my arrival. *Adhira may have brought the rains*, Chandrabai thought, *but she brought something else as well.*

The *devadasis* entered the main section of the temple, the younger girls carrying burning incense and garlands of marigolds. The courtyards and dance hall overflowed with pilgrims and devotees, town people and villagers, court attendants and, between the two central columns at the front of the dance space, the Raja, seated on a woven rug of deep red wool. Simple white *dhotis*, bare chests, jewel-colored saris, the crude silver bangles of the villagers, and the filigreed gold of nobles all mixed together. Such is the strength of our dance and our faith.

Chandrabai craned her neck to find Mahendra, but she saw no sign of him. People jostled to see the dance space. Children pushed their way through rows of legs for a better view. Chandrabai tried to clear her mind of her sour thoughts and opened her ears to the sounds around her. The plaintive melodies of the *sarangis'* strings filled the spaces between the deep and vibrant beats of the drums. Saiprasad-ji and two other priests, dressed in ceremonial orange, chanted from the scriptures, their voices spiraling above the chatter of the eager crowd.

In honor of Lord Krishna, who wears a peacock feather in his hair, the *devadasis* wore blue and green and gold. The eyes of the young ones sparkled like water in silver bowls. Chandrabai took her place beside them, seated at the back of the dance space, losing hope of Mahendra's seeing her at all. And then the legendary story of the birth of Krishna, the most special of children, began.

Jayarani was wicked Kamsa the King, her feet hitting the stone floor with haughty assurance. On the day of his sister's wedding to a nobleman, an oracle predicted that her eighth child would kill him. Rage widened Jayarani's eyes and tightened her lips. Kamsa threw the couple in prison. Watching her mother, Chandrabai had a thought: *What if Adhira, Gandar-ji's child, was an incarnation of a deity?* Chandrabai observed this well-known story in a whole new light.

Jayarani's arms described the bars of the prison in which the couple's first child was born, and the next, and the next. And each time, Kamsa took the child and killed him. Then the eighth child was born, and he was Krishna. His skin was dark as a cloud, and his face was radiant. Finding the prison guards in a deep sleep, the nobleman escaped with Krishna.

Rain fell in torrents that night, the same way it had on the night of my birth. Chandrabai pictured me in the arms of her dancing mother. The river waters rose. Placing Krishna in a basket upon his head, the nobleman entered the river. Jayarani's body swayed with the waves. Suddenly, a ten-hooded cobra sprang from the water and spread one of its hoods over the basket, protecting Krishna from the rain. Chandrabai struggled to find new meaning in the dance. Was the cobra Mahendra, violent but protective?

The nobleman reached Gokul, a village in which a cowherd's wife had just given birth to a daughter. Quickly, he slipped into their home and replaced the girl with Krishna, then hurried back to the prison with the cowherd's child. The guards heard the child's cries and alerted the King, who rushed to the prison. Just as he clasped the infant to his chest, he felt the child slip away. Chandrabai sought me out through the crowd, wondering if I, too, would slip away, if I was a threat or a protector.

Krishna's voice mocked the King from the sky, telling him the child who would kill him was now growing up in Gokul. Kamsa sent a she-demon to Gokul. When little Krishna saw her, dressed in beautiful clothes and offering to feed him, he happily took the milk from her breast. The milk was poisoned, but Krishna smiled and ate, and in so doing sucked the life from her.

With a swirl of gold, blue, and green and a flash of eyes, Jayarani concluded her dance. She bowed to Bapu, to the priests, and to the crowd. Chandrabai was lost in a whirl of thoughts when a sudden glimpse of a slight form next to Manavi-ji at the back of the hall jolted her back into the moment. Mahendra! She stood at once.

The crowd had risen as well, anxious to take the sacred dust from the *devadasis*' feet, to touch, if only for an instant, the divine. Chandrabai looked helplessly across the mass of devotees. A few of them were attempting to throw themselves onto the dance floor, to roll their bodies in the area in which Jayarani had danced. A line was forming in the doorway, bulging in areas like an overfed snake. The devotees and pilgrims eagerly held out their offerings. Turning away, Chandrabai pushed past the younger girls to leave the dance hall through the back doorway, taking with her a shawl under which to hide. She doubled back around through the courtyard and ran into the kitchen to collect the bowls for her grandmother and Mahendra.

Her head covered with her shawl, she pushed her way through

the crowds, going against their current, trying not to spill the contents of the bowls. She emerged at the back of the hall, where a small cluster was gathered in a corner: Manavi-ji, Mahendra, Ma, and Hari Dev. There was an air of gravity in the way their heads leaned close together. Chandrabai hesitated a moment to join them, but her grandmother looked up and motioned her close. Chandrabai then noticed me sitting in Manavi-ji's lap.

"I brought you food." Chandrabai set the bowls down in front of Mahendra and Manavi-ji. "I'm sorry, Girija-ji—I didn't know you would be here, too."

"That's all right. I will eat later. You're sweet to have thought of them."

Chandrabai blushed and sat across from Mahendra. She could not raise her eyes to meet his, but instead looked at his long, lithe fingers as they twisted in his lap. She searched for something clever or poetic to say but could think of nothing.

Manavi-ji brushed a finger gently on Chandrabai's cheek. "Mahendra has come to say good-bye."

Chandrabai snapped her head up. "Good-bye? But he's only just now come back!" Now she looked across at Mahendra, but his eyes avoided hers. Chandrabai looked down at me and scowled. But when I smiled, she could not direct any anger at me. Instead, she put out her index fingers for me to hold on to for balance and stood me up.

"Where is he going?" She directed this at Manavi-ji.

Mahendra replied. "To fight. I have been preparing for a while."

"Fight? The Muslims? Does Guru-ji know?"

Mahendra winced, his lips tight. "To fight for all of you. And to save Adhira from what Bapu would have her do."

"*Beta*," Ma said gently, "are you sure you need to leave?"

"Yes! Sitting around here and dancing—where will that get us? With all due respect . . . ," he said, lowering his eyes and nodding slightly toward Manavi-ji and Chandrabai.

Ma sighed, and they sat in silence for a moment. Chandrabai heard her heart pounding in her chest and ears. She let go of one of my hands, I teetered, and Mahendra reached out to hold me up. Chandrabai watched me laugh and curl my fingers around his.

"Bapu thinks Adhira is lucky," Mahendra said, "but he is wrong. The rains came when she was born, but what good has happened since then?"

Ma shook her head. "Hush!"

"No, really, Ma. I am doing this for all of you."

No, you must stay—you belong here, Chandrabai pleaded silently.

Mahendra rose. "I'll come back whenever you need me. I promise."

Chandrabai closed her eyes, praying that those words were intended for her, not Ma. When she opened her eyes, she saw his form in the doorway. He had paused, waiting for her. She jumped up and ran to him, shaking off Manavi-ji's hand as she tried to pull her back down. As she approached him, he turned slowly to face her. She stopped two paces from him. Behind him, in the courtyard, devotees sat and squatted in lamp-lit clusters with their plates of food, eating noisily and calling out to small children who ran and gathered around them like sand eddies around rocks. Behind her, she knew Manavi-ji and Ma and Hari Dev and I were sitting still and quiet, with two plates of untouched food. And in the middle, below the stone carvings of peacocks and dancing nymphs, she stood and raised her eyes to Mahendra's. He looked back at her, his soft brown gaze reflecting her confusion, her uncertainty, her desire, and he reached his hand out as if to take hers right there, in front of everyone. She held her own hand out, anticipating the warmth that had traveled through her when she had held me, but before they could touch, the temple bells erupted in syncopated peals that resonated throughout the chambers and courtyards. It was midnight, the birth hour of Lord Krishna.

"The lake at sunset," Mahendra said quickly. "Sundaran will tell you whenever I am back. Find me at the lake at sunset." He hoisted his bag onto his shoulder, hesitated, and then added, "Good for you for not dancing today. Don't let my father tell you what you are. He is under Adhira's spell, but I will make sure it is broken."

But I wanted to dance! Chandrabai thought. She closed her eyes and winced as though she had been dealt a blow. And when she reopened them to say something, anything, Mahendra was gone. A disappearing act, as Bapu would say.

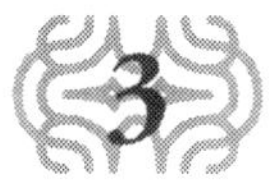

Gandar

1556

Mango!" My favorite. I had run into the temple kitchen before Bapu could stop me. The yellow-red fruits sat invitingly next to Sundaran on the cutting stone.

Sundaran shook his head and put his hands around them. "Sorry, baby, these are the last ones. We have to save them for offerings."

Bapu caught his look. Last mangoes. No more fruit coming from the court. Until when? I swallowed the saliva that had gathered in my mouth in anticipation of the sweet slices. Instead, I savored the sweetness of knowing that Lord Krishna would partake of the offering.

Bapu had faith. "The rain will come, Sundaran. The rain will come."

Sundaran pinched his lips and shook his head. "Have you heard the news from Delhi?"

"What news?"

"The Emperor died. Fell off his roof while looking at the stars. And now his son Akbar is on the throne."

Bapu shrugged. All these political happenings meant little to him.

Sundaran stirred a pot of lentils that sat on a pile of glowing coals. "Akbar is only thirteen, but they say his regent has plans for him to invade our Princely States."

"Thirteen?" Bapu laughed. "We are scared of a thirteen-year-old?"

But he thought of Mahendra, and what destruction *he* might be capable of if he were given free reign and the entitlement of an emperor. At the same time, a heaviness spread in his chest. He had not seen his son since Mahendra's departure, and he assumed no one else had, either.

"I know, Gandar-ji, but the armies are massing. And Akbar was born in Hindustan. He is a son of this land. He has a strong following. Not like his lazy father." Sundaran ladled some lentils into a bowl of rice and handed it to Bapu. "Here is your meal."

Bapu took the bowl. "We must believe in the power of our devotion."

He shared his food with me, letting me reach into his tray with my fingers. Afterward, he carried me over the hot stone floor and brought me to the relative coolness of the dance hall. I lay down on the floor by the gate to the outer sanctum, on a piece of red quilted cloth, and Bapu told me a story.

"Not long ago, there lived a princess. Her name was Mirabai. Except she was not a princess in her heart. When she was three, just a bit bigger than you, someone gave her a doll of Lord Krishna. It immediately became her favorite thing. She kept it with her at all times and, when she was a little older, decided to love only Krishna. She started writing poetry and songs about Krishna. Her family married her to a prince, but still she adored Lord Krishna. When she sang her songs, she would not notice anything else. She became famous; people heard about her music and poems throughout the land, and she became known as a saint. Eventually, she left her family, the prince, her home, and all her worldly possessions—all her things—in search of Lord Krishna himself. That, precious one, is devotion."

Bapu looked down at me. I had fallen asleep, but I had heard his every word. Bapu rose and danced softly without his bells so as not to wake me, banishing thoughts of invaders pouring into the temple.

"Gandar-ji!" The priest's bellowing voice suddenly echoed through the temple. A moment later, he entered the dance hall.

Bapu widened his eyes and motioned to me in silence.

"Oh, my apologies." Saiprasad-ji lowered his head but not his voice. "I hadn't realized you had the little one with you. Although not so little anymore!" The priest shuffled toward me as I lay sleeping.

Bapu smiled. "Yes, she is growing up quickly. Just more three years, and we can start her formal training. Although, truth be told, I see no reason to wait even that long."

"I'm glad you mentioned that." Saiprasad-ji sidled so close that Bapu could hear his labored breath. "I wasn't going to say anything for a while, but you might want to secure Manavi's blessing sooner rather than later." Here, he looked up at Bapu meaningfully.

Bapu raised his eyebrows.

"Surely you've noticed Manavi has not been dancing lately, no?"

Bapu nodded. He had, in fact, noticed that Manavi-ji had not been at the temple in a few days. When he had seen her, her face was drawn and she tired much more easily than before.

"I don't know for sure," Saiprasad-ji said, "but I think it is serious. She is hiding something. Chandrabai tells me she can no longer leave her quarters. It's best you not wait, if you see what I mean. Especially since Chandrabai is still without child. Not enough girls to ensure our prosperity."

Bapu nodded again, slowly. He realized with shame that he should have asked after Manavi-ji's health. He had assumed her illness would be a passing one, and that she would return to dance, as she had always done. If she did not, and the worst came to pass, her daughter, Jayarani, would become the matriarch. Jayarani's own daughter, Chandrabai, was straying, Bapu thought. He knew Jayarani could not fill the role of *devadasi* matriarch with anything close to the integrity her mother had brought to it.

"I will leave you be." Saiprasad-ji backed away. "Please let me know what you decide to do. Let Lord Krishna be your guide."

Bapu heard me call out to him in a voice still laden with sleep. He came over to me and rested his hand on my head. There was no question for him as to what he would do. There never had been. Nor did he consider for a moment discussing it with Ma.

A little while later, we stood at the entrance to the *devadasi* quarters with Chandrabai, who had agreed to direct Bapu to Manavi's room. Bapu had never entered these quarters. No man had. Chandrabai hesitated.

Bapu spoke quietly. "It is all right, Chandra."

Chandrabai nodded, her eyes on the ground. She fingered her skirt nervously.

"I must see your *dadima*," Bapu said. "You are not doing anything wrong."

I had been with Ma several times to the quarters. I tugged at my father's *dhoti*. "Bapu, I know where Manavi-ji is."

But neither Chandrabai nor Bapu heard me. Nodding again, Chandrabai held the gate open for us. "Over there, with the red curtain."

Bapu reached down and took my hand before stepping into the courtyard around which the *devadasi* quarters were laid out. Bapu reasoned to himself that the circumstances warranted his presence. Still, he felt a trespasser. Chandrabai left our side and disappeared behind a curtain a few doorways from Manavi-ji's. Bapu raised his eyes and looked around.

The ground was swept clean. It was early afternoon, rest time. Only the occasional muffled voice, the jingle of bells being put away, and the clink of coins being counted broke the silence. In the middle of the courtyard lay silk and cotton saris set out to dry, held down with rocks. Bapu wished that someone other than Chandrabai would see us. It did not seem right to him to be bringing his request to Manavi-ji in such a clandestine way, when instead it was an occasion for celebration. I tugged on Bapu's hand, and he let me lead him to the red curtain.

"Manavi-ji!" he called out, his voice too loud. A crow responded hoarsely, hopping into the shade. In the silence that followed, Bapu briefly considered turning around and leaving. But he knew, and I knew even then, that this was something he needed to do, for his own peace of mind, for the knowledge that he was fulfilling his duty.

"Guru-ji?" came Manavi-ji's weak voice.

"Yes. Please forgive me for coming here. It is important."

"It must be. I'll be ready in just a moment."

Then something fell to the ground. At the sound, Bapu wondered if Manavi-ji needed help. But he could not enter until she invited him in. The next few moments seemed like an eternity, but eventually she called for him. Pushing me ahead of him, he pulled aside the curtain and entered her room.

As Bapu held the curtain, a shaft of sunlight fell on Manavi-ji's bed. For a brief moment, it illuminated twisted bedsheets and a blanket spilling onto the floor. The bed was empty, but it held the shadow of a recent presence. She had left her bed hurriedly, so as not to be seen in it. It embarrassed Bapu to have such an intimate glimpse into her room. He let the curtain fall, and the room became dark. From the other side came Manavi-ji's voice, thin but warm as always.

"Guru-ji, I am here, on the rug."

Bapu and I blinked away the dimness and the spots of sunlight that still danced in front of our eyes. He let me guide him toward the back of the room, where I had been many times with Ma. The darkness began to recede. The cloth hangings on the walls came into view, as did piles of costumes and clothes, and Manavi-ji's low table covered in pots of cosmetics and combs. A sickly, unpleasant odor hung in the air. Manavi-ji sat on a woven rug amid tasseled cushions. Her gray hair, which Bapu had only ever seen in a long braid, cascaded loosely down her shoulders and back, framing her hollow face and startlingly light eyes. She had pulled a maroon shawl around her shoulders and a dark blanket over her legs. She struggled now to push it down to cover her feet. They appeared in a way Bapu had never seen before. The skin was dry, whitish toward the soles, cracked at the heels. The toenails were yellow and uneven. Bapu averted his eyes. It seemed to him that these feet could not be the ones that thousands had bent to touch over the years, the ones that had made her seem weightless and had created such beauty.

Manavi-ji continued to try to push the blanket down with her hands, but she could not reach her feet. She was desperate to hide the soles from Bapu's view. To show one's teacher the soles of one's feet is a terrible sign of disrespect. Bapu did not know what to do to alleviate her shame. Had he reached down to help her, he would have aggravated it. Their shared anguish filled the room. I stepped forward, took hold of the blanket's end, and covered Manavi-ji's feet as gently as I could.

She wiped her face with her hand and looked up. "Guru-ji." She motioned to a space on the rug just in front of her.

Bapu sat across from her, but I pulled a cushion to her side and sat next to her. Both of them watched me awhile.

Bapu finally broke the silence. "I am sorry to come like this. I had hoped to invite you to our home, but Saiprasad-ji told me . . . " He was unable to say the words aloud.

"That I cannot leave my quarters?" Manavi-ji asked, raising an eyebrow.

Bapu nodded. He looked down at her hands. Her fingers were slightly fanned, resting in her lap as though they had fluttered down from a dance position for just a brief pause.

"Adhira has grown so fast!" Manavi-ji said, smiling at me.

Bapu looked across at me, at my feet dangling off the cushion. They were soft and vulnerable, so different from Manavi-ji's. As he watched, however, Bapu noticed that I was tapping my heels in a rhythmic pattern from a dance composition of his. He glanced up at Manavi-ji. She had seen as well.

"Yes, she is already learning," he said. "Just from watching. She has a gift. Just like you did, nah? People say you were dancing by the time you were three."

Manavi-ji nodded slowly, and the smile faded from her lips. Bapu had a sudden memory of bringing Padmini, then age five, to Manavi-ji's mother, the matriarch at the time, to be blessed as a *devadasi*. That blessing, Bapu thought, had done little good in the end. But this time was different, he told himself.

"You've come about her." The harshness of her voice stung Bapu like a handful of pelting sand.

"I know it is very early, Manavi. But . . . "

"You're right. I don't have much time." She looked at Bapu with an unusual directness. "I am glad you've come to me with Adhira. There are some things I have wanted to discuss with you. About the *devadasis*."

Bapu thought he had reason for relief. "I'm happy to hear you say this. This is a critical time. The political situation, all that." He waved his arm in the direction of the doorway, the desert, and everything beyond. "And I am concerned that some of the *devadasis* are not setting a good example."

"Chandrabai? Yes, she has been distracted. Her heart"—and here Manavi-ji did the unthinkable and took Bapu's hand in hers—"her heart is not in the dance, not in Krishna."

Bapu's hand trembled in hers. She held it a moment longer, and then propriety prevailed and she let go. Bapu drew his own hand in. The weight of the emptiness it now held astonished him. A moment later, I wriggled off the cushion and put my own hand in Manavi-ji's still-open one. I felt a warmth, a connection to something vast and timeless. I looked up at Manavi-ji and she smiled at me, then turned my hand around and tickled my palm. I laughed and dropped back onto the cushion.

But inside my father, anger welled. "Chandrabai is a *devadasi*. Her heart can be only for Krishna. She committed herself to him as a wife. Why do I even have to tell you this?"

"You don't," Manavi-ji said quietly as I played with her jade bangles, pushing them up and down her arm.

The two of them were dancing a *bandish*, a fixed composition, but each was straining to bring it to a different end. Just two at the time, I was unable to intervene and too young even to understand that such a thing would be possible.

"Then think of everything that position is giving her, Manavi. As it gave you. She will never be a widow. She will never lack for anything. If the love of dance is not enough for her, surely these other things should be."

Manavi-ji glanced at me and chose her next words deliberately. "Guru-ji, sometimes these things are not enough."

Bapu's anger mixed with quiet desperation. He thought of war elephants charging, Jaisalmer falling. I watched him and Manavi-ji in turn, feeling the weight of the unsaid, and feeling at the center of it. Across the room was a wall hanging depicting a deer drinking from a stream. I went to it and imagined dipping my feet in the cool water.

"Guru-ji, look around you," Manavi-ji continued in a lower voice. "You yourself mentioned the political turmoil. Who knows what will happen after you and I are gone? That time is coming. Soon. Let

Adhira take her gift out into the world. It will do more good there than here in the temple. Let her make that choice."

"Choice?" Bapu struggled to keep his voice measured. "You sound like Girija! We do not choose our lives, Manavi. We do what we are meant to do, and we do so with joy."

"Look at Adhira." Manavi-ji was relentless. "Don't you want her to be happy? You speak of joy. . . . "

"She will be a *devadasi*!" Bapu thundered, then composed himself. "That is what will give her joy. Isn't that what made you happy?"

Manavi-ji was quiet for a long while. I remained below the wall hanging, my toes feeling the water lick at them, my hands running along the deer's soft back.

Bapu tilted his head. "Manavi, what is happening? Have you lost your faith?"

"Why do you think Padmini left?" she asked, prying at a closed door to which Bapu had long ago lost the key.

"Padmini is no one to me." Bapu sighed. "Padmini spoke of this temple as a prison. A prison! It is a place of worship, of learning, of creation. What kind of prison is that?"

"The girls don't ask to be *devadasis*, Guru-ji."

"We have had this discussion before. None of us asks to be what we are. By dancing as *devadasis*, our daughters live a free life. Their spirits are free. Their souls. This is what Adhira deserves."

I wandered back to them, pushing my toes into the cracks between the slabs of stone on the floor.

"That is a decision you are making for her." Manavi-ji smelled of sandalwood and sadness.

"It is not I making that decision. It is what is meant to be. The decision was made when she was created. It is merely my role to ensure that it comes to pass."

"And yet you need my blessing for that. Adhira wasn't born of a *devadasi*. Her fate isn't so easily sealed. We—you and I—are making the choice for her."

"It is not a question of fate, Manavi." Bapu's voice grew hard again, one stone hitting another. "It is a question of what Adhira *is*. There is no choice. Only the illusion of choice."

I wanted it to stop. "Bapu?" I tugged at his arm. He looked into my eyes silently.

"It's nothing, Adhira," Manavi-ji said, stroking my hair. "Just grown-ups talking." She looked back at Bapu. "And what will happen if I don't give my blessing?"

"It is your duty." Bapu stood, reached down for me, and picked me up with difficulty. His muscles strained, but still he held me. "Will you give Adhira your blessing, Manavi? Yes or no?"

Manavi-ji sighed, looking even more worn than when we had arrived. Sorrow tinged the edges of Bapu's anger. She shook her head slowly, in a gesture that to Bapu could have signified either resistance or resignation. He did not care for a clarification. Before Manavi-ji could say anything else, before she could refuse her blessing out loud, Bapu set me on the ground, took my hand, and led me back to the red curtain and the dazzling sunlight beyond.

Days later, Manavi-ji passed into her next life. The soft rays of dawn were tinging the white blossoms of the *neem* tree in the temple garden a delicate pink-orange, and I was watching a peacock strutting through the bushes in search of a morning meal. Bapu saw the bird approaching me, and he opened his mouth to warn me to move back. But I was not afraid, and the bird meant me no harm. Lord Krishna was not far, playing his flute, a peacock feather in his crown. The peacock pecked at the hard ground. Then it suddenly lifted its head, fanned out its majestic tail, and pierced the stillness with its eerie screech. The sun caught the iridescent plumage and set it ablaze in a frenzy of blue and green and gold and silver. In that instant, something changed irrevocably. I felt a warmth in my chest, as if a part of Manavi-ji's soul had settled there for me to keep.

Bapu fell to his knees. I ran to him, and he drew me in. His body convulsed as he buried his head in my hair. I know his mind spun with images of Manavi-ji over the past twenty-five years. Manavi-ji practicing in the early morning, her face a mirror of peace while her feet churned up the dust brought swirling in by a summer windstorm. Manavi-ji surrounded by pilgrims scrambling to take the dust from her feet, their faces alight with adoration. Manavi-ji lighting the oil lamps at dusk, her slender body stretching to reach the ledge above the main shrine, her long black braid swinging at her back. Manavi-ji playing the coy and lovely Radha to Bapu's Krishna, glancing at him mischievously from under her imagined veil as the two of them spent an afternoon of dance together. And Manavi-ji in her room, her maroon shawl wrapped around her thin shoulders, her hair loose, shaking her head slowly.

Bapu lifted his head and, through his tears, saw that my eyes were dry. I knew Manavi-ji was already dancing the cosmic dance with Lord Shiva. I put my arm around Bapu's neck, and from this he found the strength to rise up from his knees, take my hand, and walk toward the temple, from which heart-rending wails already drifted into the garden.

Manavi-ji's funeral took place the next morning. All temple activities and rituals were suspended for the day. It was still dark when Bapu and I arrived for him to pay his private respects. Manavi-ji's body lay on a mat under the *babul* tree in the courtyard. She had been placed between two thick roots, which held her in their embrace. At her side, a small oil lamp burned, the flame taut in the still air.

Bapu eased himself to his knees, his swollen joints protesting painfully. I watched him look down at the face of this woman who had been so many things to him. The whiteness of the sheet, the pallor of Manavi's skin, were reminiscent of Saraswati, consort of Brahma and goddess of learning and rivers. Saraswati and her white clothes, her white swan. Saraswati, the source of true knowledge, the life-giver. I thought of her flowing hair while my father thought of the knowledge she had been trying to impart to him when he had last seen her. The tears that had come so easily to him the day before, when Manavi-ji's death was something in the air, evaded him now that the tangible reality lay before him. This time, however, my own eyes felt moist, not for the death of Manavi-ji but for the passing of what I felt, even then, was an era of which my father was the lone remaining vestige. He recalled the warm, solid feel of her hand holding his for a brief moment, the only time they had touched in the twenty-five years in which their lives had been intertwined.

"Manavi," he called softly to her, so as not to disturb the silence. "Have you really gone?"

The stillness of dawn answered him.

"I know you tried to prepare me," he continued in a whisper as I knelt by his side. "I was not blind to the signs. Others may think I deny the fragility of life, but that is not so. And now I have seen life sucked from the wisest and most beautiful of beings. I know you will continue to dance in your next life, but what shall we do without you here on this earth? The temple has lost one of its pillars. Others have but the shallowest of foundations. You knew that—I know you did. You may have thought you were not granting your blessing for Adhira, but you did. Adhira has something of you in her, and in her you shall continue to live and dance. Go in peace on your journey."

He lightly touched the tip of the flame from the oil lamp, then brought his fingers to his forehead, his lips, and his heart. As the sky lightened in the East, he prayed, kneeling by Manavi-ji's side, until the distant but steady beat of a *pakhawaj* coming from the citadel reached our ears. It was time for the city to grieve. A crowd was massing along the side of the courtyard.

Bapu bent low. "Farewell, Manavi-ji," he whispered. In my head, I repeated the same words, while in my heart I welcomed her. As we rose, a subtle breeze stirred the flame by her side. It was the slightest of movements, but it gave us joy: Manavi-ji would never be far. Bapu took my hand and backed away, indicating to the waiting crowd that they could approach.

I know Bapu would have preferred to retreat to the desert for the rest of the day, but Manavi-ji deserved all the respect in the world, and so he attended her funeral. It passed, however, in a blur as he sank into his thoughts. The wails and moans that rose from the crowd like undulating dunes seemed shallow to him. He wondered if anyone truly understood what had been lost. Like the *devadasis* who sat in a circle, a weeping huddle of shaking shoulders and rocking bodies, his mind was focused on this loss, not on what we all had gained during Manavi-ji's lifetime. Such is often the way of grief.

Bapu and I joined the procession that accompanied Manavi-ji to the cremation grounds. Hanging from the end of the bier on which she rested was a long, leafy branch. It trailed on the ground, and as the bier carriers began their walk toward the temple's gates, it brushed away their footsteps.

Then Bapu caught sight of Ma. She held her sari over her head, hiding her tear-stained face behind it. Bapu did not at first recognize the tall young man, wearing a bright red turban, tied in the Rajput style, and a warrior's mustache, who walked next to her. But the young man held Hari Dev protectively by the shoulder and Ma by the elbow, and Bapu realized it was Mahendra. Unexpected gratitude flooded his chest.

The crying, pushing crowd filled the cremation grounds around the funeral pyre. People chanted, sparks flew from the dry wood, smoke billowed up toward the pyre's roof. The bittersweet smell of burning *neem* wood was thick in the air. Bapu held in his mind an image of Manavi-ji dancing as the flames consumed her body. Through the crowd, he once more saw Ma and Hari Dev. Mahendra was a few steps behind. They settled on the ground beside us, and Ma rested her head on Bapu's shoulder. Surrounded by my family, I cried—not for the loss of Manavi-ji, not even for my family, but for me, for all the changes I felt coming. Overhead, vultures circled.

Bapu rested his hand on my back and looked over at Mahendra, wondering if his son had come to his senses. Perhaps, he thought, there was still hope for him. He kept his gaze on him, determined to give him a smile or some sign of welcome should he turn his head to our father, but Mahendra kept his eyes on something, someone, else. Bapu followed their gaze over the huddled heads to the *devadasis*. As he watched, Chandrabai turned toward Mahendra, and their eyes locked with a tangible force that took Bapu's breath away. Manavi-ji's words about Chandrabai's heart came back to him. This, he realized, was what she had meant but had not said. His anger mounted. His son not only felt that he could find something better to do than dance but had the temerity to try to lure a *devadasi* away. In an instant, all of Bapu's good feeling toward Mahendra evaporated, like a drop of rain on hot stone. Against my back, his hand was stiff.

That evening, after the meal and after I was asleep, Bapu watched Hari Dev help Ma set out a dozen little oil lamps along the walls of our home's courtyard. To keep Manavi-ji's spirit alive through the night, Ma said. A small fire burned in the fire pit, and from it Hari Dev was lighting the lamps that Ma handed him. It was too dangerous for her, with her limited sight, to handle the fire herself. Mahendra sat in a corner, cleaning a dagger. He still wore his turban. He put down the dagger and helped Hari Dev place the lamps on the higher parts of the wall. Mother and sons worked in silence.

Bapu wanted to do something as well, to be a part of their world, but he could see that he was not needed. His stomach was knotted, his chest tight. He approached Ma and the fire. Ma's eyes shone with tears, and her skin glistened from a combination of perspiration and the oil she used to protect herself from the wind and sun. Bapu wanted to fall into her arms and rest his head in the damp crook of her neck. He wanted to tell her that the wise grieve neither for the living nor for the dead, for they are not deluded by temporary changes. The Mahabharata teaches this, that experiences come and go and the ultimate reality lies only in the eternal.

What he did say was something entirely different. "I took Adhira to see her. Manavi."

Both Ma and Mahendra raised their heads toward him. Mahendra's eyes narrowed.

"And?" Ma's face betrayed her hope.

"And nothing. She gave her blessing. As she was supposed to do."

"No!" Ma's hands flew to her face. She shook her head. "No, that was not what she was supposed to do."

"What do you know?" Bapu raised his voice. He wondered what he was doing, instigating an argument now, yet he continued. "This is no concern of yours."

Hari Dev began to cry, and Mahendra put his arm around his shoulders. His eyes were still on Bapu.

Ma's voice became tight and low. "She is my daughter, too. It is every concern of mine."

"Enough!"

Hari Dev's cries grew louder, and he began to flail his arms.

Bapu scowled at him, wondering why the boy could not compose himself. Spurred by an urge to put an end to the hysterical noise, he wheeled around and slapped him across the face. Hari Dev let out a hiccup of surprise that halted his cries. There was a brief silence, and then Hari Dev's shrieks filled the air again. His face grew red, and he struggled to breathe. Ma rushed instinctively to him, not even needing to see her way to her son. It was happening, the first time in so many months. Bapu had been mistaken in thinking that Hari Dev had outgrown these fits. Poor Hari convulsed on the ground in Mahendra's arms, unable to control his limbs. His head shook, his eyes rolled back, a thin rope of saliva trickled down from the side of his mouth, glinting in the firelight. The sight of it disgusted Bapu. He backed away. No one noticed.

Mahendra and Ma lowered Hari Dev to the ground, where they held him down firmly. Bapu watched as they moved together without needing to exchange a single word, as they had done so many times before my arrival. This time, Bapu knew it was his fault. He knew he had brought on this fit by raising his voice to Ma and his hand to Hari Dev.

Hari Dev's convulsions subsided. His head lay still, and he breathed more easily. Ma and Mahendra cautiously let go of his arms and legs. His body was spent, bathed in sweat, his crooked legs folded at awkward angles. The legs that had never danced to the compositions in his head, the compositions Bapu would never know were there. Hari opened his eyes and looked up at Mahendra, who was still bent over him. The oil lamps threw dancing shadows on the red turban, and Hari Dev reached up to touch it.

He spoke weakly. "Why are you wearing that?"

Mahendra put his hands under Hari Dev's arms and pulled him to the wall, where he helped him lean back. "It's the turban of a warrior," he replied, throwing Bapu a defiant look.

Hari had more questions. "Do you still know how to dance?"

"Of course. Would you like a story now?"

Hari Dev nodded.

"I will tell you about Ma, where she comes from. We are the sons not only of dancers, but of warriors as well."

Ma squatted on the ground, silent. Bapu watched, disbelieving, from where he stood as Mahendra took a few steps back and found a clear space in front of our brother. Mahendra held his palms together and bowed toward Hari Dev and Ma.

My brother crossed the courtyard, back and forth, wielding an imaginary sword. It was an ancient time, and several powerful warrior kings ruled the land. Upon learning that these warrior kings had killed his parents, one Parashurama, an incarnation of Vishnu, vowed to annihilate them. Crisscrossing the patch of ground, Mahendra traveled the earth with his ax, killing the kings and freeing their people. For the first time, Bapu saw clearly that other side of his son. He glanced at Ma, wondering if she was thinking of her sword-maker father, of the harm he and his swords had inflicted, but her face was impassive, her eyes closed.

A great disorder descended upon the earth. Without warriors, mankind was helpless against the demons. Mahendra's eyes opened wide, the pupils dark and intense against the whites. The gods gathered at the oasis of Mount Abu, Ma's ancestral home, whose magical power Bapu had himself felt, and asked a great sage there to regenerate the warrior race to rid the earth of demons. That the gods were at the mercy of the warriors was not lost on Bapu, and this enraged him. He wanted to put a stop to Mahendra's dance, but it is inauspicious to interrupt a dancer telling a story of the gods.

His hand indicating a flowing beard, Mahendra became the sage who built a fire. Then he became Lord Indra, who carries his bow and arrow so proudly. He reached down, deftly plucked some blades of grass, twisted them into a figure, and tossed them into the flames. From them slowly emerged a figure holding a mace. He was given three kingdoms. Another spin and Mahendra was Lord Brahma, Creator of the Universe, one hand outstretched in welcome, the other held up as a symbol of strength and courage. Then he was Lord Shiva, one hand raised in a gesture of blessing and protection, the other holding aloft a small drum. Then he was Vishnu again. Each time, he fashioned an image and tossed it into the fire pit. Each time, a figure emerged, bearing a weapon, and was given a territory to rule.

The newborn warriors set out against the demons. As soon as a demon was slain, a new one emerged from his blood. In the pushing and pulling of his upper body, Mahendra showed their struggle. But the gods were watching over their creations and began to drink the blood shed from each slain demon. Soon, the very last demon was killed. The gods rode their mounts into the sky, Mahendra's feet their galloping hooves, and there was much rejoicing on Earth. Thus were the leaders of the great fire-born Rajput clans created.

"You see, Hari," Mahendra said, catching his breath as he finished his dance, "this is where Ma is from—Mount Abu, where these four clans were born. It's a very important place. There are other warrior clans, too. Thirty-six altogether."

"And where do the others come from?"

Bapu had kept silent the whole time, impressed despite his anger by the way in which Mahendra had told this story. His son had not forgotten everything he had taught him.

Now Bapu answered Hari Dev's question. "Ten clans come from the Sun, and ten from the Moon. And another twelve from foreign lands."

Bapu glanced at Mahendra and caught his look, a look that betrayed Mahendra's surprise that Bapu knew the origin of the martial races.

"Here in Jaisalmer," Bapu said, pulling Hari Dev onto his lap and trying to forget his recent fit, "the Rajputs are of the Bhatti clan, one of the Lunar clans descended from Lord Krishna. They are proud and brave, but they can be headstrong and foolish. They have a streak of evil in them and can be treacherous allies."

Many of these words were beyond Hari Dev's comprehension, but Bapu continued nonetheless.

"Some of them work for the Raja, and they are honorable. But some of them just care about themselves, and growing rich. They spend their time stealing cattle and training falcons, and they make their living through forced levies on caravans traveling to Delhi. They are the most feared of all desert marauders. They are respected, but not for the right reasons. Your brother thinks he can be one of them."

"And can he be? The kind of warrior who works for the Raja?"

Bapu looked up at Mahendra, who was now standing, scowling

at him and adjusting his bag on his shoulder. "No. He cannot be any kind of warrior. He can dress like one, and live like one, but he cannot be one. He will always be a dancer."

Hari Dev yawned. "I don't understand, Bapu."

"No, *beta*, I don't suppose you do."

Bapu watched Mahendra leave without a word. Hari Dev's body grew heavy as he fell asleep. Somewhere in the distance, a jackal howled. Ma stared unseeingly in silence toward the place where her older son had been standing. Here one moment, gone the next—it was my brother's way, to keep everyone guessing as to his whereabouts, to hide in the imagination.

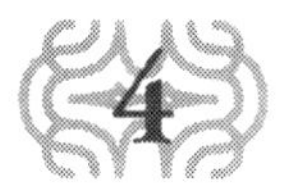

Girija
1557

Ma stepped out of the house, carrying me on her hip. She blinked, her dimming eyes adjusting with trouble to the searing whiteness of the sunlight. Over twenty years in the desert, and still she was not accustomed to its tremendous contrasts. The oven-like heat of day and the cold fingers of night. The short bursts of plentiful rains and the endless, barren years of drought. And everywhere the dust, a gritty layer covering the jars of water and pots of food, forming miniature dunes at the corners of the room, swept in by Vayu the Wind through the doorway. Always something to clean, she thought, something to cover, something to put away. This was not what she had imagined when she had left her native home in the oasis of Mount Abu at the age of fourteen.

Eight-year-old Hari Dev tugged at her skirt.

"Yes, yes, we're going to the market." She pulled the skirt from his hand.

"Will you buy me a surprise?" His voice was full of little-boy eagerness.

"Fine. Whatever you want. But just one."

"Are there many foreign people there now? Is Mahendra there? Is it dangerous?"

As far as Ma knew, Mahendra had not been home in the eight

months since Manavi-ji's funeral, and Ma feared the worst. She set me down, unable to carry me for long. She worried that I would get tired walking to the citadel and back, but she had managed to convince Bapu to let me spend a morning with her instead of at the temple. She was not going to leave me with anyone else. Her grip on me, while often invisible, was always as strong as iron, a force through which I felt her soaring hopes for me, for our family, a force that at times came near to rivaling that of the deities themselves. Bapu thought she lacked in faith, but he was wrong. Hers was simply a faith of a different kind at the time, a faith in herself, in each of her children as humans.

"I don't know," she said, driving the worry from her voice. "Let's go find out." She tucked her long, still-black braid of hair into the waist of her skirt, in the front.

Hari Dev set off. Ma held on to my hand with one of hers, and his shoulder with the other. Hari pushed a rock out of the path, clearing the way for her. I wiggled my fingers in her hand. Her mood softened, and she realized too late how tightly she had been gripping Hari Dev's shoulder. He had stopped in the middle of the road and refused to go forward.

"Hari, *beta*, please keep walking." Ma tried to sound as gentle as possible as she gave him a little push.

"Ma, why are you sad?"

"I'm not sad. Keep walking." But Ma knew he would not believe her.

"No!"

Ma knelt and placed her hand under my brother's chin. Only there, up close, could she make out the worry on his face, the question in his large brown eyes. She brushed his hair from his forehead.

"Hari, we have to continue. I promise I'm not sad. It's just . . . I have to do something today that I don't want to do. You know how sometimes I ask you to clean some pots and how you don't like doing that, but it's something that must be done?"

In her hands, Hari Dev's head nodded.

"Well, your Bapu has asked me to do something I don't want to do, but I will do it, and everything will be all right. Please, can we continue to the market now?"

Hari Dev nodded and began to walk again, counting his steps under his breath. Ma took my hand and followed him, once more holding his shoulder. It was a relief that he did not ask what it was she had to do. For how would she have explained to our sweet Hari Dev her repulsion at hosting Saiprasad-ji for dinner, even if it was only once a year? The thought of his presence in our home brought back painful memories of her childhood in Mount Abu, the types of memories one implores the gods to take away, of sour breath and searching hands in the night, of the bearded silhouettes of her father's friends rising above her. But Bapu insisted they still were in Saiprasad-ji's debt, for he was the one who had found them that day twenty-three years earlier when Padmini had arrived much too early, Bapu's dry hands cradling Ma's spinning head in his lap, the swirling sand sticking to her damp face and flying in her eyes as her insides contracted.

Saiprasad-ji had taken our parents in. While Ma had recovered, Bapu had danced at the temple. In return for the priest's hospitality, he had begun to teach the *devadasis*. Of course, under the benevolent gaze of Lord Krishna, he found his home. He grew accustomed to the temple and its rituals, and they to him. Before Ma fully realized what had happened, Bapu had made the decision to settle for good in Jaisalmer and become the temple dance master. Ma reminded him of his promise to his father—he had never made any promises to her—to travel and bring the tales of the gods and goddesses to people far and wide, as his father and grandfather had done, but he had found his place. Our place.

"Ma, why are you so slow today?" Hari Dev took her free hand and pulled her forward. "You said there was nothing wrong."

"No, no, there's nothing wrong, *beta*. Let's go." Ma sought solace in the knowledge that at least the priest would bring with him Bapu's monthly payment from the court. For a few days, she would not have to count out the coins so carefully. These things mattered to her.

The sounds and smells of the citadel were starting to surround us, filling Ma's senses in a way that sights could not. Dogs barked, bullock cart wheels creaked. Bangles on women jingled, men laughed. Acrid odors of goats and mangy dogs mingled with urine and the smoke of cooking fires.

Hari Dev shrank against her legs. "Ma, what's happening?"

I curled my hand around her fingers, and she picked me up. A crowd was gathering up ahead, at the foot of the incline leading to the citadel's main gate. Excited chatter streamed from all directions. We were pressed into the throng of bodies. Ma recoiled at their hot, damp touch. Somebody coughed and spat, the thick, juicy sound close to her ear. An announcement, people were saying. Something important the Raja was to tell the people. Everyone hazarded a guess. The Raja's daughter was getting married. Jaisalmer was under imminent attack. The Muslims were coming. The annual tax on crops was being raised. No, it was being lowered.

Ma held Hari tightly by the wrist, trying hard at the same time to shield me from the surging elbows and shoulders. Carried along by the crowd, we arrived at Chauhata Square, the Court of Public Audience. In front of us rose a wall of backs. We were close enough to see the perspiration stains spreading darkly on cotton, to smell the odors of a crowd on a hot day: coconut hair oil, stale spices, animal dung. Everyone was facing away, watching the palace balcony where a court official would make the announcement.

Hari Dev strained away from Ma, pulling at her hand. "Ma! I just saw Mahendra *bhai*!"

"Mahendra? Are you sure?" Held against her body, I felt a jolt in her chest and her heart beat a little faster. A little bit of hope. She wondered if Mahendra somehow knew about the dinner.

Hari Dev jumped up and down for a better view of our brother, whom I could now see. "Yes, it's him. He's with someone. And he's wearing a turban!"

"Who? Who is he with?"

"I can't see now; there's someone in front of him. Oh, wait, it's a . . . oh!"

"Well, who?"

"I think it's Chandrabai, Ma. But they've moved away. I can't see them anymore. Is Chandrabai supposed to be here in the citadel?"

Ma thought back to something Manavi-ji had mentioned about Chandrabai and Mahendra. Even as she had dismissed it, she had known it might well be true, though she hoped not. She wondered if it was possible that the woman Hari Dev had seen was Padmini, our sister who had left the temple to marry before he was born. He had never met her. And yet Ma knew that Hari Dev would not make such a mistake.

Hari Dev pulled us forward. "We have Adhira with us, Ma. Maybe that is why Mahendra is here. She brought him to us. Let's follow them!"

Ma shook her heard. "Hari, don't talk nonsense, please! Adhira can't 'bring' anyone to us." But I know that a small part of her believed he might be right.

The crowd seethed around us. Ma followed as Hari Dev led us along the walls of the women's quarters at the back of Chauhata Square, where the crowd was thinner. The court announcement had lost its importance to Ma.

"What is she wearing?" she asked Hari Dev.

"Who?"

"The person with Mahendra. What is she wearing?"

"I don't know. Something blue. Why?"

"No matter."

From high above us, behind latticed windows that Ma was unable to see from that far, came the tinkle of bangles and women's laughter. Somewhere, behind those windows or others like them, Padmini lived. Ma closed her eyes for a moment, reveling in the knowledge that, for this brief instant, all her children were near her, even if two of them did not know it. The tension in Hari Dev's shoulder coiled, as though he were ready to let loose one of his fits. She quickly reopened her eyes. He would not last much longer in such a crowd, and there was still the food to purchase. She gave him a push, and he led us toward the market, the sound of the crowd echoing through the narrow stone streets, then fading as we moved away.

As we approached the marketplace, however, new sounds and smells, both familiar and strange to Ma, greeted us. The recent arrival of a caravan from Persia had attracted merchants from all around, including foreigners. Pieces of straw from carts carrying animals for sale caught in Ma and Hari Dev's sandals, pricking their feet. Raucous voices, the piercing shrieks of peacocks, and the manic chatter of monkeys rose in a nearly tangible cacophony from the square, magnified by the stone walls. I looked around, drinking in the sights and sounds of the market.

In order to reach the back, where the regular merchants sold their goods, we had to walk past many other carts, laden with exotic items from distant lands, places with names that Ma thought rang of adventure, like Kandahar and Shikarpoor. When she was growing up, her brothers had spoken to her of these places, of experiences she now knew she would never have: rivers rushing loudly over stone beds, the wind whispering through fields of rice and tea, snowflakes melting on her skin in the mountains. It was not enough for her to visit them in her mind, but this was as close as she would ever come to those places and sensations. Many of the goods were from Afghanistan and Persia, the land of the Muslims. Bapu, impervious to their splendor, had told her to keep away from them, but she could not.

"One day, Adhira, one day you will be able to buy these things for yourself," Ma whispered into my ear. "You will marry a nobleman who will adore you for both your beauty and your intelligence. You will advise him on political strategies, and he will lavish you with sweets and coffee and gems. The entire court will respect you. Come, let's explore the mysterious things here. Hari Dev, let's find your surprise."

Sweets and coffee and gems—those I have now had. As for the rest, Ma did her best, given the circumstances.

"But what about Mahendra? Where is he?"

"Don't worry. We will see him at dinner."

Holding on to the rough edges of the carts, Ma bent down, trying to see the wondrous items. One caravan had brought plump dates and round raisins. Next to their glistening and sticky piles lay mounds of brown nuts. Ma let her fingers linger on them. They rattled dully as she shook them. Dried apricots and figs bore the scents of faraway orchard gardens. Hari Dev noticed the apricots and clamored to have one as his surprise. Remembering how sweet they'd tasted when Bapu had given her two after my birth, Ma bought a handful and gave us each one. Hari Dev held his and took a very small bite of it, smiling. He would make it last a long time. I would make mine last forever.

"Don't you want to eat it?" Ma asked me.

I shook my head.

"Why not? It's very tasty and sweet."

"No, for Lord Krishna." And I held the apricot away from her.

Ma said nothing. This was what Bapu had already taught her daughter, she thought: to deny herself a simple pleasure for the sake of Krishna. A little piece of her hope fell away, trampled under the dusty feet of the shoppers in the marketplace. I did not want it that way. But from above, Lord Krishna smiled at me.

We neared the back of the square and came to the goods from other parts of Hindustan. Ma fingered the rolls of chintz and silk and the bales of sprigged gossamer. She held up muslins and silver and gold brocades, rubbing them to her cheeks and then to mine. She marveled at the cardamom pods and saffron threads, cloves and black pepper, dried chilies and cinnamon sticks. Their smells tickled the insides of her nose and brought tears to her eyes. She held me out to breathe in the spices as well. They stung my own eyes, and I began to cry.

"Ma, why are you doing that?" Hari Dev asked.

"So she learns that there are other flavors in life."

When we finally arrived at the Rajasthani products, Ma let Hari Dev lead us past sugar candy from Bikaner, iron implements from Jaipur, and Jaisalmer's famous camel saddles. And then she stood still. A glint of sunlight bouncing off metal caught her eye. *Sirohi* blades from Mount Abu. The flash of light brought back memories of her childhood. She wondered which of the swords her father, swordmaker to the royal family in Mount Abu, had made, which ones those dreadful fingers had caressed, and if he was even still alive. She thought of the *sirohi* blade she had carried away with her when she had left home, and which all these years had lain, wrapped in cloth, at the bottom of the trunk that held our family's blankets. She had taken it on impulse, stealing it from her father's workshop—his prized sword, the very first Rajput blade—taking an object of protection from a man who had never protected her. Object of protection, or of destruction. It lay beneath the blankets, muffled under their softness, a reminder to Ma of what she had escaped.

The market was filling with people. The announcement in Chauhata Square was over. Ma hurried us to the food stalls, tripping on uneven stones, alarmed at how much of the morning had already passed.

"Akbar's army has defeated the Afghan king!" someone cried not far from us.

"The Afghan king?" said another voice. "I thought he had an army of one thousand five hundred elephants!"

"Had, yes. No longer. Akbar had the elephants captured and the king beheaded!"

"*Hare Ram!* What if he takes Jaisalmer?"

"Ma, who is taking Jaisalmer?" Hari Dev asked. "What does that mean? And I'm tired. My legs hurt."

"Let's sit down," Ma said.

She let Hari Dev lead us out of the way of the shopping women and sat at the base of a wall, placing me in her lap. I still held the apricot, crushed and sticky now.

"Don't worry, Hari. No one will take Jaisalmer. We are safe. This is a strong place."

"How do you know?"

Ma hesitated. "Well, there is a story . . . "

Hari Dev reached over to take my hand. "Tell us, Ma."

"Right here? *Beta*, it is so crowded and getting late already."

"Please, Ma!"

"All right," Ma said, leaning against the wall, pulling in her feet and motioning for Hari to do the same. "A long time ago, a prince named Rao Jaisal came upon a sweet-water spring on a hill in the desert. He was looking for a new place for his capital. On the hill, Rao Jaisal met a hermit who warned him that the new city would be destroyed two and a half times. Despite the warning, the warrior prince Jaisal moved his capital to the hill. Then, over one hundred years later, the hermit's prophecy came true."

"What's a prophecy?" Hari Dev asked.

"It's when someone knows what will happen in the future."

"Can that really happen?"

"No," Ma said quickly.

"Then how is this story true?"

"It's a part of the legend of Jaisalmer. Just listen. In a wild attack, the princes of Jaisalmer captured a treasure caravan of over three thousand horses and mules belonging to the Sultan of Delhi. Angered, the Sultan, who was a Muslim, attacked Jaisalmer. The men of Jaisalmer stood bravely on the ramparts, defending the city. Days became weeks. Summer gave way to winter. Little by little, the commander of the Muslim army became friendly with one of the young Rajput princes. Every evening, they met under a *khajeri* tree and played chess. After each game, they shared a goblet of wine, then returned to their command posts."

"So Rajputs and Muslims can be friends!" Hari Dev clapped his hands.

"Listen! The siege on Jaisalmer continued for seven years. Then the commander's brother fell ill, and the Rajput prince invited him into the fort to recover. The commander, in return, decided to lift the siege. But his brother saw how terrible the conditions were in the fort, where there was hardly any food and people were dying. So the brother convinced the Persian army to attack. Jaisalmer fell, and twenty-four thousand women and children performed *jauhar* in Chauhata Square, dying in flames. The men then put on their saffron war robes, took lots of opium, and charged to their deaths. The commander's forces occupied the city."

As he listened, Hari Dev began to suck his thumb. He never wanted to hear about anyone dying. Ma did not notice. Her mind was in the story, and she was oblivious to what was immediately around her, hearing instead the screams of the women and children in the fire, and smelling the sweet, pungent, metallic odor of opium mixed with blood.

"After two years," she continued, absently stroking my hair, "the commander's forces grew tired of desert life and abandoned the citadel. A few years later, a branch of Rajputs tried to restore life and order to Jaisalmer. Then they raided a camp of the Sultan of Delhi, starting another battle. Ten years after the first *jauhar*, the second one took place."

"Ma," Hari Dev interrupted, "I don't want to hear about fires."

A dog scavenging for scraps came to sniff at my apricot. Hari Dev threw the rest of his own apricot away from us, and the dog limped over to eat it, leaving mine—Lord Krishna's—untouched.

"Shh! No more fire," Ma said. "Then, just twelve years before your Bapu and I arrived here, the final part of the hermit's prophecy came true."

"Ma! Stop! Why are you saying these things?" Hari Dev's voice trembled. "You said nothing would happen to Jaisalmer."

"Oh, *beta*, I said Jaisalmer is a strong place. Even if things happen, the city survives. Maybe it changes, but it survives. Don't be afraid. It's just stories. Let's get our things and go."

It was not "just" stories. The gateway to the city still holds the hand marks of some of the women who dipped their hands in dye and pressed them against the wall before perishing. And the sweet-water spring Rao Jaisal discovered lies below the well in Chauhata Square. But Ma knew that she should not have frightened Hari Dev with the violent tales of Jaisalmer's past. She stood with me and patted Hari Dev's head. She tried to imagine Chauhata Square full of women, children, blood, and flames. Was it duty that drove the women to the flames, or fear of what might otherwise happen to them? She wondered, not for the first time, nor for the last, what it felt like to be ablaze. Standing there in the citadel, she felt something akin to fire coursing within her, in a way she never felt at home, let alone in the temple.

Hari Dev tugged at her hand. "Ma, let's get what you need and go home, please."

Ma was rolling out the gram flour dumplings when Bapu returned from the temple. The sun was beginning to set, shadows lengthening across our home's courtyard. Through the doorway, Ma could hear Hari Dev playing with me. She turned toward us, two small silhouettes in the sliver of light. These were the only times we could be confident Hari would not have one of his fits. Watching over me gave him peace of mind. She heard my giggling laughter rise and fall, and then Bapu's footsteps. They sped up as he crossed the courtyard, eager to see me, and then stopped as he bent to pick me up.

"Hello, my blessed little one," he said. To Hari Dev he said nothing. His shadow fell across the doorway. The stiffness that had disappeared after my birth had begun to return to his movements, but neither he nor Ma made any mention of it. Thankfully, it had not yet affected his dance.

Ma closed her eyes, suddenly weary. Our home was not large—three rooms and the kitchen area—but our lingering at the market had taken all morning, and she had not readied our home for the evening. She had not yet put away the bedding or Hari Dev's wooden toys, nor had she swept the floor or started burning incense to perfume the air. She knew she had failed and that Bapu would be displeased. But, she thought to herself, the dumplings, lined up on the stone slab in front of her, had taken some time to make, and she had picked over the rice and lentils more slowly than usual, her fingers feeling every grain of rice, sure to remove every last stone and insect.

Bapu stood for a moment in the doorway, holding me. He was taking in the state of the room. Ma drew a breath, ready to counter any complaint. But when Bapu spoke, he was smiling.

"Dumplings! I thought you did not like to make them, that they take too much time."

"I don't. But I thought you wanted a good meal tonight for Saiprasad . . . ji." She made an effort to refer to the priest respectfully, which she usually could not bring herself to do.

"Of course I do." It was the closest Bapu would come to thanking her.

He set me down by Ma and walked over to the sacred *puja* area. Ma sat still, the dough drying stiffly on her hands. Bapu picked up the bronze statue of Nataraja, Lord of Dance, and dusted it off with a corner of his *dhoti*. He brought it to his lips, then placed some flowers around it. Their smell filled the room. He rearranged the cushions on the floor and then lifted the rug in the eating area, beat it with his hand, and placed it back down.

Ma winced. That area was for her husband to sit in and rest and eat the food she brought him. It was not his place to perform such a household chore. And yet she sat rooted to the floor next to me, where I played with the spoon she had been using to add water to the dough. *Let him do it,* she thought. *This was all his idea anyway.* But guilt gnawed at her heart, the knowledge that she was not being a proper wife.

Ma rolled the last few dumplings. When Hari Dev shuffled through the door, looking for me, she rinsed his hands in the hand-washing jug and asked him to carry the dumplings to the fire pit in the courtyard. Carefully, two by two, he carried them out as I watched him. Ma scraped the dry dough off her own hands.

Hari Dev stood in the doorway. "Ma, why is Bapu sweeping the floor?"

Ma turned around. Bapu was crouched at the far end of the room, brushing the floor with the straw hand broom.

Ma rushed to him as a shout escaped her. "No!" It was only after she had pulled the broom from him and Bapu had teetered for an instant from the force of the gesture that, standing so close to him, she caught the sadness and surprise on his face. Unable to look him in the eye, she swept the floor furiously, her own eyes filling with tears. She had let her husband, our father, the dance master, squat on the floor with a broom. Her tears streamed hotly down her cheeks as she pushed the sand and dust toward the door. Hari Dev began to cry. His sobs caught in hiccups in his throat. I dropped my spoon and ran to him, wanting to end what was beginning. Ma dropped the broom and covered her face.

Bapu came up behind her, and she let herself fall against him. They were the same height, and her head rested on his shoulder. Reaching over her, he touched her cheek with uncharacteristic gentleness.

"Girija, this is something we must do. You know that."

"Why? Why must we pretend to be what we are not, to have what we cannot afford?" Ma did not bother to lower her voice.

"What can we not afford? We have everything we need. This is our life. I just want our home to be clean and worthy of our guest."

"Isn't it usually clean enough? Look!" Ma pointed to Hari Dev and me as we watched them, holding hands. "Our children play on the floor. If it's worthy of them, isn't it worthy of Saiprasad? And the things you wanted for tonight's meal, they are expensive. The goat meat. The silver trays. I had to borrow those. They don't belong to us."

Bapu pulled away from Ma.

"Borrow! Who from? We cannot serve Saiprasad-ji on someone else's dishes!"

Ma stood and turned toward Bapu. She raised her eyes to his. Her lips no longer quivered. She spoke steadily. "Not just someone else. I borrowed them from Chandrabai. They used to be Manavi-ji's."

"That is even worse!" Bapu paced across the room. "We cannot defile a *devadasi*'s dishes. You must take them back at once!"

"Defile! Your own wife and priest will defile the dishes? How can you say such a thing?"

But Ma knew not to expect an answer. Nor did she want one.

She turned away. Hari Dev pressed up against her legs, his head against her waist, sucking his thumb, still holding my hand.

"Why don't you show your sister your elephant collection?" she suggested to Hari Dev. "I think Mahendra may be bringing you a new one tonight."

Bapu had settled wearily on the cushions. "Mahendra! What makes you think he will show his face tonight, of all nights?"

By the time Saiprasad-ji's labored breathing in the courtyard announced his arrival, Ma had stored away the bedding, cleared the floor, and lit the incense and oil lamps. I slept in the room I shared with Hari Dev. He lay beside me, under the same wool blanket. When Ma checked on him, he was still awake, happily twisting curls of my hair in his fingers.

Ma envied us our quiet peace. At every sound from outside, she went to the doorway and listened to the night, expecting to hear Mahendra. But it was merely a lizard burrowing into the sand for the night, the scratching of a stray dog scavenging for food by the embers of the fire pit, and finally the priest.

Saiprasad-ji panted, wiping his forehead with the end of his shawl. "*Namaste.*" His damp face caught the light from the lantern.

"Come in, please." Ma moved aside, flattening herself against the wall to let him by.

Bapu bowed his head. "Yes, please, welcome to our home. Thank you for honoring us this evening."

"Well, you know, since my wife, poor woman, passed away, it is not often I have a good woman's cooking," Saiprasad-ji said without sadness. He folded his stomach over his crossed legs on the rug. *You certainly have someone's cooking*, Ma thought as she brought in a tray of water. She gathered her shawl to her as she bent to offer him his cup, unsure of the direction his eyes might be straying.

"Your home looks . . . lovely," Saiprasad-ji said. Ma thought with unnecessary shame of the threadbare patches in the rug.

Bapu bowed his head again. "Thank you, thank you, Swami-ji. We are fortunate to live in such comfort."

Ma excused herself to tend to the goat meat on the fire. Outside, the air was crisp and clear. Free, she thought, of the smoke of incense, illusion, and ingratiation. She squatted by the dying embers for warmth and looked up. Bapu had often sat with her and described the stars studding the sky like so many small diamonds. She heard footsteps from beyond the courtyard.

"Ma!" Mahendra dropped lightly to the ground by her side. He smelled of opium and wide-open spaces. "The night is full of stars, glittering and winking at us."

"Mahendra." Ma put her hand on his and squeezed it. Warmth filled her chest. "How did you know?"

"The cook, Sundaran. His brother runs one of the taverns in the citadel. I get word through him."

They sat quietly for a moment. Ma wondered about the woman who had been with Mahendra earlier, but she knew questions would drive him away. Then Saiprasad-ji's bellowing laughter broke the silence.

"So he's already here," Mahendra said.

"Yes. But . . . what is this news about the emperor?"

Mahendra bit his lip. "It is bad."

"Come. We can talk about this inside. Better than listening to that priest all evening."

Mahendra collected the meat onto a copper plate, then lifted the clay pot of yogurt. Ma set her face into a smile and followed him inside.

From the tension in the room, Ma knew immediately that both Hari Dev and I were awake. She crossed toward Saiprasad-ji, who had taken me on his lap between his large hands. I felt their heavy moistness around my whole body. Hari Dev was pressed against Bapu on the floor cushions, his thumb in his mouth, emitting small sucking sounds. Ma turned toward Bapu for an explanation.

"Adhira woke up and Saiprasad-ji wanted to hold her," Bapu said. "I wish you could see how happy she looks on his lap."

Ma knew this could not be true. I looked over at my father, and for the first time in my recollection I struggled to accept his words.

"Such a beautiful girl," Saiprasad-ji said. "Soon she will be dancing for us on those pretty little legs, nah?"

In a violent movement, Ma wrested me from his hands. My heart beat loudly against hers as she held me close.

"Girija!" Bapu's voice was trimmed with anger. "What do you think you are doing?"

Something primal coursed through Ma's blood. A vision of the *sirohi* in the adjoining room flashed in her mind, and she struggled to control her voice.

"I must feed Adhira before we eat." She willed Bapu not to protest, not to remind her aloud that I had eaten just before the priest arrived.

"Saiprasad-ji." Mahendra's voice sounded from close to the floor. He had put down the pot of yogurt and bent to touch the priest's feet. Ordinarily, he detested performing this gesture. Silently, Ma thanked him. She wrapped me in a blanket, took Hari Dev's arm, and brought us back into the safety of the bedroom. From there, we could hear Bapu as he turned his attention to Mahendra.

"At least you remembered the importance of being home tonight to host our priest," he said.

In the bedroom, Girija stroked my back. We did not hear Mahendra's response.

"Mahendra, what a man you have become!" Saiprasad-ji's voice carried easily into the bedroom. "You could be our emperor," he joked.

"Give me a sword, and I will behead anyone who attacks!"

Mahendra's desire to speak about political affairs was palpable in his voice.

"Oho! Such fire in you!" Saiprasad-ji laughed.

Bapu bristled. "Too much fire, Swami-ji. Too much for his own good."

"Emperor Akbar is younger than I am!" Mahendra's excitement would not be dampened by Bapu's words.

Ma pulled a blanket over Hari Dev and me and returned to the main room, drawn by the discussion.

"This is it," Mahendra was saying. "We have to do it now. Overthrow these foreigners."

"*Beta*," Ma said, sitting at the edge of one of the cushions, "Akbar was born here, in Hindustan. He is a son of this land, not a foreigner."

Saiprasad-ji's eyes narrowed at her. She ignored him.

"So what if he was born here, Ma? He's the son of foreigners. And he does not shy away from battle."

The room was silent as Mahendra paused.

"He has many enemies, and they all want to take our land. We should pit them all against each other and just get rid of them. Once and for all. And then tackle him ourselves."

"Since when do you know so much about war strategy that you can sit here and lecture us?" Bapu waved an arm at Mahendra.

"Since speaking with some of the brave warriors who are engaged in battle themselves. At least they are doing something useful." Mahendra's voice wavered for a moment, losing its conviction.

"What are you saying?"

Ma sat by and waited for the collision she was powerless to stop. Bapu and Mahendra were like two bullock carts gathering speed as they headed down a citadel alley from opposite directions, neither one looking up to see the other one coming.

"I'm saying . . . " Mahendra's voice was strained but measured as he straightened his back to stand tall. "I'm saying, at least they are trying to do something. To protect our lives and ways and people. What do you do? Just dance your own life away in a little temple, lost in the desert."

That was how my brother saw our temple. Something little, lost.

He never did see that the inside was so much larger than the outside, that it was a doorway to the universe.

"Mahendra! How can you speak to your father that way?" Saiprasad-ji came to life, but his voice was weak and alarmed.

Bapu drew a breath before unleashing his anger. Unwilling to be present for what was coming, Ma stood and went to finish the food preparations. Behind her, as she carved the jackfruit for the end of the meal, Bapu's voice filled the air.

"How would you know what I really do, Mahendra? You speak so loftily of our lives and our ways, yet you spit in their face. Go play in the sand with your so-called warriors! Their brains are so addled with opium, I doubt they would even recognize the enemy if he joined them around their campfire!"

"Bapu—"

"Let me finish." Bapu's voice was low and growling, like a wolf's. Mahendra needed a reminder, and he was receiving it. "The stories of the gods, the tales of their valor and courage in the face of obstacles and evil, are important—no, necessary—lessons for everyone. Especially"—he waved his finger toward Mahendra—"in this time of war. They help strengthen our Hindu faith. And faith, my son, is what builds unity and resistance. It is time you understood this. If you cannot, you do not belong in this house."

Ma flinched but said nothing. Mahendra glared at the floor. In the silence that followed, Ma brought out the food, feeling her way from the kitchen to the dining area with her feet. Platters of goat meat, bowls of yogurt, the gram flour dumplings, and jackfruit. It was often her hope that food would defuse some of the tension in our home. And here was more food than any of us had seen in a while.

"Very well said, Gandar-ji!" Saiprasad-ji sputtered. "Art and faith. Let's eat to them!"

"Your father's right, *beta*." Ma placed a hand on Mahendra's trembling shoulder. "That's why the Raja sends a monthly payment for your father, right? It is important to the state. Come, eat."

They ate in near silence. Ma ate with them. It was an arrangement that she and Bapu had come to years ago, despite Bapu's more traditional preferences. She ate with the rest of the family, not after.

Mahendra's sullen anger lent a bitter taste to her food. Saiprasad-ji, however, ate heartily. After sucking the sweet bulb of jackfruit flesh, he belched loudly and pushed his tray away from him, signaling the end of the meal. Ma rose to clear away the food, but Mahendra jumped to his feet.

"Ma, sit and rest. You've done enough tonight."

He stacked the trays and took them outside, where Ma heard him rinse them off with the jug of household water kept by the pots of flour and lentils.

"What a strange boy you have there!" Saiprasad-ji said. "All manly about wanting to go fight in battle, and yet here he is, doing a woman's work!"

Shame filled Ma as she thought of Bapu sweeping the floor earlier in the evening, and she hurried outside to join Mahendra. She found him laying the platters out to dry at the edge of the courtyard. She squatted next to him and gently took a platter from his hands. "Thank you, *beta*, but I can finish this."

Mahendra let go of the platter and sat back. "That meal—it was expensive, wasn't it?"

Ma nodded. It surprised her that Mahendra would think of this. But money was very much on his mind.

"Ma, do you have what you need?"

"We are managing just fine. Please don't worry."

"I do worry, Ma. About you. I want to know you have everything you need. Not Bapu. You."

"I told you, Mahendra, there is nothing we need. Nothing I need. We get Bapu's payment from the court."

"I know, but . . . I don't think you'll be receiving that for much longer. The state is starting to put all its money into the army."

"The court will support us," Ma insisted. But her conviction was vanishing. "Now please be quiet about this."

The flames of the two oil lamps on the wall danced and flickered in the evening breeze, shifting shadows.

"Even if the court supports Bapu, that won't save Adhira."

"What do you mean?"

"I'm going to bring you money, Ma. Enough money for the family, and even to give to the temple, if that's what Bapu wants." He dropped his voice. "Enough so that Adhira won't have to become a *devadasi*." In his mind, it all worked out perfectly.

"Oh, Mahendra." Ma felt for his hands with hers. "You know that for Bapu, this has nothing to do with money, right?"

"Money will help," Mahendra insisted. "It has to. If I bring enough before Adhira turns five, maybe Bapu won't start her training."

Ma wanted to believe him. She said nothing of the hours I already spent with Bapu at the temple every day.

"In the meantime," Mahendra continued, "what about Padmini? Why can't she do something?"

"Mahendra, you are a good son. But we are managing."

"But she could help; she should help, no? I thought you said her husband was rich! Why don't you go talk to her?"

Ma shrugged. "It's not so simple, *beta*. You know how your father is."

"But you could go anytime, couldn't you? Bapu doesn't stop you. Is it because of your eyes? I can send someone to accompany you."

Ma sat back on her heels. "You're right, he doesn't stop me. He doesn't stop you, either. Have you seen her?"

It was good for Ma to be speaking about Padmini. Mahendra was the only person with whom she could do so. Bapu pretended she no longer existed, Hari Dev did not even know of her, and Ma thought at the time that I was too young to hear of this sister. As for the *devadasis*, none knew how to speak with Ma of the daughter who had turned her back on the temple. Over the years, her firstborn had gradually become a collection of memories.

"No, I haven't seen her, but . . . " Mahendra's voice drifted out past the opening in the courtyard wall.

"But what?" Ma leaned forward.

"I tried to see her. Twice. Both times, a servant told me she was out, but somehow it didn't seem right. I think she was avoiding me. I haven't tried again."

His words extinguished Ma's nascent hope like two fingers pinching the wick of an oil lamp. "So . . . that wasn't her with you today."

"With me? When? Where?"

Ma lifted her head toward the sky, then turned back toward Mahendra. "In the citadel. I went to the market. Hari Dev thought he saw you with a woman."

"No . . . I was alone. He must have been mistaken."

But they both knew Hari Dev did not make mistakes. They sat in silence, the weight of Mahendra's lie hanging between them.

Finally, Mahendra rose. "I can't stay any longer."

"Will you go inside and say good-bye to your father?"

"He doesn't understand."

"You're right, he doesn't understand. There are some things you don't understand, either."

"Hmph. Wait and see. He'll be surprised. Something is brewing. I've been spending time with—"

"Shh! I don't want to hear it. Do what you feel you have to do, but please say good-bye to your Bapu."

"Ma, I can't."

He picked up his camel-skin bag and slung it over his shoulder. Once, when he was still living at home, Ma had opened that bag and found a collection of foreign items—a crude opium pipe, a dagger, a handful of strange coins. She had fingered each one with wonder and envy. The bag itself had smelled of dense smoke and camel dung. Something deep inside Ma had stirred, something she thought she had buried long ago. A yearning for adventure. Quickly, she had pushed the items back into the bag.

Now Ma stood and reached out once more to hold Mahendra's hand for a moment. His skin was rough and his palm marked by a long scar. She traced its edges with her finger.

"I'll see you again soon, Ma. Give this to Hari Dev tomorrow when he wakes." He placed a small sandalwood elephant in her hand.

"Nothing for Adhi?"

Mahendra looked down to the ground, then back up, and shook his head. What he had for me was not anything on which I could ever lay a hand.

Ma felt the elephant's trunk and listened to Mahendra's footsteps fading into the darkness beyond the courtyard wall.

"Girija!" Saiprasad-ji had come out and stood a few paces away.

Ma took an instinctive step back.

"Thank you for your hospitality," he continued. "The meal was wonderful. I look forward to the next one."

"Of course. Thank you. We look forward to hosting you again." She said the words without thinking, her mind roaming the desert with Mahendra.

The priest left, and Ma stepped back inside, only then remembering the payment that was due. She called out to Bapu, and he answered wearily from the sitting area. She walked over to him and tripped on a small cloth pouch beside him. She picked it up; it was alarmingly light. A small handful of coins jingled loosely inside. Ma stored it quietly in the chest in the bedroom, under the spare blankets and shawls, a few layers above the *sirohi* blade. Mahendra's words about the state and the army echoed in her mind.

Bapu was still sitting when Ma returned to the main room. She bent toward him and held out her hand. "Come, let's go to sleep. It's been a long day."

Bapu rose without taking her hand. His face was close enough that she could feel his breath on her. She placed her hand where it fit neatly in between his shoulder blades and pushed him gently toward the bedroom. They undressed in silence, and quickly, because of the cold. As they removed their layers of clothing, Bapu's mind was elsewhere. *Ekhatu.* A composition played with only one hand. That is what my parents were: two hands playing separate compositions.

Once under the wool blankets, Ma lay on her side and faced Bapu. She traced the contours of his face with her fingers.

"Where are you?"

She could not remember a time when they had spoken in anything but a whisper at night. Even in the time before we children had started arriving, the nights they had spent out in the open on a hastily spread blanket, they had kept their voices low. Marauding bandits, desert jackals, and something humbling about the sky itself made them remain as quiet as possible.

Bapu sighed. "Girija. They are going to take our art from us and bring it into their debauched courts."

"The Muslims?"

"Yes, of course the Muslims. Do you know what happens in those courts? Terrible things."

Ma did not know, and she doubted that Bapu did.

"There, they dance just for entertainment," Bapu said. "A prelude to the repulsive acts of their bodies. Brahma, Vishnu, Shiva—there is no place for them in those courts." There were tears in Bapu's eyes.

"Repulsive acts?" Ma said. "What about what Adhira will have to do if you force her to be a *devadasi*? Do you think it is any different from what happens at those courts?"

"How dare you say I am forcing Adhira to be anything?" Bapu sat up, and his voice rose. Ma thought of us asleep on the other side of the wall. She put her finger to her lips, but Bapu would not be quiet.

"And the difference is that the *devadasis* are married to Krishna. They are sacred. Their next lives will be blessed."

"What about their current lives? And maybe it is not as bad as you think, Gandar." She tried to believe what she was saying, but it was difficult. "Akbar's father, Humayun, was an arts patron. Painting, poetry. Akbar will surely support dance. Besides"—she paused, weighing the wisdom of what she was about to say—"you don't have to look to the Muslim courts for signs of . . . what did you call it? Immorality?"

"What is that supposed to mean?"

"Don't tell me you haven't noticed Saiprasad. Didn't you hear what he said about Adhira's legs? She's just three years old!"

"What are you saying, Girija? Saiprasad-ji is a priest; his love is Krishna. He does not have those . . . urges."

"Of course he does! He's a man. He was married, remember?"

Bapu turned toward the wall. "He is a priest." He could not forget Saiprasad-ji's comments. "And I wish you would call him Saiprasad-ji. Is it so difficult? How do you think it makes me look when my wife disrespects the priest like that?"

Ma knew he did not really expect an answer. Between them, unspoken thoughts gathered and settled for the night, their presence palpable in the darkness.

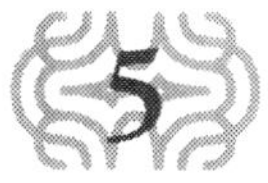

Gandar
1558 and 1531

Darkness had not yet lifted entirely, and Hari Dev and I were still asleep. Bapu sat up. During my waking hours, he devoted himself entirely to me and to dance, but when I was asleep, he took the time to do other things. He swung his legs over the edge of the low bed, and his knee cracked loudly. He sat still, hoping he had not awakened Ma. Then he sensed her absence. Extending his arm to her side of the bed, he found emptiness. He rubbed his eyes and in so doing was reminded of the pain in his swollen knuckles. It was nothing, he told himself, just morning stiffness. He refused to believe that it might be the return of the joint pain he'd been having before my arrival. He denied this, as he denied so much, in order to pursue his life's purpose. He stood, and his knees and ankles felt well enough for his weekly meditative walk to Bara Bagh, the royal burial ground.

Bapu stepped into the courtyard outside the house and immediately saw Ma's seated silhouette leaning against the wall, a soft black shadow against a hard gray backdrop. He paused for a moment, thought of going to her, then decided against it and squatted at the water jug. Even from across the courtyard, he could tell she was staring into space. In one of her moods, he thought. Ma never complained out loud, but neither did she hide the faraway look of sadness that clouded her eyes now and then. And ever since Mahendra had stopped living at home, the look of sadness came more often. Had Bapu paid closer attention, he would have noticed that some days, that look was replaced by a softening of the corners of Ma's eyes and a slight internal smile, and he might have understood that my brother was present more often than he, Bapu, saw him. But mostly these days, Bapu avoided looking too closely at Ma's face, lest he see familiar shadows.

Now he lifted the lid and tipped the jug, receiving the precious water in his cupped hand. He splashed it onto his face, taking a gulp to wash out his mouth. Then he filled a camel-skin pouch, tied it shut, and with the same cord tied it into the waist of his *dhoti*. He was ready. He would have to approach Ma now. It did not seem right to him just to leave.

"Walking? To Bara Bagh?" Ma called out to him.

He went over to her. "Yes."

Ma sighed. Bapu saw that she did have that look. "Why always to there?" she asked.

"I like it. It's peaceful."

Ma nodded, and asked the question she asked every week. "Take some food?"

Bapu gave her the same answer as he did every week. "No. Better to cleanse the body and mind just to bring water. I'll be back by midday."

Ma nodded again. Bapu stood for a moment, feeling he ought to say something, anything. But he turned and set out, and Ma listened to that familiar sound, footsteps receding.

The union between my parents was an unlikely one. The gods have their ways and their reasons, but this was something that had perhaps taken even them by surprise. Deep inside, each of my parents knew this. Each wondered now and then if they hadn't tempted fate by joining their lives. They had taken a quiet leap onto a new path together, each one leaving behind the well-worn one that had lain ahead. From then on, Bapu tried to steer his course back, with Ma at his side, but the road was uneven and filled with unknowns. Even when I was only four, I felt a confusion within me, a sense of yearning when I was with Ma and an equal sense of something missing when I was with my father.

Bapu made his way past still-sleeping homes, skirting the western walls of the citadel. In the muted predawn light, the walls were smoky gray, waiting for Surya to breathe color into them. A goat bleated plaintively as Bapu walked by.

"Don't worry," he whispered to it. "The rains will come again soon." He walked on, feeling a bit foolish for having spoken to a goat, although there is no shame in doing so. It was the sort of thing Hari Dev did all the time. Then a furtive shadow in a turban rounded a corner up ahead of him and caught his eye. The young man started down the path toward him, noticed him, and stood still. Bapu would have recognized my brother's slight form anywhere, having spent years watching him closely, grooming him to dance. They stood rooted in place, many paces from each other. The sight of Mahendra brought Bapu a mix of anger and sadness, and also pride and joy. They mingled within him like whole spices sizzling in a pot, each one releasing its own aroma, and Bapu knew not what to think of their combined flavor. He had not realized just how much he missed him, how much he wanted to know what Mahendra was doing. He took one step forward, but in that moment Mahendra turned and hurried back around the rounded wall of a bastion.

Bapu turned away from the citadel, and his confusion. A bustard spread its great wings and lifted its heavy body over a dune. Walking in the desert like this reminded my father of his days as a *kathaka*, wandering from village to village with his own father, dancing the stories of the gods. He missed the old days, when people in each village had welcomed him. Things had been easier for him then. But the fact that his work was more difficult now made it all the more important to him.

He walked on toward Bara Bagh, trying unsuccessfully to banish thoughts of Ma sitting alone. He was not blind to the fact that the years of what was, for her, a solitary life in the desert—after a childhood in the verdant Aravalli hills—had sapped her of her energy. And now there was no longer Manavi-ji to sustain her energy with friendship. It was this energy that had first caught Bapu's attention, when Ma was a young girl and he was nearing thirty.

He remembered with vivid detail the day he had arrived in the town of Mount Abu after days of walking, lost, parched, and alone. The dry *khajeri* trees and stunted acacia shrubs had given way to strange, tall trees with dark, glossy leaves, heady smells, and heavy fruit bursting with juice. Tufts of moist green grass had appeared under his feet, soothing his burning soles. He had eaten some of the fruit along the way and had let the sweet juices run freely down his chin. This was a Bapu I would never see with my own eyes. Eventually, he stumbled upon a town. Overwhelmed, he sat down on a rock and closed his eyes. The wind carried on it the smell of flowers and nearby water.

He opened his eyes again, and before him stood an older man, bare-chested, with thin legs, silver hoops adorning his ears, and a yellow turban on his head. He carried a sword.

"I'm sorry" was all Bapu could say, as he struggled to move back.

"What for?" The man's voice was sharp.

"For being in your way."

"You were not in my way. In fact, you look as though you do not *know* your way."

"True." Bapu allowed himself to smile. "I have been walking many days. Tell me, is this Mount Abu?"

"This is Mount Abu. You're from the desert, then? Shouldn't you be with the other *kathakas*, the ones who were here a few days ago?"

"They were here? Do you know where they went?"

The man shook his head. "No. They stayed two days and danced for us. They told the story of the game of dice. One of my favorites. And they brought news of the death of that scoundrel Babur, the so-called 'Emperor.' Then they left."

Bapu remained silent, not wanting to talk about the deceased Muslim emperor Babur, whose lazy son Humayun had been left in power, with this man whose hand had not once left the hilt of his sword. Humayun, Bapu now thought as he walked toward Bara Bagh; Humayun, who was now dead, leaving his own young son Akbar on the throne.

Abruptly, the man with the sword turned around. "Follow me."

Bapu could do nothing but follow the man to his home, where several women served him the most extravagant meal he had eaten in years. Mounds of steaming rice, roasted eggplant, grilled goat meat served on wide, green leaves. More and more food, and with it cups of a sweet, alluring liquor. Several times, Bapu looked up from his food to offer thanks to this generous family. On one of these occasions, his eyes met those of the girl who was bringing him a piece of melon. He was surprised; the other women kept their eyes downcast when they approached him. This one looked straight at him, defiant yet somehow still shy. Caught for an instant by her gaze, Bapu was astonished at the depth of her eyes, and for a brief moment detected in them a surging energy that sent a strange bolt to the very pit of his stomach. She dropped the platter, which clattered to the floor. The melon fell heavily on Bapu's foot, and the girl took two steps back, then turned and hurried to the kitchen. *Too much liquor*, Bapu thought, his head spinning.

To keep his head clear, he turned to speak with his host, who explained that he was the sword-maker for the royal family of Mount Abu. After the meal, he took Bapu to his workroom. Rows of sheaths and long, curved blades inlaid with gold wire rested against the mud walls, their metal hilts gleaming in the light of an oil lamp. Bapu recognized them as *sirohis*, the favorite swords of the Rajput princes.

"What is this one?" Bapu pointed to a sword that hung on the wall, resting on two metal hooks. It looked ancient, as though it had a story to it.

The sword-maker swelled with pride. "Ah, this one." He ran his hand against its tarnished hilt. "This one is special. They say this was the very first Rajput sword. Of the first four warriors who emerged from the fire sacrifice at Mount Abu, one was created by Brahma. That warrior stepped out of the flames holding a sword—this one. It's my inspiration for every *sirohi* I make."

Bapu had heard stories of *sirohis* cutting off heads and piercing hearts, and he hurried out of the room, his host laughing behind him. The memory of that laugh struck Bapu now, as he approached Bara Bagh. He had heard that laugh since then—Mahendra, who shared the laugh and the love of swords with Ma's father. And now, instead of dancing, he was wielding a sword somewhere in the desert.

Bapu now looked around at the canopied monuments to the dead scattered throughout Bara Bagh. Here rested the kings and queens of Jaisalmer, their children and parents, their brothers and sisters. The royal burial grounds breathed history. Out there, past, present and future all overlap in one perfect, timeless moment. Fragments of wars, sieges, and droughts, as well as times of peace and plenty, hang in the hot air like ashes around a pyre. And what lies ahead? Bapu wondered. When the next cenotaph of white marble is erected, will the carvings at its base show Muslims, Hindus, war elephants, divine dancers? From a dark place in Bapu's mind came an image of Mahendra lying wounded on a battlefield. He blinked it away and turned his thoughts to me instead.

The day was clear and windless. Bapu wished he could have brought me with him, so that I might witness the rugged beauty of the desert, watch the flocks of spotted sand grouse on their winter migration, hear the jackals howling at dawn. There the presence of the gods is tangible. But Bapu knew I was still too little. And Ma, she would have enjoyed the serenity of Bara Bagh, but Bapu knew she would not make the long walk. It was just too much desert for her. And yet she had done it before.

That evening in Mount Abu, after showing Bapu his creations, the sword-maker led him back to the main room. Bapu looked for the girl and found her among a cluster of women lighting small oil lamps. Her laughter rang above their voices, her thick braid swinging against her back, the curled end brushing the bare skin between her emerald-green blouse and flame-orange skirt.

"Come," the sword-maker said. "It is time for stories."

They stepped outside and settled onto some mats beneath the eucalyptus branches, for Bapu had finally learned the name of these fragrant trees. He had never seen such large leaves; he was used to the smaller, spinier leaves of desert trees. Everything was different in Mount Abu. Bapu was looking forward to sitting still and learning some new stories. He saw that several dozen people had gathered, sitting or squatting on the ground and watching him expectantly. The women brought out lamps and placed them in an arc in front of Bapu and his host. Beyond them, eyes and nose rings and bangles flashed. Only then did it occur to Bapu that it was he who was expected to be the storyteller.

The food and drink had slowed his movements and muddled his mind in a way that he did not habitually allow. He stood up uncertainly and breathed the cleansing scent of eucalyptus. As he stepped forward amid the lamps, Bapu caught a glimpse of a figure hurrying up to the crowd and hesitating a moment before settling in among them. A flutter of orange cloth and a pair of eyes behind the flickering flames. Again a flash traveled through his body like a lightning bolt. It jolted him out of his stupor, and he began to dance. In honor of this magical town nestled amid the hills, and to thank his host for his hospitality, Bapu danced the story of Krishna and the Govardhan Hill.

Bapu bowed and became seven-year-old Krishna, bright-eyed and playful. Pouting and shaking his head, he disagreed with his father, who explained to him that a festival would honor Lord Indra, who provides the rain for the crops. No, Krishna said, the festival should honor Govardhan Hill, which provides the pasture for the cows. His arms described the greatness of the hill, and he convinced the village elders to prepare for the Govardhan festival.

With a turn, Bapu became Lord Indra, proud and regal on this throne. Aware of the girl's eyes on him, he avoided them, afraid he would falter and lose his balance. Insulted, Lord Indra paced, his strong step and gold armbands reminding all of his might. He plucked an arrow and, his feet drumming the ground to gather intensity, aimed his bow at the skies, summoning the clouds of devastation. Bapu found himself seeking out the girl now, and amid the lamp flames and the sparkle of jewelry, his eyes found hers, which offered him an instant of steadiness. With a resounding stamp of his right foot, he released the arrow and let loose torrents of rain upon the village. The bells on Bapu's ankles whispered the softness of the first drizzle, then grew louder as the rain fell more heavily, until their frenetic ringing indicated the unrelenting torrents as Bapu's arms described the ropes of rain.

The girl's gaze wavered for a moment. Bapu remembered where he was. He became the terrified villagers, watching in horror as their land and cows became submerged. Bapu felt another gaze on him, that of an angry father, the sword-maker. The villagers built a boat, rowed to a corner of dry land, and performed a fire ritual. Hands clasped in prayer, Bapu begged Krishna for help. And Krishna, though merely a boy of seven, lifted the hill above the floodwaters with his hand and held the hill for seven days and seven nights, without food or drink or sleep. Bapu held the pose, his body immobile but his mind and heart racing. In time, Lord Indra called off the rains and begged forgiveness from Krishna. The villagers returned to their homes without fear, and Krishna gently placed Govardhan Hill back on the ground. The festival took place as planned.

Bapu could not clearly remember the rest of the evening, except for some of the stories with which the musicians and singers filled the night air. He watched in wonder, dizzy from the drink and the roar in his chest. And then, some time later, he awoke. He was lying on the mat beneath the eucalyptus tree. The musicians, the villagers, his host, everyone had disappeared. A single lamp burned by his side. Drums still beat in his head, and his mouth felt like the desert floor. The scent of jasmine filled the air.

"I have brought you water," the girl said, her voice right by Bapu's ear. He wondered why she insisted on remaining in the shadows. He did not know then that hers was always a world of shadows.

She answered his thoughts. "My father doesn't know I am here." She pushed a clay bowl of water toward him, her slender wrist extending out of the darkness. Without thinking, Bapu reached out and placed his hand on her arm, pulling her into the pool of light. She stiffened but, unwilling to spill the water, stepped forward. He took the bowl from her, drank from it, and set it on the ground. The water traveled down his throat like a newly fed river after a drought. His fingers still held her wrist amid her silver bangles, and he pulled her down so that she was sitting opposite him. Her fist was clenched. She looked, impossibly, as though she might hit him. Her skirt spilled around her in pools of green and orange. He noticed the white jasmine blossoms in her hair, fresh despite the late hour. He looked at her face and was puzzled to see that her eyes, so dark that the pupils disappeared in their depth, were staring straight ahead of her, just past his head. He turned to follow her gaze. Was someone watching them? Only the swaying branches in the night. He turned back toward her.

"You cannot see."

"I can see well enough." Her arm, which had slackened in his grip, stiffened again, pulling away. "Please let go."

Bapu let go. The silver border of her skirt caught the lamplight for an instant, dangerously close to the flame, and then she vanished. Bapu finished the water and lay down, looking up through the fluttering leaves. Sleep evaded him. His mind kept turning back to the girl. She was still a child—or was she? She looked to him to be about fourteen years of age, but it seemed to him that she had experienced a lifetime. He wondered what had brought her to him. Perhaps, he thought, she had simply wanted to see him again. But no, she could not see well. In fact, she had seen very little of his dance. Bapu understood this now. Those eyes, which he had used to steady himself, had looked through him the entire time. He felt foolish for thinking she had somehow been moved by his performance. And yet she had. For seeing is not everything. And this was Ma in the days when dance spoke to her heart in a way that made it leap for joy, not shrink in sadness, as it did by the time I was born.

A loud whistle above my father awoke him. The sun was already high above the horizon. He stood and stretched and heard the shrill sound again. It echoed painfully in his head.

"Mynah birds," a male voice said.

Bapu turned to see his host sitting on a log.

"They're everywhere this time of year," the sword-maker continued. "Whistling and chuckling as though they own the place. Intelligent birds. They can be trained to speak. One of my sons kept one for a few months and taught it to torment his sister. 'Girija, go away,' it would say." He laughed. "But then one day Girija caught the bird—I don't know how, with her wretched eyes—and went into the forest with it. When she came back, the bird seemed to have forgotten how to say those words. It followed my son around and repeated other things he taught it, but never those same words, and never her name."

Bapu smiled as he sat in Bara Bagh, remembering this conversation. Hari Dev had a similar ability. He could tame wild animals with a look and a whisper. But Bapu did not see the value in this. What good, he thought, would it do to his crippled son? He shook his head. He did not allow himself to dwell on thoughts of what he perceived as failure.

"Girija. That is your daughter's name?" he asked the sword-maker back in Mount Abu.

"Yes, you noticed her as well, hanh? Poor thing can't really see, but she's got other attributes, that's for sure!" The sword-maker laughed as he set off.

Bapu followed him in silence back to Ma's home and accepted a cup of milk. He heard voices in the kitchen but saw no sign of her. Girija. Her name was musical, like the call of a bird. Another young woman brought him a bundle wrapped in cloth, some figs, and a goatskin pouch of water. At the edge of town, Bapu bid my grandfather farewell.

For a long time, however, he was unable to leave. Fingering a eucalyptus leaf, he paced back and forth. He remembered his promise to his dying father a few years earlier, always to travel the desert and bring the great stories to the people, always to put Krishna before anything else. He turned his back on Mount Abu, but his feet were heavy as they carried him downhill.

Barely had he stepped into the forest when Bapu heard the crack of a branch behind him. He stood still. The sword-maker had warned him of wild boars and leopards. He turned slowly, but there was only the path leading uphill and a bulbul bird hopping into the shade. He continued walking, singing aloud, until the sun grew hot and the trees cast isolated pools of shade on the hardening ground. Sitting below a jacaranda tree ablaze in purple flowers, he opened his bundle of food and ate.

"I am at peace with my decision," he said out loud as he lay down to rest, but his dreams were full of dark eyes and slender arms.

When he awoke, Ma was sitting with her back to him. Her hand rested on a long, thin, cloth-wrapped bundle. Her hair fell down her back in an undulating cascade. Bapu reached out, expecting to find nothing. But his fingers encountered silken softness. She stood up, deftly braided her hair, and handed him the pouch of water.

"Drink. We have a long way to go. I will hold your arm." She rested her fingers lightly on his forearm. In the other hand, she held the bundle. It was all she had brought.

They set out. Questions welled in Bapu, but he dared not speak, fearing that the sound of his voice would break the spell and cause her to vanish. Instead, he asked her to keep quiet, too. She nodded, and they walked in silence. He watched the ground, making sure to step far from roots and rocks that could trip her. Thus she became his *sangat*, his accompaniment, the steady beat of her footsteps echoing in time between his own.

Remembering this long walk with Ma, Bapu now realized the sun was arcing toward its zenith and it was high time he left Bara Bagh and returned to the temple. He took a drink of his water, turned toward the shimmering shape of the citadel that rose from the sand in the distance, and started off toward it. All those years ago, Ma had walked for days with him, holding on to his arm. They had spent the nights sheltered by villagers, sleeping side by side as though they were meant to be together.

Eventually Ma began to speak, and Bapu let her do so. He learned that she could see shapes, large swaths of color, and changes in light. An illness had swept through Mount Abu the year of her birth, taking with it the eyesight of many of the elderly and newborn. If she held something close to her eyes, she could distinguish more detail. In order to follow Bapu, she had asked her cousin, a child, to accompany her. She had sent him back before Bapu could see him.

One morning Bapu awoke before Ma, no longer able to contain his curiosity. Very quietly, he peeled back several layers of cloth on the long object that lay by Ma's side. Within them lay the narrow, sharp length of a *sirohi* and a tarnished hilt. Bapu recognized it as the one from the sword-maker's wall. The first Rajput sword. Quickly, he covered it and stepped back. He thought of Ma's clenched fist. But she stirred and smiled at him.

Bapu never asked about the *sirohi*. Walking home from Bara Bagh, he still did not know why she had brought it, nor did he know where it was. He did not like to think of it in our house, for it was a symbol of another world, the world of warriors. It did not please him to be reminded that it was perhaps his having accepted Ma as the mother of his children that had set Padmini and Mahendra on the wrong path. Until the end of his days, he would believe this. Hari Dev, he thought, was his punishment, and I was his chance at redemption.

Bapu was now approaching the citadel, on the other side of which lay the temple and our home. His mood had darkened. What had started out for him as a pleasant memory of his time in Mount Abu had led to sobering thoughts about his work ahead. Now he hurried so as to have time to dance in the temple for a while before rest time.

He was circling the base of the citadel, approaching the main entrance, when he saw Chandrabai ahead of him. Her head was covered, but he recognized her gait, as he had with Mahendra. His son. The *devadasi.* In an instant he saw again the look that had crossed between the two of them at Manavi-ji's funeral. It was now a Tuesday, begging day for the *devadasis*, and therefore it made sense for Chandrabai to be in the citadel, asking for alms for the temple. And yet. It was an improbable coincidence that he had glimpsed Mahendra in the morning and now Chandrabai. The two of them had arranged to meet in secret, and Bapu understood this now. This was as far, however, as he let himself carry this thought. He struggled to control his voice as he called out.

"Chandrabai!"

Chandrabai turned around with the look of a frightened deer. But within moments she regained her composure and smiled.

"Gandar-ji. Have you been walking?"

"Yes, to Bara Bagh. Tell me, any luck today? Have people been generous?" He glanced at the empty begging bowl in her hands.

"No, Gandar-ji. Everyone is tightening their purse strings. I will go back out in the evening." She looked up at Bapu, and now her face was pure and placid, like the surface of Ghadisar Lake, revealing nothing of the muddy waters below. For she had indeed been with Mahendra and not begging for donations after all.

Once again, Bapu did not know what to think, and this made him uneasy. It was difficult for him to fathom that Chandrabai would be anything but truthful with him, her teacher, yet even he could not deny the growing sense of deceit that was rising around him.

There was only one remedy for his discomfort. Bapu stopped for a moment at home to collect me before continuing on to the temple. He found me playing with a pile of dried lentils while Ma felt for stones in the day's rice. He wished he could voice his fears to Ma, but he did not want to get mired in an argument with her.

"We'll go to the temple now," he said in her direction.

I looked up at him. "Me too?"

Bapu smiled at me and held out his hand. "Yes, of course you too, Adhi. Come."

I stood. "Ma comes too?"

Ma said nothing.

Filled with a heaviness I could not explain, I let go of Bapu's hand. "Bapu, can we dance here instead, for Ma?"

Bapu let out an impatient puff of air. "No, Adhi, I need to pray at the temple. Don't you want to see Krishna? Ma will be fine here."

Ma shook her head almost imperceptibly, as if to herself, and Bapu, tugging me out of our home, pretended not to notice the tightness of her lips as she ground her hand into the rice.

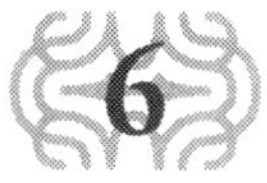

Mahendra

1559

Weary from another day without food, Mahendra walked eastward. Already the deep blue sky of evening had blended into the desert's blackness. There was no horizon, only the sense that he was walking toward the end of the world and might at any moment fall off. It was always his way, to walk toward darkness instead of toward the light, even when he felt in his heart that he should not. Now he glanced behind him and wished he could head the other way, toward the lighter sky, where Shukra, the evening star, shone reassuringly. But Sikander had promised him that this was the night he would, after three years, finally introduce him to Sikander's warrior band, and Mahendra was to meet them outside the village of Devikot, by the dry water tank a full day's walk from Jaisalmer. The lack of water in the tank—it had been five years since the last real rains, five years since my birth—would ensure that no one else would be near.

Five years. Bapu had begun my formal training, and Mahendra felt time was running out for him to bring home enough money to change the course of my life. To save me, as he saw it, and to save himself. He tried to quicken his step. Hunger stabbed at his stomach, and fatigue weighed down his legs. The wind picked up and swirled sand around him. He reached into his bag and pulled out the familiar cloth: a scarf that Chandrabai had given him at their last clandestine meeting. He wrapped it around his nose and mouth. It still bore traces of sandlewood and her sweet perspiration, which now overwhelmed him with memories of their last encounter, of her soft eyes beneath him, of her naked shoulders and breasts. He was seized with a desire to turn back, to go home, to lose himself in her. Then Bapu's face loomed before him. He pushed forward.

Mahendra had a plan, and he told himself it would work. It had to. Sikander had repeatedly assured him that his "brothers" would fully accept and respect him. They would treat him as one of their own, he said.

"Don't worry," Sikander had said. "I know you can fight. You're a man now. And now you look more, well, weathered. If you can convince me, you can convince them. Believe me!" And Sikander had laughed wholeheartedly, as though he had just made a good joke.

The cool night air raised the hair on Mahendra's arms, and he pulled his shawl more tightly around him, tucking the ends of the scarf below it. Night had almost fully fallen, and he did not know how much farther he needed to travel. Fear tightened his throat. A small form darted past him, spraying his shins with sand, its lithe body and pointed ears dark in the waning light. A desert fox on the hunt. Then the smoky smells of domestic evening filled the air. Meals were being cooked and homes heated for the night. My brother was not far from Devikot. As he stood still to determine the direction of the smells, something else caught his attention. It was the sound of a hand drum being played erratically, a deep and strong sound coming from somewhere other than the village. Its music stirred hope in him, and dance, as music always did. Mahendra resumed walking, correcting his course to head toward the drumming.

Kicking sand in front of him with every step to scare away any creature that might be lying in wait, Mahendra finally saw the orange glow of a campfire and the flickering shadows of men crouching and standing around it. The hollow sound of the hand drum grew louder, and with it the wind carried hoarse voices and raucous laughter. Mahendra hurried forward, then stopped short, smelling the sharp odor of horse manure and hearing uneasy snorts. He had forgotten that the warriors' mounts would be surrounding them, beyond the light of the fire. He stood still in the darkness, the men and their fire a few dozen paces away. Dark forms rose around him. Manes shook and whipped against thick necks still coated in perspiration. Snorts grew louder and closer. Hooves stamped dully on loose sand. Mahendra wanted to call out to Sikander, but his voice was caught deep down in his throat.

"Eh, who's there?" an angry voice called out.

In an instant, the camp was astir. The drummer dropped his instrument, leaped to his feet, and pulled out his dagger. Others followed him, blades glinting in the firelight. The men, shouting to each other, stood at the edge of the dancing light, brandishing their daggers and calling out to their horses. Two shadows darted forward, and an iron grip closed on my brother's arm as the cold, sharp edge of a dagger dug into his throat. Sour breath layered with the sweetness of opium blew into his face.

"Who are you?" a rough voice demanded as the fingers around his arm tightened. "You think you can make off with one of our horses?"

Mahendra's voice came out as a squeak. "No. No!"

The man laughed, but the sound was far from comforting. "What's this, Nono? Is that your name? What clan are you from? Who sent you?"

A second voice, this one behind Mahendra, whispered urgently to the first one. "Eh! Don't waste time with questions. Just kill him off and let's finish the food."

Sweat streamed from Mahendra's temples.

"Guryal, don't be a fool!" hissed the first voice. "What if there are others out there?"

Mahendra was dragged across the sand, his shaking legs unable to support him. He willed some strength into them. If this was Sikander's band, he thought, he was not making a good impression. And if it wasn't, this was the end.

"So? What is it that's disrupted our dinner?" Sikander's smooth voice, laced with only a tinge of tension, called out. At the sound of it, Mahendra drew a breath and regained control of his legs. He and his captors were only a few paces from the light. He would not let Sikander see him being dragged like a wounded *chinkara*.

"Sikander!" Mahendra called out as he struggled unsuccessfully to free his arms.

"We've caught a horse thief!" said the one called Guryal, holding the dagger to Mahendra's throat. "Why does he know your name?"

Mahendra finally wrenched his right arm free. "I'm not a horse thief, you idiot! Take this dagger away from my neck before you regret it."

"Are you threatening us?" Guryal growled, although he did remove the dagger. The three men stepped into the light.

"Ah, Mahendra!" Sikander's eyes were laughing from beneath his scarlet turban. Despite his mirth, he looked, as he always did to my brother, warrior-like. His cummerbund, also scarlet, was fastened tightly around the waist of his white cotton tunic. His dagger was tucked into it. "It's all right, Mulraj, you can let him go."

Mulraj and Guryal stepped back, arguing. "Who is this, Sikander? Why do you know this horse thief?"

Mahendra, rubbing the welts on his arms, protested. "I told you, I'm not a horse thief! Sikander, didn't you tell them I'd be coming tonight?"

"Ah, yes, right. Has it already been a fortnight? Good thing we decided to stop near the tank. I'd been thinking of pushing on a little farther tonight. I guess you would have been wandering for quite a while then, no? Ha ha!" He motioned to the fire. "Come, have some food. I think there's still a whole goat leg, unless Nasir's already sunk his teeth into it."

The mention of food made it hard for my brother to maintain his scowl. His mouth watered at the sight of the roasted goat, or what was left of it. Around the fire squatted a dozen or so men, gnawing meat off bones, smoking opium, and drinking a strong-smelling liquor. Some still held their daggers at the ready, although most had returned them to their waistbands when Sikander had recognized him. All wore turbans similar to Sikander's, albeit varying in cleanliness. Their hostile eyes, rimmed in red as though to match their headgear, returned Mahendra's gaze silently.

Mahendra stood awkwardly, looking to Sikander for direction, but Sikander had turned his attention to his opium pouch. A grunt sounded at Mahendra's feet. A stocky man squatted by his side, chewing on some goat meat and motioning to the remaining leg with a greasy hand. The man nodded at Mahendra and moved sideways on his haunches to allow him room to sit. Grateful, Mahendra squatted by him and helped himself to the meat. It was the tough and stringy meat of an old goat, but he did not care. It was warm and tasted good. Mahendra ripped off long strips with his teeth, barely pausing to chew them. Someone handed him a pouch of liquor, and he drank thirstily of it. The liquid burned his throat, and he coughed some of it out while the men laughed at him. The drummer returned to his instrument, the hollow beat of the hand drum filled the air between the crackles of the fire, and everyone appeared to forget about Mahendra. The liquor settled warmly in his stomach, and he feared it might put him to sleep. He turned and spoke to Nasir, the grunting man, in order to stay awake.

"How long will you be camping here?"

"Mmm. As long as Sikander says we are." Nasir picked meat out from between his yellow teeth. "A caravan is going to pass through the tax checkpoint near Devikot soon. We'll attack it there and take the payment."

"Eh, Nasir!" Guryal shouted out. "Why are you telling him our plans? What if he's a spy?"

"Calm down, calm down." Nasir waved a leg bone dismissively toward Guryal. "Sikander wouldn't let a spy come near us."

Across the fire, Sikander sat with eyes closed in a state of opium-induced torpor. It was not clear how, exactly, Sikander would prevent a spy, or anyone, for that matter, from approaching the camp. It seemed more likely that Guryal would run out, behead anyone who happened to be passing by, and ask questions later.

"Don't mind him." Nasir turned back toward Mahendra. "He explodes easily but doesn't cause much damage."

Mahendra tried to laugh. "I see. But the caravan, it'll be a Muslim one, right?"

"Muslim, Hindu, does it matter? All of them have to pay the tax collector when they pass his checkpoint."

This was when another man might have heeded the voice in his head that warned him that something was not as he had believed. But not my brother. "But doesn't the state need that money? You know, for the fight against the Muslims?"

From across the fire, Mulraj laughed, his stained teeth glinting in the firelight. "Listen to this boy. 'Doesn't the state need the money?'" He mimicked Mahendra in a high-pitched voice. "What do you think we're doing? Risking our lives every day to turn over everything to the state? Are you a fool?"

"But . . . " Mahendra sat back, crossed his legs, and turned to Nasir for explanation. "What are you doing with the money, then?"

"Eh, speak up, Nono," Mulraj shouted to him. "I want to hear what your brilliant ideas are."

Nasir shot Mulraj a look. "Mulraj, shut your mouth."

"Mulrash, shutyourmouth," Mulraj repeated, lying in the sand. His pipe fell out of his mouth. The other men, like him, lolled around, seemingly unaware of, or at least uninterested in, the conversation. The opium was taking hold. Several times before, opium had been pressed upon Mahendra, but he had never smoked it himself. He knew others—Chandrabai, Ma—might might not believe it, as the smoke of others often seeped into his hair and clothing. But Bapu had always said, "Respect your body, for it is a vessel for communicating the divine. Do not feed it poisonous substances." At first irritated with himself for listening to Bapu, Mahendra was now grateful that he had.

"Are they always like this?" he asked Nasir in a low voice.

Nasir laughed, then held a finger to one nostril and noisily blew out the contents of the other onto the sand. "Don't worry," he whispered. "They're taking the night off. We just pulled off a very successful raid. Sikander told us all to rest tonight. Everyone here's a tremendous fighter."

"Ah." Mahendra was not convinced. These men were not what he wanted them to be, but, much like Bapu, he had chosen what to believe, and he would not accept anything that stood in the way of that belief.

"But Mulraj is right," Nasir continued. "We can't turn over the goods to the state. That would, in fact, be foolish. What do you think the state does with the money collected at the checkpoints?"

Mahendra shrugged. He waited for Nasir to continue.

Nasir picked his teeth again, peered at the shred of meat on his fingernail, then ate it. "By the time the collector takes his share, the treasurer's office dips into it, and the accountant records what he wants, less than half lands in the state's coffers. But we can use that money for weapons and horses. Well, and, of course, a little for other important needs. But the Raja should be thanking us!" Nasir paused to poke the edge of the fire with a twig. "Besides, there are enough other state taxes. Tax on this thing, tax on that thing. Tax on land and agriculture, on water and alcohol and houses and camels, tax on shops."

"I know," Mahendra said. Our family, until then, had been fortunate to receive payment from the state, rather than owe tax upon tax, like everyone else.

"And now," Nasir continued, the liquor loosening his tongue, "the Muslims are imposing another tax for Hindus. Who do they think they are, taxing our people? The *jizya*—it's shameful. To have to pay a tax for not converting to their religion! We can't let this happen in Rajasthan."

"Never!" Mahendra agreed. At last, he thought, here was someone aside from Sikander who was addressing the real problem.

"So, it's Mahendra, right?" Nasir said. "What do you think of this Akbar emperor?"

Mahendra was glad to be asked something. Here was his chance to impress someone.

Mahendra sat up and picked up a small stick that lay beside him. "*Pffi!* Who cares about Akbar? He's just a puppet. Bairam Khan, his regent—now, that's who *really* holds the power. And he won't give it up anytime soon."

"You think not?" Nasir looked sideways at Mahendra.

"We have to be really careful. All he wants is to widen the frontiers of the Muslim-controlled territory. Soon he'll try to enter Rajasthan. We need to get rid of them all." He dug the stick forcefully into the sand.

Nasir frowned. "I don't know. I hear Akbar's very intelligent. Maybe he's biding his time. You know, to figure out who to trust and how to rule."

"Intelligent?" Mahendra raised his voice. "He can't even read!" The words were out of his mouth before he realized his mistake. The others were listening after all. Eleven pairs of red-rimmed eyes, including Nasir's, glared at him.

"Not that that's a measure of intelligence, of course," Mahendra hastened to correct himself.

"Well, it's a trait I'd like to see in an emperor." Sikander emerged from his opium cloud. "An emperor who can't read or write for himself is one who must rely too much on others."

Mahendra felt bolder now. "Exactly! That's exactly what I meant. He may be an excellent soldier, but how can he hope to rule without being able to study history or read maps? This is to our advantage."

Mulraj was listening again. "Fine, maps are important," he said. "But why should Akbar care about history? What's done is done. He'll be trying to build his empire into the future."

Sikander flapped an arm. "Mulraj, what are you doing? Trying to provoke Mahendra on purpose? Any good leader must know history to understand what he's up against." Here, Sikander chuckled. "If he knew that Rajasthan's resistance to invaders is the stuff of legends, he might change his mind."

"Yes." Mahendra nodded vigorously. "Take the city of Chittor, for example. Not far from here. Everyone has tried to conquer it, but no one has succeeded yet. This Akbar can't read about the failed strategies that others attempted. So let him try his turn and see what happens."

A story was welling up within Mahendra in the way stories still did at times, no matter how hard he tried to suppress them. It was one of his favorites. He wanted to tell it in the best way he could, through dance. He looked around. All the men were watching him, listening. In their eyes, behind the opium smoke and layers of distrust, he thought he discerned some curiosity.

Sikander nodded at my brother. "Mahendra, you know the story, right? Tell them. They like stories." And he chuckled again.

Mahendra took hold of the stick again and held it tight, lest any graceful movements of his hands betray him. His voice would have to suffice to tell the story. One stray dancer-like movement, and the men would set upon him like jackals. He set his face into an impenetrable mask to immobilize his eyebrows, took a breath, and began speaking.

"It was 1302, and Delhi was in the hands of Sultan Alauddin Khilji, from Afghanistan. Like others before him and after him, the Sultan wanted to move west into the region of Gujarat because of the fertile soil there, but in order to do so, he had to cross, and take hold of, Rajasthan. In particular, the princely state of Mewar sat in his way. So he attacked its capital, Chittor. But, as you well know, Rajputs are indomitable. They held the fort for eight whole months, fighting off the invaders. Finally, the Sultan said he would lift the siege if he was allowed to gaze, just once, on the face of Rani Padmini, the lotus-faced wife of the King of Mewar, whose beauty was legendary. The King agreed, on the condition that the Sultan be able to see only her reflection in a pool, which in turn would be reflected in a mirror.

"When the Sultan saw Padmini's beauty, even twice reflected, he was love-struck. The King accompanied his enemy to the main gate of the fort, and just as the huge wooden doors were dragged open, the Sultan's soldiers captured him. In exchange for the King's safe return, the Sultan demanded Padmini's hand in marriage. To save her husband, Padmini agreed to this ransom, and the Rajputs organized a procession of palanquins to transport her.

"The palanquins arrived at the Muslim camp. Each palanquin was carried by six slaves, who in fact were warriors in disguise, and each palanquin carried a seventh warrior. Padmini's uncle, pretending to be Padmini, requested a final, private meeting with the King. As soon as he left the King, all the warriors burst forth and attacked the Muslim camp. A massive battle ensued. Some say five hundred Rajput warriors were slain. Some say fifty thousand. Rani Padmini threw herself into flames, rather than fall into the hands of the enemy. Many died, but Chittor and its king were saved. The fort, Chittorgarh, stands strong to this day, and always will."

Mahendra's heart was beating fast as he fell quiet. The expressions of the men around him had changed. Their eyes had narrowed and filled once again with suspicion. Sikander was slowly, almost imperceptibly, shaking his head. Mahendra looked down and saw the stick lying on the ground. He did not know what he had done, what they had seen. His hands shook. The rest of his body felt like lead. The silence was deafening.

Guryal grabbed one of Mahendra's hands and spread out his fingers. Even in the faint light of the dying fire, their smoothness was a stark contrast with Guryal's hands, etched with years of fighting. Those hands, which, like mine, could be flowers awakening to the sun, a river rising over its banks, a tree reaching to the sky. "Look at these hands! Just one scar, and baby soft. You call this a warrior? Sikander, what are you trying to do?"

"Guryal, let him go!" Sikander pulled Guryal away, but Mahendra stopped him.

"No, Sikander, Guryal has a right to suspect me." This was Mahendra's chance to prove himself. *Veera.* Valor. One of the nine sentiments. He had portrayed it in dance many times. He thought he could do it again here. "Guryal, I will fight you if you'd like."

The other men moved closer, smiling hungrily like jackals approaching a carcass. Guryal put his hand to his dagger, then looked over at his leader. Sikander said nothing.

Guryal dropped his hand. "No, I have a better idea. Have you seen him ride a horse, Sikander? A warrior's horse? No? Then he'll ride one right now."

A rock dropped into Mahendra's stomach. He had been on camels before, many times, but never on a horse. Not a single warrior he had encountered so far had allowed him to ride his horse. He looked out toward the mounts. In the dimness, their dark forms stirred restlessly. He thought of how our brother, Hari Dev, would have no trouble riding a horse, even a wild one. He would lean down, wrap his arms around the horse's neck, and whisper to it in its own language.

"Well?" Guryal prodded him.

Mahendra looked at Sikander, who nodded. He had no choice now.

"Fine. I'll ride one of your horses. But I'll choose which one."

Mahendra stepped out of the firelight, toward the horses. All the men were watching him closely. But within a few steps, they would lose sight of him. The darkness would be a challenge once he was on the horse, but at least it would hide the fact that he did not know how to mount one. Horses do not kneel down like camels.

Mahendra paused a few steps from the horses. Their nervousness permeated the air. The moon was out. The white horses stood out in their brightness, and even the hides of the black ones shone. Their backs were bare; beside each one lay a saddle and a pile of blankets. Mahendra's heart sank even further as he realized he would have to ride without a saddle. He had no idea how to put one on a horse. On each head, the points of the horses' distinctive ears curved inward like a pair of *sirohi* blades. Eleven long, broad faces turned toward him, watching. Mahendra took one step forward, and three of the horses did the same. They were not tethered, for there was nothing to tie them to, nor was there any need. These types of horses, Marwari horses, are known for their homing instinct, for bringing back riders who become lost in the desert. There are three ways in which a cavalry horse leaves a battlefield: victorious, carrying his wounded master to safety, or eaten by vultures after laying down his life for his master.

Mahendra's stomach heaved, threatening to send back the goat meat. He swallowed hard. Behind him, most of the men had sat back down around the newly fed fire. They did not really care what happened to him. He could run, but there was nowhere to go. He took another step forward. The horse closest to him, a proud black one, shook his head and neighed.

"It's all right?" Mahendra's whisper came out as a question.

The horse neighed again and drew back his lips, exposing long teeth. Mahendra took a breath, and the dancer in him took over. Out of his mouth came dance syllables, which he recited as he stepped forward toward the horse. *Kita taka tun tun na tete dha.* The horse's ears twitched and pitched forward, as if to better pick up the whispered sound of the consonants. Mahendra repeated the syllables. *Kita taka tun tun na tete dha.* The horse lowered his head. *Kita taka tun tun na tete dha. Dha dhin dha kita dha dhin dha.* Mahendra was just two steps away from the horse's head. He reached out his hand again. *Kita taka tun tun na tete dha.* The horse nuzzled Mahendra's hand with his lips. His breath was warm and moist. Up so close to the horse, Mahendra could see how long his legs were. Long legs to keep the horse's body away from the scorching sand. He put his hand on the horse's flank. *Dha dhin dha kita dha dhin dha*. Mahendra reached up farther and caught a handful of mane. It was rough in comparison with the hair on the horse's side. Rough and tangled, but easy to hold on to. *Kita taka tun tun na tete dha*. Tugging on the mane, my brother took a leap and threw his right leg over the horse.

The instant he was on, tension shot through the horse's body. The horse threw himself back violently and whinnied. The others, quiet until now, joined him as they pawed the sand. Mahendra gripped the rough hair with both hands and tightened his hold with his knees. His mouth was dry; when he opened it, no sound came out. The horse bolted, jolting him back. In a moment they were careening into the darkness. Mahendra was thrown forward and back, his neck painfully absorbing the impact of every step. The sounds of the other horses, the voices and drumbeats around the fire, all fell away. Mahendra lowered his torso, leaning down toward the horse's neck. In terror he closed his eyes tight, willing the horse to stop. It didn't even slow down. But out of the fear ringing in Mahendra's ears emerged the rhythm of the horse's pounding feet as it galloped over the sand. It was a syncopated four-beat rhythm, with the slightest of pauses, barely perceptible, while all four feet flew in midair. One two-three four pause one two-three four pause. *Dha ge-tet te - ta ge-tet te - dha ge-tet te - ta ge-tet te -* .

Mahendra laughed, but the sound was carried away on the wind. He slid easily into the rhythm and dared to open his eyes. He was surrounded by shades of black. Below him, the horse's body was a gleaming silver-black. Farther down, the ground was a shade lighter, with occasional coal-colored clumps blurred by speed and flying sand. Ahead of the horse and man, dunes loomed like impenetrable shadows. Above him, the endless sky sparkled with stars. Mahendra's hair streamed back as he lifted his head to look up. He was one with the horse, with the ground, with the sky. Dance in such a way that you become one with everything, Bapu had taught him, as he taught me. Finally, Mahendra understood what this meant. This was his dance. He wished Chandrabai could see him now, a warrior and his horse, masters of the world. One day, he thought, once he had saved me, once he had proven himself to Bapu, he would ride away with Chandrabai like this, her arms around him, clinging to his back, leaving everything else behind.

The horse leaned in to the left and circled back, slowing down to a canter. Three beats now, the right hind leg, then the left hind in tandem with the right fore, then the left foreleg. Then a brief pause, and the cycle repeated itself. *Ta ki ta - di ki ta - ta ki ta - di ki ta.* Mahendra's body adjusted easily to the change in rhythm. In the distance, the campfire burned orange like a single ember in a coal pit. The horse headed toward it, unbidden. Mahendra was not ready to return. He wanted to fly again, to feel time hold still while he careened through space. But he did not know how to tell the horse to do what he wanted. He watched as the campfire grew larger. Now the horse slowed again, to a trot. Diagonal legs moved together synchronously to define two beats, over and over again. *Taka taka taka taka.* Shadows moved around the campfire. *Taka taka taka taka.* And now a walk, four beats again, but this time regular. No pause. *Dha ge tete ta ge tete dha ge tete ta ge tete.* The horse's rib cage expanded and contracted in a gradually slowing rhythm. By the time they reached the edge of the firelight, both man and horse were breathing evenly.

The horse came to a standstill. Mahendra leaned down. "Thank you," he whispered into the horse's neck.

He slid down, landing triumphant in the dancing pool of light. The men were staring at him, surprise, even admiration, on many faces. Mahendra met Guryal's scowl.

"That's Lakhan," Guryal growled. "Who told you to take my horse?"

"Guryal, leave it be," Mulraj said. "How was he to know which horse was yours?" He chuckled. "Heh, I can't believe Mahendra rode Lakhan! Of all the horses! Congratulations, Mahendra." And he slapped Mahendra on the back.

Guryal spat in the sand and walked over to Lakhan. He gave the beast a rough shove, and the horse trotted back toward the others. Still scowling, Guryal followed him. Mahendra made no attempt to conceal his satisfaction as he watched Guryal's retreating back.

Sikander, a faint smile playing on his lips, nodded and motioned for everyone to sit. The fire was dwindling, smoldering embers brightening to orange with every breath of wind, then dying again. Mulraj threw some gnarled and dry *khajeri* branches onto the fire. The shriveled leaves curled in the flames, and the branches crackled. Sikander tossed a blanket to Mahendra. The rough wool smelled of horse sweat and smoke. Mahendra pulled it around his shoulders, while, in our home, I slept under another blanket, one that smelled of incense and cooked lentils, with Hari Dev curled around me. On the horizon, Surya began to lighten the sky, pulled by his seven horses. *Kita taka tun tun na tete dha.*

Chandrabai
1561

When Chandrabai woke, she noted with relief that it was still dark. She pushed off the heavy blanket and lay back. Cooler air settled softly on her. She wondered how much time remained before dawn, whether she should hurry back to her quarters right away. Beside her, Mahendra snored lightly. These mornings were easier for him—no one would come looking for him here in the hut, the use of which he had secured through an acquaintance of Sundaran. No one would look for her, either, but the other *devadasis* expected her at the morning ablutions.

She closed her eyes and ran her hand over her belly. It still felt no different from before, despite the changes that were taking place beneath her skin. She knew it was unusual to be twenty-one years of age and carrying a child for the first time. She would not be able to hide her condition much longer. And my brother would want to know whose child it was. She would be unable to tell him. Two months ago, she had been with him, and with her patron as well. But Mahendra would need to know. If the child was not his, she thought, he would not care what happened to it. But if it was, and it was a boy, he might one day want to take him away. And if it was, and it was a girl . . . Chandrabai squeezed her eyes more tightly shut, afraid to picture what might happen. For if it was a girl, she would have to give her to the temple.

A jackal scrambled and growled outside.

Mahendra stirred and yawned. "Is it time?"

Chandrabai felt around for her clothing. "I think so. You had better go quickly, then."

"Don't worry, no one will see me. And really, what will happen if one of the other *devadasis* does? Nothing. It's just my father I need to avoid."

Chandrabai sighed. All this secrecy irked her. But then she felt guilty for this thought, for she was withholding her own secret.

"When will you come back?"

His hand reached over and caressed her side. She sat still, wondering if he could feel anything different.

"I don't know. Soon, I hope." His fingers trailed toward her front.

She stood. "But when? Six months? Less?"

Mahendra laughed in the darkness. "You'll miss me, hanh? I'll make sure to come as soon as I can."

"No, no, that's not what I meant. I mean, yes, of course, come when you can, but, you know, don't put yourself in danger. Wait longer if you need to."

Mahendra rolled over onto his back. "What are you trying to tell me, Chandra? What is wrong?"

"Nothing. It's just that you never tell me where you are going, or what exactly you are doing. It's all just adventure this and fighting that. Smells in your clothing and a glow in your eyes."

"Is that what is bothering you? Don't worry. I can't tell you exactly what I'm doing. But it's for you, and for our families."

Chandrabai's stomach tightened. Maybe he did know.

"And one day, when we have fought back the invaders, I'll take you with me," he continued. Chandrabai wondered if these invaders were ever actually going to come to Jaisalmer, but she said nothing. She could not picture Mahendra as a victorious warrior. What she could picture easily instead, what she imagined for her future, was a wealthy man like Samarjit, Padmini's husband. She had never met Samarjit, but she knew he was a painter in the Raja's court, and Padmini was said to live in a large house in the citadel. When Mahendra spoke like this of taking her away from the temple, Chandrabai imagined herself as Padmini, and Mahendra as Samarjit, living together in luxury. Like everyone else at the temple, she still had no idea of the true conditions of Padmini's life.

"Well, I wish we could stay together now, but you should go," Mahendra said, his tone of voice changing. "It will be light soon."

Relieved to be leaving, and ashamed to be relieved, Chandrabai let Mahendra embrace her in the dark, and then, a scarf over her head and a plain peasant's sari draped around her, she crept back down the path to the temple. A familiar uneasiness spread in her stomach, and she headed for the temple kitchen.

On the ledge above the pots of dry goods, she found a covered bowl of cooked rice. Sundaran had left it for her. Promising herself to find a way to thank him, she ate a few scoopfuls to quell the heaving in her stomach. A bell rang, and she hurried back to her room before the others rose. She rumpled the blanket on her bed, hid her peasant sari under it, and climbed in. Her stomach settled as soon as she lay down. The simple furnishings in her room emerged from the shadows as daylight grew. They stood in stark contrast with the rich embroideries and plush cushions of her imagined future in the citadel. Then she remembered: Today the new Raja was being crowned, after the recent death of his father. She was expected to be present to confer good fortune on him. She sat up, and immediately her stomach churned. She lay back down. The day loomed ahead like an insurmountable dune.

"Chandrabai, are you in there?" Jayarani-ji's voice sounded from outside. The corner of the curtain moved to the side, and Chandrabai saw the silhouette of her mother peering in.

"Yes, Ma. I'll be coming out soon."

Jayarani-ji entered and came to sit at the edge of Chandrabai's bed. She put her hand on Chandrabai's forehead. Chandrabai pushed it off.

"Ma, stop! I don't have a fever. It's my leg again," she lied.

"Again? Where is the pain? Perhaps I should call someone. Maybe this is related to, you know, why you haven't conceived yet."

"No, no. There's no need. I'm sure it will pass."

"But can you dance? And what is that smell? Like . . . opium?"

Chandrabai pushed her sari farther down into the bed. "I don't smell anything. And no, I'm sorry, I don't think I can dance."

Jayarani-ji stood and patted Chandrabai's leg. "No matter. But you must come to the coronation anyway. There must be as many of us as possible. Can you at least walk?"

Chandrabai nodded. She would now have to pretend to limp all day to keep her cover. She sat up again, pretending her slowness was due to her leg.

Her mother took pity on her. "I will have one of the girls bring you some food here. Rest for a while longer, and keep your strength for later on." She left.

Chandrabai felt better after eating some more rice and lentils. Her stomach settled, and she was able to contemplate the rest of the day with more composure. She now regretted having led her mother to think she could not dance, yet she was quite glad to be free of that responsibility for the day. Still, to assuage some of her guilt, she decided to go to the temple to help with the morning rituals, although, unclean, she would not be able to offer a special *puja* to Lord Krishna or enter the inner sanctum.

The temple was still mostly empty. One of the younger *devadasis* was sweeping the courtyard, the broom swishing the ground with rhythmic regularity and demonstrating to the newest arrival, a thin, sad scrap of a girl, the proper manner in which to move the sand and grit out of the temple. The new girl had been dropped off, on the brink of starvation, by her parents. They could, or would, no longer care for her. In the past few months, some light had returned to her eyes, and she showed some promise in dance, but she had yet to show any true gratitude for being alive.

Chandrabai thought to speak to the girl but stopped short at a sound coming from within—the sound of my voice. I was singing. I loved early morning in the temple, when everything was clear and fresh and I could picture my voice spreading to the pink-orange sky, enveloping all beings, reaching out to my Lord Krishna. Chandrabai paused in the courtyard simply to listen, for despite the turmoil within her, our chants of devotion always lifted her heart.

I poured out my song, like water from a bowl, until I was empty of it and the temple was full. Movement resumed around me. The swishing of the broom, which had paused, started again. A lizard skittered across the courtyard. Bapu appeared at the temple entrance, saw Chandrabai, and beckoned her to join him. Chandrabai slowly crossed the courtyard, limping.

"You have come early," Bapu observed, glancing down at Chandrabai's leg but saying nothing about it. Hari Dev appeared behind him, holding a cluster of dry leaves.

"Yes, I wanted to spend some time with Lord Krishna." This was the truth.

"Wonderful. Why don't you join Adhira? She is conducting a *puja*, but I am sure she will not mind if you are there, too."

She's just a little girl, Chandrabai wanted to protest. *I am by far her elder. Shouldn't I be the one who minds or doesn't mind?* And yet when Chandrabai entered the outer sanctum, she did so humbly, feeling she was disrupting something sacred. I knelt in front of the entrance to the inner sanctum, my head bowed, my hands joined at the palms in front of me. I felt, too, as though something had been disrupted. I wished I could lay my eyes upon the statuette of my Lord Krishna, but, having not gone through my dedication ceremony to become a full *devadasi,* I wasn't yet allowed into the inner sanctum where Krishna resided. Instead I stayed still, whispering a prayer, imagining that I was becoming one with the temple, with its walls and pillars.

When I felt a warmth on my forehead, like the hand of Krishna himself, I picked up a stick of cassia incense and waved it in circles, making the swirls of smoke dance. Chandrabai watched me in silence, wondering if there was something truly divine about me. She imagined me as an *apsara,* a celestial nymph come down from the sky in a bolt of lightning. I like to think this notion was of help to her in her times of uncertainty. Those around me whose faith—in dance, in Lord Krishna, in the future, in themselves—has wavered have found in my own faith a source of strength, conviction, and purpose. This, I hope, is what the gods intended. But I don't know if they intended my growing sense of apprehension about becoming a *devadasi.*

Chandrabai heard a noise behind her; it was my father, come to watch me. "An inspiration, no?" He smiled encouragingly.

Chandrabai took a few steps back. She wished she had stayed in her quarters.

Bapu followed her. "You are right. Best to wait until Adhira has finished for you to go in to do your own *puja*. And you will be dancing later tonight, yes?" He looked at Chandrabai pointedly.

Chandrabai had forgotten to limp. She tried to make up for it now, exaggerating her imaginary pain and rubbing her leg for effect. "No, I'm so sorry, I don't think I can dance today."

Bapu contemplated her for a few moments, and his silence unnerved her. Chandrabai was about to ask to be excused, when he motioned for her to follow him. When they had entered the dance hall, he told her to sit. Hari Dev sat-squatted in a corner, tearing up a bunch of leaves and arranging the pieces into neat piles. He paid no attention to her or to Bapu. Chandrabai lowered herself gingerly to the ground and crossed her legs beneath her with feigned difficulty.

"Don't mind him. Now, listen, I know you have heard the *Bhagavad Gita* many times, Chandrabai—Lord Krishna's teachings to Prince Arjuna as the Prince wavers, caught between duty and his own desires. Let me remind you of how they begin." And before she could protest, Bapu was dancing.

He was Prince Arjuna, the great warrior and archer, about to go into battle. His back was straight, his body proud. Chandrabai sat a little taller. Arjuna rode in his chariot with Krishna, who was both his advisor and his charioteer, Bapu's feet beating the rhythmic pattern of hooves on sand. Arjuna was about to fight for his clan's rights against his cousins, the Kauravas, who refused to share the kingdom. Chandrabai watched Bapu but saw Mahendra.

The chariot came to a standstill as Arjuna surveyed the opposing army. His shoulders fell as he saw it was full of familiar faces: his friends, his relatives, his uncles and cousins, even his guru. Chandrabai knew that, as a warrior, Arjuna had a duty to lead his troops in this war against his family. But how could he do this, kill his relatives and his guru? Holding his hands out before him and shaking his head, he told Krishna that he could not fight. He would prefer to retreat to the jungle for the rest of his life than to take aim at his kin. And with great solemnity he laid down his bow.

In the next moment, as he rose from the ground, Bapu spun around and assumed the stance of Krishna, wise and protective. Anger tightened Chandrabai's chest. She did not want this lesson now. Krishna said, "My dear Arjuna, give up this weakness, as it does not befit you. It is your duty to fight in this battle. While this may mean slaying your kinsmen, you will be doing it for justice and the greater good. Fight for the sake of fighting, without considering happiness or distress, loss or gain, and by doing so you shall never incur sin."

In one turn, Bapu was Arjuna again. Conflicted between his duty to kill his enemies and his duty to show reverence to his teachers and elders, Arjuna paced back and forth. In the end, bowing deeply, he surrendered completely to Krishna and implored him, hands clasped together, to take him as his disciple and show him the right path.

"And you know what happened in the end, Chandrabai," Bapu prompted her, as he came to sit by her side.

Chandrabai felt a deep fatigue. "Yes. Of course I do. Arjuna was finally convinced that he must fight. With the perfect clarity and detachment of the enlightened—"

"He fought in the battle, as was his duty," Hari Dev said, without looking up, at the same time as Chandrabai.

She said the words she knew so well, but they meant little to her. She knew, however, what my father was trying to say to her. He knew of the turmoil within her.

They sat in silence for what seemed to her like an eternity. The smell of incense curled into the room. Eventually, Bapu slowly rose to his feet. "I know you will do the right thing. Why don't you go perform your *puja* now?"

Chandrabai stood as well. She wanted to leave the temple, but Bapu's eyes were on her, so she returned to the outer sanctum. I finished my prayers and wiped the sand and dust out of the crevices in the carvings along the doorway to the inner sanctum. A sliver of sunlight shone through a crack in the wall. I pointed it out to Chandrabai. She frowned.

"I wish someone would repair these cracks. Everything is crumbling."

I told her that the ray of light might be Krishna sending us a slice of the heavens, but she gave me a strange look. We watched the particles of dust dancing in the light, and Chandrabai wondered in silence if my ability to see things differently would change once I was introduced to some of the duties of a true *devadasi*. She hoped that it would not. As for me, I tried to live fully in that moment, grateful for the sun and the sky and the sand, resisting, with the only means I had, the walls slowly closing in on me.

Bapu left the sanctum, and as soon as he did, Hari Dev hurried over to us.

I put my arm around his shoulders. Because of his legs, he was barely taller than I. "Did you think of some new ones?"

Hari Dev nodded.

Chandrabai looked at both of us. "New what?"

I explained to her that Hari Dev was constantly making up new dances in his head, layering the footwork with the mathematical patterns that gathered and swirled in his mind, and then sharing them for me to give life to with dance.

"Can I see?" she asked.

Hari Dev looked over at me, then at Chandrabai, with wide eyes. "Nooooo!"

I had to laugh. "No, *didi*, this is just between us. Don't tell Bapu. He doesn't believe that Hari can think up dance patterns."

Then I took my brother's hand and pulled him into the dance chamber. Chandrabai hurried through the motions of her prayer to Lord Krishna, and what had started out for her as a genuine desire to pray now dissipated in the air like a cloud of smoke.

Later in the day, the churning in her stomach returned. Hoping she would be able to overcome it, she set out anyway for the citadel with the other *devadasis*. She knew she could have feigned incapacitating pain and stayed back, but she could not bring herself to carry her untruth further. She could not dance today, that was a fact, even if not for the reason she had stated, but she would attend the coronation and do her part to confer good fortune on the Raja.

As Chandrabai climbed the steps to the gates of the citadel and wove her way through the narrow streets to Chauhata Square, trailing behind the other *devadasis*, her stomach heaved, perspiration collected in her palms, and her head pounded. She tried to remember to favor one leg, but hoped that, as the crowd grew thicker, it would be less noticeable if she stopped doing so. Most of the *devadasis*, with the exception of her mother, Jayarani-ji, paid little attention to her, happy to be out in the city. And even Jayarani-ji would be busy soon, preparing to dance.

It was evening, and although the sun had not yet set, the citadel was festooned with little oil lamps. The flickering wicks danced in front of Chandrabai as her head began to spin. Drums were beating up ahead, and a thousand voices resonated in her ears as the crowd pushed forward. Jayarani-ji held her by the arm and pulled her along.

"Come, *beti*, you can stand up in the front, near the court attendants. It will be less crowded there."

In time, they reached Chauhata Square. Chandrabai had begun to feel sharp pains in her belly and wanted only to sit down. But there was nowhere to do so. Jayarani-ji kept hold of her arm. Two palace guards came toward them, and Jayarani-ji spoke briefly to one of them. They nodded, and she turned toward her daughter.

"Stay with these men, *beti*. They will make sure you are safe. I must go prepare for the dance. I will come looking for you afterward."

Tears sprang to Chandrabai's eyes. She did not want to be left alone, even with the guards. But she nodded. She was a grown woman, soon to be a mother; she knew she had to be able to manage on her own. She followed the guards, who led her to a less crowded area, below the stairway leading to the Raja's private balcony, where the coronation would take place. She leaned against the wall. People watched her, whispering. Some recognized her as a *devadasi*, but she did not care. One of the guards handed her a clay cup of water, careful to maintain propriety and not touch her hand, and she sipped it slowly, gratefully. Some of the churning subsided.

She looked around. She rarely had occasion to watch events from this vantage point. A few paces away, a cluster of women stood. The jewel tones of their clothes, the silver- and gold-filigreed borders of their saris, and the gems on their arms and necks flashed in the sunlight. A similar cluster of men stood a bit farther off, their turbans freshly tied, their mustaches newly waxed. A ring of guards held the crowd back. Next to Chandrabai, a few of them chatted, discussing Emperor Akbar's recent marriage to the daughter of the Raja of Amber to seal an alliance with the court there. The Raja had agreed without a fight. The alliance guaranteed peace and some measure of continued autonomy. Chandrabai wondered what Mahendra would think of this type of arrangement.

The drums grew louder as the moment for the coronation drew near. It was then, just as her mother and the other *devadasis* were beginning their dance, that a flash of pain stabbed Chandrabai. She doubled over and cried out, but there was too much noise around her for anyone to hear. The guards who had been assigned to stay with her were craning their necks to see the dancers. Chandrabai needed to get away from the crowd, lest she fall to the ground and get trampled. She mustered what little strength she had to drag herself along the wall, to the cluster of women. They stood with their backs to her. She reached out to touch one of them, the closest one, on the elbow.

The woman wheeled around suddenly. For a brief instant, her eyes were angry and fearful, but they softened to look at Chandrabai more questioningly. Although the woman's head was covered, and although there was something different in the set of her jaw—for it had been ten years since she had seen her—Chandrabai recognized my sister.

Chandrabai struggled to stand up straight. "Padmini?"

Padmini pulled away from the other women and held Chandrabai by the shoulders. "You are a *devadasi*, yes? I recognize you."

Chandrabai nodded, the pain intolerable.

"Let me look at your face. You're Jayarani's daughter!" Padmini exclaimed. "What is wrong?"

Chandrabai could say nothing. Tears streamed down her face now, while a liquid warmth spread to her lower body. She understood now what was happening. *Matra*, a beat in the musical cycle. Now a lack of beat, a silenced cycle.

Padmini took her arm. "Come, come to my home. It is not far. Don't worry, I'll take care of you."

The sounds of the crowd fell away; even the walls of the surrounding buildings seemed to Chandrabai to move back. She was aware only of the sticky warmth, my sister's fingers gripping her arm, and, through it all, despite the pain, a spreading sense of relief as the once-*devadasi* led her away and the never-to-be *devadasi* left her body.

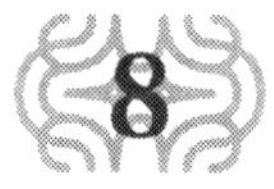

Adhira

1563

Bapu remained seated at the edge of the bed, unmoving. "I will be ready in just a few moments, Adhi."

I stood in the doorway, shifting my weight from one leg to the other. The sun would be up soon, and I worried that I would miss the magical start of the day. Bapu was becoming slower and slower. He beckoned to me and pointed to his legs. I knelt in front of him and rubbed his calves, as I did every morning, kneading their tightness with my fingers. His hand rested a moment on my head, and I looked up at him, past his bony rib cage to his face. My Bapu looked nothing like the dancer that he was in the temple. At times like this, he frightened me.

He smiled, but even in his lips there was weakness. "Maybe you should go ahead. I'll join you soon."

"But Ma . . . " Ma never liked me going to the temple alone, especially before the others were up.

Bapu shrugged. "You are a big girl, nine years old. What is there to worry about? Go—let Ma be."

My heart jumped, for I wanted nothing more than to greet the morning alone in the quiet of the temple, without his shadow over me. I skipped out of the room, then tiptoed past Ma in the kitchen. Guilt gnawed at me, as when Bapu did, or made me do, something I knew Ma did not approve of. But I pushed the feeling aside. I parted the bead curtain at the front door as quietly as I could. Ma heard me anyway.

"Adhira! Where are you going?"

My mind wanted to stop, but my body could not.

"To the temple. Bapu's coming soon. All right?"

I did not wait for an answer but ran all the way to the temple in the dusty gray morning. There, I slipped through the badly closed gate as the guard snored, and then sat in the courtyard, against the wall, catching my breath. Above the temple hung the type of quiet that comes only in the absence of people; the *devadasis* had not yet entered the temple with their sighs and yawns.

In three days, I would be one of them. Every time I thought of this, of my approaching dedication ceremony, I felt a quiver just below my ribs. Like a cocoon about to break open, I was about to take a new form. Finally, I would be able to enter the temple's inner sanctum, to come face-to-face with my Lord Krishna, to perform my duties to him. But as the day approached, my mother seemed farther and farther away, and the space between her and Bapu had widened to a deep, dark pit. Their arguments had dwindled to nothingness, and I feared, in a stomach-aching way, anything that could silence Ma.

I sat for a while longer, relishing the quiet, the knowledge that I was alone. Not even Saiprasad-ji was there. I was thankful for this, then remorseful for thinking this way. But I could not help it—something about the priest troubled me, and more so with every passing year. As I thought about him, my elation subsided. I was not ready to admit it to myself, but a part of me understood, even then, that my dealings with the priest, and perhaps with the world beyond the temple, would change once I was a full *devadasi*, and this gave me pause.

I stood and ran in circles around the courtyard, my arms outstretched, feeling the air rush past my arms and hands, banishing these thoughts from my mind. The flame-orange light of the rising sun slanted into the courtyard through the gateway. I held up my fingers in the shaft of light. It filtered through them and threw their long, tapering shadows onto the floor. I reached out toward a flower

I could see clearly, and at first my hand was just my hand, traveling through the air. And then, the instant I picked the flower, my hand became the flower itself, and I watched my fingers opening one at a time, like petals shyly greeting the new day. I felt the earth, the desert, the temple awakening through me, from the stone floor, still cold from night, to the tips of my fingers, warm with life. I stood in the long rectangle of sunlight and watched the swirling motions of my hands. They were brief spring butterflies, fluttering in the quiet of dawn. I held my fingers together, thumbs in, and turned my hands into blades to slice through the still-cool air. I could make my hands into the hands of Shiva the Destroyer, or Vishnu the Preserver, or Brahma the Creator. They could be anything.

This was my favorite time of day in the temple, so full of promise and newness. It belonged to me, and only me. The creatures of the night had retreated to their holes; the creatures of the day were not yet out. It was my time to be alone in the temple, to do as I pleased, to be serious or playful, as the mood suited me. The sky lightened. The silhouette of the *babul* tree inside the temple began to take on texture, ridges and knots in the trunk appearing slowly, every detail brightening until my eyes could discern the black trail of ants marching up the dark gray bark, the white thorns on the branches. Little by little, all the wondrous details of creation were revealed. The rising sun breathed color and warmth into the sky and the temple: blue purple pink orange yellow.

The morning call of a gray partridge—*kee-uck!*—broke the silence. The bird stood in the shadow of the wall, its soft, gray-brown plumage blending into the gray-blue smokiness of the corner still untouched by the sun. It darted its head around, pecked at the ground, skittered across the courtyard. It turned back to look at me, inviting me to follow. All at once, I was a gray partridge, too. I bent down and held my arms to my sides like folded wings. I ran fast, with small steps, and moved my neck side to side. The partridge trained an eye on me, observed me for a moment, then seemed to shake its head. *Kee-uck!* It flutter-hopped back across the courtyard and through the gateway, as if it had no time for this nonsense, its long, lean shadow trailing behind it. I laughed out loud.

I skipped across the inner courtyard and into the dance hall, careful not to set foot on the cracks in the stone. I did not know why I did this, just that I should. Some days I dared myself to step on a crack on purpose, but then I worried that something terrible would happen that day and I'd be the one to blame. It was irritating, this self-imposed rule. But in three days I would go through my dedication ceremony and would no longer need to follow it. This was the first of the two big ceremonies. The second one would happen in few years, when I became a woman. That one held even more mysteries.

Bapu and the *devadasis* had told me a lot about my dedication. I would be formally married to Lord Krishna and become . . . what was that word Bapu had used? *Auspicious.* Bapu told me every day that I already brought good fortune, but I was not sure then what he meant. I knew the rains had been plentiful the summer I was born, but nothing since then had seemed particularly fortunate. Some clouds had taunted us the year I turned four, skidding across the sky as though hurrying to a better place.

I hoped that by becoming a *devadasi*, I would truly become auspicious. I thought that perhaps then Hari Dev's legs would get better, and maybe Mahendra would come back for good, and Ma would smile again. So I told myself that it was just for a little longer that I needed to avoid the cracks. I could manage for just three more days. Besides, there were far fewer cracks in the floor of the dance hall and the outer sanctum. I had never seen the floor of the inner sanctum, where Lord Krishna resided, but I knew it had to be perfect.

In the entrance to the dance hall, facing the doorway to Lord Krishna, I held my palms together and bowed. I closed my eyes, and the soul of the temple, the force that compelled me to dance, seeped into me. I did not know then what it was, or if the other dancers felt it the way I did. It was exciting yet terrifying. I walked slowly to the center of the hall and held my cupped hands out, holding an invisible mound of flower petals. The animals and dancers and flowers adorning every surface of the carved pillars and walls surrounded me. I prepared to dance the *rang manch ki puja*, the coloring of the dance space, to awaken them.

From the moment of my first step, my body smiled, thanking me for setting it free. I stood still for a moment, my hands still cupped, my eyes closed, and I let my body sway ever so slightly to the right, to the left, to the right, to the left. My feet carried me across the floor to the four corners of the dance hall, the four corners of the earth. Kneeling in front of the entrance to the inner sanctum, I let a handful of flower petals cascade down as an offering to Krishna. They felt soft, like feathers. I placed flowers on the floor, rang a little brass bell, offered him incense. I folded my hands to form a conch shell and blew into them, and in my mind I heard its deep, soul-stirring sound. I held my fingers to my ears in reverence, recognizing the long lineage of teachers who had passed down the dance, beginning with Lord Shiva, Nataraja, Lord of Dance. I rose with my hand to my heart and invoked Brahma, Vishnu, and Shiva, the trinity of great gods.

That was when I felt something change in the air, which felt alive with presence. When I opened my eyes, I thought I saw a thousand deities looking down at me. They seemed to have stepped away from the walls and to have taken on color and movement. They were seated on the heads of cobras, emerging from lotus flowers, surrounded by auras of light. They held maces, conch shells, garlands of pearls. On their heads were peacock feathers, crescent moons, third eyes. I faltered for a moment, wondering if I had really called them forth. Yet they were there, nodding at me, encouraging me to continue. My fear was great, but my joy at having such an audience was greater. I looked for Lord Krishna. Had he come out of the sanctum to watch me? I could not find him among the faces that surrounded me. I thought perhaps he was avoiding me, as a groom-to-be avoids the sight of his bride until the marriage ceremony is complete.

I ended the *rang manch ki puja* with a bow. "*Namaste*," I said aloud, greeting the deities. My voice sounded small, but the deities must have heard it, for they nodded in silence. I did not know then what to do. Like Bapu, they seemed to expect something of me. For a moment, I was angry. Why couldn't they just let me dance? Why couldn't everyone just let me be? But I believed in these deities; I could not disappoint them.

Bapu had taught me so many compositions, so many stories, yet now, with all the gods and goddesses watching me, I could remember nothing. Lord Shiva waved a hand at me, encouraging me to dance. I looked up at him, anguished. He smiled at me, picked up his small, hourglass-shaped drum, and began shaking it. From the drum came a steady, hollow beat as the beads at the ends of the cords tied to its center struck the leather heads. The sound echoed throughout the dance hall as I remembered what Bapu had taught me, that the first syllables of language had come from Lord Shiva's *damaru*. And here he was, Lord Shiva himself, giving me the gift of language. All I needed to do was to turn it into dance. I bowed, and my feet moved to mimic the sounds of the drum. It was easy. They knew what to do. Soon my arms and hands followed and I was making up stories. I was a deer drinking water, a girl combing her hair, a hunter on his horse. Up among the carved figures of the temple walls and pillars, the deities watched, smiling.

I felt I had been in their company before. It was not something I could actually remember, but rather a sense of familiarity with this moment. And then I saw it: a peacock stood in the entrance to the sanctum, its long blue-green tail dusting the floor. Its crest of blue feathers hovered over its head like a crown, and it looked at me seriously, perhaps even a little sadly. Manavi-ji. I returned its gaze. My fingers, in their sudden stillness, tingled. I stopped dancing, squeezed my eyes shut, then reopened them. The peacock was still there. But the gods and goddesses who had been watching me had faded away. The bird and I were alone.

Had it come from the inner sanctum? Was this my future husband? I had danced stories from Krishna's life so many times, often showing him with a peacock feather in his crown. I remembered a peacock in the temple garden, a piercing shriek, and tears on Bapu's cheek. Light gray eyes and long gray hair. Infinite wisdom, infinite sadness. I felt I was supposed to understand something from all this, but what? I remembered fragments of Bapu's conversation with Manavi-ji, and how she had never answered his plea for her blessing. Was it right for me to become a *devadasi*? Did I have to? The weight of the unknown came crashing onto me. What was I to do? I understood then that I could, I had to, take the beat that was given to me and lay upon it whatever shape I wanted. I could decide for myself.

I sat on the floor in the middle of the dance hall, facing the peacock, which had not moved. I wanted to cry.

"What am I supposed to do?" I whispered. "Sometimes when I dance, strange things happen."

The peacock cocked its head to the side, as if to hear me better.

"Some of these things are really nice. Like you. But some are . . . " I could not find the right word. "Too much" was all I could say.

"What's too much? Who are you talking to?"

Chandrabai walked into the dance hall, a broom in hand. She turned back toward the sanctum. The peacock was gone.

"No one."

Chandrabai laughed. "Talking to yourself, then? That's not a good sign!"

At the sound of her laugh, I realized that I had not heard it in a long time. I wanted to tell her what I had seen.

"There was a peacock."

"A peacock?"

"Yes. It reminded me . . . of something. Or someone."

"Who?" Chandrabai was looking at me oddly, and the words slipped away from me.

I shrugged. "I don't know. It was just a feeling. As if someone I knew was here."

Chandrabai sat down next to me. "Are you sure there was really no one? I mean, aside from me coming in?"

I saw lines of worry on Chandrabai's face. "No, no! Like who?"

Chandrabai took my hand in hers. "Sometimes Saiprasad-ji comes in when one of us is alone."

My heart beat loudly in my ears. That wasn't at all what I had felt, but now that Chandrabai said this, an uneasiness welled in my stomach. I tried to steer the conversation away from talk of the priest.

"So? It's the temple. Of course the priest is sometimes here."

Chandrabai shook her head slowly. "It's just that sometimes . . . well, sometimes he tries to . . . to have things he should not have." She let go of my hand and stood. "So, just make sure you're never alone with him. All right?"

I nodded, but my heart still pounded and my stomach still

churned. Chandrabai began sweeping. Sunlight now spilled into the hall through the pillars, lighting the entire floor. *Devadasis* trickled into the chamber. The temple was awake. From somewhere nearby came Saiprasad-ji's cough. Then the priest entered. The *devadasis* bowed to him. I bowed, too, but my stomach clenched.

"Ah, Adhira!" Saiprasad-ji switched his thick gold ring from one finger to another. "I know I can always count on you to be here early. Where's your father?"

"Not here yet, Swami-ji." It was the proper way to address him. Swami—knowledgeable one, master, owner of oneself. I did not really know what all this meant, just that I should call him Swami-ji. And that Bapu might be a while longer. He had looked so tired when I'd left home, blinking sleep from his eyes.

"You came here alone?" The priest sounded pleased as he asked me this.

And I was proud of having come alone. "Yes. All by myself." From behind him, Chandrabai was looking at me pointedly, shaking her head. "But usually Ma makes me wait and come with Bapu," I quickly added.

"She's just being protective. You're lucky to have such a mother. But soon you'll be a full *devadasi*, nah? And then she won't be telling you what to do anymore."

She doesn't, I thought. But I wished that she sometimes would.

Chandrabai put down the broom. "Right! In three days! Adhira, would you like to see your outfit?"

Before I could answer, Chandrabai was leading me out of the dance chamber. When they were out of earshot of the priest, I paused and tugged on Chandrabai's hand. I knew I was not allowed to see my outfit before the ceremony.

Chandrabai shrugged. "Why not? Come, you'll like it."

We were breaking a rule. I felt a sense of foreboding. The peacock, Chandrabai's words about the priest, my fear as I danced before the deities—were these warnings to me, a little girl making a dreadful mistake?

I followed Chandrabai to the storage room, where she rummaged through some piles, then emerged with a bundle. She removed the outer layer of coarse cotton and revealed a skirt and blouse of deep pink-red. I touched the garments' silken softness and traced the patterns of gold and silver thread that weighed down the hem of the skirt and the trim on the cropped blouse. The outfit came with a see-through length of fine muslin that I would wear wrapped around my shoulders and covering my head. I had never seen any outfit so beautiful.

Chandrabai smiled. "And we'll have to pick out your jewelry. But I need to put this back now. Your Bapu will be here soon."

I followed her back to the dance chamber, thinking of jewelry. I hoped for the kind of ornament that lay along the part in one's hair. That was what girls usually wore to their wedding. I hoped for ivory bangles, dangling earrings that would swing and dance below my lobes. A nose ring studded with droplets of diamonds and rubies. These were the things I desired, and this feeling of desiring was new to me.

Then Bapu arrived, and the day took on its familiar shape. Throughout the day, however, silk and jewels danced in front of me, troubling my concentration. I wanted to reach out and take them, wrap myself in them and feel like a princess. But then I would think of the peacock, gazing at me with deep, sad eyes. Maybe Lord Krishna was disappointed in me for wanting all these things. Perhaps it was not . . . what did Bapu say? *Appropriate.* Perhaps it was not appropriate for me to want things. I knew deep inside that all I should want was to love Lord Krishna. Like Mirabai, the saint about whom Bapu had spoken. Was I, like her, capable of true *bhakti*, true devotion?

In the evening, I waited outside the temple gate for Bapu to finish his prayers. The wind had picked up. Sand swirled through the gateway. The sky was as blue as ever, shifting to violet in the west. The evening star was out, winking at me. I winked back. It almost felt as if the rains were on their way, even though it was months before they were due. If they came at all.

Bapu joined me and took my hand. "Are you all right?"

We always walked home hand in hand. I greatly enjoyed these moments, walking like this with Bapu, the way I had seen other girls do outside the temple. Inside, Bapu was my teacher, with expectations higher than fortress walls. But at the end of the day, spirits lifted by dance, he was gentler, and for the brief walk home, he was a different kind of father.

"You seemed distracted earlier today," he continued. "I was worried that you were not feeling well."

"No, I'm fine. I've just been thinking."

"About what?"

About what? The priest wanting what he shouldn't have, and what Chandrabai had said, and the upcoming ceremony, and the peacock. Bapu sat down and leaned against the wall. I sat next to him. I picked a dry blade of grass. It came loosely, easily, out of the earth. I did not know how to explain to Bapu what was churning inside me like a nest of snakes.

"What is troubling you?" The quietness with which he asked the question made it even harder to answer.

I began in a place that might make sense to him. "You know that story about Mirabai that you told me? I was thinking about it today."

"That is good. Mirabai was a very special woman. She was not born to serve Lord Krishna, yet she did. She devoted her life and her soul to him."

"Is that what I'm supposed to do?" I asked him, although that was not exactly what I meant.

Bapu took my hands in his. "Adhira, you are doing just what you are supposed to be doing. Has someone told you otherwise?"

I thought of Ma, the way she bit her lip when I talked about my dance, or the way she held on to me some mornings, as though she did not want to let me go. But Ma had never told me to be any different than I was.

"Mirabai didn't care about things, right?"

"Things?"

"Like . . . bangles. And nice clothes."

"No, she did not care about those things. She left all that behind." And then Bapu seemed to understand something. "You don't think you have to leave everything behind, do you?"

I was not sure what I thought. Bapu held me close. I felt the boniness of his chest through the thin cotton of his tunic. He smelled of stale oil.

"You belong to the temple, Adhira. To us. You must not leave," Bapu said into my ear.

The idea of leaving had not been troubling me, but for some reason I felt some relief at Bapu's words. I remained in Bapu's arms until I could tell that he did not know what to do. I pulled away and helped him stand up. I wanted to go see Ma and tell Hari Dev I would always be with him. "I won't ever leave!"

And I put my hand back in Bapu's. We turned out of the temple and onto the path home. I skip-hopped a few steps, and the sudden freedom was exhilarating.

The night before my dedication ceremony, I hardly slept. The moon was full. It lit up the courtyard outside our home when I stood in the doorway in the middle of the night, shivering from the cold air. It was unusually bright, illuminating every corner. The pots of lentils, rice, and flour; the branches of the *khajeri* tree; the fire pit—everything seemed alert, quiet but awake, in anticipation of a great event. I wondered if things would look the same the next night. Then Hari Dev crept up behind me, pulling me back inside, telling me I would catch a fever standing out in the cold. I let him take my hand, pull me back into the hut. I always did what my brother asked, because his requests were so simple and brought him such happiness.

The next morning, in contrast with the crisp, clear stillness of night, all was a blur. Hari Dev helped Ma clean our home, to ready it to receive people in the evening after the ceremony. Sand flew in the air as he swept the floor. Bapu and Saiprasad-ji were going back and forth, back and forth from the temple to home, discussing preparations, telling me to rest, planning the ceremony. In the midst of all the activity, there was nothing for me to do. The temple was being cleaned and purified with water and cow dung; I was not to go there until just before the ceremony. At home, I felt in the way of the brooms and food preparation. And Ma was being strange, as though she did not want me nearby. So I decided to go to the lake and spend some time there alone until I needed to go to the temple to dress.

Through tight lips, Ma said yes, I could go to Ghadisar Lake, if I took Hari Dev with me. Hari Dev put down his broom and joined me in the doorway. He took my hand in his, and together we set off. I was happy for this time with him. I knew it was special. By the evening, I would be a *devadasi* and things would be different. Hari Dev knew this, too. In acknowledgment, we walked in silence. Hari's hand held mine tightly.

It was midmorning. There was little activity around Ghadisar; it was too hot. We walked up the path to the arched gateway to the lake. A cluster of women squatted in the shade of a *khajeri* tree, saris pulled over their heads and tucked into their waists. Their laughter was rough. They paid no attention to us, to me. I wondered if that would change after this day. I imagined walking down paths as a *devadasi*, everyone hushing their conversations and bowing to me. Some doubt clouded my imagination for a moment: this was not what happened to Chandrabai when she walked about outside the temple. But I brushed away this thought, pushed it into the place where all my unanswered questions swirled together. I wished they could answer each other and leave me alone.

I walked with Hari Dev through the archway. Ahead, down the many stone steps, the lake stretched out, long, wide, the blue-green water still as a mirror, an occasional bird feather floating motionless on its glassy surface. The water level was low, but there was still enough. Around one of the pavilions in the middle of the lake, a ring of grasses grew, their roots happily submerged. When the lake was full, they disappeared underwater and the pavilion appeared to float on the surface. I often wondered where the water came from, since it so rarely rained. Hari Dev had told me it came from the ground. But the ground was so dry! Deep underground, Hari Dev had said. It made little sense to me until he explained it as an invisible river. This, I could understand. Saraswati, the river goddess, traveled below the surface of the earth to feed the lake that supplied the water to the city of Jaisalmer. I remembered seeing her among the deities in the temple, a white swan at her feet, a string of white pearls in one of her four hands. Perhaps it was that swan that had left a few feathers behind.

I pulled Hari Dev by the hand, and we walked down the steps. "Twenty-six!" I announced when we reached the last dry step. I knew he had counted them, too.

We sat down. Hari Dev still had not said anything, still held my hand in his, as though he would never let go. The silence, comforting at first, was starting to worry me, and I felt a return of my uneasiness. I watched his eyes follow a flock of green parrots as they rose in a frenzied cloud from the canopy of a pavilion and flew over the embankment. And as I watched, a few tears trickled down his cheek and caught on the wiry hairs that had recently sprouted above his lip. He made no motion to wipe them away, so I did. I knew that Hari Dev's emotions were usually a reflection of those, visible or concealed, of the people around him. Rarely did they seem to have their origin within him. So his current sadness was unsettling.

Still staring across the water, he answered my thought. "Because you're leaving."

"But I'm not going anywhere! Bapu said so himself. I'm not even going to live at the temple until a few years from now, after the next ceremony, the coming-of-age one. And even then, we'll still see each other a lot."

"Not really. Men aren't allowed in those quarters. Besides, you'll be busy. With people."

Hari Dev made a face. I asked him what he meant, and he turned to me.

"Do you know what it means to be a *devadasi*?"

No, I wanted to say. But I needed to comfort him, if only for my own sake. "Of course!" I forced lightness into my voice. "I'll be married to Lord Krishna, and later on I'll move into the *devadasi* quarters, and I'll start doing some of the chores at the temple. And people will come to watch me dance—me and the other *devadasis*, of course—and I'll help in all the celebrations, and through me everyone will feel closer to Lord Krishna. And I'll bring good luck. Oh, and my patron will buy me clothes and give money to the temple. And Ma will be happy to see me so happy. And Bapu, of course, will be happy, too. Won't you be?"

"Did no one talk to you about the people you'll have to visit? The men? What a patron wants?" Hari Dev still had a strange look on his face.

"What men? What's wrong, *bhai*?"

Hari Dev shook his head. "Nothing." He turned his gaze back to the water.

I did not ask any more questions. I knew I was skirting a great chasm and just one more step might put me over the edge. In my imagination, I had arranged the pieces of my life after the dedication in a certain way, and the image I had created was mostly pleasing to me. Yet Hari Dev was threatening to disrupt it, to skid across it like a lizard skids across a pattern in the sand, scattering it, uncovering the rocks and pebbles beneath. I knew I might discover something I did not want to know. So I kept quiet, too.

Hari Dev's words were still in my mind that evening. They added to the staggering weight of the dedication outfit itself. I walked slowly, awkwardly, pushing the gold and silver–encrusted hem forward with my bare foot before placing my toes on the ground. Even with Jayarani and Devika walking by my sides, holding my elbows, I worried that with my next step I would trip on the skirt and fall forward. The skirt rested heavily on my hips, the cord pulled so tightly that it cut into my skin. I'd heard stories of girls whose skirts had fallen down in the middle of their dedication ceremony, or when they started to dance, because they had not been tied tightly enough. The image now struck me as funny, and it was such a relief to think of something lighthearted that I giggled aloud. Devika jabbed me in the ribs, and I stopped.

We finally reached the entrance to the dance hall. The thin layer of muslin that covered my head brushed at my nose and turned the world pink-red. When I glanced down, I could see my nose ornament: a ring of fine gold with a small pearl between two rubies. If I wiggled my nose, I could move the ring. When I shook my head, the gold earrings that dangled from my lobes jangled against my jaw.

"What are you doing, wiggling and jiggling like that?" Jayarani whispered loudly to me. "Stand tall and straight, and don't move."

I tried to hold still. Nothing seemed funny anymore. I felt the gaze of Ma and Bapu, of Saiprasad-ji, of the other *devadasis*, on me like a pressing weight. Through the fluttering red-pink cloth, I could see a statuette of Lord Krishna on the floor at the front of the hall. He had come out of the sanctum for me, so that I could become his bride.

I breathed with difficulty, my dry throat closing. I wanted to run from everyone, but I could barely walk. I just wanted to continue to worship Krishna in my own way, to dance in freedom. I did not want to do whatever it was that Hari Dev thought I would have to do.

This was not right. I had not been born to be a *devadasi*—my mother was not one! Maybe, I thought, I could say something; maybe it was not too late. I looked up at Jayarani, praying that she would understand. But Jayarani mistook the tilt of my head for an indication of readiness; she squeezed my hand once and let go.

"Good luck!" She and Devika left my sides.

I watched them take their places at two corners of the hall. The empty space in the middle awaited me. I had filled it with my dance hundreds—no, thousands—of times happily, yet now it felt foreign and frightening to me. I closed my eyes and thought about everything Bapu had taught me, about how special I was. I clung to that thought as I walked forward, toward the statuette of Lord Krishna.

The hall was quiet save for the jingle of my jewelry, the thudding of my heart, and the cawing of birds overhead. I raised my eyes to my Lord. He was standing with one foot crossed in front of the other, his flute in his hands, a peacock feather on his head. On his mouth a gentle smile played, reassuring. He looked younger than I had expected. I dared to smile back. Maybe this would be all right.

Jayarani, Devika, Chandrabai, and Dhani, another *devadasi*, sitting in the corners of the hall, began to sing. I let the sound of their voices fill my ears. Saiprasad-ji's voice joined them, and Bapu's, adding deep, rich layers to the beautiful sound. The voices rose and fell, wrapped themselves around the pillars, and slid back to the floor. I joined them, because it was impossible not to. Singing returned the regular beat to my heart, gave me the courage to look up, to seek out Bapu's approving nod.

And then I saw Ma, sitting next to Bapu. Ma was so rarely in the temple that the sight of her here, in this setting, at this moment, caught my breath. I could no longer sing. Ma's head was turned slightly away, as though she were trying to be elsewhere. *Ma!* I wanted to shout. *Look at me—I'm still your little girl! Don't be mad at me!* But Ma did not move, only twisted her hands in her lap. Beside her, Hari Dev sat quietly, one hand on Ma's shoulder, watching me intently. His lips moved, and I wondered what he was counting.

I longed to reach out and hold Ma's hand, to have her hold mine and be with me through what was happening. Bapu lifted my veil, and everything became brighter. He put his hand under my chin and raised my face. Never had I seen such a soft look in his eyes. Surely, I hoped, it had to please Ma, too, for Bapu to be so happy. Maybe Ma was just not feeling well. *That must be it*, I told myself, knowing it was not.

Bapu tied a sacred thread around my neck, and thus I was bound to Krishna. A warmth spread where the thread lay lightly, just above my collarbone. We sat down and Saiprasad-ji came forward, then sat cross-legged in front of me. He held a necklace of red beads in his hands.

The priest turned to Bapu and Ma. "Are you willing to dedicate your daughter to Lord Krishna?"

Ma lifted her head but said nothing. Her eyes were trained on something that lay past me, in another world. I had seen her like this before, usually when she and Bapu were discussing Mahendra. I wanted to shout out: *But I'm not like Mahendra, Ma! I'm not leaving.*

Bapu spoke for both of them. "Yes, we are."

Saiprasad-ji turned to me. "From now on, you cannot claim the right of wife with any man." He went on, uttering the words Bapu had told me he would say. But I could not concentrate on them now. Some of them reached me, some did not, as I watched tears slide down Ma's face and fall on fists clenched so tightly the knuckles were white.

"You must fast and beg on Tuesdays and Fridays . . . shall not speak any untruth. . . . You must offer shelter to the shelterless . . . water to the thirsty. You yourself will eat only after proper worship of your Lord Krishna. . . . Are you willing to follow these principles? Adhira? Are you willing to follow these principles?"

"Yes, I will follow them." Somehow I had made both my brother and my mother cry in one day. I wondered how this could possibly be auspicious. I lowered my eyes. I did not want to see either of them, Hari Dev or Ma. While my head was bowed, Saiprasad-ji tied the necklace of beads around my neck and placed a wooden begging bowl in my hands. I was grateful for something to hold.

My eyes stung, and I squeezed them shut. Everyone rose. I was now ever-auspicious, and it was time for me to make my first trip outside the temple as a *devadasi*. I was to visit five houses and collect their offerings. I led the procession, the other *devadasis* singing behind me. We crossed the courtyard, and I could barely see where I placed my feet. It was by feeling the indentation under my sole that I knew I had stepped on a crack.

As we made our way down the hut-lined path from the temple, we passed clusters of people, animals, bullock carts laden with merchandise for the market, the usual street scenes. But that day, everyone made way for the new *devadasi*. Everyone bowed to me. It was, in fact, just as I had imagined earlier when I'd sat by the edge of Ghadisar with Hari Dev.

Except now I did not care. Already I missed my brother, and he was only a few paces behind me. In each home, I was received with bows, warm water washing my feet, handfuls of rice in my bowl. People looked at me with eyes both beseeching and pitying, hands greedily reaching out but careful not to touch, heads bowed in respect yet cocked in curiosity. Everything swirled around me, and I felt like a bird caught in a sandstorm.

When we reached our home, it was full of people. Women and children filled the courtyard, eating and laughing. Ma was in the kitchen, and neighboring girls were carrying out trays of food—where had it all come from? I wondered—and Bapu was talking to a group of strange men. My head was light, my feet heavy. The floor looked close, then far again. I thought I saw Mahendra enter the kitchen, and then I heard a low wail.

"I don't feel very well," I said aloud, to no one. To anyone.

Jayarani and Devika lifted me up and placed me among cushions on the floor in the sitting area. Someone brought me water, someone fanned my face. I looked toward the cluster of men gathered around my father and wondered if they were the men Hari Dev had mentioned. They did not seem to pay much attention to me. Some looked over at me quickly, then turned back to Bapu. I did not understand that they were speaking about me, haggling over my price. I strained to look through the crowd into the kitchen. Through the doorway, I saw Mahendra—it was definitely him—holding Ma in his arms. Ma's shoulders were shaking, and she was making strange sounds. I tried to get up to go to her, but my head spun and I fell back to the floor.

From the cluster of men, a form approached me. He was strikingly tall. He looked down at me, smiling. He reached into his cloth sack and pulled out something; it looked to me like it had a head. As he bent closer, I saw that it was a wood-and-cloth doll. The man held it by the waist and danced it across the floor. When it reached me, it bowed.

"Greetings, little lady," it said. I knew it could not speak. I looked up at the man who held it, the man who later would bid the highest price for me. He was squatting on the floor next to me, but still he was tall.

"Do you like this?" he asked me. Up close, I could see that he had a scar across his face. It reached from one of his light green eyes to the corner of his mouth, pulling the lips up into a crooked, permanent smile. I did like the puppet, with its white wooden face, painted eyebrows, and cloth dress. But I wanted to do something, anything, to show that I could make my own decision. That others couldn't always know what was best for me. So I shook my head.

"That's too bad. I'll find something else for you." He brushed my face lightly with his hand, and the look on his face turned to one of alarm. I wanted to tell him it was all right, that I would not tell anyone that he had touched me, a *devadasi*. But he was already standing.

"Girija-ji! Someone! Adhira's very hot!" the man shouted, and now all I could see were two knees, clad in orange cotton. Red-and-green slippers, toes upturned. Shouts and screams and then silence. And the packed-dirt floor, rising, rising up to meet my head.

Girija

Early 1564

My mother sat on the floor, wondering what to do. Listless, purposeless. Simply less. No one needed her this afternoon. I was dancing with Bapu. Hari Dev was out collecting leaves and herbs for the curative potions he made to heal wounded animals. Mahendra had not been home since my dedication the previous year. Ma's thoughts drifted to Padmini, of whose existence I was still unaware. Had I known of her, I would have encouraged Ma to seek her out. As it turned out, Ma had the same idea. Padmini was twenty-nine. She had been gone twelve years. Now that Bapu had his *devadasi*, Ma thought, maybe it was time for everyone to forgive.

The afternoon heat beat down on the roof with almost audible intensity. The light outside the doorway was blinding whiteness to Ma, its uniformity disturbing. Her eyes were getting worse. She was no longer able to discern from indoors the shadow thrown by the courtyard wall or the dark shapes of the storage pots that held our family's food supplies. They had been swallowed by the sun's light. For so many years she had held her ground against the desert, but now it was consuming her world.

She sighed, rose, and made her way outside, to sit at the foot of a tree. A lizard scratched its way up the rough bark. The afternoon wore on. Insects hummed. Shadows traveled slowly across the ground.

Then suddenly came the sound of someone approaching.

A male voice sounded. "Hello? Girija-ji?"

Ma stood. "Yes?"

"It is Uttam. Is it all right if I come into the courtyard?"

Uttam-ji! Ma wondered what my patron could possibly be doing at our home. She pulled her sari over her head and motioned to the house, trying to think of something she could offer him to eat.

"Of course! What an honor to have you visit. Please come in." She listened for the sounds of his guard or servant.

"No, no, no need for that. I just wanted to drop off something for Adhira. I came alone," he added.

He approached her, then squatted on the ground like a commoner.

Ma felt for a clay cup and the lid to the water jug. "Let me at least give you some water."

He accepted the cup. "Thank you. I was up in the citadel, doing some business, arranging for the sale of some sheep wool."

Ma nodded. She did not know how to speak with this man, this man who had paid such a large sum to the temple for the honor of my virtue when the time came for my coming-of-age ceremony. She wanted to dislike him, but here he was, squatting on the ground with her, chatting. He had done nothing to make me dislike him, either, and I kept by the side of my bed the doll he had left for me, somehow reassured by its presence every evening.

"How is Adhira?" he asked.

"She's well, thank you. Although, truth be told, she is not home very much!" Ma laughed wryly.

"No?"

"No. She is home only for occasional meals, and at nighttime. The rest of the time, she is at the temple."

Uttam spoke softly, as if to himself. "No wonder she is such an exquisite dancer."

There was a silence. Ma realized she had been anxiously fingering her bangles. She stopped, and the silence grew deeper.

Uttam broke it suddenly. "Do you have everything you need?"

"Need? Yes, of course." Ma wondered what he was implying.

"Really? Food, furnishings? Everything? Please do not be offended, but Adhira has been looking . . . thin."

Of course she is thin, Ma thought. *There has been no meat in months. Sometimes we have no vegetables. I am rationing the food money.* But she could not tell him this. She could not tell him that the court had suspended Bapu's payments two years earlier. She had always been the one to handle the money, Bapu never wanting to bother with such a mundane matter. Ma had not told Bapu that the money had stopped coming from the court, so surely she could not tell this man.

"Of course she is thin. She is growing fast and dancing a lot. Don't worry, Uttam-ji, she is healthy. The illness last year was nothing serious."

He made a clicking sound with his tongue. "No, that isn't what I meant. Adhira is lovely. I want to make sure her family is well and happy."

Tears threatened to spring to Ma's eyes. She turned her head away from him. "Yes, we are all well. Our older son, Mahendra, has been sending home money to supplement my husband's income." That part was true.

"Ah? And what does he do to make this money?"

Ma hesitated. "He's . . . " She regretted mentioning this, another truth she was hiding from Bapu.

Uttam stood. "No matter. As long as you are cared for. I must go. Please give your husband my greetings. And here, I brought another doll for Adhira. Perhaps she'll like this one; it has legs that can dance." He gently placed a package in Ma's hands and walked briskly out of the courtyard.

Ma was still sitting there, wondering why it was so hard for her to accept help, when Bapu and I returned from the temple. Quickly she hid the package amid the food pots. She would give it to me later, when Bapu was not present, to avoid his disparaging words about toys.

I called out, bursing with news. "Ma! Ma!"

I rushed over to Ma, who smiled and reached up for my arm. My arm, which was, in fact, bony and thin. Even for a ten-year-old.

"What is it, *beti*? What is all this excitement about?"

"Bapu taught me some new steps!"

Bapu entered the courtyard. "She learned three new pieces today."

"Show me!" Ma mustered whatever cheeriness she could. "Let's go inside so I can see better." In fact, as had always been the case, she would see very little of my dance.

In the months that had followed my dedication, I'd kept watch for the confusion I'd felt that day. It returned at times—for example, when Uttam-ji brought me gifts of stunning outfits and jewelry, silk brocades and delicate pearl-and-ruby necklaces. It returned, too, when I caught a clouded look in Ma or Hari Dev's eyes. As a result, I started to spend less time at home. I had not forgotten Hari Dev's words, but for the moment I lived each day safe in the love of Lord Krishna. I knew that this was temporary, though, and the only time I did not worry about the future was when I sought refuge from my questions in the blue sky of dance. At the temple, especially on days when Saiprasad-ji was busy or away and Bapu was either resting or teaching me, I was happy.

We went inside. My feet began tapping out rhythmic patterns on the hard floor. Ma felt her way to the cushions along the wall and sat down. Bapu sat by her and recited the words corresponding to the sixteen beats of *teental*.

Dha dhin dhin dha
dha dhin dhin dha
na tin tin ta
tete dhin dhin dha

I danced, knowing the timing was perfect and the sounds of my feet clear. I had no hesitation; I made no errors. I couldn't have, for I was a vessel for the divine, simply pouring out the dance of Lord Shiva for the benefit of Lord Krishna.

"That's wonderful, *beti*." Ma clapped her hands. I saw her pride but knew that just beneath it lay her dismay. She rose and went to the kitchen.

I followed her, full of dance and music, and peppered her with questions. I wanted to trample that dismay with proof of the dance's perfection.

"Did you see how it all ended on *sam*? The first beat of the next cycle? Bapu said the end of one thing is always the beginning of another. And he's going to teach me more, too."

Ma stretched out the dough for the evening's *chappatis*, her back to me. Her graying hair, neatly plaited, snaked down between her shoulder blades.

"There's no hurry, *beti*." She spoke down to the dough in her hands.

"What do you mean, Ma? I just want to learn more."

"I know. Just don't—nothing." Ma turned, put a floury hand under my chin and bent to see my face. I watched her search it for traces of fatigue, of unhappiness, half hoping she would find them. I flinched under her gaze, not wanting her to sense the part of me that wanted to throw my arms around her and cling to her forever.

"I'm glad you're enjoying your lessons." Ma turned back to the work surface and pounded the dough into flat disks with the palm of her hand. She wondered what she was supposed to say to me. Don't feed your father's hopes? Don't show so much pleasure in dance, or you will be the end of this family? Don't break my heart?

I left the kitchen, my heart smaller, and joined Bapu where he was sitting in the main room, kneading his feet. A moment later, Hari Dev returned for the evening meal, his arrival preceded by the step-drag, step-drag sound of his gait. He pulled aside the bead curtain and smiled at me, his entire face lighting up. I felt its glow, melting away the traces of Ma's distress. I asked him if he wanted to see what I had learned.

"Yes, show me!" My brother's enthusiasm was genuine. And so I showed him, ending the dance patterns with a flourish. But, I said to him, there was one thing that I did not understand. Bapu had said it was five beats, a one-beat pause, five beats, a one-beat pause, and five beats. I added them up. That made seventeen, not sixteen.

Hari Dev dipped his hand in the washing jug. "Actually, it is sixteen. See, from one to two is one beat. From two to three is two beats. So from sixteen to seventeen is sixteen beats. It's the spaces between the numbers that count as the beats." He dried his hands on a cloth.

Bapu shook his head. "Hari. Let her just enjoy the dance without thinking too much about numbers. And there is much more to the dance than numbers."

"But, Bapu, I just want her to see how the numbers work. They all fall into place so nicely." This, to him, was the beauty of dance.

"I know, but remember you have an unusual ability with numbers. And Adhira is just barely ten."

"Well, but really, she's entering her eleventh year," Hari Dev began as he sat down next to me. But Bapu quieted him with one look.

"I'm eleven years old?" I didn't think I wanted to be that old. I wanted to remain forever in this magical place, a full *devadasi* yet still free to devote all my time to dance and Krishna, and not to whatever it was that I felt ineluctably closing in on me.

Bapu was firm. "No, you are ten. And in fact, there is something we need to discuss about that."

"What?" Hari Dev and I asked in unison. He took my hand in his.

Ma entered the room with platters of food, feeling her way along the walls with her elbows. She knew what Bapu was going to say. He had mentioned it to her earlier.

"It is not proper that you two are still sharing a bed."

Something in me fell. There was little point in arguing, but I asked Bapu why not, and reminded him that two bodies stay warmer when together. It was disrespectful to contradict Bapu, but I knew what effect the additional separation might have on Hari Dev. What I had not expected was my own feeling of apprehension. If he was no longer there, did that mean a space was open for someone else?

Hari Dev himself said nothing. Neither did Ma as she rested her arm briefly on his narrow shoulder, feeling the bones under his skin.

"That may be so," Bapu said, his voice stern, "but Adhira has been dedicated to the temple. Soon she will be a full *devadasi*. Hari is practically a man. Even if he cannot care for himself. He can sleep on the floor."

I heard a familiar sound. At fifteen, Hari Dev no longer put his thumb in his mouth when he was upset, but now he sucked on his lower lip.

I had to speak up. "But what if he has one of his fits? He likes to be close to me."

"Adhira, this is not something we are going to discuss. I have made a decision."

"Yes, Bapu." There was nothing more to say. I resolved right then to do whatever I could to provide my brother with my presence, no matter what Bapu said. I did not have to listen to him. I felt bad for having been away from home so much. I moved closer to Hari Dev, our hands still clasped.

Ma set the food down on the mats between the cushions. She had no appetite, and so she merely sat quietly as we ate. *Chappatis* made of millet. Lentils. Millet mixed with yogurt and spices. It was the same thing almost every day. Ma wished someone would complain—maybe then she would feel able to ask Uttam-ji for help. But Bapu never really noticed what he ate, and Hari and I were grateful for whatever Ma gave us. Mahendra would have said something, but Mahendra was not there. And what about Padmini? Ma wondered. She imagined that Padmini ate meat every day.

And so, right then, an idea came to Ma with an unusual suddenness: she would go find Padmini and ask for her help. It was not right, she felt, for a near stranger to offer help. Family should help first. There was no need to wait any longer. And it would give Ma a purpose. She would not even tell Bapu. After all, she had not told him about the suspension of his payment. Now that that act of deceit was done, it seemed easier to commit others, ones that to her seemed harmless—acts that protected Bapu and his dignity—for while she wrestled with sadness and anger for which she blamed Bapu, this was always at the forefront of her thoughts, and would be until the very end.

The next day, Ma headed to the temple to find Chandrabai. She had decided to ask her to accompany her. She could not rely on Hari Dev to be her eyes, for what good would it do him to learn he had a sister he had never known? And Jayarani had mentioned to Ma that Chandrabai had seemed unhappy recently. Ma hoped a day away from the temple would lift her mood. She knew nothing of the true cause of Chandrabai's sadness. That it related to Mahendra was something she suspected, but she could not know of the child who never was, or of Chandrabai's mixed emotions surrounding the loss.

The walk to the temple was one that Ma knew like a part of her own body. With the help of her walking stick, she did not take long to get there. The heavy gate groaned as she pushed it open, but that did not awaken the watchman whose snores drifted to her ears from the guardhouse. The air was still. It was early afternoon, and the temple itself seemed asleep. Bapu and I rested on mats in the outer sanctum. No sounds even emerged from the kitchen. Brittle weeds, sprouting untended between the flagstones in the courtyard, poked at Ma's soles. Then she came to the dance practice area, in full sun at this hour. Here the hot stone floor was smoother, worn by generations of dancing feet. At the front, where Bapu and the dance masters before him always taught, the floor dipped slightly. Such is the power of art that it can wear away stone.

Ma continued to Chandrabai's doorway. "Hello?"

"Hanh, I'm here. Who is it? Come in!"

Ma pushed aside the curtain and stepped into the room. It was dim, a relief to her eyes. She waited a moment to let them adjust.

"Girija-ji? What are you doing here? I mean, of course you're welcome, but I wasn't expecting you."

Ma paused, taking in the room. "Well, I needed to take a walk."

A little table by the doorway dripped with shiny shapes. Jewelry and coins. And there was a smell, something smoky that reminded her of Mahendra. Chandrabai rose from the bed across the room and came toward her. Ma stepped forward gingerly, feeling her way with her stick.

"Don't worry what you step on, Girija-ji. I know, I should really clean up," Chandrabai said.

Ma reached the other side of the room, and Chandrabai took her arm gently and helped her sit on the edge of the bed. The air now smelled of coconut sweets.

"Come sit here, Girija-ji. Tell me why you came."

"I . . . " Ma wondered now if it was a good idea after all to confide in Chandrabai. Perhaps, she thought, it was not right to burden Chandrabai with her worries.

"Tell me, please?"

Thoughts of Mahendra and memories of Manavi-ji filled Ma's head. Something inside her trembled, as though an inner wall were crumbling. Chandrabai took her hand, the way her grandmother used to do.

"I'm thinking . . . of going to see Padmini."

"Oh. Why?"

Ma did not like the sharpness of the question. Instantly, she regretted coming. "What does it matter to you? It's none of your business why I want to see her."

"I'm sorry, Girija-ji. Forgive me."

They sat in awkward silence.

Ma broke it, turning toward the doorway. "It's a personal matter. A family matter."

"Oh, I see. Why are you telling me this? I mean, that you want to see Padmini?"

"I was hoping you would accompany me." Ma stood. "Listen, forget I asked you. This was a bad idea. I'm sorry. I'll just go."

"No, no!" Chandrabai swung her legs off the bed and took Ma's hand again. "Are you sure you want to go? If you are, I'll take you."

Chandrabai's face was close enough for Ma to detect something troubling. She was not certain whether it was worry or sadness or something else, but it made her uneasy.

"Yes, I'm sure." But she was beginning to wonder if she really was.

"Then we'll go tomorrow."

The next morning, they set out down the road toward the citadel. Chandrabai, holding Ma's arm, guided her, awkwardly pulling her in or pushing her away from perils in the road. Gradually, they fell into an even step. Ma listened to the sounds of life unfolding at the city's edges. A bleating flock of goats, bells clanking at their necks, heading in the opposite direction. Scattered. Disorganized. The scrape-slap of the goatherd's stick trying to keep them in order. The clatter of pots and spoons in myriad kitchens, indoors and out. The cheery chirps of larks and starlings, newly arrived from the Himalayas. The sounds echoed a larger world beyond the confines of her own, and the possibilities that life still held.

"This is an adventure."

Chandrabai said nothing, and Ma was reminded of her strange behavior the day before.

"I like adventures," she continued, determined to remain cheerful.

At this, Chandrabai let out a little sound, not quite a laugh. "So Mahendra is just like his mother!"

"Mahendra? Have you seen him lately?"

"No, no. I just mean I've heard he wants to be a warrior or something."

"Yes, he does."

They turned down a narrow street, toward Chauhata Square and the palace. The sun was not yet high enough to shine down into this street; the stone walls of the houses on either side still retained some of the night air, and it breathed coolly on their skin.

Ma needed something to take her mind off her worry. "Tell me what you are seeing."

"There are lots of servants here," Chandrabai said. "Men and women. There's a washer man carrying a large basket on his head. He's wearing a white *dhoti*, and a red-and-blue cloth on his head. There's a man, almost naked, with his hair in a knot. He is coming toward us. He has a sacred thread around his chest. He's carrying a bundle, and he has a gourd hanging from his shoulder. He's walking with a stick."

The *tap-pause-tap* of stick on stone sounded as the brahman passed them. He smelled of sweat and sandalwood. A few more turns, a few more steps, and they arrived. In front of them was a tall, wide door, tightly shut. Ma reached out and felt its geometric carvings, the solid woodenness of it. *Behind this door*, she thought, *lies a different world.* Chandrabai reached up, took hold of a brass knocker, and banged three times on the door. The knocks echoed emptily. As Ma waited, her hope dangled precariously from a thread of silk.

Chandrabai was about to knock again, when a thin voice called out to them.

"Coming!"

The door opened, slowly, quietly. An elderly woman, shoulders hunched, peered out. Her surprise came out in an audible hiccup.

"Miss Chandrabai! The madam isn't expecting visitors now. I mean, you, of course, but . . . "

The old woman turned toward Ma, a combination of curiosity, fear, and circumspection on her puckered face.

"It's all right, Sajana. Bring us to Padmini," Chandrabai said. For of course she had been to this house before.

The old woman shook her head slowly. "I can't. I must tell Madam first." Her voice betrayed her fear.

Chandrabai put her hand back on Ma's arm and guided her over the high doorjamb. "No. This is the madam's mother."

The matter was settled. Without another word, the old woman opened the door wide and stepped aside. Ma and Chandrabai entered a large courtyard, rimmed with several stories of balconies. Small arches and cutouts in the walls of the roof terrace cast eyes of sunlight on the shaded courtyard floor. The women removed their shoes and followed the servant across the courtyard, shaded stone and sun-bathed stone alternately cooling and warming their bare feet. They passed through a carved doorway and up a steep staircase. Chandrabai held Ma's arm tightly. The house was quiet. No sounds of servants, of cooking or cleaning. No sounds of children.

At the top, the old woman showed them through another doorway, then melted into the shadows. The room exuded a richness of color and fabric. The hard quiet of still stone downstairs gave way to a softer, muted quiet of carpets and wall hangings. Chandrabai guided Ma to a divan at the end of the room. When they sat, geometric patterns on the carpets came into Ma's view. They were different from what she was accustomed to seeing. The straight lines and angles were foreign.

"Muslim," Chandrabai said quietly. She sat still, but her hands twitched restlessly. They waited. And then.

"Ma?" A small voice sounded from behind, and though it had been years since she had heard it, Ma recognized it at once. A tall form, draped in green, stood in the doorway, leaning against the wall. Ma pushed away Chandrabai's hand, which was resting on her arm to hold her back, and walked toward her daughter.

"No!" Padmini's cry dealt a blow to Ma's stomach. She stopped short.

"Chandra, what have you done? Why did you bring her here?" Padmini's voice broke.

"She wanted to see you, *didi*. She's your mother."

They stood still. Time stood still. Ma remembered what Hari Dev had once said about approaching a frightened animal. Move very slowly. Let it come to you. Let it feel it is in control. *My daughter is not an animal*, she thought now, yet she lowered herself to the floor, sat on the carpet. She had learned to trust Hari's advice. "Just sit and talk to me, Padmini. Please."

My sister took one step forward, then sat down as well. She held the end of her sari over her head, covering part of her face. Ma thought it odd that Padmini should keep her head covered in her own home. Padmini had always been proud of her beautiful features. Flaunted them, in fact.

"Where are the children?" Ma hoped this subject would lessen the distance between them. She knew there had been children. At least two of them.

"At their lessons."

Of course. "Are they well?"

"Yes."

Silence.

"And your husband?"

"He is well."

Silence.

"And you?" Ma kept trying.

"I'm well."

Except, of course, Ma could tell that was far from the truth. She turned to search for Chandrabai and saw her form sitting a little to the side. She could not make out her expression. She wished Chandrabai would say something.

Padmini cleared her throat. "What about Hari?"

"He's well." Ma thought to leave it at that, then changed her mind. "Hari is a sweet boy—man now. So imaginative. So good with numbers and living things. And his sister."

"Adhira." Padmini's voice, flat until now, took on some shape as she said my name. "I heard she's a beautiful dancer. Started learning at the age of two." She let out a wistful sigh.

"Yes. Your fa—" Ma started, then stopped herself. They were making some progress. She started over. "Adhira's learning fast. And she seems to find so much joy in it."

They sat in silence again. There was no mention of Mahendra, or of his attempted visits. Nor did Padmini ask about Bapu.

Ma tried again. "Manavi-ji—"

"Yes, Chandrabai told me."

"Of course," Ma murmured.

Manavi-ji's presence hung in the air above them, like a rope bridge. Ma and Padmini clutched at each end, wavering.

Ma took another step. "Samarjit, he's still painting?" What she wanted to ask was, *Is your husband good to you? Are you happy?* But now she feared the answer.

"Yes, the court is very happy with his paintings. He's there now, with the Raja, showing a set he recently finished."

"Where does he do his painting?"

"There's a room over there. It faces the south, and sunlight comes in. He's set up his studio there."

"May I visit it?" Ma hoped to find some common ground with Padmini. And besides, she was genuinely interested in Samarjit's artistry.

Padmini hesitated.

From behind Ma came Chandrabai's voice. "Please take her, Padmini. While she can still see a bit."

"Chandra!" Ma interrupted her.

"I can show you, if you'd like." Padmini had risen, still clutching her sari. She left the room without waiting. Ma hurried after her, Chandrabai's hand once more on her arm. They followed Padmini around the balcony that rimmed the courtyard and into another chamber. Like the rest of the house, it was dim.

"He likes to keep the curtains closed when he's not here painting," my sister explained. "I'd rather not open them now."

"That's all right." Ma was glad for the dimness, which enabled her to see the contents of the room better. She felt her way around. Two heavy wooden tables, strewn with paper made, Padmini explained, from jute fiber and palm leaves. Clay pots of colored paints, some dry and cracking, some covered with clay plates. A jar of brushes. The room breathed art and creation. It reminded Ma of the dance practice room at the temple, despite the contrast between the richness of one and the starkness of the other. She fingered the coarse hairs of the brushes, held up a pot of paint to her nose. It smelled metallic.

"Does he make the colors himself?" she asked.

Padmini was standing several paces away. She remained there. "Yes. Sometimes it takes days to prepare and mix the colors. He uses minerals, cinnabar, some vegetables, indigo, lapiz, conch shells. Precious stones, even gold and silver."

Ma turned back to the tables. An unfinished painting on cloth lay stretched on one of them. She bent down to look at it closely. Brilliant red, blue, and green predominated in a foreign-looking landscape. Trees blossomed amid pink, eroded rocks. Shadows stretched across them, giving them new dimensions.

"These seem—different," Ma said.

"Yes, he has been learning from a Persian painter. It's the style the court likes now. But he still paints a lot like he used to. You know, processions and elephant fights, court scenes and deer hunts. Also the animals and flowers of the area. These paintings here are ones the Raja didn't want." Padmini motioned to the walls around them.

Ma walked slowly, looking closely at the paintings hung at eye level, her face a finger's length away from them. Each one depicted a miniature world. She saw them in a way she could not see what surrounded her in her own world. Noblemen and warriors, musicians and dancers, each rendered in exquisite detail. Every jewel in every turban a dot of brilliant color, every mustache a twisted or trimmed coil of individually painted hairs.

As Ma moved from one painting to the next, commenting on the detail of one, the brilliance of another, Padmini followed her, drawn into the paintings herself. Gradually, the space between my mother and my sister lessened, until they stood together in front of a canvas, just two paces apart, Padmini behind Ma. On it, a procession made its way down a wide street. Three warriors on horses led the way, and behind them a long column of courtiers in quilted coats shot through with gold and silver. Amid them, an elaborately decorated elephant carried a prince under a red canopy.

Ma stepped back so that she was beside Padmini. In the shadowed room, entranced by her husband's paintings, Padmini had become more careless with her sari. Now it slipped back on her head, exposing her thick black hair and the careful part in the middle. Exposing a blotchy, scrambled scar that spread from her cheek toward her ear, and down the side of her neck. Lost in contemplation of the painting, she was unaware that her sari had slipped, or that Ma's failing eyes were focusing on the terrible burn that had marred the beautiful canvas of her face.

The last bit of hope within Ma plummeted. Memories of the softness of Padmini's skin as a child, the unblemished expanse of her cheeks and neck, came rushing to her. The scar was Samarjit's doing. Ma understood this at once, for it could be the only explanation for Padmini's behavior, like a skittish bird, in her own home. Her thoughts crashed together, deafening her. All these years, she had struggled with her hopes and fears that Padmini had found happiness outside the temple, when in fact there was no happiness to be found here. All these years, she had thought she had protected Padmini, spared her from a life she did not want by encouraging her to follow her heart. And now this.

With immeasurable restraint, Ma contained her rage and sadness. Swallowing the cry that threatened to choke her, she moved on to the next painting. In it, a prince was meeting with a trusted minister, the two beturbaned men standing in confidence on a white balcony, overlooking hills and valleys. By the time Padmini joined her, she had replaced the sari over her head, a silver border now covering the area where the burn had been. Was. Ma stepped back. Chandrabai placed her hand on her back, and Ma leaned into it.

"I think it's time we left," Chandrabai said quietly.

Padmini shook herself as if waking. "Yes, of course," she nodded politely, in the manner of a hostess who had welcomed strangers simply for a viewing of her husband's paintings. She called to the servant. "Sajana! Come see our guests to the door, please!"

The return through the room, down the hall, around the balcony, down the stairs, and across the courtyard was a blur to Ma. By the time they reached the main door, Padmini had vanished, as quietly as she had appeared. The old woman hastily shut the door, and Ma and Chandrabai were once again in the busy street. The bleating and jangling of goats, the fragments of conversations, the smell of cow dung and smoke filled the air. Shafts of sunlight slanted down into the street.

Despite the brightness, Ma pushed away Chandrabai's hand. "You knew! All this time, you knew!" She did not even care how Chandrabai might have come to know.

Chandrabai said nothing but gripped her arm and walked forward.

"Are there more? Does she have more burns?" But Ma knew the answer before Chandrabai spoke again.

"Yes. Her arms."

"How do you know?"

"Three years ago, Padmini helped me. I've seen her several times since then."

"Gandar is right," Ma said with bitterness. "Adhira is probably best off at the temple. I pushed Padmini and Mahendra to create their own paths, and what good has come of that?"

Chandrabai took her arm. "It's not your fault, Girija-ji."

Ma let herself be led through the streets. Images of Padmini cowering under Samarjit's hand obscured the shapes and colors that actually surrounded her. For a fleeting, mad moment, her mind went to the *sirohi* that lay nestled in the trunk in her bedroom at home.

Home. Ma suddenly longed for the stillness, the safe quiet of our home. This outing was far from the adventure she'd had in mind in the morning.

When they had passed through the main gates and stood at the base of the citadel's curtain wall, Chandrabai paused.

Ma pushed ahead. "What is it?"

Chandrabai hesitated.

"Why are we stopping? I want to go home. Please, Chandra."

"Well. It's just . . . well, we have a little time, and there is something I wanted to show you. Something you might like to see. I mean—" She stopped, self-conscious.

Ma almost laughed at the bitter irony. She had had enough seeing for the day.

"I'm sorry," Chandrabai said. "There's something that might interest you, one of the shops."

"In the merchants' quarters? How can you be thinking of shopping now?"

"It's not what you think, Girija-ji. I know you're upset. But please trust me."

Ma stood her ground. "I've seen enough."

But it was not fair, really, to blame Chandrabai for the situation at Padmini's house. It was Ma who had insisted on going. Chandrabai had, in fact, in her own way, warned her. So Ma surrendered. She needed some time to regain her calm before she could be with anyone else, especially Hari Dev. He would know in an instant that she was upset, and then his questions would begin.

"Let's go, then."

Chandrabai pulled her along, quickening their step. They approached the merchants' quarters. In close succession, because the shops were crammed together, came the flowery scents of the garland-maker's stall, the clanging banging of the blacksmith making sickles, augers, knives. The clayey, damp smell of pots and vases forming in the potter's hands. And finally, heady mixes of myrrh, camphor, and unrecognizable herbs. Here, Chandrabai helped Ma up the small ledge that set off the stall from the street. A young child poured a powder onto a scale that hung from the ceiling.

"Jagadhar-ji!" Chandrabai called into the dimness of the stall. "I've brought someone I'd like you to see."

An elderly man approached, shuffling his feet, and stepped into my family's life. "Eh, Chandrabai! It's good to see you. It's been a while, no?"

"It has." Chandrabai changed the subject: "This is Girija-ji, our guru's wife. She has trouble with her eyes. Can you help her?"

The man approached Ma and looked into her eyes. His gray beard and mustache came into her view. He had kind lines at the corners of his eyes and mouth. Ma had to smile at him, and the lines crinkled as he smiled back. "Born with sight," he announced. "The fever took most of it a long time ago, right?"

"Yes, when I was an infant. But recently it's been getting worse."

"Edges blurring, details melting into background, sunlight blinding," he recited, as though reading off a list. "You're not eating well enough. You must eat more *kair*. Eh, boy!" he called out to the young boy who had been measuring out powders and twigs. "Bring this lady a pouch of *kair*, please, the dried ones."

The boy said nothing but went toward the back of the stall.

"Mute. But fast!" said Jagadhar-ji. "It's just as well he can't speak. I talk enough for both of us!" He laughed. "And he makes up for my slowness. A perfect match."

The boy returned with a pouch. Jagadhar-ji took a few dried berries from it and placed them in Ma's hand.

"Steep a handful of these in water overnight. Pour off the water in the morning, then boil them in fresh water—you don't need very much—and eat ten of them, three times a day. With *ghee* is best. But of course you can eat them alone, or just with salt. This will stop your eyesight from getting worse. I can't fix it for you, or even bring it back to where it was, but this will prevent worsening of the condition."

Ma rolled the berries in her fingers. She did not want to spend precious coins on a remedy that might not work. And now she wondered how important it really was to be able to see well. How quickly things can change. "Thank you," she said to Jagadhar-ji, and handed him back the pouch that he had pressed into her hand.

"Don't you understand? You must take these. Please don't worry about payment. Start with this amount, and come back in ten days and we'll discuss the result."

Tears formed at the corners of my mother's eyes. She tried to blink them back, but this time they spilled onto her cheeks, warm trickles that soon became rivulets. *Karuna*, compassion, one of the nine sentiments in life, as in dance. Sometimes it comes from within, sometimes from Krishna, and sometimes from strangers. Ma's legs gave way and she sat down on the floor, her tears flowing freely. They dripped into a clay plate and fell into a small mound of red turmeric, each one rolling through the powder and then joining the others in a growing swirl of red water.

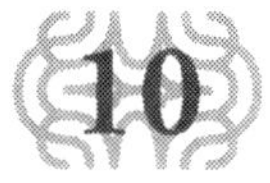

Hari Dev

Mid-1564

Hari Dev watched droplets of water falling into turmeric. They gathered a dusting of red powder, rolled to the center of the dish, and dissolved once they reached the moist, darker patch. If a drop was too big, he watched it lose its form right away and create a round, damp spot where it fell. But if it was just small enough, just light enough, it would roll, and the red particles would dance and swirl on its surface for a few moments, holding on in a fine balance before mixing with the liquid to create something new. My brother enjoyed those moments, watching the unpredictable patterns of each individual drop with the certain knowledge of what would, in the end, happen to it. Yet the way the red liquid swirled also troubled him. He had seen this before. He did not recall cowering in the dark corner as I was born and the rain came in torrents, but he did think of beginnings and endings, and of the unknown.

"Eh, boy!" Jagadhar-ji called out to him. "We need the mix."

Hari Dev followed the old man's eyes to a figure at the entrance of the stall. It was a woman. Her head was covered and bowed. Hari sensed a feeling of imminent flight about her. She looked familiar to him—indeed, he saw her often—and he thought perhaps he knew who she was, but he could not see her face to be certain. He thought of who might need the mix, he thought of the *devadasis*, and thus inevitably now he thought of me. Behind her, the street teemed with people and animals newly arrived with a caravan, but she had brought with her a muffled quiet. Hari Dev stepped slowly to the back of the stall, where the pots, trays, and pouches of ingredients were stacked on shelves. He had been working here since his fifteenth birthday—eighty-three days, he had counted—since the boy he had replaced, the mute boy who had brought Ma the *kair*, had fallen ill.

Jagadhar-ji is a good man, Ma had said to my brother. Go help him and he will teach you. Do it for me, *beta*, please, she had said, stroking his head. Do it so that I know you will be able to take care of yourself. Hari Dev could tell that something in her had changed. She was acting like a desperate mother fox, fiercely guarding her pup against a danger she could smell. He had held back his questions. He was learning that questions sometimes yielded answers one does not like. He knew part of it had to do with me. And if there was something else upsetting Ma, he preferred not to know what it was.

So he had started working for Jagadhar-ji. By the fifth day, he knew where each ingredient was located. Now he went through the items he needed for the "mix." The secret mix. The one nobody really spoke about. Dried *adatodai* roots: fourth shelf up, fourth pot. A pleasing symmetry, he thought. Four times four, sixteen, like the beats of *teental*. Cloves, basil, and black pepper were near each other in covered pots on the first shelf, the one Hari Dev could reach easily without the stool, sweet and pungent smells together. Gum of the *dhak* tree, for its astringent properties: sixth shelf, at the end, in the small pot with a spoon in it. Hari Dev disliked this one; the spoon handle made his fingers sticky. Crystals of thymol extracted from the *ajwain* fruit, to cool a wound and prevent infection: in a covered tray on the third shelf. And ginger root powder, yellow-white and strong-smelling: in a large pot on the counter.

Hari Dev dragged the stool back and forth across the floor, repeatedly climbing up onto it carefully, holding on to the vertical ropes strung at regular intervals from ceiling to floor, to reach each ingredient. His thin frame swayed, finding the balance that his legs could not give him. He set the pots and trays on the counter by the ginger and lifted the hand balance from its box. The woman's furtive eyes watched him. Just like Jagadhar-ji had shown him, he wiped the two little pans clean with a cloth, and hung the balance from a hook that jutted out from the wall above the counter. Jagadhar-ji usually held the balance in his hand, but Hari Dev was to use the hook—always!—lest the tilt in his own body affect the measurements. It was one of the many things Jagadhar-ji had done so that Hari Dev could work here, like the ropes he had installed to help Hari find his balance as he climbed the stool. It was one of the many things that made my brother feel safe at the shop, where order, careful measurement, and defined tasks provided his mind with things to focus on and prevented him from wandering too far into the dark and frightening disorder that hovered at the edges of his concentration.

The shop had become his refuge just in time, for by then I rarely had a chance to be with him. We still slept in the same room—albeit no longer in the same bed—but we both knew it would be only a short while until I became a woman and received quarters of my own at the temple. I worried what the gods had in store for him then.

Jagadhar-ji rested his hand lightly on Hari Dev's arm. "Work quickly, please. I don't think she wants to be waiting long."

Hari Dev nodded and measured out the ingredients, leveling off the spoonfuls with a flat blade, pouring the powders into neat mounds on the scale. Then he lifted the lid from the box next to the scale where the brass weights lay, appreciating how perfectly organized they were in their compartments. He could not read the numbers engraved on each weight, but he knew what they were based on their placement in the box and the feel of their weight in his hand. The littlest one was the size of a lentil, the biggest one the weight of Bapu's bag of ankle bells.

Organization, along with measurement and weighing, was Hari Dev's responsibility at the shop. If anything was missing, he would search the stall until he found it, or an explanation for its absence. When something went missing, there was always an explanation. A customer had bought a bunch of *neem* bark strips, and the purchase had not been recorded, for example. A clay plate had fallen onto the floor and broken. In these cases, Jagadhar-ji would correct the mistake in the ledger, or the potter would be summoned for a new plate, and order—along with Hari Dev's peace of mind—would quickly be restored.

Creating the mixes of ingredients was even more satisfying to him. If he took five berries from one jar, then crushed and mixed them with a powder in a plate, he knew the berries would be gone from one place but would still exist in another form. The jar might now contain only 234 berries instead of 239, but if anyone were to ask him where the five missing berries were, he would be able to point to the plate and say, *Here they are, mixed into the powder*. Nothing, he knew, could really disappear completely.

Which was why Mahendra's absence was so unsettling. It is true, Mahendra appeared to be nowhere. Part of Hari Dev thought it was not possible, that Mahendra must be somewhere. But another part remembered a story: Rajput clans, the sky unending above him, a red turban. That part of him also remembered our father saying that Mahendra could dress like a warrior but could not be one. Yet Hari Dev could see as well as any of us that Mahendra's heart was not in the dance. And so perhaps that was why he had disappeared. Neither one thing nor another, Hari Dev reasoned, Mahendra must have fallen into the nothingness between categories, and thus ceased to exist.

"No, no, no," Hari Dev said aloud, and pulled his mind back to his task. The woman was now sitting on a stool, her back to the street, her head still bowed, and Hari Dev wanted to reach out and stroke her. But he knew that would not be right, not respectful. Instead, he stood back as Jagadhar-ji poured the ingredients into a clay mixing bowl and pounded them together. Strike-strike-strike-crush-crush. Under the pestle, they mixed and crumbled into a light brown, coarse powder.

Jagadhar-ji turned toward the young woman. "How long has it been this time?"

"Two days," came the whispered answer.

"Two doses, then. Mix each one in a cup of clean water. It doesn't taste very good, but you must drink it all. One dose today, one tomorrow. Best to do it after eating something."

The woman nodded once, slowly.

"You may feel the effects as soon as tomorrow. And there will be blood." Jagadhar-ji paused and knelt down so that his head was level with hers. "I know you already know all these things. Are you sure you want to do this again? It doesn't seem to me like a good idea."

Another nod, this time more forceful.

"All right." Jagadhar-ji stood up. "Hari, could you get me two of the small pouches down there?"

Hari Dev knelt on the floor. He was just two paces away from the woman's feet. As he reached for the two jute pouches, he was drawn to the pattern on her brown sari: white dots clustered together to form neat, curling flowers. He counted quickly. Twenty-nine dots per flower. One after the other, the flowers waved and disappeared into the folds of the sari. And from under its tattered edges, the woman's ankles and the tops of her feet were visible. Smooth, the skin well cared for, but the soles toughened. Hari Dev could see the rough area on her heel as he pretended to untangle the strings of two pouches. She had a dancer's callus.

Hari Dev hurried to his feet and gave Jagadhar-ji the pouches. The old man filled them, turned to the woman. In a single movement, she took the pouches and pressed some money into his hand. Then she was gone, disappearing into the dusty throng. Hari Dev looked up at Jagadhar-ji, who nodded back to him. He knew, too, who she was. Chandrabai. In those days, my brother still understood more about the *devadasis'* lives than I did. But there were still many things he did not know. He wondered whose baby it was that Chandrabai did not want. And he wondered what the baby would have become. A boy like him, with crooked legs? A healthy boy? A girl? A dancer? The question clung to Hari Dev's mind for the rest of the day like a lizard on a wall, forgotten at times, but when remembered, still there.

The slit of orange sunlight on the wall by the jar of camphor oil thinned to nothingness, and shadow swallowed the entire street. In the temple, I performed the evening *puja*, lighting three sticks of incense in the dance chamber, bathed in the fiery glow of the setting sun. In the shop, Hari Dev began to put away the pots and trays of ingredients, the measuring instruments and the mixing bowls. He was in charge of returning everything to its proper place. Piles of plates refilled the piles of plates-shaped gaps on the shelves. Hari Dev shook each jar of powder gently to even out its surface. He counted and folded the jute pouches, wiped surfaces clean, swept the floor. Around him were the sounds of shops shutting down for the night, including the sudden nonsound of the blacksmith's hammer, silenced after a full day of striking metal. The swish of brooms sweeping the day's refuse into the street, the clanging of bottles taken down from counters, the hollow thuds of empty pots stacked on top of each other—everything signaled the end of the day. The air was cooling, and Jagadhar-ji finally gave my brother permission to go home.

Hari Dev set off. These, for him, were perfect moments of controlled freedom. His destination fixed at either end, he was like a single bell on a string. Some days, the string might be pulled taut, and he would hurry home as efficiently as he could. That meant 1,492 steps in total. Other days, the string might lie more limply, might even loop around itself a few times, and he would take a detour or two. He liked, for example, to stop by the milkman's shop to see if there were any leftover curds for him to bring home to Ma and me.

Tonight, Hari Dev was hungry, as we all often were of late, and he decided to head straight home. He started counting his steps. When he reached ninety-four, an unusual sound interrupted him. It was the singing of many hoarse voices. Rough, smoky, raw. They sounded like jackals and hyenas at the edge of a campfire. All heads in the street turned toward the sound at once, like a flock of birds changing directions in unison. The sound grew louder as a jumbled group of men stumbled around a corner a few shops away, spilling untidily into the street. There were eight of them. They slapped each other on the back, laughing and shouting. Then they turned away from him, pushing each other down the street, their red turbans moving up and down and sideways without rhythm.

Hari Dev was uneasy. They had disturbed the street's evening routine. *His* routine. He turned his back on the retreating band of men, but he could not continue his walk home. Something had caught his attention, something about one of the turbans, the slender body beneath it and the steadiness of that man's gait amid the rumble-stumble of the others. Hari Dev turned back toward the shop and the men and followed them.

Beyond the merchants' quarters, just past the leather worker's shop, lay a neighborhood of taverns and gambling houses. It did not take long for the men to arrive there. Jagadhar-ji had walked Hari Dev to its edge one day, pointed to an outcropping of thorny bushes, and instructed him never to go beyond them. Never! So now my brother paused. The bushes were so close that he could see their individual thorns, even in the descending darkness. The bushes were still thick from the ten days of intermittent rain that had fallen earlier in the summer. Hari Dev knew he should be home by dark. It was not the darkness itself that he worried about, nor the crawling creatures that emerged from the sand, but Bapu's anger and Ma's sadness, one growing louder just as the other grew quieter day by day, as though it were imperative that their combined volume remain constant. Yet here was Mahendra, reappeared, it seemed, from nowhere, and about to vanish through the doorway of a tavern.

Hari Dev desperately wanted to know what lay beyond the door. At that moment, it was worth it to him to venture beyond his limits if it meant finding a world in which people could be something different. Teetering at the edge of manhood, afraid of losing me and searching for that which would hold him steady, he was compelled to take a few more steps forward. Now he was definitely past the bushes. He paused again. Nothing happened. The loud men had been swallowed by the tavern, and the street retained no trace of them. He began to think that perhaps he had imagined them, but then he remembered how he felt when Bapu said he imagined things—a choking hardness in his throat—and he knew. He knew what he had seen. He continued until he was right in front of the door and placed his hand on its dark woodenness. He felt the vibrations of voices and disorder from the other side. He removed his hand, wondering if perhaps this was not a good idea after all. But the door suddenly swung open, spat out an unsteady man in an unraveling turban, and remained ajar. Hari Dev stepped in.

Immediately, he felt a quivering-quavering loss of control. Dimness and layer upon layer of rumbling noises. His heart beat faster, but something was different than usual, and he focused on that. This time, it seemed to be happening around him, not in him. It was as though for once his surroundings were experiencing a "fit," as our family called them, but his body was not. He imagined that he was the one spinning in circles in the eyes of the men who sat, lay, slouched, rolled among the seats and cushions. They were clustered in varying numbers—an average of five per cluster, Hari Dev calculated—around low tables. Nine tables. On each table was an oil lamp and several clay cups, some full, some empty, some overturned, some broken. The flickering light of the lamps shone in gleaming eyes, reddened faces, pools of spilled liquor. It threw dancing shadows on the walls, shadows of arms raising cups, of hands slapping shoulders, of heads thrown back. And everywhere shouts, grunts, laughter, coughs.

To test his limbs, Hari Dev took two steps forward. His body listed, then followed. He looked around for Mahendra, but it was impossible to make out the features of any given man from where Hari Dev stood. Since he felt invisible in this place, he snaked his way among the clusters of men, stepping over outstretched legs, walking sticks, and swords. He reached a doorway and realized that this room opened up onto another. And then another. In the third room, he found him.

Mahendra and seven other men were throwing dice on a table. Each throw ended with a cheer or a shout of anger, and much waving of arms and raising of cups. Hari Dev recognized no one but our brother, who wore, like the other men, a red turban. Mahendra's eyes glowed with a wild energy as he threw the dice. The raucous men and the dice combined with Chandrabai's sari and the lightness in Hari Dev's head to bring forth images of a story he had once watched Mahendra dance. He thought of the story now, to steady his mind.

It was the story of Duryodhana, eldest of the one hundred Kaurava brothers, whose body was made of thunder. Determined to win the kingdoms of his cousins, the five Pandavas, he challenged the eldest of them, Yudhishthira, to a game of dice, intending to win by unfair means. The game proceeded, and Yudhishthira lost first his kingdom, then all his material wealth, then that of his four brothers, and finally himself.

When Duryodhana reminded Yudhishthira that he had not yet lost everything, Yudhishthira staked his wife, Draupadi, and the wives of his four brothers to win back all his losses. When Duryodhana, determined to humiliate Draupadi and the Pandavas, ordered her to remove her sari, she clasped her hands in prayer to Lord Krishna. A miracle occurred, and as the layers and layers of Draupadi's sari were pulled off, others formed, so that she could never be uncovered. Mahendra's arms had shown the never-ending lengths of cloth unraveling, unraveling. Standing tall, Draupadi addressed the blind King, father of Duryodhana and his ninety-nine brothers, and shamed him for allowing a chaste woman of his own family to be so dishonored. Struck by her words, the King stood and commanded his sons to stop, for fear of a curse befalling them.

Images of Mahendra as Draupadi danced in front of Hari Dev's eyes as he struggled to blink them away. He looked for Mahendra's red turban, but there were turbans everywhere. White dots formed flowers on Draupadi's unending sari. Twenty-nine dots per flower. The dots jumped off the sari, multiplied. Soon there were so many that they began to merge, clouding Hari Dev's vision with their whiteness. The men, the cups, the flaming wicks of the oil lamps fell away, to the bottom of a well.

Or maybe he was falling. He could not tell. His throat was closing up, and he could not speak. *Not here!* he thought. This was not a safe place, not safe at all. He searched for something steady, something his mind could cling to, a rope ladder that would lead him out of the well. The dots were still there, dancing in front of him, twenty-nine and twenty-nine again and again. He focused on them, tried to create some kind of predictable pattern. This was his succor, his faith. Twenty-nine dots. Two and nine. Trying to fit them into sixteen beats, he counted two, then nine, then two, then eight, then two, then seven, and so on, until the final one landed on *sam*, the first beat of the next cycle. As he recited the pattern and counted it on his fingers, his throat opened up.

"Mahendra! *Bhai!* Help!" he shouted, hoping his voice would manage to travel all the way out to where our brother was standing. In front of his eyes, Mahendra's face now filled the small space between the dots. Hari Dev focused on it and pushed the dots away. They began to recede to the edges of his vision, and Mahendra came closer, his face distorted with fear and anger. Hari Dev had never seen these so clearly on Mahendra's face. No matter his mood, Mahendra had always presented to Hari a mask of tranquility. But in this place, among the gang he still wanted to believe was noble, he had to maintain an appearance of ferocity. Hari Dev saw the dots closing back in. His back met the ground with a jolt. He poured all his strength into staying present in the room.

"You little thief!" Mahendra was shouting as he pulled Hari Dev up by his arm. "Did you really think you could get away with our money?"

"No! No!" *What money?* Hari Dev clawed at the fingers that held his arm like iron. *This cannot be Mahendra*, he thought.

"Nono? Is that your name?" asked Mahendra-who-wasn't-Mahendra, his breath foul with fermented date-palm liquor.

Laughter from the table of men behind him.

"Get out of here at once! No, wait, I will take you out myself. Don't move!" Mahendra turned to the other men. He did, in fact, appear to have become someone else, but it was an act. In this way, my two brothers collided, one trying to save me and to lose himself, one trying to let go of me and to find himself.

Hari Dev saw a dagger tucked into the Mahendra-man's cummerbund. Now he closed his eyes. The dots danced madly. He gave up and thought instead of me. (In the temple, I was watching the incense smoke swirl around my fingers, as Hari used to twirl my hair around his, and I said an extra prayer for him.) But now, instead of the softness of my hair, the grace of my fingers, all he saw were mustaches and red-rimmed eyes. All he heard were the shouts and terrible laughs of wild men.

Mahendra pulled Hari Dev up, then pushed him through the doorway to the second room, then the first, then the main entrance. Hari no longer cared who the man was. As long as he took him away from there.

They were outside. The air was cold, clear, quiet. The door closed behind them, muffling the shouts, laughter, broken cups, spilled liquor. Hari Dev breathed deeply, and the dots receded, but he still trembled. The sky was a deep purple; the entire neighborhood had fallen into shadow. A man threw some coals on a small fire down the street, and the flame winked like an eye. Mahendra put an arm around Hari's shoulders. Mahendra, who was still, after all, Mahendra.

"Hari, what are you doing here?" Mahendra's voice was more recognizable as his own now.

"Looking for you."

Mahendra looked back at the door before pushing him forward again. "Well, you found me. Can you walk?" And, not waiting for an answer, "I'm taking you home."

They walked away from the tavern, back toward the merchants' row. Questions tumbled around in Hari Dev's head like drunken men. He sorted them, the most important ones first.

"What are you?"

"What? What do you mean?"

"I mean what *are* you?"

"I'm your brother."

"You are now, but what about in there?"

"I'm always your brother, Hari."

"Oh. You didn't seem like it. What about those men? Who are they?"

"Just men."

"But what kind of men? Do they dance?"

"Ha! No, they don't dance. They're not important, Hari. You can forget about them."

Hari Dev did not forget about people. Mahendra knew that. Was that what happened in there? Hari wondered. People tried to be forgotten?

"I didn't forget you when you were there, *bhai*. Did you want us to forget you? Because I didn't forget you, I didn't!" Hari Dev had to run-walk now to keep pace with Mahendra. He looked up and saw mostly angry eyebrows, a clenched jaw, and distant eyes. But Mahendra's hand on his shoulder was gentle.

"I didn't forget you," Hari Dev said again, louder.

"Shh! Stop shouting!" Mahendra looked around, here, there, like a nervous horse.

They passed Jagadhar-ji's shop, and Hari Dev recognized the voices rising and falling, floating out from the living quarters above the shop. Something occurred to him. "What are you afraid of?"

"What nonsense are you talking? I'm not afraid of anyone, you hear me? I am my own master. Just like Akbar," Mahendra added in a quieter voice.

"What does that mean?"

"Nothing."

"No, it means something. What is it?"

"I said nothing. You wouldn't understand."

You wouldn't understand, you wouldn't understand. Hari Dev hated hearing this. "Whatisitwhatisitwhatisit?" Loudly again. On purpose. His voice echoed in the darkened street. It was almost time for the curfew.

"All right." Mahendra could never resist Hari Dev's pleas for long. "But walk faster, please. Akbar's the Emperor. You know that, right? He managed to get rid of the people around him who wanted his place. So Akbar answers to no one now. He's his own master. And so am I. All right?"

Hari Dev did not like the tone in which Mahendra delivered this information. Nor did he like talk of ridding oneself of people. He wondered if Mahendra had gotten rid of someone, maybe killed someone. He did have a dagger. Hari Dev focused on being one's own master. "If I was my own master, I'd be the Kotwal," he said.

"What are you talking about?"

Hari Dev pointed to a man up ahead, patrolling the near-empty street. "See, he's working for the Kotwal. He's making sure that nothing bad happens. The Kotwal and his men are in charge of peace and order."

"I know who the Kotwal is, Hari."

"Oh. Well, he came to the shop today to check the weights and measures. To make sure they weigh and measure the right amounts. That's what I'd like to do."

"But the Kotwal works for the Emperor." Mahendra's voice was mean.

"Oh. If you were the Emperor, then I could work for you. That would be nice." And then, "Ma sometimes imagines you as the Emperor."

"That sounds like something she would do." There was a smile in Mahendra's voice. This made Hari Dev happy. Then the smile faded. "But it's not possible."

"Maybe you could start out being the Raja of Jaisalmer. Emperor Akbar married the daughter of the Raja of Amber. Isn't that nearby? If you were a Raja, then the Emperor could marry your daughter one day, and then you would be like a son to him, and one day you could be Emperor!" The logic of this was delightful to him.

Mahendra, however, was not delighted at all. He stopped walking, turned to face Hari Dev, held him by the shoulders, and looked into his eyes in a way that made Hari Dev uneasy. "Hari, the Emperor is Muslim. Do you know what that means?"

Hari Dev shook his head. Something about one god and a prophet, and beyond that, he did not know. None of us really did.

"You shouldn't be happy that Akbar has married a Rajput princess," Mahendra continued, although this hardly seemed to Hari Dev like an explanation. "It's his way of infiltrating Rajasthan. Do you understand? He knows he can't win the land through battle, so he's trying to break apart the Princely States of Rajasthan by forming alliances with some of the Rajas. Marrying their daughters is just a part of this plot. In any case, I can't be a prince. I wasn't born one."

Hari Dev pulled away from Mahendra, whose voice had become hard and cold again, like a stone in the desert night. Hari Dev did not know what "infiltrating" meant, but avoiding battle seemed like a good idea to him. And he was confused: Why did Mahendra think that he could not be a prince but could be a warrior? There was no logic in this.

"Well, if you can't be Emperor and you won't be a Raja and there is no one to fight, what are you doing? Why don't you come home and dance, like Bapu wants? Teach the *devadasis*. Help take care of Adhira. Or get married."

"There are many more battles to fight. Besides, I can't get married." Now his voice was hollow and bitter, like a gourd.

"Why not?"

Mahendra scowled. "Because the only woman I would marry is Chandrabai, and she's married to Lord Krishna. She won't ever leave. She's under Bapu's spell. But don't tell anyone that. What I just said."

Hari Dev said nothing. Nothing about having seen Chandrabai earlier that morning. Nothing about the baby. He wondered if Mahendra could be the father. It occurred to him that Mahendra might not even know of this baby's existence—or, by now, nonexistence. All these thoughts he kept to himself, as he had done with so many, all his life.

They walked in silence for a while. In the night air hung pockets of cooking smoke and unfinished conversations. Now my brothers were descending the long, sloped flagstone steps, down from the fort's main gate. One step down and three steps forward. One step down and three steps forward. Hari Dev reached over to hold Mahendra's hand. The turbaned men who had been with Mahendra did seem unimportant to Hari now. Maybe, he thought, it was a good idea after all to try to forget them. But how to do that? We all carry in our minds memories of people we wish to forget. Hari knew there were people in Ma's mind, for example, that she had not managed to forget, even after twenty-six years.

"Ma misses you. I'm glad you're coming home," he said aloud.

"How are her eyes?"

"Not good. But Jagadhar-ji gave her some *kair* for them, so at least they're not getting worse. He's really nice."

"And do you have enough food? Are you and Adhira eating enough?"

"Sometimes." Hari Dev could not lie and say yes. He wondered why Mahendra was asking all these questions if he was coming home anyway.

"Don't worry, Hari, I'm going to make sure that you and Ma and Adhira eat well."

"And Bapu, too?"

"Yes, of course. Bapu, too."

This did not convince Hari. "After Adhira's coming-of-age ceremony, she won't live with us anymore." He spoke to the stars as much as to Mahendra. "She'll live at the temple. So Ma won't need to feed her."

Mahendra's voice warmed. "I know. But that is not for a while, probably two years. I can help take care of her until then. Maybe even afterward. And so can you."

Hari Dev was not sure how Mahendra would help take care of me, but he liked hearing the words. He still hoped I would not have to leave. It was cold now, and he shivered. Mahendra removed his wool shawl and wrapped it around him. It was warm from his body. His hand holding Hari Dev's was warm, too. Hari Dev held on tightly. In this way they reached the path that led home. Just outside the courtyard wall, Mahendra slowed down. He stopped at the entrance. The light of the hut beckoned, but something else made Hari Dev stop as well. Bapu's shouting voice flew across the courtyard like a slap.

"Where? Where did you say he is working?"

"At the medicine stall." Ma's voice, steady, quiet, floated more slowly. Mahendra's hand squeezed Hari's. Something in the hut crashed to the floor. Hari Dev's legs trembled. It was coming back. He looked around for something to count, organize, occupy his mind. The leaves on the *khajeri* tree, outlined against the moonlit sky.

"With the merchants? Down there in that disgusting alley? No wonder he has disappeared!"

"What is that supposed to mean? Jagadhar-ji takes very good care of Hari. He wouldn't let anything happen to him." Ma's voice was cracking, like a clay water pot. Soon it would break.

"And why did you send him there at all? He does not belong there." Bapu's voice was thunder.

"And just where does he belong? Tell me that. Where does any of us belong?"

Bapu said nothing, for he had no answer to give. One hundred and thirty-one leaves on the small, forked branch.

"It makes him happy to work there," Ma continued. "He can be useful. He can help people. It's all coming apart, Gandar. Why can't you see that? I have to make sure my children are safe."

Still not a word from Bapu.

"Why are we arguing now? We have to find our son." Ma's voice finally broke, water spilling out of the pot.

Hari Dev willed his legs to be strong. He tugged on Mahendra's hand. "Come on! We have to stop them."

But Mahendra shook his head, and Hari Dev understood finally that he was not coming home after all. He let go of Mahendra's hand and backed away from him. Ma's crying subsided, and now only heavy silence came out of the hut, sliding thick as mud across the courtyard.

"Why did you come back then, *bhai*?" Hari's own eyes filled with tears. My poor little big brother.

Mahendra pulled a leather pouch from his satchel. "Because I need to give you this."

Hari Dev took it in his hands and, not expecting its heavy weight, dropped it. It fell with a jingling thud. "Money?"

"Yes. A lot of it. More than usual. Give it all to Ma, and make sure Bapu doesn't know."

"But where is it from?"

"Don't worry about that. Just give it to Ma. She will understand."

The bag sat heavily between them. Hari Dev did not want to touch it again. "Someone died," he said.

"What? Who?"

"I don't know. Someone died, and that's why you have this. I'm not taking it."

"Hari, please take it. For Ma. For Adhira."

Hari Dev thought of the sweets they could buy for me, the pretty clothes. The meat to make Ma stronger. He picked up the bag with two hands. His stomach heaved. He was tired. His mind wanted to rest, his legs were giving out. All he wanted, all he needed, was to fall into a soft, quiet place where he could let go. He sat down.

Mahendra squatted on the ground, and his strong arms wrapped around Hari Dev. His beard prickled Hari Dev's cheek.

Mahendra took back his shawl and gave him a push. "Good. Thank you. Now go home. Hide the bag in the lentil pot and go home. Don't tell them you saw me. You can tell Ma tomorrow."

"Where do I tell them I was?"

"You'll think of something. I have to go."

"But I don't want to lie!"

"Sometimes we have no choice." And Mahendra was gone.

Hari Dev carried the bag to the lentil pot, quietly removed the clay cover, and lowered the bag of money into its wide mouth. He was shivering again. The lid slipped from his hands and fell loudly into the pot.

"Is that him?" Ma's voice reached the doorway before she did.

"It's me, Ma."

"Hari! Are you all right?"

He nodded. Folds of cloth muffled his "I'm sorrys" as Ma pulled him into their home. He wondered what to tell them. All the things he was not supposed to mention crowded his mind. The tavern, the turbans, Mahendra, the bag of money, the brown sari and white dots, the no-baby. Lizards on the wall, red- and yellow-eyed. He could think of nothing else. He lifted his face briefly, caught Bapu's glare, and turned away.

Ma pushed Hari Dev gently toward the sleeping room we shared. On the floor lay his bedding. He turned and looked up at Ma in the dimness. She nodded slightly and left the room. Instead of lying on his bedding, he slipped under the comforting weight of the blankets on my bed and edged his way to the middle until he felt the warmth from my body. I shifted and turned my head to him, and my hand found his. Our fingers laced together, and he stroked the hard smoothness of my fingernails. The dots faded away.

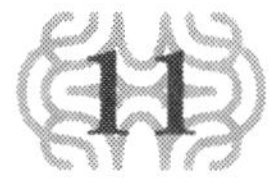

Mahendra

Late 1564

The deep, smooth blackness of Lakhan's coat gleamed with perspiration. It was midday, the most difficult time to be out in the desert. Yet Lakhan, my brother's mount, did not mind. The horse, Lord Indra's gift to humankind. Mahendra was often blind to the signs of the gods all around him, but he did recognize the perfection of this creature. Lakhan galloped over the dunes, nearly flying past clumps of brittle vegetation, his long, slanted legs kicking up the hot sand. The muscles of his neck rippled under his coat as his head nodded to the rhythm of his gait. Every time he rode his horse like this, my brother felt like a warrior. Of the whole band of Sikander's "brothers," he was the one who had inherited Lakhan. He was twenty-three and had the best horse. To him, this was proof enough that he was a warrior.

He slowed Lakhan to a trot. They were approaching the temple; he did not want to alert everyone to his presence, yet he needed to keep the horse nearby. Thieves could lurk anywhere. Mahendra remembered the day, five years earlier, when Sikander's men thought he was a horse thief, and when his dancer's hands had threatened to betray him. How things had changed since then! he thought. But in fact, while he told himself, even told others, that he was his own master, deep inside there was a doubt that had never vanished.

Mahendra caught sight of the temple, and his stomach quavered.

He brought Lakhan to a standstill, and from the temple garden where I was sitting, I heard the horse snort and shake his mane. The sound cut through the quiet stillness that hung in the air. My heart smiled to think of my brother so close by, and I willed him to step into the temple. I knew that he could feel it drawing him in, calling him home. If only he could have surrendered willingly to it. But it was not to be. Instead, he urged Lakhan on in our direction with reluctance, stopped him by the *babul* tree, slid off the horse's bare back, and tethered him. The small, spiny leaves offered little shade, but it was all there was.

Then Mahendra stood for a moment. It was still a while until he would meet Chandrabai. He looked back at the temple and decided he would just go rest there for a few minutes, to get out of the sun. The coolness of the stone chambers was inviting. I headed inside as well, keeping out of sight. I knew Mahendra was not ready to speak with me.

"Ah, here you are again!" Sundaran's head and bony chest appeared to my brother from an opening in the kitchen wall.

Mahendra smiled, reassured by the presence of another person. "Yes. I need to see her."

Sundaran nodded, sucking in his lips. He beckoned Mahendra around to the doorway and handed him a cup of water.

"Is something wrong? Is she all right?"

"Chandrabai? Mmm, yes. I suppose."

"You suppose? What does that mean?"

Sundaran shook his head slowly and narrowed his kind eyes. "Nothing. I'm sorry, I didn't mean to worry you." He picked up a coconut and banged it against a stone.

Mahendra wanted to question the cook, but he could not bring himself to upset the man who for years now had so faithfully and discreetly sent word of important goings-on through his brother at the tavern.

Mahendra decided he would speak to Chandrabai directly."You'll tell her I'm here, right?"

Sundaran cracked the coconut open, avoiding Mahendra's eyes. "Yes, of course. The lake at sunset, as usual?"

"Thank you. And my father is not here, right?"

"Not here. Resting at home."

Bapu was spending more time at home now, and I knew his days of dancing were coming to an end. From within I felt a desire to see Mahendra return to us. I sensed his heart wavering, and I hoped I could sway it. I suppose one could say that now it was I who wanted to save him.

Mahendra nodded to Sundaran and crossed the courtyard. He saw not the tranquil reassuring solidity of the walls, not the beauty of the sunlight filtering through the archways, not the hand of Krishna descended to protect us, but the yellowing weeds sprouting from between the stones. He wondered what the gardener was doing, if not pulling out weeds. Shame on him for not doing his job. Then he wondered why he even cared about the state of the courtyard. He took off his sandals and hurled them one at a time over the rear wall. He closed his eyes for a moment, so as to reduce the contrast in light when he entered the temple, and then stepped into the outer chamber. He reopened his eyes.

Instead of cool, smooth stone, his feet encountered rough sand and grit. The chamber had not been swept. For a brief instant, Mahendra panicked. Had something happened to the *devadasis*? But no, he knew Sundaran would have said something. In fact, just then, he heard the jingle of bangles. Quickly he slipped behind a pillar, and from there, wedged between the wall and the carved figures on the pillar, he waited for whoever it was to leave.

Mahendra listened to the sound of bangles crossing the chamber and then fading. He peered out from behind the pillar and saw, through the doorway to the dance hall, a young girl in a red skirt and yellow blouse. *Adhira*, he thought. Mahendra had not seen me since my dedication the year before. I looked different to him somehow. I knelt in prayer, then stood and bowed, for I was going to dance. Mahendra let out a sigh of exasperation. *Isn't there any time she does not want to dance?* he wondered. Of course there was. Many times I wanted to stay with Ma, help her with tasks around the house, but lately her silence and the distance she had put between us were frightening. The very fact that she no longer tried to keep me with her made me seek out the temple and dance simply because in them, I could let go of these thoughts and find peace.

Now, as I stood in silence myself, Mahendra felt he would have to stay there in his tight hiding space until I was done. He regretted having entered the temple at all. I thought of going to speak with him, but what could I say? My best way to communicate, to reach the Mahendra within his shell, was through dance.

In the hall, I sang. It was a simple melody, one that Bapu taught all his dancers, a meditative chant to Lord Krishna that Mahendra knew well. He listened, and from the first syllable, my voice filled the temple. It was to Mahendra a pure clarity, a limpid sound that fell around him like tinkling diamonds. He heard it echo peace, devotion, simple faith in Lord Krishna, just as I hoped to convey. It carried him into a place that was vast, clear, and free, a place that reminded him of the winter desert at dawn. Yet it was tinged with something heavier, a melancholy that I couldn't fully suppress and that brought tears to his eyes. Involuntarily, he thought of Manavi-ji. He wiped the tears away. He had not cried in years—what right did I, a ten-year-old girl, have to call forth tears now? He looked out from behind the pillar and saw me dancing. My bare arms were thin, almost frail. He felt I still danced beautifully, but my movements, in contrast with my song, seemed less free than they had been before. Anger at Bapu welled within him; he had brought enough money now to support the family, yet clearly, he thought, Bapu was still bent on turning me into a *devadasi*.

And yet his concern was not simply for me. His heart was bigger than that. He thought back to the day of my dedication ceremony, when he had held Ma, sobbing, despondent, the extent of her despair scaring him. Faced with her immeasurable sadness, he had not known what to do. Despite her near blindness, Ma had never seemed to need anyone, but that day she had told him repeatedly that she needed him to stay, that he could not leave again, even if it meant giving up the money he brought back on occasion. But bringing back money was the one thing Mahendra felt he was doing right, and so he had left again, gently prying Ma's hands loose from his tunic, promising her he would visit her again. And he had kept his promise.

The slapping sound of heavy footsteps entering the outer chamber announced Saiprasad-ji's arrival. The priest was in conversation with the accountant. The two men crossed the hall, and Mahendra prepared to make his escape. But then the voices stopped moving. Only the accountant was speaking. His nasal voice droned on. Mahendra wondered why they were standing still. Carefully, he looked out from behind the pillar. Saiprasad-ji was staring through the doorway to the dance hall, where I was still dancing, although now in silence. The accountant was listing out something and pointing to his ledger, but it was clear to Mahendra that the priest was paying no attention. He was transfixed by me.

Mahendra's disgust with the priest bubbled within him, this time an even deeper revulsion than usual. Why, he seethed inside, was Saiprasad-ji staring at his sister? He should have been used to seeing me dance. To seeing all the *devadasis* dance. Mahendra had memories of the priest looking at Chandrabai the same way. Nothing had changed. He was about to step out of his hiding place, when the accountant finally caught the priest's attention. The men resumed their conversation and walked out of the chamber, heading toward the kitchen.

Tears stung my eyes. Just when I thought the frailest of threads had reconnected my brother to me, the priest had broken it.

When he was certain the men were gone, Mahendra slipped out from behind the pillar. "Adhira?" he called softly. He was not sure he even wanted me to hear him, for he was at a loss for what he would say to me. I heard him, but I gave no answer. The chance was lost. He was not here for me. When Mahendra looked into the dance hall, I had vanished.

The dance hall was clean, swept. Everything looked the same to him as it always had. This space could not be affected by the changes going on in the world, or even by the changes taking place in the rest of the temple. Nothing grew in this hall. Nothing died. Not even grasses or weeds. To me, this was a sign of the glory of the temple, of the divine touch of Lord Krishna, but to Mahendra, it was a paralyzing trap. *No wonder*, he thought, *Bapu is oblivious to reality. This hall in which he spends so much time is a timeless world.* Mahendra left quickly.

He was still behind the temple, sitting on the ground and collecting his thoughts, when Lakhan snorted and lifted his head from the dry grasses. A few moments later, there were footsteps and a tapping sound. He jumped to his feet, fearful that one of his "brothers" had followed him. A figure appeared, carrying a stick, picking its way over the stones that lay strewn across the seldom-used path. It was Ma.

"Mahendra!" She waved her walking stick in his direction. "Is that you? I heard a horse. What are you doing here?"

Mahendra went over to her. "I could ask you the same thing!"

Her head was covered, but the beginning of her hairline was visible. Wisps of gray framed her face. Mahendra took her arm. With her free hand, she reached out to touch his face, and he held it to his cheek. "Would you like to touch something magnificent?" he asked her.

"Other than you?" Ma laughed. "What did you bring?" The hope in her voice was palpable.

Mahendra led her to Lakhan. "It's all right; this is Ma," he said softly to the horse. He held Ma's hand out and placed it gently on the horse's flank. The horse twitched but stood still. Ma smiled and left her hand there. She said nothing, merely leaned into the horse, until her forehead rested on his side. She breathed him in. Mahendra understood. Lakhan's flank, so strong and solid yet so soft, felt like courage, protection, freedom, and comfort all at once. His animal smell was wild yet reassuring. After a few moments, Ma lifted her head and turned back toward Mahendra, smiling.

They left the horse, walked back together toward the rear wall of the temple, and sat down in silence at its base. A sand beetle scuttled over a rock. "I didn't expect to see you back here, Ma."

Ma laughed again, but this time it was a hollow sound. "And you? I assume you're waiting for Chandrabai?"

Mahendra swallowed.

"I know I'm not the only reason you've been coming home, Mahendra," Ma said. "And I have spent some time with Chandrabai. I put the pieces together."

Mahendra's face flushed, and he was glad Ma could not see it.

"*Beta*," Ma continued, "I know you haven't asked me, but I have to tell you I don't think it's a good idea."

Mahendra spat on the ground. "You're right, I didn't ask you!"

"But listen to me anyway. If you want to be with a woman, there are lots of other pretty ones around. Why don't you come back, settle down? Give me a grandson to play with."

A grandson. I could do that with Chandrabai, Mahendra thought.

"We know enough people who'd be honored to have their daughter marry you. Many people still respect your father, and they'd happily give their daughter to his son in marriage."

"Ma, what are you saying? You don't sound like yourself. Settle for something I don't want?"

"*Beta*, I—"

"I came to see Chandrabai. There, I said it. You were right. Do you think that I've risked my life so many times to collect money that I'll just hand over to another family as a dowry?"

Ma said nothing, merely bowed her head toward her hands.

Mahendra changed his tone of voice. "Ma, what's wrong? What's happened to you?"

"I know you care about Chandrabai, *beta*, and I'm not saying that in itself is bad. But sometimes it's not a good idea to follow one's heart. I followed mine, at least I thought I did, and . . . " Ma let her voice trail off as she turned away from Mahendra. Then she turned back to him. "Your sister Padmini followed hers, too, and that was a great mistake."

"What do you mean?"

Ma sighed. "I was able to see Padmini. A few months ago. You were right—she was avoiding us. Samarjit has done terrible things to her, Mahendra, and I think she's ashamed."

"What do you mean, terrible things?"

"I saw a scar. A bad burn. On her face."

"That bastard burned her? I knew it! I knew he couldn't be trusted with her! And you're letting this happen?"

Ma reached for Mahendra's hand, but he was in no mood for hand holding. He stood up. "I'll go set him straight!"

Ma shook her head and remained seated. "I know. I was upset, too, when I found out. I was furious. My insides hurt from it. I tried to think of a way to stop it. To change it. But what are you going to do? March into his home and threaten him? Kill him?" She raised her hand. "Hush. I know the places your mind goes. But all that would do is get you into trouble and make Padmini a widow, and her children fatherless. There's nothing we can do. We're all human beings. We make our decisions, and we must live with them."

Mahendra's shoulders sagged. This was not the Ma my brother was used to. But he was gone so much, he had not seen the progression of her change. "Ma, do you know, I used to think you were like Draupadi. You used to stand up for the things you cared about, and for people who suffered at the hands of others."

Ma shrugged. "I'm not Draupadi, *beta*. Lord Krishna is not going to come to my rescue if I confront Samarjit."

Mahendra was unable to sit idly there, listening to Ma. He stood and looked around for something, anything, to break or throw. He found a broken branch, grabbed it, and swung it with all his strength against the *babul* tree. It broke with a crash and sent splinters flying in all directions. *Raudra*, anger, another of the nine sentiments. This was one with which my brother was only too familiar. Birds scattered from the tree, screeching. Lakhan reared and neighed. Mahendra kicked the broken pieces of the branch, stomped on them, and ground them into the sand with his feet. He was perspiring when he returned to sit next to Ma.

"Do you feel better now?"

He glared at her. He was ashamed that he did feel better, and angry that he felt ashamed.

Ma changed the subject. "How are things in the city?"

"Fine." In fact, they were quite good, as even I had heard. The death and destruction that Mahendra had expected, had even hoped for, had not touched the city yet, and still seemed so distant as to be imagined.

"You don't seem happy about that."

Mahendra did not respond.

"I heard that tax . . . what's it called? The one that Hindus had to pay? It's been abolished, right?"

"The *jizya*. It wasn't just Hindus who had to pay it; it was all non-Muslims. Yes, it's been abolished."

"Don't sound so disgusted, *beta*. This is a good thing. It means there's some kind of peace, that Emperor Akbar isn't trying to divide us. Right?"

"How can you believe that nonsense? He just removed the tax to give the illusion of tolerance. Besides, the rest of Hindustan is still a complete mess. The Muslims aren't even united themselves. The Persians, the Turks, the Afghans, they're all fighting each other. We have to get rid of them all now, when they are weak. But now no one here in Rajasthan wants to do anything because everyone's been tricked into thinking everything is just fine. Everyone needs to wake up!" Mahendra was pacing now.

Ma sighed. "*Beta*, there's too much fight in you."

"And I thought there was fight in you. I see I was wrong."

Ma picked up her walking stick. "That's not fair, Mahendra. I've just learned that sometimes one has to compromise. I pushed Padmini to do what she wanted, to go against your father, and it was a terrible mistake. And now you are out there, doing whatever it is you do, and trying to find your own way. I just don't want that to be a mistake as well." She stood. "Promise me one thing."

"What?"

"Just promise me you won't try to harm Samarjit."

"Now you're the one being unfair. You know I can't go back on a promise to you, Ma."

"I know. That's why I'm asking you. Now promise me."

Ma had turned toward Mahendra. There were lines in her face that had not been there the last time he'd come home. He was twenty-three. She was forty-seven. More than twice his age.

"I promise."

"Thank you." Ma walked a few steps along the wall, heading for the temple entrance, and then turned back. "You know Chandrabai has a patron, right? She can never be entirely yours."

"I know that!"

"I'll see you when you come by later," she called to Mahendra, her back already to him. Her silhouette receded. My brother stood there, envying the certainty with which she could make statements about what was to come. He had a sack of money to give her—one that would be too heavy for her to carry now—so of course he would see her later. But first he needed to see Chandrabai. He headed toward Ghadisar Lake.

The battlements of Jaisalmer's fortress were beginning to cast their shadows on the sloping ramparts. Mahendra sat in the rectangle of shade by the wall of the arcade under which he and Chandrabai met. It has always saddened me that Ghadisar Lake was, for my brother, like the temple dance chamber, a paralyzing place. Every day was the same there, and that to me was its magic. The birds changed with the months, the trajectory of the shadows shifted with time, but when one cycle ended, a new one began again, identical, proof of perfection in the universe. But Mahendra saw it with different eyes. The blending of one cycle into another to him was like the rotation of an irrigation wheel, endlessly turning but going nowhere.

This day's midafternoon stillness was particularly stifling to him, as though every particle in the air were conspiring to make him wait. His body prickled from the heat, and from the anticipation of being with Chandrabai. He wanted simply to melt into her, to lose himself in her and forget Ma's words. A grandson. And Sundaran's strange look. Chandrabai had never had a child. Maybe there was something wrong with her, he thought. Maybe she was ill. His stomach tightened, and his desire for her grew.

A falcon swooped down and skimmed the surface of the lake with its talons. The powerful sweep of its wings sent ripples across the water. The bird came to rest a few paces from Mahendra, fixing him with a piercing look. Each gray-brown feather in its plumage was clearly delineated in white. The small, narrow feathers on its head all pointed down to its yellow beak, drawing attention to the sharp, clawlike hook at the end. Mahendra waved the bird away.

"Go! Fly away, be free. Go hunt or something!" he said aloud. The bird hopped once, twice, and then spread its wings and flew over the wall. Mahendra took some pleasure in imagining it spotting a lizard, catching it midflight with its talons and hitting it against a rock, ripping it open with that beak. After so many years, this was still the nature of the energy that coursed through him. But within another cycle of day and night, it would change.

Chandrabai stepped through the arcade, dressed as a village woman in a yellow sari, one end pulled up between her legs and tucked in at her waist, and the other end pulled over her head. When she sat next to my brother, silently, her soft, well-cared-for features contrasted with the rough cotton of her clothing and the cheap silver armbands she had put on.

Chandrabai rested her head on his shoulder. "I missed you." This was as much intimacy as she would allow them in daylight.

Mahendra sat still, his body on edge at the tantalizing presence just a breath away from him. He imagined brushing her skin with his lips.

"Let's go to the hut. Please," he whispered into her hair. It smelled of coconut oil.

Chandrabai shook her head. "Not now. Wait until dark."

"Why? So what if anyone finds out? Ma already knows."

Chandrabai said nothing.

Mahendra slipped his arm around her and rested his hand as close to her breast as she would allow. "If you left and came with me, we would not have to hide like this."

Chandrabai lifted her head. "I told you I can't leave."

"Can't, or won't?" But he had heard the answer many times.

Chandrabai shrugged, looking out toward the water. Under his hand, her rib cage expanded and contracted. She turned toward him, and he was relieved to see a hunger in her eyes.

"We'll go to the hut tonight. I promise."

"Let's go now."

"No. I won't risk it. Your father could find out. . . . "

Mahendra threw his hands in the air. "So what? What is the worst that can happen? He will cast you away, and you will be able to come with me."

Chandrabai's eyes watered.

"I just want you to have the courage to leave," he said.

She let go of his hands. "You mean like Padmini?"

"Yes! I mean, no! What are you implying? Padmini did have the courage to leave. She just—" He stopped. The words were coming out all wrong. Nothing he said sounded the way he meant. He wondered why Chandrabai was mentioning our sister. And then he understood.

In horror, he turned to her. "Chandrabai, look at me. Do you think that I would hurt you? Is that what you're afraid of?"

Chandrabai shook her head, slowly, wordlessly, avoiding Mahendra's eyes. Mahendra could not tell if she was saying no or indicating that he simply did not understand. It was true—he did not understand. He put his head in his hands and closed his eyes. A hot breeze carried on it the faint slapping sound of wet clothes being beaten clean on stone and the pungent odor of rotting plants at the water's edge. And then, the clear scream of a falcon, high in the sky. Mahendra looked up at the bird soaring in wide circles.

He stood up. "I'm going." Where, he did not know. But he was driven to move, to leave this place. Chandrabai sat with her arms wrapped around her knees and said nothing. Mahendra took a few steps back but could not go. His body still ached for her. He sat back down next to her. Her face was still turned away, but something about her stance was softer. He pulled the sari gently away from her face and unveiled a slight smile.

Chandrabai turned to him and laughed. "I knew you wouldn't actually leave!"

Mahendra's delight at seeing her smile again temporarily pushed aside his irritation at her certainty regarding his actions. Emboldened, he put his arm around her again.

"Not here," Chandrabai giggled, but she did nothing to stop him.

Ma's words from earlier in the day came back to him. "Let's have a child together!" All at once, this seemed to him like the right thing to do. Raise a son, teach him he could be anything. Mahendra thought he would be a wonderful father, much better than Bapu. He thought that perhaps with a child here, a boy, he would manage to stay. Or maybe with a child, a girl, Chandrabai would be willing to leave. To give the child a chance at something different. He did not know that three children so far had not even received the chance to live.

Chandrabai's smile faded as quickly as it had come. "I don't think that's a good idea." She looked unwell.

"Why not? Imagine how handsome and clever he'd be!"

"Mahendra, I have a patron. And there are other men. How would you even know if a child of mine was yours?"

In his excitement, Mahendra had not thought of this. "I would know. A father recognizes his child."

Chandrabai shook her head. "No, it won't happen."

"Are you saying you won't let me be a father?" Mahendra's voice rose.

"No. I'm just saying I won't be the mother of your child." And yet, inside, she had started yearning for a child to keep. And so her next words astonished her as much as they did him. "Find someone else if what you want is a child."

"What if you become pregnant? What then?" Mahendra thought he had found the crack in Chandrabai's plan. He tried to pry it open. Chandrabai winced.

She thought of her repeated visits to Jagadhar-ji's shop. "I don't think that will happen."

"No!" Mahendra stood, his balance uncertain. This could not be. Not again. "No. You don't control me. You don't control what I can be. I make that choice. I—"

And here my brother stopped short, for something was dreadfully wrong. Chandrabai's face was too close to his. His hands were gripping something. Her shoulders. He had lifted her off her feet and was shaking her. The sari had slipped off her head. Her nostrils were flared, her lips trembling. Fear and disgust flashed from her eyes. And something else, something that hit him hard in the stomach. The disappointing and unsurprising realization that she had been right.

My brother loosened his grip, and Chandrabai fell back to the ground. She continued to stare at him as she stood and gathered her sari around her. She looked as though he had hit her in the face. Had he? He would never know. But it did not matter. Mahendra's anger would emerge in irreversible violence one day—that much was certain. Chandrabai knew it. Mahendra now knew it.

In that moment, my brother understood that he could not willingly change himself, nor a *devadasi*. And it was this moment, this letting go, that would soon enable his actions to allow me to free myself, when he had given up on doing so himself.

Slowly Chandrabai backed away from him, and when she reached the broad sunlight beyond the arcade, she turned and ran, a billow of yellow cloth in the white light.

12

Hari Dev

Late 1566

The sun had just started to rise on the day of Dussehra, the festival celebrating the victory of good over evil. The morning started in the way most mornings did. Hari Dev hurried to the temple garden to catch the exact moment when the yellow flowers of the bitter melon plant opened. Each flower stayed open for just a single day. He wanted to witness this birth, the beginning of this short life. All over the desert, every day, little existences are begun, lived, extinguished. Another cycle, along with that of our own lives. It did not seem right to him for no one to pay attention. Tendrils unfurl, unlikely green shoots pushing their way through cracked and hardened soil, and then are trodden by camels. Insects emerge from translucent eggs, scuttle across the hot sand, and are eaten by lizards. Flowers open and wilt. Small lives, each with some purpose, opening and shutting all over the desert. Hari Dev understood that there is something sacred about being able to witness these beginnings that are ends and ends that are beginnings.

The garden was awakening. Hari Dev smiled to himself, to the world. And then he noticed Chandrabai, sitting on the bench by the wall, her growing belly resting on her legs. She waved.

"Hello, Hari!"

He remained where he was, squatting amid the low *jharber* shrubs, whose leaves he dried and sold to local goat-keepers. He smiled back. "Hello. Not sleeping?"

She rubbed her belly. "No. The baby is too busy punching at my insides! The garden looks lovely. Even without rain. You must be taking good care of it. Better than the last gardener!"

Hari Dev nodded. "I like it."

"I can see that. I guess it was lucky, somehow, that the old gardener was dismissed. Although it's too bad we couldn't pay him any longer."

"I feel sad that he lost his position, but now I get to plant and grow whatever I like here. Some of the plants are good medicines, or good for the skin, and I sell those to Jagadhar-ji." He was pleased with how well all the pieces had fallen into place.

Chandrabai nodded with a slight smile. Neither of them mentioned her visits to Jagadhar-ji's shop, or the fact that finally, this time, she had changed her mind.

"Not many flowers for tonight's festival, though," he said, looking around. "Not enough rain."

"That's all right. Don't worry. I don't think people will be caring much about the flowers with the burning of the effigies. There is much more to be excited about."

Hari Dev let her words reassure him and tried not to think about the burning. Ma's stories of Jaisalmer and people perishing by fire threatened to invade his mind. He picked one of the few flowers, a marigold, and brought it to Chandrabai.

She took it from him, careful not to let their fingers touch, and brought it to her nose. "You like plants, yes?"

"Yes. I like how they start over every year. New beginnings."

Chandrabai nodded. About to give birth to a new life, she understood. "How old are you now?"

"Seventeen."

"Seventeen. First beat of the next cycle of *teental*. Maybe time for a new beginning for you, too?" She laughed, and her voice had a teasing ring to it.

Hari Dev shrugged. She didn't know that ever since he'd turned seventeen, he'd been worried about what might happen that year. He wondered if some pattern in his life was really about to repeat, or change. There are other musical cycles, not just the sixteen-beat *teental*. There is the ten-beat cycle. And the seven-beat one. He reminded himself of these things in order to reassure himself that nothing about this year was out of the ordinary.

Chandrabai pushed herself to a standing position and yawned. "The sun is up. I should go back. The others will be worried if I'm not in my quarters."

Hari Dev nodded and gave her a little wave. She waved back and headed toward the temple. He sat on the ground, among the bitter melon flowers. They were not opening yet. He prodded the earth beside them and pulled up an *ashwagandha* root, shaking off the crust of dried soil. It flaked away and disintegrated into sand and dust between his fingers. He scraped at the root with his fingernail, exposing its pallid flesh. It was moist, almost milky. My brother wondered at the way the plant was able to create its own moisture.

He wondered, too, if this could possibly be what would cure him of his fits. For that was the other reason for his interest in plants. Many of them held the cures to illnesses and unwanted conditions, and finding the right one, or the right combination and dosage of several, might put an end to his ailment. Jagadhar-ji had given him some ideas and suggested that the *ashwagandha* root might help. It was known, he said, to have a calming effect, to aid in the normal functioning of the nerves. Mixed with *ghee*, it was also given to feeble children, to help them grow. And, Hari Dev knew from his time in Jagadhar-ji's shop and the whispered conversations he had overheard between Jagadhar-ji and some of his customers, it had certain properties that were of special interest to men. What they were, exactly, my brother was not certain of, but he was beginning to have some ideas, and he wondered if the root might have the additional benefit, in his case, of reversing the effects of whatever it was that had caused his lower body to be less functional. And so he was eager to experiment with the *ashwagandha* root, despite its pungent odor, which I could smell as I approached him.

"What *is* that smell?"

Hari Dev turned. I stood behind him, wrinkling my nose. I wore a yellow skirt and blouse. Hari thought I looked windblown, like a flower that had tumbled across the garden and come to rest by him. In fact, I had come to him with purpose.

He laughed. "It's this root." He waved it at me.

"Ech!" I took a step back. "What are you doing with it? It smells like horse soo-soo!" I surprised myself with those words, and they made me giggle. I covered my nose and mouth.

"I know! Better watch out, or you'll smell like that, too!" Hari Dev lunged at me, brandishing the offending root.

"Noooo!" I stumbled backward. "Get it away from me! Hari, really, please don't do that!" It was no longer funny. Hari Dev stopped.

"I was just teasing, Adhi. Here, look, I'll put it in my bag. No more root, no more smell." He closed the flap on his goatskin bag.

I asked him why he needed it.

"Because Jagadhar-ji said it might help with my fits. Make them go away."

"You haven't had any in a long time."

"I know. But I'm afraid . . . "

"Afraid of what?" We sat down together under the *babul* tree.

"Afraid they might come back. When you go live in the *devadasi* quarters."

I squatted by him. "Maybe," I said, fingering a pebble and rubbing off the dirt with my thumb, "maybe I don't have to go through the ceremony."

Hari Dev cocked his head and looked at me.

"Bapu is not speaking to me," I told him.

"Since when?"

"Just yesterday. I told him I wouldn't dance at the festival."

Hari nodded. He did not need to ask why. But I tried to explain it anyway, if only to remind myself.

"It's just not right. They're using gunpowder this year in the effigies. For the first time. I heard Saiprasad-ji say so. It's bad enough with the usual fire. Why do we need gunpowder? I don't want to dance in the middle of all that." But it was more than that, bigger than that. Hari Dev reached out to take my hand. His was rough but gentle.

"No one will care about the dance then. There will be no real worshipping. It has nothing to do with Krishna." I stopped, feeling a tumble of words welling and not wanting to upset Hari. He sat back on his heels, a sad look in his eyes.

"I just don't want to feel used," I whispered to the pebble on the ground.

"I don't think Bapu will let you not do the coming-of-age ceremony, Adhi," Hari Dev said, squeezing my hand.

I shrugged and picked up the pebble again. "I could still dance. Just not . . . with all the rest."

"But wouldn't you still, you know . . . "

It was awkward to be discussing my coming-of-age with him. I had already felt changes in my body, and they frightened me. I said nothing. Hari Dev was not used to uncertainty on my part. I wondered if it had been fair of me to come to him. But I needed to speak with someone, and he was the only person I could go to. I had come to him planning to ask him to be at the temple with me during the festival, but now I felt I couldn't make him complicit in my defiance.

The moment was reminiscent for both of us of our brief time together three years earlier, before my dedication ceremony, when we had sat on the banks of Ghadisar and spoken of my future without really speaking of it. Hari then had realized how little I knew of what awaited me. Things he knew because he had overheard so many conversations between Ma and Manavi Auntie, Ma and other women, over the years. It was a brief, contemplative moment of quiet, the tantalizing pause in a dance pattern before the final frenzy of movement. After the dedication ceremony, things changed. I was home less. We were separated at night. Ma became more quiet, more distant. And here we were again, brother and sister, just before the next step in my journey.

But no, this is not the same, Hari Dev told himself. It was Dussehra now, a time for rejoicing. Hari wanted to make sure that I was happy, too.

"Look," he said, pointing to the newly opened yellow flowers. "Look how pretty they are."

I touched a flower gently, nodding.

"New ones come out every morning," Hari Dev said.

I asked him what happened to the old ones, whether they died at the end of the day.

"Well, yes, they wilt. But others open up." He worried that his attempt to cheer me up was not working. "What's happening inside?" Hari Dev nodded toward the temple.

I told him everyone was running around, getting things ready. There wasn't even room for me to dance. It was crowded, and Saiprasad-ji was there.

Hari Dev stood up, held his arms out at his sides to indicate the priest's large belly, and imitated his waddle.

"Hari, stop it!" I looked across at the temple and shook my head at him. But his imitation was so funny that I had to laugh. And so he continued, now jutting out his lower lip and crossing his eyes. He slapped his feet on the ground and limp-waddled to the *babul* tree, where he made a show of lowering his imaginary, fat self to the ground, pulled his legs under him, and closed his eyes in mock meditation. I laughed out loud, and I know Hari felt the sound wrap around him like a warm shawl at night.

He still felt the warmth later that afternoon, at Jagadhar-ji's shop, while I helped with the festival preparations at the temple. He worked quietly, pulling down pots of ingredients for the various concoctions, but in his head he developed musical cycles, keeping the rhythm, inscribing all his movements within the cycle.

"I need some dried *ber* fruit, some *guggul* resin, and some *khajeri* leaves," Jagadhar-ji now said.

Hari Dev dragged his stool back and forth, held on to the ropes, and deposited the last pot on the counter exactly in time with the last beat of the cycle he had chosen. He gave a satisfied little nod. It amused him that he could create so much in his mind, unbeknownst to others who assumed he was incapable of complex thought.

"Thank you. And now will you go to the potter and ask for a few plates?"

Hari Dev's heart leaped. The potter's shop! He would have the opportunity to watch the girl who worked there, the sweet creature who had recently appeared in his thoughts at night, as he lay alone under the blankets on the floor, a few paces from my bed. He turned to Jagadhar-ji, wondering if the old man knew, if he was sending Hari Dev on purpose, but Jagadhar-ji, kind man, just waved his hand.

"Go, quickly. I broke some plates this morning, and we need new ones."

Hari Dev hurried down the street, then slowed as he approached the potter's stall, for his limp was more pronounced the faster he walked. The girl was there, bent over the potter's wheel, her lips parted in concentration. Hari Dev hung back and watched her. She took a new ball of clay, and he started to count, knowing she would have turned the ball into a bowl by the time he reached 856. Her bangles jingled on her slender wrist, and her chest rose and fell evenly. He watched her push her hair, damp and curly, behind her ear, and drank in her presence like a cool cup of water. When she was done fashioning the bowl, she set it aside and rubbed at her forearms. Some hardened clay fell away to the ground in fragments, exposing clean and inviting skin. Like the dirt falling away from the *ashwaganda* root in the garden.

"Hari!" The potter was motioning to my brother to come closer. "Jagadhar sent you? Need some plates?" the potter called. The girl looked up briefly, glanced at Hari Dev, and returned to work.

Hari Dev hurried over to the potter, took a stack of five plates, tied with a rope, and carried them gingerly back, his face hot. He did not turn back.

Jagadhar-ji took the plates from Hari. "Perfect. It's a quiet day today. Take the rest of the afternoon off if you'd like. It's a festival day."

"Jagadhar-ji?"

"Yes? Is something troubling you, *beta*?"

"Is tonight's festival . . . dangerous?"

"Well, Dussehra is always a raucous festival. Everyone likes to celebrate the victory of Rama over evil King Ravana."

"I heard there will be gunpowder."

"Yes, someone got ahold of some gunpowder from the Muslims. The effigies will be filled with it. It might get rather hot!"

The regular ordeal of festivals, with all the crowds and noise, now seemed preferable to Hari as he contemplated the thought of fire being set to gunpowder.

"Don't worry, *beta*. Just keep your distance and all will be fine. Now go—I don't need you anymore today."

For the rest of the afternoon, Hari Dev tried to keep his fear at bay, thinking instead of the girl at the potter's wheel, the bend of her elbow and the tendrils of hair. In the evening, he held on to the sound of her bangles and the whir of the wheel as he sat among the shouting, singing, spitting, chewing crowd waiting for the dance performance. Ma had asked him to take her to the festival. She wanted the excitement, the sound and the heat of the blaze. An adventure. So Hari Dev had brought her, holding her arm, guiding her and feeling her blood coursing while his felt heavy as gram flour paste. Surya was riding low in the sky, throwing long, narrow shadows on the sand. Because of the burning of the giant forms of Ravana and his son at the end, this was the only festival dance in the year that took place outside the temple itself. The space around the effigies was wider than usual.

Hari Dev wondered if Mahendra was anywhere near. Dussehra involved the celebration of a battle and the worship of weapons; these were things that would appeal to Mahendra. But neither Hari Dev nor I saw him anywhere.

The crowd was loud, restless. Their roughness disturbed my brother. Up on the dance platform, the musicians were taking their places, settling on a rug with their *pakhawaj* drums and stringed *sarangis*. Bapu was up there, too, sitting cross-legged. I sought refuge in a different, more tranquil place. I wish I had been able to take my brother with me.

Hari Dev felt a moist hand on his arm, a large hand pushing him to the side. He looked down and recognized the thick fingers, the gold ring engraved with a peacock's head and encrusted in emeralds. Saiprasad-ji was forcing his way through the mass of bodies toward the dance platform. A few moments later, he climbed the steps of the platform to sit by Bapu. From the ground, all the people on the platform seemed like puppets, tiny compared with the towering effigies of the ten-headed demon king Ravana, his brother, and his son, which had already been rolled out to the right of the dance platform, although a good sixty paces away.

Voices echoed unpleasantly in Hari Dev's ears. He felt uneasy, even with Ma. He looked around for other comforting faces and at first saw none. The shadows lengthened and closed in on him. He tightened his grip on Ma, more for himself than for her. But then, to his left, at the very front of the crowd, Mahendra appeared. His hair was loose, wild. He wore no turban. Next to him was Chandrabai's patron. The two men, close enough to touch, inhabited two separate worlds.

Hari pulled Ma forward. "Come. I see Mahendra."

With a deep breath, he pushed their way through the seething, perspiring mass of bodies before him and emerged at the front, where a rope of jute blocked their way forward. Hari nearly toppled onto Mahendra, who wheeled around with his arm raised, as though to strike.

"It's me!" Hari Dev cried out.

Ma clung to him and lost her balance. "What is happening?"

Mahendra stood firm and held them steady. Before he could say anything, the drums started up, and Saiprasad-ji, from the platform, motioned to everyone to sit. Like a shifting sand dune, the crowd settled on the ground. When everyone was seated, the crowd quieted down. On the dance platform, the drummers were building up momentum for the story of Rama and Ravana.

In the presence of Mahendra, Hari Dev's fear eased. He liked this story, in part because it so clearly encompasses the nine sentiments, the *navarasas*, of humankind. In this way, it emanates a sense of completeness. There is love, and anger, and fear. There is disgust, and wonder, and valor. There is humor and compassion. And there is *shanti*, or peace, in the final victory of good over evil.

Ma pulled her sari around her shoulders. "Tell me what is happening."

Hari looked to Mahendra, but our older brother nodded for him to narrate the story.

Hari Dev complied. "Jayarani just took seven steps onto the dance platform."

"What is she wearing?"

"Orange and red."

Ma nodded. "She is Sita, virtuous wife of Rama."

"She is using her arms to show the trees, four of them, around their home. And now she's showing how long her hair is. Oh, there is another *devadasi*, I can't tell who, being the golden deer. Sita has put her hands together and is asking Rama to catch it for her. Jayarani is Rama now."

"He will do anything for his wife," Ma murmured.

"He is drawing a circle around the cottage and asking Sita to stay inside for safety. Now I think he is leaving to hunt the deer."

Ma nodded, knowing full well the appeal of that which lies beyond a boundary. Hari Dev saw her place a hand on Mahendra's arm.

"Rama is holding a bow," Mahendra joined in. "He has found the deer."

As the drums hastened their tempo, Rama felled the deer with an arrow. But the deer was under the orders of Ravana, the evil, ten-faced demon king of Lanka, and it took Rama's voice to call out for help.

"Rama's servant is with Sita," Hari Dev continued. "He hears the cry and leaves to find his master. And now Ravana is coming to Sita, dressed as a hermit. She doesn't know what to do."

"She wants to help the hermit," Ma said, "but at the same time, she has to obey her husband and stay near the cottage. But finally she decides to go outside the circle, right?"

"Yes," said Hari. "Oh, that's strange."

"What?"

"Saiprasad-ji is leaving the stage—he just walked twelve steps off—even though the dance is not over."

"Oh, so what?" Ma asked. "Keep telling me the story. What does it look like? I don't want to know how many steps Saiprasad is taking. Tell me what the dance looks like."

"I'll do it," Mahendra said. "Jayarani is Ravana, and she is grinning madly, a wild look in her eyes. I can see it from here. Ravana is lifting Sita into his chariot, and his horses gallop up over the billowing clouds to his land of Lanka."

The musicians called forth images of Rama's anger, his determination to rescue Sita, the gathering of the monkey general Hanuman and his army of monkey warriors. Jayarani as Rama indicated with arching arms the bridge he built to reach the kingdom of Lanka. The musicians gave life to the nine days of fierce battle between Rama's and Ravana's armies. Hari Dev watched Ma as she closed her eyes and lost herself in the frenetic sounds. He looked around for Saiprasad-ji, but the priest was gone.

"Now it's the tenth day," he resumed. "Ravana has lost his sons, his brothers, his friends, and millions of warriors. He is furious. And sad. Jayarani is being both of them, fighting. She is doing it very well. It looks like her feet are flying over the platform. Rama just cut off the main head of Ravana, but another just grew back. Now Rama is slashing that one, and another, and another. Five, six, seven, eight. Each time, another one grows back and Ravana is stronger. Rama understands that Ravana has found the . . . what is it called?"

"The nectar of immortality," Ma murmured.

"Yes. And it is all in a pot or something in his stomach." Hari Dev paused to contemplate the unlikely nature of this proposition.

"Rama takes his most powerful arrow," Mahendra continued, "and throws it at Ravana's stomach. The musicians are leaning back to get out of Jayarani's way, she is so fierce. The arrow entered Ravana and destroyed the vessel of nectar. Ravana has fallen to the ground."

The music quieted down.

"Sita is back. Her orange and yellow sari is in shreds. She is smiling, rejoicing, and walking toward Rama. But he holds up his hand."

Ma nodded. "Sita has lived with the enemy, and Rama cannot take her back."

"Sita is on the ground, crying," Hari Dev said. But he could not bring himself to say the rest aloud.

"It's all right, Hari," Ma said. "Just a story. Sita promises Rama that her heart had been only for him. But Rama stands firm. Sita, in her grief, decides to end her life in fire. When the fire has been built, Sita dances slowly around her husband and approaches the blaze. She joins her palms and prays to Agni, lord of fire, to protect her and show her husband that she is pure. With this, she steps into the fire.

But Agni rises and lifts her from the flames, unharmed. He presents her to Rama, who receives her without question. For he knew of her virtue and merely wanted the world to see it, too."

The sun was just slipping behind a dune when the dance performance ended. The crowd rose in eagerness, stretching numb legs and rousing sleeping babies. It was time for the burning of the effigies. Hari Dev's chest tightened as the bodies pressed in close to him, straining at the rope, pointing to the effigies, which were being wheeled closer on massive carts. The ten heads of Ravana caught the rising wind and caused the whole effigy to teeter precariously. Glancing at Mahendra, Hari Dev saw with relief that our brother was holding Ma solidly by the shoulder.

An arrow described a fiery arc across the darkening sky. Hari Dev lifted his hands to cover his ears, but nothing could have kept out the booming explosions that followed. He felt each one, in rapid succession, in his chest. The very ground trembled. The crowd erupted in screams. The sky turned smoky dark, and shards of wood, shreds of burning cloth, swirled down. Darkness closed in on Hari Dev, and he had trouble breathing. He did not know then that it was the same for me, that I shared that moment, in a different dark place. He wrenched himself free from the bodies around him, dropped to his knees, and crawled under the rope to the clearing. He knew it was dangerous, getting closer to the flames, but it was the only way to escape the crowd. Once on the other side, he ran as fast as he could, pain shooting into his hip. He ran past the dance platform, away from the flames and shouts. The ground and sky were spinning around him. He was counting every step, trying to stay focused on his feet, but his vision was growing blurred. *Bedham*, breathless, as in a dance composition with no pause. In his mind was a single thought: to reach me before he had one of his fits and fell into complete darkness.

Then Hari Dev realized he had no idea where to find me. The thought paralyzed him. He fell to the ground. He was on rough sand. Every intake of breath was a sharp pain in his side. His eyes were watering from the smoke. Explosions continued in the distance; he had run farther than he thought he could. Looking around, he recognized the dry, spiny bushes, the narrow path that cut through them, and the wall that seemed to melt into the now near-black sky. He was behind the temple. Knowing this immediately made him feel calmer. Surely, he thought, he would find me there.

With a plan and destination in mind, Hari Dev stood up. The bushes scratched at his skin as he walked down the seldom-used path, but he did not mind. Sometimes he welcomed slight pain, as it proved to him he was fully there. Hari skirted the wall, rounded the corner, and found the main temple gate. The watchman's hut was empty. He crossed the courtyard in the dim light of the half moon, slipped his sandals off, and stepped into the temple. He knew as soon as he entered that I was not there.

"Adhira?" he called out anyway.

"Hari Dev?" Bapu's voice answered him.

They appeared to each other from opposite ends of the chamber.

"Hari, why are you here alone?"

"The fire, the noise."

Bapu put an arm around Hari Dev's shoulder. Hari Dev could not remember the last time he had done that.

"A little too much, nah? But they are finished, *beta*. The effigies fell over, but enough people helped to throw sand over them that the fire was put out and no one was hurt. So no need to worry about that. Now, tell me, have you seen Saiprasad-ji? He disappeared during the dance."

Hari Dev shook his head. The priest was the last person he cared about right now. Or any time.

"Bapu, I'm looking for Adhira. Was she with you before you came here?"

"No." Bapu's face hardened. "She made a terrible choice today: not to dance. She told me she would be here, dancing for Krishna, but her place was with the other *devadasis*. I am going to look for Saiprasad-ji."

Bapu gave Hari Dev a little push, the kind Hari Dev despised: a gentle yet irritating push with the hand at the base of his back. Hari Dev shrugged it away. Then Bapu pulled him back.

"Where is Ma? Did you leave her alone?"

"No."

"Well, then with whom?"

Hari shook his head. He could not bring himself to tell Bapu that Ma was with Mahendra. Nothing was right at that moment. No one was where they were supposed to be. Darkness clouded his eyes again and blurred with his tears. He wrenched himself away from Bapu and ran as best he could to the entrance of the *devadasi* quarters. There he called out again.

"Adhira?"

Only the silence answered him. At a loss for what else to do, he headed home. Perhaps, he thought, he would find me there. The darkness was dense now, and he wished he had a torch. The half moon cast only a slight, silver light around him. As he passed the path down to Ghadisar, he paused. The lake was deserted at night; he could not imagine that I had gone there. But something, someone, drew Hari Dev down the path toward the arched entrance. Perhaps it was Vishnu the Protector pushing him down that path. Framed in the archway was a clear patch of deep blue sky where a single star twinkled. The water spread like an inky pool. I had noticed this about it as well. Hari Dev was about to turn back, when he thought he heard a slight sound. It was something between a cry and a whimper. It sounded to him like an injured animal. It came from below, at the water's edge. Hari Dev ran down the steps. Twenty-six of them. The water had receded even farther in the last few weeks and exposed flat stone that sloped downward.

And there I was, lying curled up at the water's edge. Like a sleeping cat, Hari thought. Except that I was not sleeping. My shoulders were shaking, and Hari understood it was I who was making that sound, even though I did not hear it myself.

I did hear him approaching. It was the first sound I was aware of, my mind having flown to the pastures of Govirdhana hill and the music of Krishna's flute as soon as I had understood what was happening to me.

As Hari approached me, he saw my bare legs, my skirt pushed up around my waist. Water lapped at my feet, although I barely felt it. His heart pounded and a loud roar filled his ears, as it had filled mine before the strains of Krishna's sweet flute replaced it. Hari reached down to cover my legs, and his eyes found something. On my exposed thigh, fading but still clearly visible, was the imprint of a peacock's head. Hari's own shoulders began to shake, and in that instant I remembered the crack I had stepped on the day of my dedication ceremony.

Hari knelt on the ground, his hands under my arms, and pulled me up until my head rested on his chest and my feet were out of the water. A dark stickiness oozed from the side of my head, under my hair, and left a wetness on his chest. Hari Dev wrapped his arms around me, rocking me gently. A trickle of blood ran from me to a small puddle near the water's edge, where it swirled, tinging it red-black for an instant, and then lost itself in the dark immensity of the lake. And my brother remembered another time, twelve years earlier, when his fear had been immeasurable.

13

Chandrabai

Early 1567

I no longer came early to the temple in the mornings, but someone else had begun to roam its chambers alone, a part of her heart finally fulfilled. Chandrabai looked up from the temple courtyard at the dark immensity of the sky. Meera wriggled in her arms, still crying. The baby had woken up and, unable to lull her back to sleep, Chandrabai had wrapped her in a shawl and taken her to the temple, so as not to disturb the other *devadasis*' sleep yet again.

Now Chandrabai walked back and forth across the width of the outer courtyard, singing softly to Meera. The baby whimpered and squirmed. Her eyes were open wide; she was not falling asleep. Chandrabai went to the kitchen to find her a piece of fruit on which she could suck. The kitchen was dark and cold and smelled of ash. She found Sundaran squatting in a corner among clay and brass pots, rubbing the sleep from his eyes. He hurried to his feet unsteadily when she entered.

Sundaran smiled. "Ah, Baby and baby!"

"Yes, I think she is hungry. Do you have anything?"

He shook his head. "Not much. Some rice with milk?"

Chandrabai nodded and waited for him to prepare it in a bowl. She set Meera down on her plump feet and held her, watched her, as the baby teetered. Although Meera was already three months, it still often came as a shock to Chandrabai that she existed at all. Meera fell back and frowned, and Chandrabai thought she saw a fleeting, impossible resemblance to Mahendra.

Meera was entirely hers, at least for now, and Chandrabai relished her simple, undivided love. She held her on her lap and fed her spoonfuls of millet and milk. The child pushed the food against the roof of her mouth with her tongue, dribbling some of it back out and swallowing the rest hungrily.

Sundaran lit an oil lamp on the floor and watched unabashedly. "Happy?"

Chandrabai nodded.

"It wasn't good, what you did those other times. I am glad you kept this one."

Chandrabai's face reddened, and she looked away.

"I am sorry, Baby. I should not have said that. I will get to the cooking now."

Chandrabai put the bowl and spoon down. "No, you are right. Don't be sorry. It just needed to be . . . the right time."

Meera nestled her face sleepily against her mother's breast. Chandrabai fashioned her shawl into a sling and placed Meera in it, secured against her hip. She felt awake, calm. For once, she looked forward to sweeping the temple and opening up the shrine for the morning. She thanked Sundaran and left the kitchen.

She entered the outer sanctum. From the garden came the gargling sounds of the watchman performing his morning ablutions. Saiprasad-ji had not yet arrived. After what he had done, he had taken to arriving at the temple even later than before, when the temple and Lord Krishna had already been awakened, and when the *devadasis* were already dancing with Bapu.

I had not told any of them what had happened. I knew it would break each of my parents. It almost broke me. Hari brought me a bitter beverage of herbs and bark to help me heal, and to help me sleep. I told Ma and Bapu that I was feeling unwell, and Hari spoke to them of a fever that had spread through Jaisalmer and that was followed by weeks of lethargy. It is a great irony that this is what caused my parents, after so many years, to spend more time together in our home. To have a common purpose: that of seeing me get well. Their silences as they rested in their own room gradually felt less formidable, and little by little, as I drifted in and out of sleep, I began to hear the hum and murmur of their voices together.

I spent my few waking hours those days, which stretched to four months, asking Krishna for advice. My body craved dance, yet I was tainted as a *devadasi*. I knew just two things: that I needed to hold on to my dance, and that I needed to leave the temple.

Shifting Meera's weight against her, Chandrabai set about sweeping the temple floor. She worked rhythmically, methodically, pausing only to scrape at the dust and sand that settled occasionally in the cracks between the stone slabs. The roots of the *babul* tree in the courtyard crept insidiously underneath, lifting and cracking the floor, every year a little more. I imagined them splitting and multiplying, gathering strength below.

Gray-blue daylight had begun to filter into the temple when Bapu and I arrived on the day of my first return. My stomach churned and my legs shook. Bapu believed this was due to general weakness from my illness.

"Ah, Chandrabai, you are here already." Bapu entered the chamber, his own gait labored and halting.

Chandrabai bowed to us in greeting, filled with relief to see me back on my feet. Bapu knelt in silent prayer. I set about lighting a stick of incense from the oil lamp that still burned by the entrance to the inner sanctum. My fingers trembled, and that day they looked just like fingers to me, not like butterflies or flowers or swords. Chandrabai watched me intently. She was struck by how tall I had grown, despite my illness. Thirteen. She knew my coming-of-age ceremony would surely come soon. Observing me, she detected a change in me. She struggled to ascertain what, exactly, it was. She saw it as a certain guardedness, perhaps, a pulling in, as though I were trying to disappear within myself and be visible to others only as a shadow. Even now, she thought, as I waved the incense in circles in front of the entrance to the inner sanctum, there was something evanescent about me, as though I might swirl into the spirals of smoke and melt into the air. Had I been able to, I would have.

Chandrabai watched me closely all morning. The other *devadasis* joined us, and we danced our greeting to the day and our devotion to Lord Krishna, led by Bapu. Chandrabai sat to the side for a while, nursing Meera. Her position offered her a view of me, and this is what she saw: I stood almost imperceptibly apart from the others—with them, yet in a different space. Only when I danced did I appear to be my full self. Then a slight smile played on my lips and my eyes saw something that Chandrabai's did not. But then Saiprasad-ji arrived, his large form obscuring the light from the doorway for a moment, and Chandrabai did see something. She saw my smile falter, she saw my eyes widen and then narrow, and she understood.

Chandrabai was seized with a desire to wrap herself around me, to hold me tight as she did Meera and shield me against what was not supposed to have happened. But in the way I moved, she understood I was already surrounded by a protective sphere. A slight change in light played around me, like the ring of brightness that surrounds a full moon before it melts into the darkness of the sky. Like the aura of light around Krishna's cloud-dark face. Chandrabai felt that by trying to reach through it, she might shatter it. She wondered if what she was witnessing was simply the play of sunlight that now streamed into the chamber, or something else. Nothing else had changed around her. Bapu continued to sing a poem to Lord Krishna; the *devadasis*, including me, continued to dance; Meera continued to drink hungrily.

Time stood still for Chandrabai as she sat alone with her realization. Meera's little hand pinched her side, and she had a memory of me at that age, in Ma's arms in the temple garden, as Ma pleaded with Manavi-ji to think about the future. Was this, she wondered, the future her Dadima had failed to change? Or was it the one that she had in fact altered?

For all Chandrabai could see was destruction. To her, this man, this priest, wreaked not only misery upon a *devadasi* sister—for what patron would accept a desecrated *devadasi*?—but also devastation upon the divine, and only terrible things could ensue. Feigning a need to tend to Meera, Chandrabai excused herself and left the dance chamber, hurrying back to her quarters. She needed to put distance between herself and Saiprasad-ji, whose oily presence she could feel even as he busied himself in other parts of the temple. She wanted space and time to think, to sort through the feelings that churned somewhere between her stomach and her chest.

Back in her quarters, she laid Meera down on a blanket and paced back and forth. She was compelled to do something, to rescue me, for the sake of all that was right, and for the survival of our divine dance. And for Meera.

Then something dawned on Chandrabai. She saw what she now believed Bapu had seen as soon as I was born, what she believed even Manavi-ji had not recognized.

"We have all been blind," she said aloud, as Meera followed her with her eyes, her fist in her mouth. "Adhira is not a dancer. She's not a *devadasi.* She is the dance. She is faith and devotion. She is the physical manifestation of Nataraja, Lord of Dance. The remover of darkness and ignorance and illusion."

The words tumbled out of her mouth in a frenzy. They came not from her own self but from elsewhere, as though spoken through her. But something else grew within her: a sense of duty as a *devadasi* to hold me aloft, like Vasudeva holding the infant Krishna above his head as he crossed the overflowing river, to carry me to a place where I would live forever.

She was still speaking aloud when I came to her quarters. I stood for a moment in front of the fluttering saffron curtain. I had seen her expression change, her composure dissolve, while I danced, and the sudden relief of knowing that someone else understood was overwhelming.

"Chandrabai," I called out, although my voice came out in a cracked whisper.

She pushed aside the curtain in an instant, pulled me into her dim quarters, and enveloped me in her arms. I sank into her pillowy, motherly softness and cardamom smell. I felt her tears on my neck, and she felt mine on hers, and soon Meera's wails accompanied our silent sobs. Chandrabai pulled back and picked up Meera, resting her against her shoulder. She wiped her eyes roughly with the back of her arm.

She looked straight into my eyes. "When?"

"The night of Dussehra."

"Does anyone else know?"

"Hari."

Chandrabai nodded, patting Meera's bare back as the baby's cries subsided. She knew Hari would have told no one.

"Chandra *didi*," I said, "I have to leave this place. I can't bear to stay."

Chandrabai nodded again. This she understood to be true. I could not stay. She fingered her jade bangles, a gift from her *dadima*. There was only one person to turn to.

"But where do I go?" My voice rose as the magnitude of the question engulfed me.

Chandrabai took my hand and asked a single, last question. "Do you still want to dance?"

I nodded.

"Then there is someone who might be able to help."

"No! You can't tell anyone, please."

"Just one person, Adhi. One person, who knows how to be discreet."

"Who?"

Chandrabai looked away for a moment, then back at me. "Your sister."

And this is how I came to know that I had an older sister.

Chandrabai went right away. I wanted to go with her, but she insisted that I wait in her quarters. My sister, she said, might not be ready to see me. I did not understand at the time that Chandrabai needed to ask Padmini first if she was willing to let me see her.

It was midmorning, the only time of day when my sister could safely welcome Chandrabai. The children, three boys now, were in school. Padmini could not risk their seeing Chandrabai, for fear that they might breathe word of her visit to their father. And of course Samarjit himself had to be out, and he often spent the mornings in court. Chandrabai, therefore, always saw the house at the same time of day, in the same light, with the same sounds of women and young children chattering in the street and the same smells of cooking fires and cow dung in the air. Today, however, she noticed more people in new clothing styles, more foreign-looking men speaking unfamiliar languages. They had arrived without the battle that Mahendra had assured her was coming, without the destruction of the city or the invasion of the temple. Other cities had fallen bloodily, but Jaisalmer still flourished. This gave Chandrabai hope that perhaps here, in the citadel, was the answer to how to save me.

Sajana opened the door to Padmini's house. Chandrabai followed her upstairs to the main receiving room and settled Meera, asleep, on a carpet. Padmini entered, and her smile illuminated her face as she knelt by the child. Her head was uncovered; she had long ago abandoned all efforts to hide the marks in front of Chandrabai, who in turn tried as best she could not to stare or appear surprised when a new bruise bloomed on some part of Padmini's skin.

Padmini stroked Meera's cheek with one finger. "What a beauty."

Chandrabai settled on the floor beside them. "Yes. I wasn't expecting such perfection."

"No one never does." Padmini sighed. "My brother has not seen her, has he?"

"No. I haven't seen him in over two years. Since that day I told you about, when he raised his fist to me."

Padmini nodded.

"I thought of you, and I realized I would always live in the shadow of his rage, no matter how much he cared for me."

"Good. It's good you did that."

They sat in silence for a while. Chandrabai thought about why she had come.

Padmini broke the quiet. "So. Tell me."

Unable to blur the edges of what she had to say, Chandrabai went straight to what had brought her to Padmini.

"It's happened. You know. Saiprasad-ji."

Padmini raised an eyebrow, and her shoulders sagged. In her look was alarm and apprehension, but no surprise. All she was asking was who it was.

"Adhira."

Padmini closed her eyes and tightened her lips, as though absorbing a blow. When she reopened her eyes, she asked simply, "Now what?"

"We have to do something."

"What, how? Who knows about this?"

"Just Hari Dev. Adhira's coming-of-age ceremony can't be far. When her patron finds out . . . " Chandrabai did not say out loud what they both were thinking. That everything, everyone, would be ruined when Uttam-ji discovered the truth.

"Who is he?"

"A man named Uttam. A landowner."

Padmini nodded. "My husband has spoken of him. He has some dealings with the court."

"Is there anything you can do?"

"Do? Like what? Anything will raise suspicion. What do you have in mind?"

"I don't know, Padmini. I was hoping you'd have an idea. There must be something. You know how your father always says we are vessels for communicating the divine? Adhira is that vessel."

Padmini said nothing. Chandrabai felt her words were coming out all wrong. She feared she was not making herself clear. She was suddenly terrified that Padmini, who had not danced in so many years, would not understand. She stood and went to the window.

"Your mother once asked Dadima to change the future," she said, looking out. "The future of everything our lives have meant is not at the temple, not with Saiprasad-ji there, not with the stones cracking and our teacher so old. . . . " Chandrabai turned back to face Padmini, and her voice broke.

Padmini held up her hand. "There is the court."

Chandrabai looked up at her through the wetness of her tears.

"The court. Samarjit has told me there are dancers there."

"The court? Have you been there?" Mahendra's words about the terrible things the Muslims did in their courts filled Chandrabai's thoughts.

"No, of course not. My husband won't allow me there. You know, in case anyone sees. But he tells me about it. He knows I would love to be there. He's not all bad, you know. He describes it, paints pictures with his words and brushes. Adhira could dance at the court. With all the Muslim guests there these days, the Raja has been looking for dancers to impress them."

Chandrabai shook her head. She could not let me dance for Muslims. She could not understand how Padmini could even suggest it.

"Think about it," Padmini said. "If Adhira is as you say, it will not matter for whom she dances. It will not matter where. What matters is that she be able to do it, with the purity she deserves. And far into the future."

Chandrabai nodded.

"What Saiprasad-ji did tainted the temple, the *devadasis*, our whole tradition," Padmini continued. "The court is not tainted in that way. No, I know what you will say. But I will tell you, the Muslims are capable of great devotion. Dance, music, poetry, painting—they are all flourishing in the court, and many of the new artists are Muslims."

"But—how do you know?"

"I do not leave my house much, but I do hear things. The temple may crumble, but the court will always exist in some form. Adhira will be safer there."

Chandrabai was not ready to believe these things. Yet she no longer believed the things that used to hold her life together, either. "And men? Do the dancers have duties toward them in the court?"

"Yes. Of course. But Adhira can't escape that anywhere. At the court, she may well become the favorite of the Raja, and if that is the case, she will be very well cared for." Here, Padmini smiled wryly. "Ma used to dream of one of us catching the fancy of a prince, of becoming an advisor in the court. She could get her wish this way."

Padmini fell silent, thinking about the effect on Ma of finding out what Saiprasad-ji had done.

"I don't know," Chandrabai said.

"Well, I don't know what else to suggest. My father's ancestors used to travel from village to village, bringing faith to the people of Hindustan. Imagine if Adhira could bring our dance and faith to a whole new people!"

Chandrabai looked around and wondered how Padmini could speak so loftily of faith and new people when her own life was confined within walls.

"And you? Do you really believe in new beginnings?" Chandrabai asked, as much to challenge Padmini as to give herself more time to consider what she knew, ultimately, would be the only choice of what to do for me.

Padmini's expression changed, and her voice became harder. "Of course! I left the temple, didn't I?"

"That's hardly a beginning anymore! How long has it been? Sixteen years?"

Padmini lowered her voice and walked her fingers on Meera's stomach. "I can't leave Samarjit. Where would I go? And the children . . . "

Chandrabai returned to sit by her. "I am not suggesting you leave. But come with me to Jagadhar-ji's shop one day. I've told you Hari Dev works there, and he might be able to make something to hide your bruises, maybe even the burn. You could go out again, have a new beginning of your own."

"No, I can't let my brother see me like this. Or Adhira."

"But Hari Dev was so little when you left. He won't even know who you are! Please?"

"I don't know."

"You know how he helped me, with the mix, each of those times. I've never known if he recognized me or not, but it doesn't matter. He's stronger than you think, Padmini. And it gives meaning to his life to help others."

"Why are you asking me this again now, Chandra? I thought you came to discuss Adhira."

"I did, and we did. But we've always done things for each other. Let's do this together."

This was how Chandrabai would make her decision. If Padmini agreed to seek help and return to the outside world, she, Chandrabai, would help deliver me to the court. *Sawal jawab*, call and response. Like a dancer and a drummer, exchanging phrases.

Padmini rose and pulled her sari over her head. "All right, then. I'll do it. I'll let Hari Dev help me. If he even can. But about Adhira: we must let this cycle reach its end before we can do anything."

"The ceremony?"

"Yes. Tell Adhira the plan if you'd like, but she should have the ceremony and go with Uttam-ji. We should not stop any of that."

"Why not?"

"Because the Raja will want her to have reached womanhood, to have a wealthy patron, to be a *devadasi* in all respects. He needs to feel he is acquiring something very special. It will make him want her more."

"But then Uttam-ji . . . He'll know, won't he, about Adhira, once they are together?"

"Maybe, maybe not. We'll have to take that risk."

Girija

Late 1567

For the six days following the start of my menstruation, as *devadasi* tradition dictated, I was isolated in a room outside the temple grounds. Ma saw me only a few times, when she took turns with Jayarani to bring me my meals. Already, even though I now stood before her, knee-deep in the lake's waters, Ma missed me. And missing me made her miss Mahendra, who had come only twice in the past three years to bring money, and it made her miss Hari Dev, who had been particularly aloof for several months.

Ma sat by the water's edge. She listened to the sounds of Jayarani rubbing my skin with oil and turmeric for my ritual bath, the cloth periodically slapping into the water and then drops cascading back down. I closed my eyes and let the oil sink into my skin, the water carrying away the past, my body being born again.

I knew what Chandrabai and Padmini had planned for me—I had even visited my sister in her home, with its shadows and heavy silence. The knowledge that I would not be a full temple *devadasi* for long was liberating. Guilt for deceiving those around me jabbed at my insides, but I tried to have faith that Krishna would understand. I would still be dancing for him.

Ma was grateful beyond words for Padmini's presence on this

day. She had never expected it. They sat next to each other, and Ma wished time would stand still.

"I'm not ready for this," she said aloud, pushing her bare toes into the water. Then, "I'm so glad you came today."

Padmini said nothing but shifted closer to Ma. "Of course. It's Adhira's coming-of-age, and I am still her sister."

"Today I lose one daughter and gain one back."

"You're not really losing her, Ma."

"Maybe not. But today Uttam will take her. Tonight she'll know the burden of a strange man in her, and she will no longer be my little Adhira."

I kept quiet, willing that burden, which I already carried, to wash away into the lake.

Jayarani gave a wry smile and went to the lake's edge to lay the washing cloth to dry.

There was a brief moment of silence before Padmini's answer, and Ma sensed that something was amiss.

"But Uttam-ji is a kind man. He'll treat her well."

"And I suppose you are a good judge of that?"

"Ma!"

"Oh, Padmini!" Ma turned to her and reached for her arm. "I'm so sorry. I should never have said that. I don't know what has come over me. Forgive me."

Padmini stroked Ma's hand awkwardly. "It's all right, Ma. It's all right."

Ma had not felt her eldest's touch in many years, and the feel of Padmini's skin against her own overwhelmed her. Words threatened to flood out of her mouth, and she had to clamp it shut to keep them in. Long ago, at the age of thirteen, she had awakened to find a friend of her father's slipping into her bed. She had shouted out, the man had pressed his hand to her mouth, and then the mynah bird her brother kept had come flying into the room and created enough of a commotion for the man to flee before doing what he had come to do. When her father had not come to chase away the intruder, Ma had realized he was complicit in the plan.

"I just wish I could protect her."

"It wasn't—isn't—for you to do that, Ma. And in any case, it is too late." Padmini stood quickly and left Ma to turn over in her mind the latter portion of her statement.

Padmini, Chandrabai, and Jayarani dressed me in a new sari—one of Uttam-ji's many gifts—and adorned me with jewelry and red powder in the part of my hair. I stood at the edge of the lake, and the hot breeze dried my legs. Ma stood apart from us, the only one who was not, nor had ever been, a *devadasi*. Unable to see me clearly, she imagined shimmering traces on my cheeks formed by tears that were not in fact there.

"She is ready," Chandrabai announced.

Ma stood and made her way toward us. She held her hand out to me and pulled me close. We held each other, and I do not know who was comforting whom. I wanted to tell her that nothing was her fault, that I finally understood what she had tried to teach me, that even though Lord Krishna would always look after me, I would make, was making, my own decisions. But the words swelled and wedged themselves in my throat. And so I said nothing, simply let her embrace me until Padmini gently pulled her away.

Ma wiped her eyes with the back of her hand and turned to Padmini. "You will come to the ceremony, yes?"

"No. I can't. People will see me . . . "

"But you came here; surely you can come to the ceremony? I thought Hari was able to help with . . . "

"He helped, but it's not perfect yet. Here it was safe; it was just the four of you. I have to go back home now. I will come visit again soon."

After we all left, Ma was more alone than ever. The ceremony itself passed in a blur for her. Not just the usual blur of colors and shapes, but a blur of sounds and feelings as well. She was numb, so numb that she began to fear there was something wrong with her body. Even at the feast afterward, the food tasted dull to her, although the kitchen girls Uttam-ji had hired had chopped okra and mustard greens in the kitchen. There were cloves, pepper, and cardamom. There were *achars* and pickles, and sweets. Betel leaves filled with spices. But by the end of the evening, Ma could not remember tasting any of these foods. As for me, the ceremony and feast themselves meant little.

After the feast, the evening continued with music and dance at the temple. Ma let herself be carried on the wind of celebration. But there were markedly fewer people at the temple than at past celebrations. In lean times, the temple, poorly maintained, had lost much of its following. Sounds echoed emptily in the chambers, so that the whole performance felt to her like an act constructed in a void.

With so many thoughts crowding her head, Ma found no words to say to me at the end of the evening, when I came to bid her good-bye. This moment that she had rehearsed so many times in her head was now too complicated, too layered. And so it was for me, too. Nothing we could say would be enough for either of us. Instead she held my face with one hand and touched my forehead with the fingers of the other, imagining that she was giving me a third eye, like that of Shiva, which would grant me wisdom. The moment was brief and yet also eternal. And then Uttam-ji and I receded into the darkness.

Ma slept fitfully that night. She and Bapu barely exchanged a word as they readied themselves for bed. "It is for the best" was all Bapu said as he blew out the lamp, but his sighs and shiftings betrayed his restlessness for a while. Just as Ma, however, was about to say something, anything, to unite their solitary sadnesses, she heard his breathing shift to the slow, steady rhythm of sleep. He was not tortured by thoughts of Uttam-ji and me—thoughts that Ma tried to banish from her mind by calling forth memories of the lake in her hometown of Mount Abu sparkling in the sunshine, of Manavi-ji's hand holding hers, of anything pleasant and reassuring. Anytime she was successful, however, anytime she started feeling the welcome weightlessness that announced the arrival of sleep, she was jolted awake by the memory of my plump two-year-old hand in her own, or the weight of my four-year-old body asleep in her arms.

She was still awake when the silence that precedes dawn wrapped itself around our home. She felt it like a tangible presence. And she felt another presence. She sat up in bed and listened. There it was again, a slight jingling, almost imperceptible, coming from outside. Ma got up and felt her way across the room, wrapping a shawl around her shoulders. She paused for a moment in the doorway. Bapu's breathing did not change. Then she listened at the entrance to the room

Hari Dev and I used to share. Only Hari's heavy breathing. Hari Dev, who at eighteen was no longer a child. She lingered in the doorway, listening to my absence. She thought for a moment of going to lie in my bed, to hold my bedsheets to her face, but there was the sound again, in the courtyard.

She went toward it. "Who's there?" she called out in a whisper. The courtyard was silver-gray-black.

"Ma! It's me."

"Mahendra!"

His familiar, rough hand took hers and pulled her down to sit on the ground, leaning against the courtyard wall.

"You need to get better at moving quietly. How do you survive in the desert, making all this noise?"

"I did it on purpose, Ma. I thought maybe I could draw you out."

For the first time in days, she wanted to smile. Mahendra put his arm around her shoulders. "How are you? Did Adhira . . . ?"

Ma held up her hand. "Yes, she's gone. Could we talk about something else? Tell me something interesting, different. Anything. There's still a world out there, right?"

"Yes, there's still a world out there." Mahendra's voice was heavy. He paused.

"What is it?" Ma asked.

"I . . . I don't know what I'm doing anymore," he said, his voice cracking. "I want to come home."

"What has happened?"

And so, as they sat in the still darkness and everyone, everything, around them slept, Ma listened to Mahendra tell her that Emperor Akbar had married the princess of Amber, the capital of another Princely State of Rajasthan. It was done. The future prince of Amber would have a Muslim father. While the Raja of Amber agreed so easily to form an alliance with Akbar, the fort at Chittor, capital of another Princely State, had fallen under attack by Akbar's forces. Chittor was a symbol of Rajput resistance.

It would survive the attack, wouldn't it? Ma asked.

But Mahendra did not think so. The Raja had abandoned the fort and moved the capital farther up in the hills. He had supplied the fort with provisions for several years, but he had entrusted its defense to two young princes, barely eighteen years old, and only five thousand Rajputs. Now the fort, which the same family had held for over eight hundred years, was encircled.

Akbar had built massive approach corridors, which snaked their way uphill to reach the fort walls. Broad enough for ten horsemen, the corridors were made of brick and mud, with planks overhead, covered in hides. Ma tried to imagine how much work, how many men, it had taken to build these, but the magnitude was beyond her. Mahendra said five thousand men had worked to build the corridors, but work was, of course, slow. The Rajputs managed to kill more than one hundred workers every day.

There was a complete lack of satisfaction in Mahendra's voice. Not long ago, he would have been delighted at such a triumph of Rajputs over Muslims. Ma had never cared for details of death and killing, but she had understood what was behind Mahendra's motivation. Now he seemed not to care anymore. And that, more than anything, was worrisome.

"*Beta*, whatever it is you've been doing, you don't have to continue." But even as the words came out, she was uncertain. Mahendra knew this and said nothing. They sat in silence, listening to the sounds of dawn. She wondered what Mahendra would do, but she did not want to push him away with questions. She wanted his closeness.

They had been silent a while when Mahendra reached into his bag and pulled out a jingling sack. Ma felt him take her hand and then felt the familiar weight of the pouch of money.

Mahendra kept his hand on hers. "Ma, this may be the last time I can do this for you."

The solemnity in his voice alarmed her. "Are you not coming back again?"

"I'll come back. But I don't know how long I can keep bringing money like this."

Ma nodded. "It's all right. I've been saving most of it. Using it wisely. We have plenty for a while. I want you not to worry about us. Also, Uttam-ji has been good to us."

"Adhira's patron? What's he like?"

"I think you'd like him. Maybe one day you'll meet him. He's a landowner and lets villagers graze their herds there for a share of the animals. He lends money, too. Jayarani says he has a long scar across his cheek; I don't know how he got it. Some form of fight. But he seems like a good man. He'll take good care of Adhira." She spoke these last words the way she had been repeating them to herself, the way Bapu had said them. But they did nothing to relieve her feelings of anxiety and guilt.

Uttam-ji was indeed a good man. My first night with him, he was kind, gentle. He never got so far as to remove my underclothes. Maybe it was because I flinched, maybe I let out a sound. At any event, he paused, pulled his hand away from me, and searched my face with his eyes. I wanted to tell him everything, but I didn't know how. As it turns out, I didn't need to. Somehow he understood, and when he did, he kept his thoughts to himself, stroking my hair with a sad smile.

Meanwhile, the sun had risen. Already the air was warming. Light and shadow replaced the uniform darkness of night outside our home. Mahendra made no motion to leave.

"Your father will be waking soon," Ma reminded him.

"I know." Mahendra still did not move.

Ma wondered if she should go in and tell Bapu their son was here. Tell him not to say anything, not to send him away with harsh words. Maybe this way Mahendra would stay. But just as she was having these thoughts, Bapu called to her. She stood up. Before she could go inside, Bapu was in the doorway.

"Girija? Are you out here?" he called. And then a moment of silence as Bapu caught sight of Mahendra.

Mahendra rose. "Bapu."

Bapu acted as though he had not heard, and asked Ma for something to drink.

"Bapu," Mahendra said again, this time a little louder.

"Has the boy fetched the water yet?" Bapu lifted up the lid of the water jar. His voice echoed in its emptiness.

"No, but he'll be here any moment. Did you not hear Mahendra?" Ma asked. That Bapu might not have heard was impossible. Bapu's hearing was still excellent.

"Mahendra?" As though she had asked him if he had heard his own father.

"Yes! What's wrong? Look, Mahendra's come to see us." She took Mahendra's hand and squeezed it.

"I don't know any Mahendra. But come, let us have something to drink."

Something was terribly wrong. Was Bapu not well? Ma let go of Mahendra's hand and went over to him, trailing her hand against the wall of the hut. She reached out to feel Bapu's forehead.

Bapu recoiled. "Eh! What are you doing? I am not sick!"

"Then why don't you say something to our son?"

"Because he is not our son."

"What?"

"This is no son of mine, Girija. No son of mine would abandon his family like this. No son of mine would abandon our tradition. He did not even come to Adhira's ceremony. Mahendra may have been born to us, but he is no longer my son." Bapu's voice trembled for a moment as he held back tears.

"Bapu!" Mahendra's voice echoed the distress to which Ma herself could put no words.

Ma leaned back against the wall as Mahendra stumbled toward Bapu.

But Bapu moved back. "No, Mahendra. It is too late. Go. You have understood one thing, which is that you do not belong here. Do not come back."

Ma found her voice, and her tears. "Gandar! Think about what you are doing! Mahendra's come back to us; he understands he made a mistake. Don't send him away. Please, don't send him away. Mahendra, don't go. Bapu will change his mind."

"I will not change my mind. I made this decision long ago. Come, make my tea," Bapu said, retreating indoors.

Mahendra gathered his bag, throwing it onto his shoulder. Ma could bear it no longer. "Mahendra! You don't have to leave. Bapu is as lost as you are. He's just trying to save his pride. Please don't leave."

Mahendra paused and went toward her. He held her briefly, and she breathed in the smoky smell of his hair. Then he was crossing the courtyard.

"Where are you going?" It was a question she had never asked of him before.

"I don't know" came the answer he had never before given, and he was gone.

Ma wiped her eyes. It was time for Bapu to know. She walked back to the place she had been sitting with Mahendra, squatted down, and felt around on the ground for the sack of money. She picked it up and went inside.

Bapu was sitting on a cushion, rubbing his legs, his dry fingers making a rough sound against his dry skin. Ma did not care that he was doing this himself, that she was shirking her duty. She threw the sack of coins at his feet, and they scattered across the floor.

Bapu grunted. "What is this? Where did you get this?"

"This is what your son Mahendra brought us. This is what he's been bringing us for eight years. Eight years! Do you hear?"

"What are you saying?"

"I'm saying that Mahendra's money is what has been supporting us for the past eight years. Not you, not your dance."

"Why? My state pension is enough. What is that boy trying to do? Shame me? In my own home?"

Bapu was pacing across the room now. And as his anger rose, hers turned to sadness. She was going to tell him the full truth now, and he would be devastated. She held back for a few more moments, delaying the inevitable. The deliverer of bad news always wishes to stop time before having to reveal the truth. She reached out for Bapu's hand, but he did not take hers.

"How could you let Mahendra do this, Girija? How could you keep this from me? I should not have let you take charge of our money. Saiprasad-ji was right: it is not a woman's business."

Ma said nothing. She could bear Bapu's anger.

But then his voice softened. "Girija." He pulled her down to sit on some cushions. "Was there something you really needed? Something you did not tell me about? Was I really not providing you and the children with what you needed? I could have spoken with Saiprasad-ji, asked for him to get my pension increased. I would have gone myself to the court to ask for more."

"No, you couldn't have done that."

"Of course I could have!"

"No, you don't understand. Please! The state cut off your payments eight years ago."

There was a sharp intake of breath. My parents sat in silence, my father unable to let Ma's words sink in, like a patch of earth so dry and parched that it cannot allow in any rain and instead lets it roll across its surface. But eventually, the water finds a crack to penetrate.

"Forgive me. I couldn't bear to tell you."

Still silence.

Ma took Bapu's hands in hers. "Gandar." She tried to see into his blank face. "You are so happy when you are dancing. You were teaching Adhira. I couldn't tell you. They cut off payments because of the war against the Muslims. Because of the fighting, all the money is going to the army. I had to feed the children, feed us. I had to—"

"Enough! Go!"

"Go?"

"Go. Away. For a little while. I need to be alone."

"Gandar, please."

"Go!"

Ma got up, withdrawing her hands from Bapu's, which had gone limp. She backed away slowly, hoping he would change his mind. She was afraid to leave him alone. Alone with the feeling that he had failed. She wanted to stay with him, but he had retreated into a shell—like the fortifications of Chittor—and she no longer had the strength to tunnel in. So she left.

When she reached the end of the courtyard, Hari Dev emerged from our home and advanced toward her. She called out to him, wondering what to say. She knew he would likely not ask any questions. Hari Dev rarely asked for explanations anymore. And in fact he ignored her call and limped across the yard and out, disappearing around the wall, headed for the refuge of Jagadhar-ji's shop. The clay collection cups he brought with him thudded dully together in his satchel. Ma did not call him back.

The next day was only my second day away. In Uttam-ji's city home, I sat alone in a sumptuous room full of embroidered cushions and silken draperies, and a wall on which hung dozens of the wooden dolls my patron liked to carve. They looked down on me stiffly, their painted faces smiling, frowning, grimacing. A servant brought me food on silver trays, water in shiny goblets. Uttam-ji had left, telling me he was needed at his other home, the one amid the irrigated fields in which he told me he cultivated crops and kept sheep. In fact, he was in the room next to the one in which he had left me, pacing as he decided what to do with me.

I had not danced in three days, and my feet felt as though a thousand ants were crawling in them. When I could bear it no longer, I rolled up the carpets to expose the sandstone floor. I found a statuette of Lord Krishna in a cupboard by the bed and placed it below the window, in a rectangle of sunshine. Looking out over the rooftops where clothing fluttered in the dry wind, I set my eyes on the desert horizon and danced, careful not to step on Lord Krishna's shadow.

Back at home, time had taken on new dimensions since my departure. It was only the second day without me, but it felt to Ma as though I had been gone much longer. The rhythm of days had been broken. Bapu had not been to the temple at all the previous day after Ma told him about the money, and he had not gone this day, either. He had left the house both mornings and come back late at night, but she could tell by the tired droop of his shoulders, by the slowness of his step, that he had not been dancing. She wondered where he'd gone, what he'd eaten. He would not let her do anything for him. She made his meals and left them out for him, the way Hari Dev used to leave platters of food for the wounded animals he cared for as a child, and with a heavy heart she brought them back in untouched.

Hari Dev himself spent little time at home, too. But that was normal. It was good he was fending for himself. My brother was on the verge of discovering his own freedom. He said very little to Ma, although he still brought her *kair* for her eyes every few days. Now she stopped taking it, threw away the berries instead. She thought they were giving her stomachaches, and she no longer cared how well she might see.

Ma was sitting in the courtyard, fingering a small pile of rice, removing hard pebbles from among the grains, when we approached.

"Girija-ji!" Uttam-ji called out to her. I remained quiet, for nothing I could say would ease the pain she was about to endure.

Ma had not expected me for at least seven days, enough time for Uttam-ji to take full pleasure in what he had acquired before allowing me to return to live in the *devadasi* quarters and limiting our relations to just a few times per month.

She rose. "Uttam-ji," she addressed him, even though she longed to speak with me directly. "Is something wrong?" She could not see the look on his face, nor mine.

"I'm afraid there is, Girija-ji. I must return Adhira to you and renounce being her patron."

Ma met this news with shocked silence, at a loss for what to say.

"You really didn't know?" Uttam-ji asked.

"Know what?"

"Adhira has been with another man."

The words fell like rocks on stone. *That is not possible*, Ma wanted to shout. But suddenly she was holding me in her arms, feeling and hearing me sob. And Ma understood what he was saying. She understood in a way that she wished she did not. If only she could have known the rest, that my tears were not just for myself, but for her, and for Bapu, and for Mahendra and Padmini, and all that was hurting them. Only Hari Dev, I knew, did not need my tears.

Ma's heart rose into her throat and choked her. She could do nothing but hold me and let her own tears flow. She did not even care that Uttam-ji, a near stranger to her, a wealthy man, was watching.

Uttam-ji coughed. "I'm sorry, Girija-ji. Adhira is lovely. I care for her deeply. But you must understand, I can't be her patron. She's been damaged. This isn't what I paid for."

Ma's head spun as she tried to keep Uttam-ji's words out. But they forced their way in, and she knew she had to pay attention. Something had to be arranged, tenuous balances had to be maintained. She would speak to Uttam-ji in a language he could understand.

"What about her honor? Our family's reputation? This wasn't Adhira's fault, not her own doing. You know this, yes?"

"Yes, I thought as much, even though she wouldn't tell me who it was or how it happened."

"I have an idea who it was. But that's no matter right now. What matters is that our family, my husband, cannot survive if this becomes public knowledge. You must help us."

"Of course—whatever I can do."

"Remain her patron in name. You can do that and still be a patron to others. You won't need to pay for any of her needs; we'll take care of her. Just please remain her patron in name, and I assure you no one outside our family will ever know the truth."

Uttam-ji hesitated.

"Please?" Never had Ma begged so many people for so much in such a short time. She did not know how much longer she could keep doing it.

"All right," said Uttam-ji. He knelt on the ground by us. "Good-bye, Adhira." His voice was sweet as music. He was close enough for Ma to see the sadness etched on his face, as clear as the scar that stretched across his cheek. He placed a hand on my back. This was the moment when the course of my life took a turn that no one—not Ma with her hopes nor Bapu with his dreams nor Mahendra with his fears nor even Hari Dev with his memories of things to come—had foreseen. The hand of Krishna opened a door, and I, his servant, decided to step through it.

For a long time after Uttam had left, Ma and I sat still. Finally, when Ma's legs began to grow numb, she helped me to my feet, led me indoors to my bed, and pulled a light sheet over me. She sat by my side, stroking my forehead, gently rubbing the area between my eyebrows, the way she used to do when I was a baby. I fell into the most restful sleep I had had in months.

Ma rose and went to the chest in the other bedroom. There was something there, under the layers of clothes and blankets, that she needed to remove from our home. Something of her father's that had brought a piece of him here, into her family. Perhaps it was her fault, she thought. Perhaps things would have turned out differently if she had not kept her father's sword. She wanted never to see or feel it again.

15

Mahendra

1568

Sikander nodded at Mahendra. "That sword has served you well, nah?"

They were sitting in a shallow valley between two dunes with the men they called their brothers, resting in the growing sliver of shade as the sun sank lower in the sky. It would be my brother's last moment of rest. He knew nothing yet of the developments with Uttam-ji; Ma had told no one. Instead, his thoughts were on a single notion: escape.

The *sirohi* was hard and cool in his hands. Its smoothness was pleasant as he ran his fingers along the sides of the slightly curved blade. Everything about it was a relief from the rough, hot grittiness of the sand.

"Yes, it has." With his plan for escape swirling in his mind, he had no words for idle talk.

Sikander sat down beside him. He leaned in to speak in a low voice, and his opium breath filled the air.

"The others are still jealous that you have this Rajput sword from Mount Abu. If I were you, I wouldn't show it off like this."

Mahendra sheathed the *sirohi* and put it down next to him. "I'm not showing it off." Nasir grunted, and the rest of the band clustered closer together, leaving Mahendra and Sikander apart.

Mahendra had been carrying the *sirohi* now for several months, since Ma had given it to him the last time he was home. After Bapu had sent him away, Mahendra walked blindly to the tavern just past the merchants' quarters. With nowhere to go and nothing to do—Sikander's band was conducting a raid three days' walk from Jaisalmer—Mahendra sought refuge in liquor. Day turned to night and then to morning, and Mahendra awoke, his head pounding, on the ground outside the tavern door. He dragged himself to Jagadharji's shop, where he knew our brother worked. There, without a word, Hari gave him a corner to lie in and some concoction to drink. Mahendra slept the day away, like a wounded animal, feeling safe for the first time in years. As night fell, Hari Dev woke him, whispered that he had to close the shop, and gave him a long, cloth-covered object, saying Ma wanted him to have it.

Mahendra had carried the sword everywhere since then, slept with it by his side, his hand on the hilt. He did not know why Ma had given it to him, nor why she even had it with her. But he felt that it belonged in his hands. He had explained his last absence to his "brothers" with a lie, saying Bapu was dying and had left the sword for him as a parting gift. Mulraj and Nasir and the others had gathered around him, wanting to touch the sword, their eyes glowing.

Sikander rubbed at his teeth with a stick. "They don't like that I keep giving you more of the crucial roles in the raids. They think it's just because of the sword. They don't understand you are stealthier than any of them."

Mahendra swallowed and nodded. Stealing up on sleeping guards in the night, catching the tax collector unawares—these had become his tasks. Wielded with enough force, the *sirohi* could slice off a head in one strike. It was supposedly a quiet way to kill, Mahendra knew, but every time he had to do it, his stomach turned. The sound of his own retching, the gurgle of blood, his heart pounding behind his ribs—these sounds filled his ears to the point he felt his head might burst.

Sikander looked at the horizon. "It will be time soon. Let's review the plan for tonight."

"Shall we gather the others?"

"No, they each know their role. I want to review what you will do."

Tonight would be the last time. Tonight's raid, on a rich landowner, would be his last. He was correct, at least, about that part. Sikander skewered him with his red-rimmed eyes, as though trying to pierce his thoughts.

"So, you will enter the landowner's home. It is your job to make sure he does not interfere with our raid."

"Who is it?"

"No matter. You don't need to know who it is."

"Why don't you ever tell us?"

"The less you know, the better. Anyway, you are to secure the inside of the home and take the valuables. Kill if necessary. Understood?"

Mahendra nodded.

Sikander blew his nose noisily into the sand. "I will come in with you. In case there are watchmen inside the home. The others will handle any guards outside. They will take the bags of grain, and the goats, and the money buried under the goat feed."

"Can they carry it all?" Mahendra feigned a genuine interest in the haul.

"Maybe not all. But we'll take as much as possible. There is likely to be a recent harvest of *bajra*, sorghum, maybe even wheat. This landowner advances money to the local cultivators and takes security of their crops. We are going to do very well, my friend!"

Mahendra felt ill.

"What's wrong?" Sikander's voice was sharp, and the others—those who were awake, at least—turned to look at them.

"Nothing. I mean, what if . . . what if there's a woman with him? I don't know if I can kill a woman."

Sikander laughed, and his laugh turned into a sputtering cough. "Ha! Such a gentleman! No, the man isn't married. There will probably not be a woman."

"Since when is that a guarantee of anything?"

Sikander stopped coughing, and his eyes bore into Mahendra. "I said don't worry. Is there going to be a problem?"

My brother shook his head. "No, no, of course not. I will be very quiet; the landowner will not hear me. And if he wakes up, I'll come up from behind and kill him quickly."

Sikander planted his sheathed dagger into the sand. "Good. That settles that." He reached into his bag, pulled out an iron tiger's claw, slipped it over his fingers, and examined its points. The first time Mahendra had seen Sikander use it, he had nearly fainted. With one swipe, Sikander had cut his attacker's face to shreds, leaving the man blinded and writhing in a pool of blood, strips of skin hanging from his cheeks. Sikander had stood over him and laughed.

Mahendra's heart beat loudly as he recalled that night. Never again would he have to see that, for tonight he had his own plan. He had orchestrated his departure very precisely. The band was used to his leaving on occasion for a few days, but he had always returned. He had to. He had proven himself worthy of the band's brotherhood, and that meant that he had earned their loyalty. If he did not return when he said he would, they would come looking for him. But tonight, he vowed, would be different.

If the landowner awoke, Mahendra planned to engage him in a fight. If he did not awaken on his own, Mahendra would make a sound to make sure that he did. He was confident he could maintain the upper hand, especially with Ma's *sirohi*, and he would control the fight in such a way that he would sustain an injury—not life-threatening, but serious enough. He would call to Sikander for help, if necessary, and Sikander would rush in and subdue the landowner. Mahendra and Sikander would escape, and Mahendra would have to leave the band for a while to recover from his arm injury. It had to be an arm injury, so that he would still be able to run. The brothers would not question his need to leave, and he would return home. After a while, he would send word to Sikander that his arm had not healed well, and Sikander would no doubt tell him he could not take him back if he could not fight, and Mahendra would be able to say good-bye to his life of falsehood and savagery.

Just imagining the weight lifting from his shoulders was almost too elating for Mahendra. He dug his hands into the cooling sand and set his face in a scowl to keep from smiling. He tried not to wonder too much about what would happen once he was home. Anything, he thought, would be preferable to his current life.

"By the way," Sikander said, not bothering to look up as he picked at something on one of the points of the tiger's claw, "did you hear that the fort at Chittor has fallen?"

"What? When?"

"About a month ago. Remember that day when you told all of us the story of the legendary resistance of Chittor? Heh, well, not so legendary anymore, I guess!"

Mahendra despised this man, this good-for-nothing bandit, and his disregard for a great Rajput city. "What happened?" He struggled to keep his voice even.

Sikander spat on the tiger's claw and polished it on his sleeve. "Oh, the Emperor's forces blew the walls with gunpowder, and Akbar himself killed the Prince. Then, *jauhar*. Three hundred women. Before the rest could join them, Akbar's war elephants charged. Thirty thousand people killed, and who knows how many thousands of prisoners. Akbar's occupied Chittor. So you see, no point in fighting them. Best just to look out for ourselves."

Mahendra's head pounded.

Sikander stood. "All right. It's time. Let's go!"

The men gathered their weapons. Each man had a dagger tucked into his cummerbund, and a wooden shield. But there were also bows and arrows, lances, maces, and the tiger's claw. *I must get away, I must get away*, Mahendra repeated to himself. It was his mantra as he loaded his weapons onto Lakhan. The more he thought about it, the more he was convinced his plan would work. He rubbed Lakhan's back. He would miss his horse, his only true friend for so many years. He had tried to think of a way to take Lakhan with him, but he realized it would be too dangerous. He could not jeopardize his own escape. And it would raise more suspicion from his brothers. He could only hope that Lakhan would not try to follow him in a rescue attempt.

The men checked the safety of their weapons, the water level in their gourds, the number of empty sacks they were taking with them, their supply of opium, and headed out of their camp. By the time the last horse had left, the only sign of their presence in the valley between the dunes would be the ashes in the fire pit, some discarded goat bones from their last meal, and the patterns of forty-eight hooves in the sand. By the next morning, all these traces would be gone, buried under new layers of sand. By the next morning, Mahendra would be gone as well.

They galloped through the dark, Sikander reading the stars to lead the way. They were headed for a village not far from Devikot, where Mahendra had first joined the band. Now that he knew he was leaving, he felt a stab of regret. He would never again hear the wind whistle past him as he rode Lakhan in the dark, a black shadow in the night. He paid attention to every detail—the horse's back rippling beneath him, the rhythmic thud of hooves on sand. Even the smell of Lakhan's perspiration.

Sikander shouted a command, and the horses came to a standstill. Their target was just ahead, the light of several torch lamps wavering in and out of view. The estate was like a small village, huts scattered among cultivated lands, with the landowner's brick home in the center. An earthen embankment separated the croplands from the more gravelly lands uphill. It was a method of harvesting every drop of surface runoff from whatever rain there ever was. As a result, downhill from the main buildings was a cluster of green bushes, and this was where the men hid their horses. Without a word, each man dismounted, wrapped jute sacks around his waist with rope—to fill with grain or jewels, and to protect himself from possible cuts—and all but Mahendra and Sikander fanned out to encircle the estate.

There was nothing to do now but wait for Mulraj's signal. Mahendra leaned against Lakhan as the horse chewed some leaves. Sikander smoked his opium pipe. Mahendra feared this man, hated him, but he owed him his life several times over. It was because of Sikander that he had been so well accepted by the band and had survived as long as he had.

Mulraj's call came: two long, howl-like cries mimicking a fox. Mahendra waited for Sikander to head out, gave Lakhan a furtive pat with which he meant to express so much more, and quickly followed Sikander. Lakhan whinnied softly, and Sikander turned back in alarm.

"Make him be quiet! And what's wrong with your eyes?" Sikander's voice came out as a low growl.

"Nothing, nothing. Just some sand." Mahendra rubbed at his tears. "Lakhan won't make another sound. Let's go."

They clambered over the embankment and, crouching low, pushed their way up through waist-high mung bean plants. A form squatted ahead of them, and my brother gripped the *sirohi* hilt, but it was just Nasir. Beside him lay two bodies in a heap, limbs unnaturally tangled. The air was filled with the smell of blood and feces. Mahendra tried to think of something else, anything else, but he could not. Now his mind could conjure up only images of swords, turbans, horses flying over sand, bodies crumpling to the ground. He tried to think of the dance syllables he used to whisper to Lakhan, but even they were gone. The dance had finally left him. He followed Sikander blindly. The torchlights were out now. There was no moon; in the heavens, the deity Chandra and his ten white horses averted their gaze.

The house was long and low. It was the nature of such buildings, but to Mahendra, it seemed it was lying in wait for him. There were no sounds from within. Another fox-like cry. It was Mulraj again, confirming that all the guards had been killed or otherwise quieted. Mahendra stood behind Sikander at the door to the house. He felt like a ghost. Bodiless. He was being pushed forward by a force he could not control. Sikander turned, gave him a questioning look. Mahendra nodded, for what else could he do? Sikander pushed the door with his shoulder, but it was latched.

The next few moments passed for my brother in a blur of muffled sounds and sights. The heavy door opening. A shocked face in torchlight. The glint of the tiger's claw. Sikander rolling on the ground with another body, a hand over a mouth. The floor slippery with blood. Another shadow, a cry. Flames leaping, burning flesh. A moan, limbs flailing. Sikander's hand on his back, pushing him forward. His own hands warm and sticky. It was too dark to see what was on them, but he knew. He felt his way along a corridor, his hand encountering paintings and tapestries on the wall. Then there was a heavy curtain in front of him. He pushed it back. He did not care what he would find; he could not imagine that it would be worse than what was behind him.

He was in the bedroom. There was a bit more light; a small oil lamp burned in the corner. A raised platform covered in cushions dominated the room. A man lay among them, asleep. His breath was even. Mahendra tried to match his own breath to it. The room was like an oasis of peace. My brother stood transfixed, forgetting for a moment why he was there. Then the fox call sounded again. He looked at the form on the bed. Thankfully still asleep. Now that he was there, Mahendra had no intention of waking the man. He had played the scene in his mind so many times, but in an instant it dissolved. From the long legs lying splayed across the bed, Mahendra knew the man was tall, stronger than he. Mahendra crossed the room, looking for signs of anything valuable that he could take with him. Anything that would appease Sikander and assure him that Mahendra had done his best. The room exuded wealth and comfort, but he could not take rugs or paintings with him. At the foot of the bed, a trunk drew his attention. It was poorly shut, overfull. He made a motion toward it, hoping it would not creak as he opened it. His foot caught on something, and he grabbed at the bed to steady himself. The *sirohi* clattered to the clay floor.

"Who's there?" The man on the bed had sat up, and pointed a long object at Mahendra. The round blackness of its opening hovered unnervingly by Mahendra's head. He could not move.

"Do you know what this is?" the man asked.

Mahendra knew. He had seen one before.

"In the time it takes you to blink, I can blow a hole in your head."

Mahendra knew that, too. And he knew, at that moment, that he did not want to die. He started to cry.

The man laughed. "What are you, some kind of weakling? Are you even a man?"

Mahendra could not speak, could barely breathe.

"*Pfft!* I don't need to kill you. You won't last long out there anyway. And I don't like to kill. That's not what I do. I'll let you go, and you will never come back. Move!" The man shoved the barrel of the gun at Mahendra's side as he slid down to the end of the bed.

A voice shouted in Mahendra's head. This was not right. This man did not have the right to decide how this would end. Mahendra had a plan! This stranger could not change that. But Mahendra's sword lay on the ground where he had dropped it, and he dared not lean down to pick it up.

Then the man swung his legs down over the end of the bed, and Mahendra saw the shadow of his foot briefly obscure the glint of the sword. The man uttered a cry and doubled over, and the gun pointed away. Seized by an impulse, Mahendra pushed it out of the man's hands and bent to pick up the *sirohi*. In that moment, he saw the man's bare foot, blood pulsing inkily onto the floor. And then the man was lying on his back on the bed, shouting and thrashing, and Mahendra was bringing the *sirohi* down on him again and again, and every time he brought it down, something else taunted him. Chandrabai running from him in her yellow sari. Bapu casting him away like a piece of refuse. Saiprasad-ji spewing spittle in Ma's face. Padmini muffling her screams under her husband's blows. Me, dancing for my Lord in the temple. Red-rimmed eyes watching his every move.

Sikander's voice cut through the thick air around my brother. The room spun. He rubbed his arm across his face. His eyes and nose leaked warm wetness. His arms were slick with sweat. Blood dripped from the *sirohi*. And on the bed, the man lay motionless as a dark stain slowly spread across the sheets under him. Mahendra's stomach rose into his throat.

Sikander rushed into the room, but my brother could not look away from the body on the bed. From the face, eyes rolled back so only the whites showed. Amid the crisscross of cuts and blood marks, Mahendra saw something in that face. A long scar, stretching from lip to ear. How well I know that scar, though I saw it for a scant few days. My brother wondered where he had heard of a man with such a scar. And then he heard Ma's voice, and he remembered. He dropped the *sirohi*, and once again it fell to the floor. This time he would not pick it up. Sikander grabbed his arm and pulled him away, and then he was stumble-running back through the corridor, through the field, over the embankment. On the bloodied bed lay my patron and his promise.

It was evening again by the time Mahendra approached the sandstone walls of Jaisalmer. He had walked since dawn. His arm throbbed. It had, in fact, been cut in Uttam-ji's room—the only part of his plan that had come to pass as he had wanted. Particles of sand clung to the damp, reddened cloth that Sikander had wrapped around it. The arm hung limply, pulling at his neck in the sling Mahendra had fashioned with his turban and tied with his teeth. His hair clung to his forehead and cheeks. His mouth and throat were parched, his feet like lead. He dragged them forward, heading home. His mind swirled with visions of Uttam-ji's body. Unaware of the turn my life was taking, of the change in Uttam-ji's role, he did not know how he would face me or any of our family. He simply knew he needed to go home to Ma. He believed she would help him, would find a way to make things right. He did not even care if Bapu was there or not. People stared at him, pointing as he descended toward home, past the path to the burial ground and past the road to Ghadisar. He did not care about them, either.

He rounded the corner and entered the courtyard to our home. His stomach lurched. Now sweat trickled down his temples into his eyes, but he could not even lift his good arm to wipe it away.

"Ma!" he called out. "Ma, help!" He could not hear his own voice, but of course our mother did. He slid down against the wall and sat on the ground, closing his eyes. Some years ago, Ma had sat against the temple wall, telling him there was too much fight in him. That fight was gone now. Now she was next to him again, reaching out for him. He buried his face in the folds of her sari, and she rubbed his back. She was humming a song, a melody Mahendra recognized. Her body was tranquil, her voice steady, for she had been expecting this.

He put his head against her shoulder. "Ma, I've done something terrible."

"What is it, *beta*?" Ma spoke as though nothing he said could be that terrible. It gave him the courage to go on.

He pulled his head away from her. "Adhira's patron. What was his name?"

"Was?"

"I killed him, Ma." As soon as he said it out loud, Mahendra felt better. It was done. Ma hesitated for a moment, then continued to rub his back. Her head was turned away from him.

"Did you hear me, Ma?"

Ma sighed. "I did, *beta*." She was quiet for a moment, and then turned her head back to him. It was dark now, but she had brought a lamp out with her, and in its light the wrinkles on her face were deeper than ever before. "It was not his fault, you know."

Mahendra wondered what she meant.

"He paid a price, expected a certain thing in return," she continued. "And when he did not receive it, he simply brought it back."

"I don't understand."

Ma turned toward Mahendra. "Why did you kill Uttam-ji?"

"I didn't know it was him. We were in his home, and he had a gun, and I had no choice."

Ma hid her face in her hands. "Oh."

"Ma, what's happened?"

She just shook her head, her hands still hiding her face.

"Ma, please don't be angry at me! I didn't know, I swear it to you. I hate myself for having done this, for having ruined Adhira's chance at happiness. I know you said he was a good man. Please don't make it worse."

"Oh, *beta*, don't hate yourself. It's Saiprasad you should hate, and maybe me."

"Saiprasad-ji? You? What do you mean?"

And then he heard words that made no sense and yet did make sense. Ma was saying that she would never forgive herself for not preventing it, but as Mahendra's anger rose in him like a fire, he was convinced it was Saiprasad-ji and especially Bapu who were stoking it. Bapu, he thought—Bapu, with his devotion to dance, with his self-imposed blinders—had ruined everyone. Everything.

"Where is Bapu?" Mahendra asked.

"Leave Bapu out of it, *beta*. Bapu has suffered enough."

"Enough? You're telling me Bapu is the one who has suffered?"

"Believe me, he has suffered. In ways you cannot understand. And he wants you back."

"He said so?"

"In his own way, yes."

"That means he has not said so. Why do you keep protecting him?"

And then Bapu walked into the courtyard, carrying a torch. Mahendra lunged at him while Ma shouted, "No, he doesn't know!"

"Know what?" Bapu stood still, looking at Mahendra, who was now paralyzed, standing between our parents. Bapu's face was weary, old. The sense of purpose that used to animate it, the sense of purpose that used to madden Mahendra, was gone. His body was bowed, as if struggling under a heavy weight. For he had in fact suffered greatly.

"Know what?" Now Bapu looked at Ma, who had risen and was leaning against the wall. "What other secrets have you been keeping from me?"

"Nothing, Gandar," Girija said quietly.

But of course it was not nothing. "Ma, you have to tell him."

"I can't, Mahendra. Please, it's nothing."

Bapu looked from Ma to Mahendra and back, his head swiveling. Mahendra did not see a father, a dancer, a teacher who had given of himself every day of his life until his very body was on the verge of giving out. Instead, Bapu looked to my brother like a confused bird. Uttam-ji's words came back to him: *Are you even a man?*

"Then I'll tell him." But even as the truth came out, even as he said the words, Mahendra felt his anger dwindle and give way to an aching sadness. "Ma just told me. Adhira—your precious priest forced himself on her before she went with Uttam-ji."

"Saiprasad-ji? Adhira? But . . . but she is living at the temple. Uttam-ji is her patron. She is a *devadasi*!"

"She's a girl, Bapu! She's just a girl, and something terrible happened to her because you let it happen. Don't you see? She's not something divine. Lord Krishna isn't protecting her. That was what *you* were supposed to do, Bapu. Bapu?"

Bapu had fallen to the ground. In the light of the lamp, his face was pale, yellow. His bony legs were crumpled under him. For a fleeting moment, he looked like Hari Dev after a fit, only much older. Mahendra felt a rush of pity for him. Pity, and a moment of recognition, that he and Bapu shared the same devastating belief that Bapu could have made things different.

Mahendra was unable to lift Bapu with his injured arm. "Ma, can you help me?"

But Ma was no longer strong enough, either. Instead, she knelt on the ground and took Bapu's head on her legs, stroking it as though he were a baby. Mahendra looked on helplessly. Bapu's breath was shallow. He looked up at Mahendra for a moment, and Mahendra caught his gaze and held it with his own eyes. *This is when you apologize*, he thought. *This is when you apologize to me, and to Ma, and to Adhira, and to Padmini.* But Bapu said nothing, simply looked past Mahendra, trying to detach himself from his body.

Mahendra backed slowly away. He could not return home; he thought the emptiness he saw in Bapu's eyes told him that "home" was gone forever. He felt, once and for all, no longer a son. Not a son, not a dancer, not a man, not a warrior, not a husband, not a father. Not even Ma needed him now. She knelt, cradling Bapu's head and singing softly, without even a glance toward him. The air hummed with insects while my family unraveled and in my quarters I sang a prayer, a *vandana* to my Lord Krishna, that he comfort them. A hawk shrieked overhead, circled once, a brown shape against the blue sky, and flew out toward the desert. Mahendra crossed the courtyard and followed it, into the space between things.

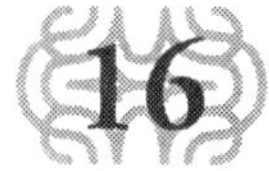

16

Gandar and Adhira

Summer 1569

Bapu sat by the edge of Ghadisar Lake, trying in vain to gather some strength from the place where he had always found peace. Padmini, Chandrabai, and her little daughter sat about one-quarter of the way around the lake, huddled in a pool of shade. They were watching him, likely talking about him, he thought, but he could not bring himself to care. Every part of his body ached, try as he might to rise above it. He felt surrounded by failures of the physical form. His own body was failing him, Saiprasad-ji's body had fallen prey to terrible weakness, I was defiled, and Mahendra, wherever he was, had been injured. Bapu did not even spare a thought for Hari Dev. After his lifetime of deep belief in the power of the mind over the body, life was finally eroding the foundations of his faith. Glancing across the diminished expanse of water—summer was half over, and still there was no sign of rain—he wondered if something was wrong with Padmini, too. He had yet to learn of her plight or know that Hari had given her the ability to hide her shame. He had simply seen her a few times from a distance, as he did now. It was no coincidence, of course, that she was always leaving places just as he arrived.

At this time on a regular day, Bapu would have been conducting the morning rituals at the temple. But ever since that day six months earlier when he had learned of what had happened to me, there had been no more regular days for him. Each day now was a new challenge, an uncharted territory that he had to cross as best he could with the dwindling hope that something better would begin on the other side. I wanted to tell him that I did not blame him for what had happened—I knew he just hadn't been able to see the danger—but he rarely spent any time alone with me any longer, and when he did, something in his eyes prevented me from speaking.

"Gandar-ji! Gandar-ji!"

Bapu looked up. Meera ran toward him, her body hurtling forward, wanting to go faster than her little legs could take her. My father had a vision of me at that age, running in the temple garden, and the memory rooted him in place. Meera nearly collided with him. Instinct took over, and he held out his arm to prevent her from toppling into the water. She looked at him shyly.

"Hello, Meera." He had never known how to speak to small children, unless he was teaching them at the temple.

"Hello. What are you doing?"

"Just sitting here."

"Meera sit here, too," she said, and dropped down on the ground next to him, wiggling her toes.

Bapu's own feet were bony, dusty, the heels cracked. It had been days since he had danced, and his feet did not miss it. This realization bore down on him with the intensity of the sun. He watched Meera's toes and thought of Saiprasad-ji's comments about my legs when I was so small. Now he could not fathom how he could have ignored them. Saiprasad-*ji*. Bapu now thought of him as Ma did: Saiprasad. Stripped of any sign of respect. Not in the way she called him Gandar, but in quite the opposite way. It repulsed Bapu to see him at the temple now. I could not bear to be in his presence, either, and in an unspoken agreement, we never found ourselves together.

Meera pointed. "Look!" A crane stood in the water, motionless. Meera rose, held up one foot, laughed, and fell over. She turned to my father. "Now you be a funny bird."

"Not now."

Meera folded her hands together. "Please?"

"Oh, all right." Bapu stood gingerly, his knees cracking. He folded his arms like wings, bent his back, stuck out his neck and head, and lifted one leg. The child laughed again, and the sound rang clear and pure, skimming the water's surface. Bapu felt an immense sadness. He sat back down.

"Go. Go back to your Ma. You should not be in the sun like this. Go." He waved in the direction from which she had come.

"Go!" he said again, with greater sternness than he intended.

Meera hesitated, then puckered her mouth into a frown and ran back to Chandrabai.

It was midmorning and getting hot. Bapu ought to have moved into the shade. But my father welcomed the discomfort of the heat and the sun's harsh rays beating down on his bare head.

Then came the rhythmic *tap-tap* of Ma's walking stick. Her shadow fell upon him, and the tapping stopped as she stood still. Bapu looked up, but the sun shone behind her and he could not see her face. She sat down on the ground two paces away from him, close enough to be companionable, but far enough to inhabit a separate space. She said nothing, just sat. She wore one end of her sari over her head, something she had been doing with more frequency, pulling into herself.

Bapu spoke the thought that had been prowling the edges of his consciousness for months. "I have lived too long."

Ma turned toward him, and her face emerged from the shadows. She did not deny what he said, but her expression was questioning.

"I am sixty-nine," he continued, as much to himself and to the gods as to her. "I have lived much longer than most people. Why? If I had left this world a few years ago, things would be different. Better. Maybe my time should have been when I was sixty. Or sixty-four." Sixty-four—four cycles of sixteen.

Ma said nothing, just listened.

Bapu's words came tumbling out, filling the space her silence provided. "I had to continue. Mahendra was not taking my place. Someone had to teach the *devadasis*."

At the mention of Mahendra, Ma's face contracted. Mahendra had not returned since that night six months ago.

"He will come back," Bapu said without conviction. "You know he always does."

Ma shook her head. Bapu thought of Mahendra's bloodied bandage and knew she was right. In the heat and sand of the desert, wounds festered easily. Something swelled in him, like an animal struggling to surface from the sand for air.

"That first day," he whispered, "that first day back at the temple was the most difficult of my life. Even more so than the day Mahendra told me what had happened. At the temple, the *devadasis* lined up as usual. I couldn't tell what they knew, what they thought of me."

For eight days he had been unable to bring himself to the temple, to face me. I had waited each of those days with the *devadasis*, wanting to learn, needing to dance.

Ma sat still, her head turned toward the water, but Bapu knew she was listening. It felt good to speak.

"Adhira," he continued. It was difficult for him even to say my name. "Adhira came and stood before me, and I could not look her in the eye. And then she danced. And, Girija, she was more beautiful than ever. When I understood she was not paying attention to me, I managed to look at her face. Every motion of her eyebrows, every unfurling of her fingers, every step she took was perfect. It was as though . . . she had become truly divine. The others stopped dancing and just watched her."

Ma nodded her head ever so slightly. She already knew all this. Bapu continued anyway.

"In that instant, I realized she owes me nothing. Nothing. Everything comes from within her, not from what I have taught her. She has no need for me, Girija." He swallowed a hard lump in his throat. "And then she stood still and looked at me. I do not know what I expected. There was no anger, no pity, no fear in her eyes, but tears fell from them. She looked at me like that, and then I could not bear it anymore. I left."

Ma breathed in, and it was a wet, muffled sound.

"I'm so sorry, Girija." The words emerged, unfamiliar, out into the open.

Ma continued to remain silent, although the wall around her

began to slip, the way a mud embankment slides down on itself when it finally rains. When she did speak, however, the words came from far away. "Not now. It's too late for sorry."

There was a rock in my father's chest. He wanted to close the distance between him and Ma, to lean against her. But he dared not. Ma drew up one knee, folded her hands on it, and rested her head on them, her face turned toward him. He expected to see anger or sadness in it, but there was neither. What he saw was a striking resemblance to me, and so he shut his eyes.

"I do not blame you, Gandar. You did what you knew to do, what you felt you had to do. But now everything's changed."

Bapu kept his eyes shut. "So what do I do now?"

Ma gathered her sari around her and shifted her position so she was sitting next to him. Her knees touched his, the soft cotton of her sari brushing against his skin. She smelled of jasmine, of the lush greenery and cool breezes of Mount Abu. She reached out and took his hands in hers. Neither one could remember the last time they had held each other like this. He opened his eyes and for the first time noticed that her hands were as wrinkled as his own. She lifted his to her cheek and held them there for a moment. He looked into her eyes, whose depth and darkness now lay hidden behind a milky layer.

"Do you really want me to tell you what to do?"

"Yes."

"Take Adhira to the royal palace."

"What?"

"She has been summoned there."

"By whom? Why?"

"By the Raja. To dance."

"Is there some ceremony taking place?"

"I don't think so. I think he just wants to see her dance."

"For no reason? What, to entertain the Raja, who stopped sending payments to the temple years ago?"

"You should feel honored, you know."

"Says who? And who told you that she has been summoned?"

"Padmini."

"Padmini?"

"Yes, Padmini, your daughter. She arranged for it."

"What business is it of hers to make such arrangements? To decide where Adhira dances? After all these years, she reappears and gives orders?"

Ma sighed. "You asked me what you should do, and I'm telling you. Padmini is just trying to help. Her husband works in the court. He has connections there."

"Her husband. The one she left the temple for?"

"Yes, of course, that husband. At the court, Adhira can show everyone the beauty of your dance. Even some of those foreigners. Let them learn from her. Spread the art of this dance."

"The Muslims? She is supposed to dance for them?"

"Emperor Akbar now has a son, and his mother is a Rajput princess. The boy, Selim, is part Rajasthani. We can't stop it anymore. You have to see this now. Besides, you saw how few people attended the last festival at the temple."

Was this, Bapu wondered, what Manavi-ji had been trying to tell him so many years ago? "I won't let her dance there. I'll dance instead."

Ma shook her head slowly. "No. You won't be protecting her that way. The Raja summoned her, not you. She's young, and you said yourself her dance is divine. That's what you should show them."

"Does Adhira know yet?" he asked softly.

"Yes. She was . . . afraid to tell you herself."

"Because she knows she should not go."

Ma let out an exasperated sigh. "No, Gandar. Because she knew that was what you would say."

"What happened to our sweet, simple daughter?" Bapu said, then realized how oblivious that question revealed him to be, just as Ma opened her mouth to berate him. He put up his hand to staunch the flow of her anger. Then he picked up a pebble and threw it into the lake. It fell with a *plop*, and a cloud of gnats rose and resettled elsewhere.

Ma nodded. "Good." She pushed herself up, leaning on her stick, and held out a hand to him. "Come, Gandar-ji, let's get out of the sun."

Bapu took her hand, and she led him away from the water's edge. He wondered if he had imagined the way she had just addressed him.

In the evening, when it was time to close the temple, Bapu lingered in the dance chamber, hoping, yet also fearing, that I would be the one to come put out the oil lamps. But Saiprasad-ji was meeting with the accountant in the courtyard, and so it was Chandrabai who arrived instead. She backed away toward the entrance when she saw him.

"I'm sorry, Guru-ji. I didn't know you were here."

"No, that is all right," he said, waving her back in.

She approached him hesitantly.

"I have been wanting to talk to you." It was difficult for Bapu to say the words, but he felt it would be even more difficult to speak directly with me. I wish he had tried.

Chandrabai looked around uncomfortably as she stood before my father. "Yes, Guru-ji. About what?"

Bapu turned from her and occupied his hands by rearranging the flowers on the shrine. "I would like you to give a message to Adhira."

"About the court summons?"

Gandar turned back to face her. "You know about that?"

Chandrabai nodded and cast her glance downward. "Yes. And so does Adhira."

Gandar looked down at the soft, faded flowers in his hands. He did not ask her anything about Padmini. He did not ask her what else she knew. He saw now that many things, many relationships, many transformations had been taking place for years without his knowledge. It was not his place or his time to try to understand them now.

"And what did Adhira say?"

Chandrabai looked up, relieved that this was his only question. "She said she looked forward to it. She said it would be an adventure. She asked to see Hari Dev before going. I told her it was just for one evening, she could see him after, but still she insisted on seeing him before." No one knew that I had decided not to return. This would be my good-bye to Hari, and he would need me to allow him to let go.

Bapu nodded. Chandrabai continued to stand before him. He wanted to say something, but his mind, clouded and swirling with thoughts for so long, was now suddenly empty. He turned back to the shrine, placing the flowers in a pile, watching the spirals of smoke from the stick of incense. Eventually Chandrabai left the chamber, and my father was alone with the echoes of the unsaid.

The next day, Bapu waited in the temple courtyard after rest time for the arrival of the guards from the royal palace. The emptiness in his mind had persisted through the night. I was going to dance for the Muslims; he thought he should have slept fitfully, if at all. Yet he woke up to find he had slept a deep, dreamless sleep, as had I. Now he felt there should be some commotion about the temple, some activity to mark the momentous nature of what we were about to do, yet it was a typically hot, quiet afternoon. Bapu wondered if maybe this was the dream, if maybe it was actually nighttime and he was fast asleep.

Then Hari Dev entered the courtyard. Bapu watched, more aware of him than he had been in a long time. His son was a man. My little big brother. His legs were still crooked, he still walked awkwardly, but there was strength in him, and our father saw this. Hari took off his shoes carefully and placed them neatly along the inside of the courtyard wall. He took no notice of Bapu as he walked directly across the courtyard and into the temple itself, where I awaited him.

I sat on the floor by the entrance to the inner sanctum. Hari knew he would find me there. When he walked in, I could read the fear and hope on his face, one mixed with the other. He stood in front of me, awkward yet manly, his hands dangling at his sides. I rose and rested my head against his chest. He had finally grown taller than I was. His chin came to rest on the top of my head, and his arms slowly rose. They hesitated, then wrapped gently around me, and we stood in silence. I heard the steady rhythm of his heart.

Finally he let go, and I saw the tears spilling from his eyes.

"You know this is what must happen, right?" I asked him. I had practiced this conversation, knowing how difficult it would be.

He nodded.

"And your heart, is it happy with Sudhali?"

He smiled and nodded again. I had seen for myself the effect that the girl from the potter's shop had on him. But it was a relief to have him confirm my hope.

"Then you no longer need me, Hari. Don't shed those tears for yourself, or even for me. I think the worst has already happened to me. If you must cry, do so for Bapu and for Ma. Theirs have been the hardest battles. And then, when the time comes, let go of them, and the temple, and be free."

Hari wiped his eyes with his hand and breathed wetly. I felt a hardness in my throat. I would miss him so much.

"Is that what you are doing?" he asked. But he knew full well the answer.

He took my hands in his, and I suddenly wished I had something of myself to give him to keep. But I wore no jewelry; I had nothing with which to cut a lock of my hair.

He saw me looking around and smiled gently. "I do not need anything." And he touched my cheek with the tips of his fingers. "Goodbye, Adhi," he whispered.

I looked into his soft brown eyes, beneath his damp lashes. "I won't be back, Hari. Ever again."

"I know. But you won't ever be gone, either." Having watched our brother be neither one thing nor another, Hari now understood that I could be with him and elsewhere at the same time. He squeezed my hands one last time, then turned and walked out of the sanctum. I heard his shuffling step recede, then his feet slipping into his shoes and their muted tap-slide on the stone floor growing fainter and fainter.

Bapu watched Hari cross the courtyard. My brother's lips moved. Bapu knew he was counting.

"Son," he called out, "she will be back; it is just for one evening." But Hari walked through the gateway and did not turn back.

Bapu had no time to ponder the meaning of Hari's worry, for the watchman announced the arrival of two royal guards. He rose to his feet, wondering what to do. He peered at the guards through the opening in the wall, regarding them with equal measures of dislike and apprehension. Each one had a sword hanging at his side, a yellow cummerbund bright against his foreign-looking white *kurta pajama*, a yellow turban wrapped tightly on his head, sequined red *juthis* with upturned toes on his feet.

I emerged from the temple, aware with every step that my feet would never touch those stones again. "Bapu."

The other *devadasis* followed me at a distance. I wore a bright pink skirt and blouse with a silver border and had put on some simple silver bangles. Something tightened around Bapu's heart. He was about to instruct the watchman to send the guards away, to say he had made a mistake, when they both stepped into the courtyard and bowed toward him.

"It's all right," I assured him. "Don't worry about me."

"Guru-ji," one of them said. "It is an honor to accompany you. Please don't hurry. We will wait."

His politeness surprised Bapu, and there was nothing my father could do but go out to them with me. I stood by his side now, my head bowed. Bapu wanted me to look up, to be proud. *These men are just guards*, he wanted to say. *They are nothing. You have come from the realm of the gods*. But no person is nothing, and I bowed my head not in shame or deference, but simply because of the solemnity and weight of the moment.

Bapu straightened himself to stand tall. "Let us go." He took the lead, walking to the gateway. Then he stopped short. In front of us, an empty palanquin rested on the ground. Its red silk curtains were pulled aside, and a tiger skin stretched across the woven seat. Bapu could not imagine riding in it. Everyone's eyes were on us, and it irked my father that these guards were making him feel uncomfortable here in the temple, in his domain. It was time for me to lead the way. So I stepped forward, and immediately the guards were at my side.

One of them reached out his arm as if to help me. "Allow us."

"No!" Bapu cried. "No one may touch her!"

The guards looked startled, then nodded and withdrew their arms. I climbed into the palanquin and helped Bapu in. He tripped on a cushion and lurched forward, almost falling onto me, and I held out my arms to catch his brittle frame. I shifted to make room for him, and the guards lifted the palanquin onto their shoulders. It rose and swayed, and the curtain fell into place, enclosing us in a cocoon of filtered red light. The palanquin was small, but Bapu made sure always to keep some space between us. I watched a slit of sunlight slanting in between the curtains and falling across the tiger skin. After a while, I turned to him and smiled, and some of the weight bearing down on him lifted.

The sounds of Chauhata Square floated into the palanquin, and Bapu parted the curtains slightly. A laughing child ran past—a brown blur, a flash of white teeth. Flutter-flying behind him, attached to a string in his hand, was a diamond-shaped piece of cloth, flame orange against the blue sky. The square was teeming with people. There were fragments of a foreign, guttural language and signs of new styles of clothing. There were more light-skinned people. But no more beggars or lepers than before.

When the palanquin came to a halt and was lowered to the ground, Bapu assumed what he hoped was an indifferent pose and refused the guards' offer to help him, although his legs were stiff and one knee joint was locked. We were in front of Raj Mahal, the royal palace. In front of us rose a massive wall. The balconies of the palace's seven stories began two stories up. Two guards stepped aside and opened a carved wooden door. With one leading the way and another taking the rear, Bapu followed me into the royal palace.

A thousand impressions came at us as we were led through hallways and past chambers. Floors of polished tiles and mosaic, smooth yet ridged underfoot. Then lush carpets, their deep red and orange pile absorbing the sounds of footsteps. Paintings of brilliant colors hung from the stone walls, illumined by shafts of light from the inner courtyard and occasional oil lamps affixed to the walls. Strains of music, some from familiar instruments and others seeming to travel from faraway places, floated out from behind curtained doors. Tapestries hung from poles. In the stairway, small statues nestled in recesses in the walls. Bapu looked for Krishna but could not find him. In fact, many of the recesses were empty. I hoped that he was not far.

The front guard pulled back a curtain and opened the wooden

door behind it. Bapu and I were thrust into another hall. At the other end, across an expanse of fabric, cushions, bolsters, rugs, and tapestries, and blurred by the haze of sweet smoke that drifted in the air, were two divans. Upon one of them reclined the Raja. Upon the other sat another man. At their feet were arranged several women in gauzy robes. A young boy whispered something in the Raja's ear.

The Raja's voice was deep and jovial, like that of a man with few worries. "Aha, so this is the famous Gandar-ji and his daughter! Let me have a look at you two."

In a daze, Bapu held his hands, palms together, in front of him and bowed. I did the same. As we did so, a tall figure separated herself from a cluster to the side of the room and came toward us. Padmini.

She stood before us, bejeweled and dressed in a heavily embroidered skirt and tunic, my sister, who had long ago turned her back to dance and now faced it again. I had not seen her since my coming-of-age ceremony. Bapu had seen her only from a distance. She had retained her gracefulness, but there was something in her eyes that unsettled Bapu, and he saw on her face the traces of what he assumed was some type of affliction.

The Raja waved us forward impatiently. "Don't just stand there like statues! Padmini, bring them to me."

Bapu and I followed her across the room. Despite his vow to stand tall, Bapu gazed downward, avoiding the Raja's face. In so doing, he caught the steady stare of one of the women who sat languidly at his feet. Jewels dripped from her neck and ears.

"So this is the divine dancer? Interesting. Let me see your face."

I raised my head and took a step forward.

"Well, very beautiful indeed," the Raja said. "No need to look so serious. This is a place of enjoyment." Then he fell quiet.

Positioned slightly behind me, Bapu could no longer see my expression, only the effect that it seemed to have on the Raja and his guest. They contemplated me in silence, and even the rest of the room fell quiet. The Raja's cheerful countenance turned to one of solemnity, as though he had been reminded, and rightly so, of more weighty subjects than pure enjoyment. For a moment, Bapu dared to hope the Raja might reinstate court support for our temple and dancers.

"Well," the Raja now said, straightening his posture and shaking his head, as though to cast off an unwelcome mood, "now that you are here, let's begin the performances. I hope you can stay awhile. His Excellency Jabir Shah Khan is here from the Emperor's court and is eager to see what Jaisalmer has to offer. And of course we are looking forward to seeing what the dancers and musicians from his homeland have in store for us."

His Excellency nodded solemnly. Bapu now understood that my dance was to be a part of something much grander than he had expected. Jabir Shah Khan looked at us with unconcealed curiosity. Bapu returned his gaze. He would not be intimidated by this foreign man and his waist-tight coat and jeweled turban. Who was he, he thought, to judge our dance?

A door at the back of the room opened, and a long line of men and women filed in. Some were dressed in familiar Hindu outfits, while others wore simpler variations of Jabir Shah Khan's clothing. Several of the women wore diaphanous layers of muslin, through which the outline of their legs was clearly visible. They appeared to Bapu as he had imagined: immoral. He averted his eyes, the only man in the room to do so.

The performers settled in a semicircle, and Padmini gestured to me to join them and to Bapu to sit to the side, where she herself sat as well. On the other side of Bapu was a short, stocky man in a simple tunic and sash. On his head was a black cap, like an overturned bowl. Bapu thought he looked like a silly child.

The man leaned in toward Bapu. "Is this your first *mehfil*?"

Bapu looked at him, confused.

"*Mehfil*. You know, this." The man gestured at the room in general.

Bapu resisted an urge to ask Padmini for an explanation and instead simply nodded.

"What is your art form?"

How could this man not know this? "I am the dance master of the Krishna temple."

"Dancer, eh? So old! I'm a poet."

The Raja and the Muslim guest were in discussion, paying little attention to the artists on the floor. I sat tall, my bell bag before me, as the musicians finished tuning their instruments and pulled slow, alluring melodies from them. The poet poked Bapu's leg.

"Beautiful, nah? Have you seen those instruments before? All from my home, Persia."

Bapu nodded at the smiling poet. He wished the man would be quiet and stop touching him. He began to worry about what I would dance. But the poet had more to say.

"I'm hoping to impress the emissary, the Raja's guest, enough that he'll take me back with him," he confided. "Akbar's court—that's where I want to go. I hear they pay poets handsomely. I've been at this court five years now, but it's time to move on. I'm headed for Akbar's court. And the girls there!" Here, the poet grinned and looked Bapu over. "One is never too old for that."

Disgusted, my father motioned for the poet to be quiet and turned away from him. He wondered what kind of poetry could come from a man with a mind such as his.

The music rose and fell in swells, and the poet was finally quiet. Bapu looked around the room. Many of the artists had closed their eyes. Some swayed with the music, as did I. He welcomed the opportunity to close his eyes as well. The melancholy strains of a flute, interspersed with the plucked sounds of a stringed instrument, lifted him from where he sat and brought him soaring over desert dunes, across desolate plains, toward mountain passes, to places he had only imagined. I found him there. He did not see me, but I chose that moment in which to say good-bye to him. Without understanding why, he thought of Ma.

The air stirred in front of him, and he opened his eyes. Two tall, slender women had risen. I saw him take in their beauty, although he did not know where to look. He felt he was committing an affront by staring at them, yet clearly they were there to be watched. From the moment they began undulating across the floor, they were grace and refinement. Their movements were unfamiliar, yet they depicted surprise, anger, longing in unmistakable ways. Around the room, the other artists, guards, and servants were nodding in time with the music, absorbed by the performance. Much more absorbed than the temple crowds ever seemed.

Now the Raja beckoned to me. The musicians quieted their instruments and looked expectantly toward me as I rose. I looked forward to dancing. Bapu moved as though to rise as well, but Padmini reached out and held him down by the shoulder. Her commanding touch shocked him into staying in place. The Muslim guest raised his eyebrow in question to the Raja.

The Raja sat forward. "Adhira. That is your name, right? Would you like the musicians to accompany you?"

I nodded and asked for the lute player to stay, and for a *pakhawaj* player to join him.

"Of course. Please bear one thing in mind, though, as you dance. Our esteemed guest is of the Muslim faith. Do not offend him with inappropriate depictions of . . . well, Muslims don't portray their god." Here the Raja looked pointedly at me, and then, seeing that I understood, past me at Padmini and Bapu.

Bapu was confused. *Of course she would not portray the Muslim god,* he thought. How could she do that? But the Raja was still looking at me, and Bapu remembered the missing statues of deities from the niches in the stairwell. It dawned on him that I was not to portray any gods, not even Hindu ones. *What is dance without the deities?* he wanted to ask. He turned toward Padmini, but she simply shrugged her shoulders. He was about to say something aloud, to explain that I could not possibly dance under these circumstances, when I responded.

"Of course. I understand."

Jabir Shah Khan clapped his hands once and smiled. "Excellent! I hear your dance is very expressive. Show me how you portray a woman waiting for her lover."

Bapu was appalled when he saw me nod. Still blind to what was possible, he watched numbly as I wrapped my coils of bells around my ankles. I knew exactly what I would do. When I was ready, I rose. Bapu saw the slight smile on my lips and understood that I was already dancing in my mind. I pulled an imaginary veil over my face and opened my hands into a lotus flower, and suddenly Bapu wanted to laugh aloud. I was going to depict Radha, Krishna's consort, waiting for her lover. No one need know who the characters were. Radha could be a woman, earthly, of flesh and blood. The Muslim would never guess the truth. I would perform before him and show him the wonders of Hindu dance and faith without even seeming to do so. Humming, I nodded to the musicians, then faced the Raja and his guests.

I stepped into the center of the dance space and bowed, holding my palms together in front of me. Ever so slowly, I brought my hands to my forehead, my mouth, my chest. Mind, breath, heart. I thanked our ancestors for their gift of dance, and in so doing I became Radha, thanking my Lord Krishna for my very existence. Radha, Krishna's favorite among the cowherding maidens. I sat, one leg folded in, one knee raised. Upon it, I rested my clasped hands. I looked up and showed with unfurling fingers the flowers upon the tree that rose above me. I gestured, palms up, to the fields and hills around me, where Krishna and I played, danced, and grew up together. Krishna, the blue-skinned one, my childhood friend, my true love. With my arms I showed how the world had pulled us apart: Krishna was gone to overthrow and kill his evil uncle, Kamsa, and I, Radha, awaited him. Krishna had departed to safeguard the virtues of truth, and I waited for him. Krishna married Rukmini, raised a family with her, fought the great war of Ayodhya, and still I waited for him.

The musicians repeated the same phrase of their melody over and over again. I was Radha, waiting with eager anticipation, one hand becoming a mirror held to my face, the fingers of the other hand lining my eyes with kohl. I smiled, pleased with what I saw. I was Radha, waiting happily, reaching up to pluck flowers from the branches above, and placing them in my hair, my fingers rippling down the length of my tresses. I was Radha, waiting impatiently, until I shed bitter tears and the tears became a lake that spread beneath my outstretched fingers. I was Radha, waiting sadly, resting my head on my knee and holding my arms out in yearning, until my mind summoned the strains of a flute and, raising my head, I opened wide my eyes and rejoiced, only to find Krishna still gone.

There were infinite ways in which to depict Radha awaiting her moon-faced lover. I had only just begun. But the Raja held up his hand and gestured to the musicians to silence their instruments.

Distressed at this further offense, Bapu watched as I brought my hands together and concluded my dance. I knew this was simply a beginning, and I bore the Raja no ill will for having interrupted me. Besides, I wanted to experience the worlds of the other dancers and musicians.

The Raja clapped his hands like a child. "Wonderful. Beautiful! I see you have many things to show us. You could fill the whole night, no doubt! But let us leave time now for the others." He glanced at his guest.

Jabir Shah Khan nodded emphatically. I returned to my place in the semicircle of artists, some of whom shifted to the side to give me ample space. My father seethed inside. He was unable to relinquish his sense of outrage. I had embodied Radha, the ultimate representation of love for God, endless and unconditional, and then had been made to stop abruptly. He wanted to ask the Raja to allow me to dance again, but the Raja was in discussion with his guest. Jabir Shah Khan was leaning over to say something to the Raja, who furrowed his eyebrows and bit his lip. The Muslim guest widened his eyes at him in warning, and the Raja nodded and held up his hand, as if to say they would discuss it later. The guest seemed satisfied.

By the time the Raja looked up, I had removed my bells and in the space in which I had danced now stood three men in stiff caps and white robes. The men began to chant and spin.

"Sufi," the poet whispered. "Like Emperor Akbar's main advisor."

We watched the men. As they whirled, faster and faster, their robes spread out, billowing around them.

"What are they chanting?" Bapu wondered aloud.

"Devotion," the poet answered. "They say that God has neither form nor gender, and none is equal to God. They let go of all notions of division and realize the divine unity."

Dance in such a way to become one with everything. The words of Bapu's father, which he had passed on to all the *devadasis.* All around the room, the artists and court attendants were swaying as they sat.

"I've been studying the writings of the poet who inspired them," Bapu's neighbor continued. "Rumi, they call him. I pray to God that one day I may be like him."

The men's robes became a swirling blur, the features of their faces no longer discernible. Their presence filled the room, pushing out almost everything else. Their chant seeped into me, into my father, who let their whirling mesmerize his eyes. The poet's words, the women's languid expressions, the Raja's haughtiness, Jabir Shah Khan's watchful eyes all fell away, replaced only by a vastness both empty and full, like an endless expanse of desert.

Eventually the whirling dancers ceded their place to musicians. The opening strains of a new melody began, slowly building in strength. Then the rhythmic beat of a foreign drum joined in. Around us, people chanted and clapped their hands. Someone began to sing in a language we could not understand. His voice bore the freshness and clarity of rainwater, and his full-throated singing pulled at Bapu's chest. He repeated the same lyrics over and over again, as I had done in my dance. Tears spilled from Bapu's eyes.

What seemed to my father like an eternity later but to me like just a flash, the Raja and his guest were stretching, some of the artists were rising, some remained in the slumber to which they had succumbed. Bapu rose, his legs stiff from being seated, his face stiff from dried tears. Padmini helped him up, and together they came to me. The square of sky outside the window behind the Raja bore the smoky-gray traces of early dawn. The musicians gathered their instruments, rubbing their eyes, and retreated. Bapu wondered how he and I should take our leave, when the Raja beckoned to us, as Chandrabai had told me he might. Padmini led us to him.

"I meant what I said earlier," he said, looking at me directly and not at my father. "Your dance was . . . transporting. You must dance again here."

Padmini spoke quickly before either Bapu or I could respond. "Yes, of course, Your Majesty."

The Raja still looked only at me. "I think you would make a good addition to the court, no?"

"An addition, Your Majesty?" Bapu blurted out.

The Raja gestured vaguely across the room. "I've no doubt you'll find the company to your liking."

I nodded. So far, he was right. "Yes, Your Majesty."

Bapu pulled me back. "Adhira! You don't have to . . . "

The Raja shifted his gaze to my father. "Yes, as a matter of fact, she does. Besides, this will be a temporary arrangement. His Excellency Khan is bestowing on her the highest honor: she will soon belong to the Emperor's court."

The words fell on Bapu like splinters of glass. As for me, Krishna caught them in his hand before they could cut me. Instead, they felt like small thorns that could only scratch me.

"In Delhi?" Padmini showed surprise for the first time.

The Raja glanced at the guest, who nodded benevolently. "Yes. She will stay here, in my court, until my daughter marries Akbar, and then Adhira will travel with her to Delhi, or perhaps Agra. I am sealing an alliance with the Emperor."

Padmini lowered her eyes. "And when would you like Adhira to come back here?"

"Well, no reason to delay. She can stay now. I can't imagine there is anything she needs that we cannot provide her with here."

Panic swelled in Bapu's throat. "Now?"

"Yes, now. We'll arrange for you to come see her in a few months if you wish, when she is well settled in. I have found it is best to wait a little." He glanced over at Padmini, as if to ask, *Will there be a problem?*

Padmini shook her head.

"Well, then, it is settled. There is a woman who attends to some of the courtesans. She'll see to it that you have what you need. First, some new clothing. This outfit of yours does not put forward your best attributes. And then you must learn the proper Muslim greeting, the *amad* and *salaam*." The Raja sat back, pleased with himself.

Bapu watched wordlessly as an elderly woman appeared from nowhere and guided me toward the door at the back of the room. Her hand on my arm was soft but strong. Bapu wanted to throw himself at my feet, to hold me in his arms, but I was already out of reach. In truth, I had been for a while. When I was halfway to the door, I turned and smiled at him, the only way at my disposal to reassure him. It would be a few more days before he would understand that I was carrying our dance into a new era, to a new people. That his life's work was taking on a greater significance than he had ever dreamed, even though it was in a setting he had dreaded. That Ma was right. That while I felt a hardness in my throat and a heaviness in my feet, this was a chance at a fresh start for me.

Padmini took Bapu's arm and guided him over to the two guards from the previous evening, and before I passed through the door at the back of the room, I watched his brittle frame as they led him back through the halls hung with tapestries and thick curtains to the world outdoors, where, under a pink sky, a new day was dawning.

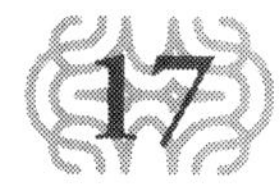

Hari Dev

Late Summer 1569

Hari Dev reached up and placed a cracked earthenware pot on an upper shelf. Two tall jugs on either side of it propped it up, like the guards who had escorted our fragile Bapu out of the palace. "Always be very careful with this one," my brother instructed the new boy. "This powder is very rare." He now had his very own assistant. Jagadhar-ji, pleased with his progress and handling of the shop, now came in only in the afternoons. Since our farewell two months earlier, Hari had been spending almost all his waking hours in the shop, freeing up Jagadhar-ji to spend time with his grandchildren and play chess with his friends in the shade of a *peepul* tree. Hari Dev did not begrudge him this. Jagadhar-ji deserved some rest. My brother was glad for the work and knew that he could call on the shop owner for help anytime he needed it. Their relationship was clear, straightforward, devoid of any mysteries or secrets or concealed emotions.

Hari Dev also had another reason to be grateful for Jagadhar-ji's absence, the same reason I knew that I need not worry about him. He glanced over at Sudhali, the lovely, long-limbed girl he had watched for thirty-two months as she molded bowls and plates from wet clay.

"Three slices?" she asked him with a smile, as she cut the flesh of a melon away from its skin.

He nodded and came to sit a moment with her at the counter. Her presence was like a salve to him, soothing the ache that my absence caused. She handed him a plate, and as she did so, her sari fell from her shoulder, revealing a patchy, pinkish discoloration of skin that stretched from just below her ear to her shoulder, down to somewhere beneath her blouse.

Sudhali followed his eyes and pulled her sari back up. "Don't."

"Why not? You don't need to hide that from me. I don't hide my legs."

She smiled. "Well, but how would you do that?"

"The way your skin is, that's why your father hasn't married you off yet, and why he's allowing you to be with me."

"I know, I know."

They sat in comfortable silence watching children playing and dogs scavenging. The street was especially quiet, for today Emperor Akbar was to take the daughter of the Raja as one of his wives. The festivities had been taking place for several days in the palace—indeed, I had danced at some of them, pieces of my choosing, with an array of musicians accompanying me—but today would mark the marriage ceremony itself, and the community feast in Chauhata Square. Everyone was gathering there. The Raja had formed an alliance with the Emperor, and this marriage would seal the agreement.

I was glad that Hari did not know that I would soon leave Jaisalmer, departing with the Raja's daughter and her retinue, headed for Delhi. I worried about leaving the desert, the rhythms I knew so well, but some of the court staff spoke to me of beautiful gardens, lush vegetation, plentiful food, and rains every single year. I wished I could bring Hari Dev with me. But instead he would continue to imagine me nearby, just beyond reach behind the palace walls. He did not know the details of the royal marriage arrangement, either, nor did he care to, but he did know that it involved some payments from the Raja to the Emperor, and some kind of autonomy for Jaisalmer in return. He had started to wonder how one could quantify the value of independence—how many sacks of coins, how many soldiers, how much gold could equal freedom?—but when his mind wandered in that direction, he changed its course and concentrated instead on the more immediate and tangible measurements of his daily life.

"What do I do with this?" The new boy held up a pot of resin.

Hari Dev stood reluctantly. "I must get back to work."

Sudhali licked the melon juice off her fingers. "I can help you. My father doesn't need me today."

Hari Dev explained to the boy the order in which the roots, powders, and resins were stored, then set Sudhali up on a corner of the floor, separating pieces of *neem* bark by size into neat piles. With everyone working, the shop was quiet. And then Padmini arrived.

"Oof, it's hot." She dropped onto one of the now-empty stools and wiped her face with the end of her sari.

Hari Dev nodded. "I know. There's something especially heavy in the air. Like maybe it's going to rain?"

Padmini accepted a cup of water from the new boy. "One can always hope so. But the sky is clear."

Hari Dev instructed him on which ingredients to set out for our sister's concealer. Mica, clay, zinc, tea extract, and nut oil. It had been sixty-four days since he had met her that first time, at home, in the days before he had started feeling as though the walls of home were closing in on him and had moved out to live with Jagadhar-ji's family above the shop. Sixty-four days, and he had made the concealer twice. It could last only about thirty days. Beyond that time, it would dry out.

He pulled a mixing bowl from a low shelf. "You're not at the wedding."

"No, I didn't feel like it." Padmini put down the now-empty cup of water.

I had not seen my sister since my first evening at the court, but I sensed her watchful eye often, in the way the servants tended to me, in the special deliveries of sweets, in the deference with which the palace staff treated me. She glanced around the shop, her eyes resting a moment on the assistant and then looking up at Hari Dev. He understood and asked the boy to leave them alone for a few moments. Sudhali rose as if to leave as well, but Padmini shook her head and motioned her to stay. Hari Dev pulled another stool up to Padmini and sat again, happy to have a few moments' rest. The crookedness of his legs put a strain on his hips when he stood.

Padmini sighed. "Mostly," she said, "I wanted to make sure you are all right."

Was he all right, he wondered? If he did not think about it too much, he was. But now that she had mentioned it, he was not so certain.

"Is Adhira dancing today?" he asked, in something close to a whisper.

"Yes. We could go watch her together if you'd like. I'm sure you could close the shop for a little while."

Hari Dev shook his head and swallowed hard. No, he did not want to see me. He had said his good-bye to me the day before I had left for the court, and it would disrupt the finality of that moment to see me again. I had told him I was leaving but that all would be well, that I would always be near him, even if we were separated by a stone wall, and that I would carry a part of him, his dance compositions and the patterns they traced, into my new world. After that day, my brother had carefully collected his happy memories of me—my singing voice, my reassuring smile, the radiance of my dance, the smoothness of my fingernails—and placed them in a corner of his mind, behind a door that he closed gently. He visited them now and then, to keep them alive, to color them with his thoughts so that they would become more vivid than his other memories of me. To see me again but not be able to be close to me would upset the fine balance he had managed to establish.

Sudhali rested her hand on his back. "It is better this way, you know," she said quietly.

Padmini looked at the two of them, envying their easy closeness. "Sudhali is right. What was left for Adhira at home?"

Hari Dev looked around the shop at the neat rows of pots, the scales. This was home for him. But Padmini had meant our parents' home, a home much changed in recent months. Bapu slept more than before, home at times of the day that, previously, he had spent religiously at the temple. Ma brought him broths and soft foods made by the girl Padmini had hired for them and sat by his side, telling him stories, remembering their days of travel across the desert. Ma and Bapu were closer now than in recent years. Hari Dev's mind wondered how Ma could have forgiven Bapu for not guarding me more closely, but his heart understood. When his mind and heart were at odds like this, confusing his thoughts and feelings, nothing was clear. Which was why he could no longer spend much time at home.

"At the court, she'll be well taken care of," Padmini continued. "And my husband promised he would keep an eye on her. As long as she is in Jaisalmer."

She saw Hari Dev's quick glance. "You've helped him, too, with this mix you've made. He's no longer afraid I'll air our private matters in the streets when I go out. So he knows he owes me something." Her little laugh was wry, dry.

Hari Dev was tired of trying to decipher the complexities that held some people together and tore others apart. And more than that, now he wondered what to make of Padmini's comment about Jaisalmer, for where else would I go? But he did not ask, for he did not want to know. He leaned into Sudhali, who stood behind him, picked up a little jar from the counter, opened the lid, and breathed in the pungent smell of cloves.

Padmini tapped the edge of the counter with her nails. "Honestly, the person I worry about right now is Ma."

Hari closed the jar. "I think Ma will manage. She is strong. Adhira said the person in need of help is Bapu." Leaving Ma behind to go live at Jagadhar-ji's had been a hard decision. But Ma had promised him she no longer needed his assistance, especially with the help Padmini had hired.

Padmini let out a grunt. "Fine, you can worry about Bapu if you want. Either way, please keep an eye on our parents. I'll be there the day after tomorrow, but right now I need to go home. My husband does not like me gone for so long. And it looks like you have a customer coming." She rose, gathering her sari and pulling it back over her head. "Sudhali, take care of my brother. And, Hari, promise you'll go see Ma today?" Padmini stood at the entrance to the shop, waiting pointedly, even as another woman stepped in and looked to Hari Dev for assistance. He nodded and rose to take the customer's order.

When he closed the shop that evening, the streets were relatively empty. The wedding feast was still underway. I had danced, a dance of hope and joy that my body created as I thought of the villagers on Govardhan Hill rejoicing after the floodwaters had receded. It seemed suitable for the occasion. In the street, the air carried a trace of moisture, but the sky was still clear. Nevertheless, the wind had picked up and blew some loose, dry grasses in swirls at Hari Dev's feet. A gust brought with it the sounds of men laughing, and he looked down the street. With few people around, he could see down to the tavern where many of the shopkeepers ended their workdays. Ever since that day five years earlier when he had gone into the tavern to look for Mahendra, he had avoided that end of the street. Now he wished that finding our brother could be as simple as walking through that door again.

But Mahendra was gone. Truly gone. Hari Dev knew now that it was, after all, possible to disappear into the space between categories. No longer a dancer and never truly a warrior, Mahendra had vanished for good.

Hari Dev turned to walk toward home. One thousand four hundred and ninety-two steps. He would not make any detours tonight. He told Sudhali that he needed to be alone for a while. She held his hand and squeezed it, understanding without his telling her that he was going to do something he needed to do, even though he did not want to. He was relieved at her lack of questions, her simple acceptance. This was one aspect of being a grown-up that he did not like: not wanting to do things, yet feeling compelled to do them anyway. He thought of how much of Ma's life must have felt this way, and this thought helped him move forward toward our parents.

He had taken 701 steps and had just passed the gate to Ghadisar Lake when he felt that something was not right. In the palace, as I danced, I had felt something, too, a piercing in my side, and I had sat down for a few moments, my head in my hands and my elbows on my knees. As I looked down, I saw the woven design of a peacock in the rug, and next to it a figure on its knees, holding a pleading hand up toward the sky. And I knew an end had come.

Hari's first thought was that Ma was unwell. He quickened his step, walk-running with his weakest leg dragging. He entered our home's courtyard, and all appeared normal. The courtyard was swept, the pots of lentils and rice neatly stacked in their shaded shelter. Too neatly. It was time to prepare the evening meal, yet there were no signs of food preparation.

"Ma!" he called out as he entered the main room. No one answered. There were no smells of food from the kitchen area. The afternoon rest time was long past; it was too late for our parents to still be asleep. At least Ma should have been up. But if she was not home, where would she have gone? Memories of his frantic search for me three years earlier threatened to cloud his vision. He pushed them away, counting the steps across the room, moving toward our parents' bedroom.

Hari Dev first saw Ma, squatting by the low bed in the shaft of light that fell in from the doorway, her arms hugging her legs. She made no sound, not even when she turned her head toward Hari Dev as he entered the room. Her face was tranquil, a smile playing on her lips, as though she were in some kind of trance. It was a look Hari Dev had seen many times on my face, on the faces of *devadasis*, in particular on Manavi-ji's face so many years back, when she was dancing a composition over and over, going through the steps and motions as though she need not think about them, as though they were a part of her, because they freed her body and allowed her mind to travel to other, faraway places.

Ma nodded gently toward the bed. There Bapu lay, as though asleep, his mouth slightly open, lips puckered around his nearly toothless gums, his arms along his sides. Hari Dev watched his chest for the telltale rise and fall of breath, but there was none. He waited a moment for some kind of feeling to take over, but that, too, was missing. Instead, there was an emptiness, a space ready to fill.

He stood willing to absorb Ma's sadness, but there was a dimension to it that he could not hold. It did not fit in the emptiness he held. It wasn't that Ma was not sad. She was. But something was holding her up, catching her sadness before it plummeted to the ground. Something was causing the tranquility of her face. Something like relief. Something like Krishna's reassuring hand. Hari Dev sat on the floor next to her and laid his head on her shoulder.

Ma rested her own head on his. “I’m surprised he lasted this long.”

Hari Dev realized he felt the same way. It was not something he would have been able to articulate, but as soon as Ma said it, he understood.

“I’ve been expecting this for several years now,” she continued. “I suppose the way everything has unraveled recently was finally too much for him.”

“When did it happen?”

“In his sleep. He lay down for his afternoon rest, and when I came to wake him . . . ” Ma opened her palms in a gesture of letting go.

The room was darkening. Night was falling. Hari Dev calculated that if Bapu had slipped away during his afternoon rest, it had already been a while. Cremation needed to happen quickly, but he had no idea how to prepare for this. It is one thing to wrap a dead jackal in cloth and carry it out to the desert. It is another to organize a funeral for the temple dance master. For one’s own father.

Padmini had said she would be here in two days, but that would be too long. Hari Dev thought of someone else who could help. “Ma, I’ll get Jagadhar-ji,” he said.

“No, not yet,” Ma said, reaching out to grip the side of the bed, as though Hari Dev were trying to pull her away.

“You can stay here, Ma. But we’ll need help planning.”

Ma turned her head toward him and nodded, gratitude written on her face in a way he had not seen before. Neither said what each was thinking—that the person who should have been planning the funeral was Bapu’s elder son. Hari got up, lit two oil lamps, and placed them in the room with our parents before leaving.

The sky was a deep purple. Dusk. As Hari Dev retraced his crooked steps to Jagadhar-ji’s shop and home, day phased into night. All around him, animals were beginning their transitions. The black, scuttling shapes of spiders and scorpions emerged from their holes, in search of smaller insects to eat. The silhouettes of larks and starlings flitted in the dry branches overhead, looking for a place to settle for the night. A wolf growled in the not-so-far distance, perhaps guarding a fresh kill. An antelope leaped across Hari Dev’s path, retreating into the deepening shadows. Below the citadel’s ramparts and along the broad steps leading up to the gate, dogs rose from their afternoon slumber and scavenged for food scraps. My brother felt the beginnings and the ends, the awakening of hunger in some and of fear in others. He felt the warmth of the sand underfoot and the coolness of the nighttime air descending. He felt the dryness of months of drought and the faint promise of rain to come. When he finally reached the front of Jagadhar-ji's home and attempted to call out to him, he realized he was sobbing.

The funeral was well attended. Jagadhar-ji and Padmini had helped spread the word of the death of the temple dance master. An entire retinue from the court—nine men, including the Raja himself—was present. I was not allowed out of the palace complex so soon after arriving, not even for my father's funeral. But I had said my farewell. In my rooms, I sat with my attendants and other courtesans and taught them some of Bapu's songs, the songs of his father before him. Hari Dev closed his eyes, opened the door to his memories of me, and called forth a vision of me playing with him in the temple courtyard, a girl of six or seven in an orange skirt, my long braid flying behind me as, laughing, I tried to dance out the compositions he called out to me. He carried this vision with him throughout the day, while in the palace, I felt a warmth behind my ribs.

At the *puja*, the temple was crowded with people, all in mourning white. Hari Dev counted about ten in one cluster, then quickly calculated that about thirty such clusters could fit in the inner courtyard, where the *puja* took place. Three hundred people. Among them, Ma and Padmini and her three boys. Beside them were the five remaining *devadasis*. The loss of their guru just one day ago already had traced months of sadness on their faces. They suffered the plight of the left-behind. Everyone else sat several paces away, beyond the immediate area of the shrine.

The mass of bodies threatened to suffocate Hari Dev, but he spent the day at Ma's side, which afforded him some protection from the crowd. Everyone recognized Ma as the wife of the dance master—not quite widow yet, not until Bapu's body had been consumed by the flames of the funeral pyre—and kept a respectful distance from her and, therefore, from Hari Dev.

Ma asked him to stay by her side. She was in perfect control of the day's events, giving instructions to some and comforting others, her sadness having given way to purpose, for she had made a decision and was methodically going through its steps. My brother's arm on hers detected no turmoil in her pulse, no unsteadiness of beat. For this he was grateful. Ma's control and balance comforted him and prevented his mind from wandering into unknown and dangerous recesses. Even his concerns about how to perform the duties of the eldest son dissolved in her presence.

"I will help you, *beta*," Ma said that morning when he broached the subject. "I will help you as long as I can."

And she did. Throughout the day, Hari Dev periodically felt close to having one of his fits, but each time, Ma was there. When Saiprasad-ji appeared, his feet slapping the floor, Ma quickly instructed Hari Dev to count the orange marigolds that had been set aside on a sheet to adorn Bapu's bier and body. There were to be 108, one for each of the names of Lord Krishna. So Hari Dev had been spared Saiprasad-ji's professed sympathy and condolences. By the time he had confirmed that the flowers numbered 108, the priest had moved on, swallowed by the crowd. Later, after the *puja*, when a line of people formed to offer sympathy and share sadness, Ma suggested to him that he calculate how many sweets from the sticky coconut mounds that had been brought in from the palace could be placed on each plate of food, to ensure that there were enough for every funeral attendee. And in this manner, Ma kept his mind focused on individual tasks until it was time for the dance. Then, in the safe confines of the sixteen-beat cycle of *teental*, he could loosen the reins on his thoughts.

In the center of the dance space, Chandrabai sat, her legs crossed. She was alone. All around was silence. She rose, slowly, as if awakened from a deep meditation. Her eyes were open wide, yet tranquil. With a simple gesture, the fingers of her right hand to her forehead, she depicted a third eye. She was ageless, unearthly, a manifestation of the divine. She was the Three-Eyed One, omniscient. She was Lord Shiva.

Slowly, Lord Shiva crossed the floor, his feet beating a simple rhythm. He traveled to the four corners, the four directions of the earth, and at each one bowed. Returning to the center, Chandrabai raised her right arm above her head, her hand turning into an hourglass drum, the *damaru*. She shook the *damaru*, and from it came the beating pulse of the universe, now awakened. *Ta thei thei tat.* But with that sound came another, and with a swift turn, Chandrabai at once turned toward it and became its creator. Now she was a dwarf, bent low, her lips pulled into a sneer. For the dwarf was illusion, ignorance, and laziness. He took three steps forward, but Chandrabai as Lord Shiva drew her right leg up and crushed him, freeing the universe of his influence. She held up both hands to her head, and her fingers rippled down, showing the matted locks of Shiva's hair, from which he released the life-giving, holy waters of the river Ganga.

Having shown the five elements—creation, preservation, destruction, illusion, and emancipation—Chandrabai arced her arms around her, creating a ring of flames, the endless cycle of birth and death. With great care, she took her position in the center of it. Her left foot was lifted, crossed slightly in front of her. Her right hand was raised in an open-palmed gesture of protection. Her left hand pointed to the dwarf, who lay, crushed, under her right foot. For Chandrabai was Shiva, and Shiva is Nataraja, Lord of Dance.

Her dance took both an instant and an eternity. For once, Hari Dev could not measure. But at the end, a weight lifted from him, like a gradual release of pressure. He turned his back on the temple to take part in the procession to the cremation grounds, leaving the temple forever. Nothing remained to bind him to the place from which he came. From now on, he thought, his life could revolve, unfettered, around the weights and measurements of the shop, the neat containers of compounds, the predictable scales. Sudhali would provide whatever comfort and balance the shop could not, Padmini would help him care for Ma, and the desert, with all its wondrous creatures and transformations, would always be there to remind him of the presence of the gods. All this would come to be, with one exception.

At the cremation grounds, the pyre was ready. Hari Dev and Ma led the procession, with Padmini close behind. As they approached the pyre, the crowd fell back and settled on the ground. Saiprasad-ji intoned the incantations to the dead, and the *devadasis*' voices rose with his, above his, clear as *puja* bells, until no one could hear the priest. In my room in the palace, I heard their mourning song and ran to the window cut into the deep stone wall. I joined my voice to theirs, sending it over the rooftops and past the lake, weaving it around and through the crowd until I could imagine it reaching my family's ears. We shared the same grief, but for different reasons. Mine was not for the passing of my father, or even for the decision on which my mother was about to act. My grief was for the dance. Bapu had entrusted me with a gift, and I knew that while I would carry it into the future and honor it with my heart and body and soul, it would inevitably change. I would cause it to be different from the dance of my father. I understood that this was the end and the beginning of a cycle, but this time this knowledge took longer to soften the pain.

Hari Dev stepped forward, leaving Ma's side, and walked around the pyre three times. Returning to her, he took the torch that the priest handed him, lit it with the sacred fire of the earthen pot, and held it out to the smaller twigs that jutted from between the branches that made up the pyre.

As the flames began to lick the edges of the pyre, a shadow fell upon the cremation grounds. The wind picked up, feeding the flames. The sky darkened. Clouds were gathering rapidly, gray-black, draining the surroundings of color. Rising from the bare ground and the lifeless wood of the pyre, amid the white-clad crowd, only the flames of the funeral fire offered any color, their brilliant reds and oranges glowing triumphantly. Billows of dense smoke rose to the sky, blending with the clouds. Waves of heat bore down on Hari Dev, and he tried to pull Ma gently back, fearing that the wind might lift the end of her sari too close to the flames. But as he did so, she resisted. Standing her ground, Ma pulled Hari Dev to her, in front of her, placing him directly in between her and the crowd. The flames rose at her back.

"You are free, *beta*," she said. "You don't need me any longer. Your life is in the citadel, and I would only be a burden to you. My place is with your father, as it has always been. I know you'll keep me in your heart."

Hari Dev felt her hands squeeze his, her lips graze his cheek, and then she let go and turned away from him. From behind him, Padmini cried out, but it was too late. Ma's body was engulfed in flames, her entire sari ablaze. Her arms reached across the top of the pyre as if to hold on to Bapu, as if entreating him to wait, telling him she would be his accompaniment this one last time. Hari, rooted in place, recalled her telling him the story of Jaisalmer, of its sackings and the ritual *jauhar* of the women. The girl from among the eucalyptus trees of Mount Abu was becoming one with the desert.

The flames had begun to dwindle, the pyre was crumbling, the crowd thinning, when the rains arrived. The sky rumbled. Lord Indra on his chariot. Heavy drops came pelting down, creating an erratic pattern of spots on the ground that quickly merged into dark brown wetness. Smoke still rose from the pyre, blacker now. The sounds of the crowd fell away, and Hari Dev closed his eyes and lifted his face to the sky, hearing only the crashing of the clouds, the hissing of the wet, burning wood, and the splashing of the rain. Raindrops fell into my brother's open mouth, pasted his hair to his head and his clothes to his body. The odor of wet earth and sodden ash filled the air. Still at the window, I breathed it in, leaning over the stone to jut my hand into the heavy drops. At my brother's feet, a rivulet of dark water trickled down from the drenched pyre and swirled into a muddy puddle, black and brown spirals turning endlessly on themselves.

He remembered a sense of fear and hope, of impending change, of ending and beginning. He closed his eyes again and searched for that same fear, his mind already summoning the numbers and patterns—my favorite compositions—with which to quell it. But he found only the hope.

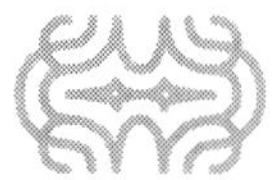

Adhira
1611

The rains come reliably here in Akbarabad, beginning every June. They swell the river Jamuna for two months, as when Vasudeva carried Lord Krishna across for safety, before finally retreating in September. On the hottest days, the rain splashes down and then rises again as thick steam from the ground, wrapping around buildings and seeping into doorways. On these days, I remain indoors, within this vast fort that Emperor Akbar rebuilt thirty years ago with sandstone brought from Rajasthan. I confess to putting my head to the walls when no one is looking and breathing in their odor. If I close my eyes and concentrate, I believe I can smell sweet, dusty traces of the desert.

Until last year, I hadn't much left from my early years in Jaisalmer. The dance, of course, but now it is trapped in my body. The day I fell from the garden wall, foolishly chasing my youngest grandchild as though we were peacocks at play, was the last day that I danced fully. My head met the stone floor with a crack that resounded in my ears before everything vanished. When I awoke here in my quarters, my children and attendants were gathered around me, but it was the look on Dayal's face that told me how much had changed. Dayal, apprentice to the finance minister, that man whom I have come to love, the father of my children, reminded me in that instant of Hari Dev.

He looked poised to absorb my pain. Behind him, in the alcove in which I conduct my daily *pujas*, my statuette of Lord Krishna sat as it always did, but it seemed to me his eyes were brighter than usual. I tried to reach out a hand to Dayal, but it did not respond. And yet, while I could not touch him, I felt something nonetheless. It was a memory from another time, a memory I had never before had. It was a memory of Hari Dev's, of his feelings the day we sat at Ghadisar Lake before my dedication ceremony.

For several months, I recovered under the care of Akbar's own physician. Movement has fully returned to my right side, and I can now walk the gardens with an attendant and correct my daughters when they dance. During those months, a flood of new memories arrived: Ma wishing I would eat the dried apricot she gave me, Mahendra crying behind a temple pillar while I sang, Hari searching the night for me, Bapu willing Manavi-ji to bless me as a *devadasi*. Lord Krishna took the dance from my body, but he gave me something in return: the story of my family, a story only I can tell.

Author's Note

This book is set in a real time and place in India's history. There are, however, a few areas in which I have taken some liberties. The city of Jaisalmer sits in what was known, in the sixteenth century, as Rajputana but is now the state of Rajasthan. I have chosen to use the current name, as a reminder that this is a place one can visit today. Similarly, Muslims would have been referred to not as such, but as Mosalmans or Mussalmans. It seemed less distracting to use the modern term. Finally, the temple dancers would not have been referred to as *devadasis* in Jaisalmer, which is in the northern part of India. There exist many different terms for such "servants of God." The term *devadasi* originated in South India but has become the main term used to refer to female temple dancers in India.

In the depiction of the dance as well, I have made some deliberate choices. These are due to a lack of precise historical information regarding when some elements of the dance, now known as *kathak*, came about. It is not clear just when dancers began to wear ankle bells, nor is it certain when they started dancing to specific musical cycles, such as the sixteen-beat cycle, although the cyclical nature of Indian classical music was already well established at the time.

Finally, I would like to attribute to Pandit Ram Narayan Misra, guru (teacher) to Pandit Chitresh Das (guru to my own teacher,

Gretchen Hayden), the quote "Dance in such a way as to become one with everything." His teachings permeate everything that dancers in his lineage study, and it is with reverence that I place these words among those uttered by Gandar, the temple dance master in this story.

Questions for Discussion

1. Where is the line between legend and history? Between what is believed and what is "true"? Do you believe, for example, that the well in Chauhata Square, a real well that one can see and touch, was built around a spring that gushed forth from a barren spot of land when Prince Arjuna, a character in the great Hindu epic the Mahabharata, struck it with one of his arrows?

2. What role do stories play in one's life and beliefs? Why do the stories of the Rajasthan cities speak so much to Girija, to Mahendra, and even to Hari Dev? Do they mean the same things to each character? What is the significance of stories to Adhira?

3. What is faith? In this story, who has faith and who doesn't? Faith in what? How are the different approaches to faith different? Are there any characters who don't appear to have faith in anything? Is that possible?

4. What is devotion? Adhira is the embodiment of devotion, but do others in the story practice their own form of devotion? To what are they devoted? To what end, and at what cost? How does faith differ from devotion?

5. To what extent is our future waiting for us to write it? Each of these characters struggles in his or her own way with whether or not one can control one's destiny, and some of them experience a profound shift in belief over the course of the story. Think of Gandar, of Girija, of Mahendra, of Adhira (is Hari Dev different?). Are they better off for having gone through this shift?

6. How much can a person truly change? Are those who are trying to be something others think they are not really capable of becoming something else? How does Gandar's stance on this differ from Girija's?

7. When does action born out of fear have positive consequences? Driving the actions of many of these characters is a deep-seated fear of what the future will bring under Muslim rule. Ignorance and assumptions combine with reality and individual personalities to spur Gandar, Girija, Mahendra, and others to act in drastically different ways toward a goal they may not realize they have in common: saving the family. But are the consequences of these actions the ones they expected? Do they, in fact, save the family?

8. When it comes to tradition, should one fear change? How does one balance the pressures of "modern" life with the requirements of tradition? How does one adapt while maintaining integrity? When does a tradition become something else completely? At the end of the story, what do you think might happen to the tradition of the *devadasis* and of kathak dance?

9. How does one reconcile the portrayal and treatment of women as both worshipped and scorned? These days, in 2014, India is very much in the news for horrifying rapes. Yet India is also a country where the Mother, the life-giver, is revered. Hinduism gives us Shakti—divine feminine creative power—and the associated goddess Kali, both maternal and enraged. How does Adhira's life reflect this dichotomy? How is the world of women portrayed in this story?

10. What makes the foreign familiar? How is Adhira's family, while so unlike ones we know now, also typical? To which character or moment did you relate the most?

Acknowledgments

Writing this book has been a journey. Along the way, I have been supported in material, intellectual, and emotional ways by a multitude of people, a veritable village. I owe particularly deep gratitude to:

Gretchen Hayden, my teacher, mentor, colleague, and friend, for introducing me to the realm of *kathak* and inspiring me always to try my best. Gretchen-ji and her husband, George Ruckert, disciple of the late *sarod* maestro Ali Akbar Khan, are the epitome of integrity and talent.

Pandit Chitresh Das, *kathak* master and guru to Gretchen Hayden, for bringing *kathak* to the United States, and for giving his insatiable energy to the Chhandam School of Kathak Dance and to his students, constantly innovating within tradition.

My writing-group partners and cheering squad—Jennifer Dupee, Crystal King, and Kelly Robertson, as well as Laura Warrell—for being there every inch of the way.

My Chhandika family—the women alongside whom I have danced, learned, and taught—for providing me with a cadre of peers with whom to share the highs and lows of juggling artistic endeavors, professional lives, and growing families.

My circle of dear friends and readers of early drafts—including

Sarah Carroll, Madeleine Dassule, Bandita Joarder, Sophia Mansori, and others—for being loyal and generous friends of the highest caliber.

Grub Street Writers, an independent writing center in Boston, for offering such high-quality workshops and events, and for providing me, and so many others, with a supportive network in a warm and friendly atmosphere.

April Eberhardt, my agent, for her unquenchable enthusiasm and tireless work, and for caring about my book as though it were her own.

Steven Bauer, an editor of incredible insight and wisdom, for helping me bring this book to the next level.

Brooke Warner and She Writes Press, for seeing a remarkable opportunity in the evolving publishing sector, and for making an innovative model a reality.

Kathy Le and her family, for sharing everything with ours, including housing, cooking, errands, child rearing, and even vacations. Our quasicommune, a self-selected family, is what has made so much of this possible.

My brother, Siddhartha Mitter, journalist and writer, for being there when I need him, and for showing me by example the importance of forging one's own path.

My parents, Sara Sagoff Mitter and Pronob Kumar Mitter, for keeping me connected to their two continents while raising me in a third, and for instilling in me the knowledge that writing is a worthy pursuit.

My daughters, Kalyani and Sanaya, for their patience, their sense of humor, their love, and their lengthy naps, and for only once pointing out that Kalyani's third-grade book was published before this one. I do believe they helped my writing take on a new dimension.

And most of all, my husband and partner on my path, Jason Duva, for his unwavering love and support, and for never once questioning. Not a single time.

About the Author

© Penny Lennox

Anjali Mitter Duva grew up in France and has family roots in Calcutta. She is a co-founder of Chhandika, an organization that teaches and presents India's classical kathak dance. Anjali graduated from Brown University and completed her Master's in city planning at MIT. She lives near Boston with her husband and two daughters. FAINT PROMISE OF RAIN is Anjali's first novel. She is working on the second, set in 19th-century Lucknow.

SELECTED TITLES FROM SHE WRITES PRESS

She Writes Press is an independent publishing company founded to serve women writers everywhere. Visit us at www.shewritespress.com.

Bittersweet Manor by Tory McCagg
$16.95, 978-1-938314-56-8
A chronicle of three generations of love, manipulation, entitlement, and disappointed expectations in an upper-middle class New England family.

All the Light There Was by Nancy Kricorian
$16.95, 978-1-63152-905-4
A lyrical, finely wrought tale of loyalty, love, and the many faces of resistance, told from the perspective of an Armenian girl living in Paris during the Nazi occupation of the 1940s.

The Rooms Are Filled by Jessica Null Vealitzek
$16.95, 978-1-938314-58-2
The coming-of-age story of two outcasts—a nine-year-old boy who just lost his father, and a closeted young woman—brought together by circumstance.

The Sweetness by Sande Boritz Berger
$16.95, 978-1-63152-907-8
A compelling and powerful story of two girls—cousins living on separate continents—whose strikingly different lives are forever changed when the Nazis invade Vilna, Lithuania.

Cleans Up Nicely by Linda Dahl
$16.95, 978-1-938314-38-4
The story of one gifted young woman's path from self-destruction to self-knowledge, set in mid-1970s Manhattan.

Beautiful Garbage by Jill DiDonato
$16.95, 978-1-938314-01-8
Talented but troubled young artist Jodi Plum leaves suburbia for the excitement of the city—and is soon swept up in the sexual politics and downtown art scene of 1980s New York.

CPSIA information can be obtained at www.ICGtesting.com
Printed in the USA
BVOW01s1123250814

363814BV00008B/6/P